I0645344

ORIGIN
OF THE
VAMPYRE

A Companion to Doctor Polidori's *The Vampyre*

The Companion Series

Stand-alone novels delving into the intrigue of the Romantics' ghost
story competition of 1816—the *Year Without a Summer*

Fire on the Water:
A Companion to Mary Shelley's *Frankenstein*

Origin of the Vampyre:
A Companion to Doctor Polidori's *The Vampyre*

ORIGIN OF THE VAMPYRE

A Companion to Doctor Polidori's *The Vampyre*

By

P.J. Parker

This one is for my little brother, JP.

"Like a star in the halo of the moon, invisible."

—Doctor John Polidori

Prologue

His shattered finger snapped as he dug it into the ground, attempting to drag the full dead weight of his body along the rough cobbled stone of the Soho alley, dark of shadow. Loose fingernails long since splintered, now ragged and worn down to exposed bone. Decaying knuckles disintegrated against the pavement—flakey remnants of flesh smearing his face as his head lolled on the inexorably slow and uncertain path.

Racked by shuddering, painful sobs, he wished only to get as far as he could from the potter's field hole in which he had been buried.

Back to the family he loved more than life, or death, itself.

CHAPTER ONE

Rachel slung her laptop bag over her shoulder and crossed 42nd Street at Fifth Avenue. The broad steps and terraces of the New York Public Library rose between the marble lions—*Patience* and *Fortitude*—that had guarded it for more than a century. Tourists gathered in the library's palatial lobby, marveling at the polished architectural detail and reveling in the air conditioning away from the blaring traffic and the sticky Manhattan humidity that had wilted the trees of Bryant Park.

Rachel wished she could take off her suit jacket, but the seven-block walk from Rockefeller Center had reduced her blouse to sweat-soaked transparency.

"Ms. Walton."

Rachel looked up and pulled her lapels together. The concierge held out a package about the size of a large boot box, wrapped in brown paper, tied with string, and covered in stamps—British.

"Thanks, Scotty." Rachel tucked the package under an arm and awkwardly signed the form the concierge tilted her way.

"Hot outside, hey?" Scotty said with a smirk only a twenty-year-old Iowa farm boy could pull off without receiving a jaded New York backhand across the face.

Rachel smiled before heading down the south corridor away from the tourists. The package was weighty and cumbersome, its contents slipping back and forth inside—perhaps the dull thud of wood on wood. She steadied it with both hands. Two floors down, where the marble opulence gave way to linoleum and white-washed concrete blockwork, she stopped and leaned against the wall to reaffirm her grip. She nudged off her jacket to catch the imagined breeze creeping along the corridor from the dehumidified book-stacks beneath Bryant Park.

And then she saw him.

Straight up ahead, standing in her bright glass box of an office set amongst the miles of archive shelving. Massive in size, Adam leaned over her desktop contemplating something on the computer screen. His buzz cut was newly trimmed and sharp. A lemon-colored polo shirt clung to the powerful musculature of his torso, leaving absolutely nothing to the imagination. The hard bulge of his tattooed biceps glistened with a cool sweat. *God, he's big*, was always her first thought whenever she saw him, instantaneously followed by, *God, I love him.*

"A present for me?" Adam asked when she walked in.

"No, it just arrived at concierge." She placed it and her laptop bag onto the desk.

He smiled. "I wasn't talking about the package."

Rachel glanced down at her blouse. Before she'd a chance to chuckle, he stepped around the desk, pulled her up into his arms, and kissed her with a warmth and passion that had only escalated since they'd first met in Montreux, Switzerland, on the shores of Lake Geneva three years ago. She melted into the gentle strength of his embrace, the excruciating heat and moist pleasure of his mouth against hers. He brushed his lips across her cheek and whispered into her ear, "*Ma chérie.*" She'd never heard a more masculine voice. His tongue was Swiss, more German-Swiss than French, but he'd started to develop a slight Manhattan nasality—a tendency picked up from the tight group of friends he'd made since joining her in New York.

She pressed her hands against his chest. "My publisher approved the commission."

"The Polidori biography? Oh, Rach, that's great!"

Rachel's smile faltered. "I don't know about being away from Helen for so long. Plus, I already have reams of data on Polidori from my research for Mary's bio." She glanced at the oversized, framed bookstore poster on the wall for *Fire on the Water: A Companion to Mary Shelley's Frankenstein*. "But I'll need to be in London for at least a month to wrap up the last five or so years of his life, after the summer of 1816."

Adam nodded thoughtfully. "Henny and I can video call you every morning and evening, and I will ensure she gets three times as many hugs and kisses throughout the day." He touched his forehead to hers. "We'll give it a week or two, so you can finish the first major slog of research, and then we'll fly over and join you, yeah?"

"Yeah, I'd like that."

He lowered Rachel to the floor and sat on the edge of her desk next to the package. "I didn't realize Doctor Polidori died so soon after the Romantics tour of Europe. Was it, um, natural?"

Rachel pulled at her blouse to fan herself. "I don't know. There's conflicting data, and a lot of speculation. He seemed to spiral after the publication of his ghost story competition manuscript."

"*The Vampyre: A Tale*," Adam said.

Rachel nodded. "But whether it was the public reception to that work, or something more complex to do with his personal life, I don't know. Yet."

Rachel stared past Adam toward the package, and he turned to follow her gaze. Stamps covered a third of the front face, most with the silhouette of Queen Elizabeth, but a few with the smiling cherub face of the future King George. But that was not what attracted her attention. The addressing, care of the New York Public Library, was florid with letters over an inch high done by an impressive, masculine hand—a beautiful copperplate reminiscent of the ancient letters she'd studied for the Shelley biography. The sender's address was written diagonally in the top left-hand corner:

Aubrey Polidori
38 Great Pulteney Street
Soho, London, W1F
England

CHAPTER TWO

Doctor Polidori settled the oars and lay back, allowing the boat to drift on. He even dared loosen his cravat. It was perhaps nine o'clock in the evening, a pleasant supper of pheasant and wine at Villa Diodati still warming his body and thoughts. An oil lamp at his knee highlighted every cushion and plank of the rowboat's interior. Yet the lapping water of Lake Geneva was, as far as Polidori could discern, impenetrably black. The shore was a thin, mist-shrouded line—blurred pinpoints of light escaping from chalets and villas through drawn curtains and shutters. The Alps rose dark and jagged in the distance, surmounted by snow that appeared ice-black in the starlight. The air was chilled and damp. Polidori pulled a cigar from his frock coat pocket, cut off the end, and lit it. With one arm cradling his head, he pressed his lips around the sweet vessel of succor, his attention on the dense clusters of stars above. A lavender-scented puff of smoke occluded the visage but a moment before being nudged aside by a breeze. He rocked amongst the constellations, hoping for inspiration.

The rain of the past week had abated; indeed there was no sign of cloud. Polidori wondered that there was no moon but knew it was best not wasted, knowing he couldn't share it with the one who made his heart ache. He closed his eyes, drew on the cigar, and held his breath until he felt light-headed. No doubt Lord Byron was somewhere thinking of him, too. Probably still chuckling at Polidori's idea for the ghost story competition.

*   *   *

After the last terrible tale from *Phantasmagoria* had been told the previous week, everyone present in Villa Diodati's drawing room had sat in horrified silence. Lord George Byron and Miss Claire Clairmont had gazed into the fire, Mary into the depths of her sherry. Percy had sipped tentatively at a thimble glass of laudanum, his eyes wide. Polidori had stood by the window, his thoughts lost in the incessant rain. He'd turned when he'd heard Mary chuckle.

"I daresay I have never heard you utter such preposterous prose, Lord Byron," she said. "The idea anyone would be frightened by that phantasm tale makes me wonder at the sanity of its author and publisher."

Lord Byron laughed. "Perhaps it lost something in the translation from German to French." He pulled Miss Clairmont into his side. "Were you frightened, my dear?" Miss Clairmont blushed. "John, come out from amongst the curtains and tell me whether you were frightened," Lord Byron said as he strode across the room and gripped Doctor Polidori's shoulders. Polidori stiffened, the familiar scent of breath on his neck, the accustomed warmth of the Lord's hands upon him. But never in the company of others. Polidori's blush went deeper than Miss Clairmont's.

"I believe any of us could write tales of horror with more impact and consequence than any of these naive ghost stories." Polidori said.

Lord Byron's hands lingered, his thumb pulling Polidori's cravat down below the collar to expose the bare, flushed skin of his neck. They held each other's gaze in their reflection in the rain-streaked window.

* * *

Polidori's rowboat suddenly skimmed the crest of a swell, and the cigar smoke idled from his mouth as his lips curled in inspiration.

CHAPTER THREE

Rachel pulled the package across the desk toward her. It was quiet in the book stacks, with Adam gone to collect Helen from daycare and promising fettucine alfredo and fresh garlic bread by the time she arrived home. She cut the string and pulled back the layers of paper and bubble wrap, stopping when she realized the contents of the package.

She flinched at a loud thud on the far side of the subterranean room. Her heart thumped in her chest in concert with the slow, dull staccato of bank after bank of fluorescent lights shutting off across the nine acres of book-stacks. She checked her watch. The darkness ratcheted nearer until nothing outside her office was visible, save for the green exit sign at the far end of the corridor. She'd spent many an evening cradled by this darkness doing research. But now, as the glass walls of the office reflected her and the document box in front of her, she only felt alone.

Again.

The box was simple in its structure, unlike the ornate trunk that had unearthed unexpected horrors related to her Shelley bio. Plain wood covered in a dark, waxy film, this box bore no escutcheon nor required any key. The lid was held shut by a simple hook latch. Several daubs of grey-blue wax were placed unevenly along the lip of the lid, each stamped with a seal to confirm the safekeeping of the box's contents, all long since broken with each opening of the box. Perhaps two-hundred years ago, Rachel surmised, noting the initials *JWP* in the wax impressions of the damaged seals.

She glanced again at the crumpled paper packaging and the address of the sender:

Aubrey Polidori.

"How did you know?" she whispered in the silence of her office.

On instinct, she opened her laptop and created a spreadsheet for her observations, then pulled on a pair of cotton gloves and photographed the box from multiple angles. Finally she nudged the delicate latch to the side. The lid creaked as she opened it, a slim wooden arm angling out to hold it high. Inside the top of the box's lip sat a wooden tray covered in a threadbare, cobalt-blue silk, and nestled within it, an envelope with her name on it. Until today, she'd never seen her name written in such lavish copperplate. The envelope was either very old, or very expensive, with beautiful blue strands of silk pressed into the pulp. She leaned over the box and sniffed, waving its scent toward her face. A faint but distinct aroma of parchment, port, and cigars. A combination she'd not smelled since working with Mary's letters. She photographed the envelope front and back, then slipped a letter opener under the flap to extract the single piece of parchment within. In the same rich hand of the package addressing was written:

You will find within all you need to complete Polidori's story.

Rachel leaned back and read it over again. The document box wasn't very large. The research she'd already done would fill it hundreds of times over with letters, newspapers, diaries, and esoteric fragments. What could it possibly contain that would adequately explain the final years of Polidori's life? And death? She photographed the parchment and slipped it back into the envelope. Then, standing, she grasped both sides of the ancient tray, fragile in its age. She lifted it carefully, but still the slim length of wood on one side, long-splintered, came off in her hand. She settled the intact portion of tray onto her desk, her face going slack as she saw what was inside the box.

Nothing.

CHAPTER FOUR

A loud banging interrupted what had been a pleasant dream.

The sunlit pebbles of Brighton Beach . . . Officers of the regiment strolling barefoot in the ocean shallows . . .

A hand pressed firmly upon his chest. It was cold against his naked flesh, sucking the warmth from his slumber.

"Doctor, quickly. A Bow Street Runner awaits you at the door."

Polidori rubbed brusquely at his face, attempting to wake. He pushed himself up onto his elbow amongst pillows and quilted eiderdowns. "Has there been another?" he said.

His valet nodded, fright evident on his features, garishly lit by the single candle on the washstand. Polidori quickly donned a shirt and pulled Wellington boots onto his stockinged feet as the valet held his frock coat high. He was still fastening the top buttons as he ran out the front door into Great Pulteney Street, his medical bag tight under his arm.

It was dark outside, the ubiquitous dull glow of London fog hanging just above the eves of the four-story townhomes bordering the street.

A bell rang in the distance.

The Bow Street Runner was blowing his whistle, waving for Polidori to follow in haste. They ran along Great Pulteney and across Brewer Street, carriage horses startled by the commotion, then down the narrow Farrier's Passage and into the cobbled stink of Smith's Court. Within moments their course had led them from London refinement to absolute squalor. The court was darkest at this time of night, devoid of the lanterns that lit the surrounding streets. Ladies never frequented here; only men who desired what a city might provide within its quiet corners and private niches. The court was empty now save for the flowery odor of opium and the salty lingering stench of masculine satisfaction.

Polidori came to a breathless halt. The Runner had stopped and bent low, holding aloft his lantern.

This was the second man this week.

Polidori squatted beside the Runner to inspect the body—an elderly gentleman, dressed immaculately for the opera. His pantaloons hung loosely at the knee, his opera slippers missing, his left foot and calf mauled with chunks of flesh ripped loose from the bone.

"A hound?" the Runner asked.

Polidori leaned in further to inspect the gentleman's head. A gash behind his ear, blood glistening. A corner of the sooty brickwork was smeared with blood and tufts of grey hair. "The cause of death," Polidori muttered. "Did you find his slippers, Officer?"

The Runner pointed to the far side of the court where the slippers lay, then retrieved them. Polidori lifted one close to the light of the Runner's lantern. It was saturated in a translucent, blood-specked saliva. "Bring him to Great Pulteney Street. There may yet be more I may learn before you locate his family and associates."

The Bow Street Runner hauled the gentleman onto his shoulder and followed Polidori. A few passers-by shuffled, wide-eyed, into the gutters in case the well-dressed burden should be diseased.

The steps to Polidori's basement were slippery from the fog. The green door, seldom locked, stood ajar. Polidori pointed to the parquetry table in the center of the room and the Runner shrugged the body onto it. The week's first cadaver still lay unclaimed on the side counter, draped in a sheet mottled by yellow-green stains, its stench barely tempered by the pickle-odor of formaldehyde.

"Do you think it was the same animal, Doctor?"

Polidori ripped open the gentleman's pantaloons, exposing the full extent of his wounds. Whatever mouth had ripped at the flesh was broad—much too large for a rat—most probably a hound, as the Runner had suggested. Polidori prodded at the muscle and sinew, attempting to nudge it back into its original circumstance. It didn't appear any was missing. Nothing eaten.

"It is merely ravaged, and not for want of consumption. At least, not of the meat itself." He took a scalpel from his bag and cut through the ragged muscle closest to the bone. He dug his fingers

into the flesh and extracted a tooth.
  It was flat.
  Decayed.
  Human.

CHAPTER FIVE

The black London cab took a circuitous journey from Heathrow Airport toward the city center. The sun had just set, the last of its red and yellow ribbons reflecting off low-hanging clouds. Rachel was familiar enough to know where she was and to trust the cabby's judgment. They coursed along the southern boundary of Hyde Park, then the tree-lined avenue between Green Park and the Queen's private gardens of Buckingham Palace. They slowed to a stop at a traffic light, and a crowd of tourists crossed the road, snapping photos. Doctor Polidori would have recognized these grand avenues, malls, and parklands. Many of the Georgian buildings of his time still defined the majestic streetscape. He might have been taken aback by the new façade of Buckingham Palace, with its now-famous balcony and the understated moments of affection it had hosted. But unless he'd have lifted his gaze toward the gleaming glass pinnacles farther down the River Thames, he might not have noticed such a great time had passed.

Rachel checked her phone, anxious to call Adam and Henny before her meeting. Anxious about the meeting itself. And the man whom it was with.

As the cab rolled along the Mall, Henny's face flashed up on the phone screen, a profusion of Titian red curls and giggles. Their conversation was punctuated by Adam's kisses on Henny's cheeks and Henny's kisses on the camera. By the time the hackney was circling Trafalgar Square, Rachel felt flushed and happy. And ready to meet *him*.

The cab pulled to the curb on Charing Cross Road, and Rachel grabbed her bag and slid across the seat. "I should be about twenty minutes," she said.

"That's okay, luv. I'm due for a tea break anyway. I'll just be over the street." The cabby flicked off his meter and pointed to where half a dozen black hackneys were parked in the deepening shadows of an immense London planetree.

Stepping onto the sidewalk, Rachel realized how much she'd missed London. Granted, she'd spent much of her time here researching the Romantics in archives and reading rooms, but there was something about the city itself that made her feel more connected to her subjects than New York ever could. The breeze was cool against her skin, a faint smell of bergamot drifting.

The bells of St. Martin-in-the-Fields began to peel. Tourists stopped to listen. Rachel stopped, too, recalling her research, the many meandering threads of study considering whether the church could be in any way relevant to her research. The foundation stone for the current church was laid almost one hundred years before Polidori's death. His home was not far from here. She wasn't certain of the timeline, but he may have been present for the demolition of the surrounding areas for the creation of Trafalgar Square. Perhaps for the removal of the bodies buried in the original churchyard.

The bells' frenetic peeling escalated. She wondered for whom they tolled.

Perhaps a wedding.

Perhaps not.

Rachel sidestepped a dawdling group of tourists and entered the National Portrait Gallery. She knew exactly where she was going: room 18. A room where she'd spent many an evening on the stiff, green leather benches, formulating her chapters and pondering the portraits of those she now considered some of her greatest friends. The mosaic floor, classic columns, and a barrel-vaulted ceiling of the gallery's entrance gave way to a modern interior. She stepped onto the escalator that would take her up to room 18.

She wondered what he would be like. Whether she could trust him. His voice on the phone had been pleasant enough. Articulate. He knew well the subject she'd come to study. But that voice had conveyed more—a familiarity. A warmth. A discrete sensuality. Perhaps it was because he shared a deep love of the Romantics.

Mary Shelley was the first to catch her eye. An enigmatic smile in oils and brush strokes. To her left was Percy Shelley, to her right

Lord Byron, both relatively handsome. Young. Taken by fate not long after their portraits were completed, never to grow old.

Doctor John Polidori's canvas was the smallest, relegated to the far corner of the portrait gallery where the light was dim. And yet it had always entranced Rachel even more than those of his famous male contemporaries. The elegance of his couture. The youth and innocence of his face. The unruly curl of his hair. But beyond anything else, Rachel always wondered what he was looking at. Something off-frame, with a yearning, a sadness, for something so close yet unattainable. His eyes glistened in reverie.

Aubrey Polidori sat on the bench in the middle of the gallery, his feet flat on the parquetry floor, elbows on his knees, chin resting atop his fists. He was the epitome of London's fashionable youth in tailored tweed slacks, a crisp white linen shirt, and a brown leather bomber jacket, very old and torn at the elbow, though Rachel sensed not by design. He stared not at the painting of his ancestor, but at the Shelleys and Lord Byron. Rachel couldn't help comparing the younger to the older, though she guessed they were both in their early twenties, just in different centuries. There was no doubt of their relation, with a shared translucent complexion and roguishly handsome features, the same longing and tear-glistened eyes. Both men were beautiful. No, handsome. No, beautiful.

Rachel cleared her throat and Aubrey shook himself from his trance.

He rose and held out a hand. "Hello, Ms. Walton. A pleasure to meet you in person." His words were measured, his voice deep and gentle with a masculine resonance that made Rachel aware they were alone in the gallery. He bowed his head slightly as he gripped her fingers. For an instant she thought he was going to kiss her hand, as old-worldly and ridiculous as that might have seemed, but he didn't. She blushed anyway, then chuckled at her foolishness.

"Mr. Polidori—"

"Please call me Aubrey."

"Aubrey." Rachel glanced at the painting of the doctor over his shoulder. "Thank you for meeting me here. Even though your letters of recommendation are impeccable, it seemed best to meet in a public space."

"I understand. A beautiful young woman cannot be too careful, in this day and age or any other." He gestured for her to sit. "Have you considered my offer?"

"I don't wish to impose. I've been offered accommodation in Wembley."

He sat down beside her. "Rachel, I wouldn't hear of it. It's only fitting you stay at Great Pulteney Street while you complete your research. The estate still has many of the doctor's papers and notebooks. Several of his samples. As well as his last diaries."

"He had more diaries?" Rachel slumped back, dumbfounded. "Surely the British Library should have them, or at least copies in their catalog."

Aubrey smiled and brushed his fingers through his hair. An errant curl fell across his forehead. "Every family has its secrets."

Rachel's stunned gaze landed on Mary Shelley's portrait. The delicate warmth of her smile. The doe-like eyes open to the world, to her own and her close confidant's imaginations, which had created creatures feared and loved by generations.

Her Frankenstein's Wretch.

His Vampyre.

"Such a wonderful friend," Aubrey muttered. His eyes glistened.

Rachel nodded.

CHAPTER SIX

Polidori hunched over the cadaver, an odor of moth balls and mulberry wine creeping from the skin. The victim's clothing had been stripped, folded neatly, and placed next to the other body on the credenza, including a silk cravat that had been knotted tight and ripped, likely in the tussle prior to death. He guessed the gentleman to be well into his fifties, with a body scarred by life and war. His left shoulder appeared gouged by a bayonet, the flesh stretched back into place long ago by battlefield stitching. Polidori ran his hands down the arms and around the torso, recognizing the dimple and bump of remnant subsurface metal fragments meant to kill. French Revolutionary War, he surmised, as the victim appeared too ancient for the Battle of Waterloo. The teeth, however, were doubtless Waterloo. He urged open the grey-stubbled jaw and slipped his fingers and thumb in behind the cheeks. The inside of the mouth was dry. Like parchment. There was a dull crack as he pressed the jaw further and pulled out the dentures. He placed them on the cadaver's hairless chest.

The chest heaved.

An arm slipped from the table to hang outstretched.

Polidori stumbled backwards in fright. He landed against the other body on the credenza, his elbow sinking into the decaying torso. An apothecary jar full of samples and formaldehyde crashed to the floor.

"My dear God." He collected his senses and returned to the gentleman—the victim. The chest slowly dropped as air was expelled through the open mouth and nostrils. Trembling, the doctor held his ear close to the mouth. No further sign of breath. He touched his fingertips to the side of the neck. They slipped naturally into two indentations from some antiquated wound. No sign of a pulse. He squeezed the hand, but no response. He held a mirror to the lips, but no fogging.

He waited, thinking hard, and then he noticed the dentures. One of the teeth was missing. He picked them up and held them close to the lantern. They were well made. Expensive. Nicely shaped teeth collected from the dead of the Waterloo battlefield. The enamel of each was strong and without blemish, groove, or decay—more likely European than British. The estate would want to keep them.

He pulled out the tooth he'd extracted from the lower-leg wound—dull, rotten, with bloody remnants of root and gum. Definitely not part of the dentures.

Polidori took out his pipe, stuffed tobacco into its head and lit it. He sat with the gentleman for the remainder of the night, his fingers lightly pressed to the wrist of the outstretched arm. The lantern guttered and the basement dropped into darkness, but still he held the cold, cold flesh, wondering if life continued or was gone. It upset him that, despite his training, he did not truly know the answer.

CHAPTER SEVEN

The cab wove through the streets and alleys around Leicester Square then into the heart of Soho. Finally they turned down Brewer and then onto Great Pulteney, pulling to a stop in front of number 38.

The ground floor of the imposing townhome was cream colored, the three upper stories brickwork, with darker bricks delineating each of the nine large sash windows—three per floor. Beside the Greek-style portico protecting the front door was a green historical marker.

JOHN WILLIAM POLIDORI
1795–1821
POET & NOVELIST
AUTHOR OF
'THE VAMPYRE'
BORN & DIED
HERE

Here.

The word jabbed at Rachel's heart as she stepped onto the sidewalk. She'd wandered this street but never entered the building, doubting any remnants of Polidori's life could still exist within its walls. Now, after talking with Aubrey, she knew her assumptions were wrong.

"Much of the home was remodeled after the Blitz," Aubrey said as he hoisted her luggage from the trunk. "But my room is almost exactly as it was. The family has always thought it best to disturb the past as little as possible."

"Your room?" Rachel said, peering toward the basement through the wrought iron fence.

"I mean, it was Doctor Polidori's room. It has the best light and is where you will stay."

Rachel shook her head, wide-eyed.

"Nonsense," Aubrey continued. "There are several empty bedrooms on the upper floors I am equally comfortable in. If you are to do justice to my ancestor's biography then you must reside in his suite. I think it will give you a better sense of him. Of who he was." He pushed his fingers through his hair again and unlocked the front door.

Rachel felt uneasy stepping into the townhome. She wondered if she was doing the right thing. Perhaps she should stay at Wembley. At the same time, she felt an unexpected excitement at being exactly—*exactly*—where her subject had researched, written, slept, dreamed.

Died.

She followed her host through the door and up the stairs.

Polidori's bedroom was at the front of the house, with dark wooden floors, almost black, and whitewashed, wood-paneled walls. The three tall sash windows were open to Great Pulteney Street, heavy cream-colored drapery pulled to the side. Centered on the far wall was the wrought iron bed frame, flanked by dressing tables and a tiled washstand. A windowed niche in the wall held a broad mahogany desk, scarified and worn. A cast iron tub, without plumbing, stood on its ball and claw feet beneath one of the windows.

"Only one bathroom in the house, I'm afraid. It's down behind the kitchen," Aubrey said. "But you are welcome to bathe in here if you'd like to use his bath."

Rachel felt flushed. His bath. His bed. His desk.

"Of course, the mattress is new." Aubrey smirked.

"Thank you," Rachel said. "I really don't know what to say. Your offer for me to stay here is so kind. So wonderful."

Aubrey checked his watch. "I'll leave you to unpack and freshen up. I usually eat at seven, but we can have dinner whenever you wish. I hope you like bangers and mash." He closed the door slowly behind him. It creaked.

Rachel sat on the edge of the bed, astonished by where she was.

CHAPTER EIGHT

Mary Shelley
Albion House
Marlow
March 1817

Darling Mary (my inquisitive Eve),
I was intrigued to hear you are expanding your original ghost story into a full-length novel. Your idea for the sea captain happening upon Frankenstein and then his wretch in the desolation of the northern ice lands adds an exciting romantic element. Peeling back the many layers of your novel, your stories within stories, consumes my imagination in the most joyful manner. I wonder that you settled upon the name "Walton" for your captain. Did it come to you in one of your dreams? It seems familiar to one who has roused my sleep of late.

Alas my original ghost story is destined not to be printed, unworthy of a longer structure. After leaving Geneva and your circle for my own tour of Switzerland and Italy I vowed to leave it incomplete. But I will admit the horror of the Vampyre demanded to be written, that I might make sense of certain occurrences during that dreadful summer at Villa Diodati. It threatened to suck the very life from me if I did not put quill to parchment. I eventually dashed off the manuscript within three days as a present of gratitude to a bon vivant who'd afforded me great hospitality. I trust it has since been relegated to a dusty box in her villa nestled in the Alps of

Switzerland and shall never see the light of day.

I have my reasons for this hope—part of an oath I made to Lord Byron after that imprudent incident where I made a scene at La Scala Opera House in Milano and was removed from the premises.

Both story and relationship have long since disintegrated from my thoughts.

Best,

John

CHAPTER NINE

Aubrey pressed a set of keys into Rachel's hand. "Feel free to come and go as you please. And nowhere in the house is off limits. You'll find most of Polidori's medical journals and private letters in the drawers of his desk. However, a few ledgers and valued personal belongings are down in the basement safe. The combo is 1-8-2-4."

"Three years after he died?"

"Um, yes."

Rachel leaned into the warmth of the wingback chair, the taste of grilled sausages still on her tongue, and took a sip of merlot. She knew Aubrey must have read every word of Polidori's writings, but she didn't wish to be influenced by his views of what each might mean.

"I have a question," she said. "The document box you sent to me in New York. It's empty."

"Is it?" His lips spread into a thoughtful smile that deepened the subtle wrinkles at his eyes. The clock on the mantle struck ten, and Aubrey rose. "I'm a bit of a night owl. I've a prior engagement in Old Compton Street to say goodbye to some old friends. You are more than welcome."

Rachel shook her head. "Perhaps another time."

He pulled on his bomber jacket and opened the parlor door. "Rachel." His gaze was penetrating, his eyes much darker than she recalled. "You're safe here. You know that don't you?" The sheen of red wine on his lips held her attention. He disappeared out into the hall.

CHAPTER TEN

Doctor Polidori dripped blue-tinted beeswax onto the flap of his letter to Mary and pressed his seal into it. The wax quickly lost its luster as it cooled. His quill stood in the ink pot beside the mangled foot and calf of the elderly gentleman.

"There is something I am missing," he muttered to himself. He gripped the cold foot, pushed his thumb into the sole then released it. An indentation remained. He removed his own boot and stocking and swung his foot up onto his knee. He gripped it in the same way and pushed his thumb into the soft flesh. It sprang back when released and flushed pink and healthy. He didn't expect the cadaver to react in the same manner, as death had most certainly overcome the gentleman. But...

"Blood," he muttered.

There was very little at the scene.

He examined again the shredded flesh of the gentleman's calf. Both tibial arteries had been severed. There should have been a lot of blood—a pool of it. He reached for his scalpel and sliced up through the remainder of the calf, following the posterior tibial artery. He needed his knife to cut through the flesh of the thigh, deep into the tough, atrophied muscles to uncover the full length of the femoral artery up into the groin. He urged the artery from the leg, alternately cutting with his knife and then his scalpel to loosen it. It should have been fat with coagulated blood, left dormant after the heart had ceased. Instead it was flat between his fingers. Like a ribbon.

"Could he have been killed somewhere else?" he said to the empty room. "The blood drained?" Polidori rang the bell for his valet, then began scratching out a letter for delivery to the Bow Street Runner.

As he wrote he reached for the flask in his coat and took a sip.
London Dry Gin with a tincture of arsenic.

CHAPTER ELEVEN

Rachel had intended on going straight to bed, to force her body clock onto local time. Instead she sat cross-legged on the bed in her pajamas, staring at Polidori's desk and the empty document box sitting on top. The window above the desk glowed from the lantern light of the townhome's internal courtyard, creating a dull aura that hugged the box, pulsing with each flicker of gaslight.

She smiled at Aubrey's cheekiness about the box's contents. Of course it was empty. A ruse to intrigue her and lead her here. She walked over to it, pulled on her gloves, nudged the latch to the side, and lifted the lid. After carefully lifting out the broken tray, which still held the envelope with her name on it, she checked the upholstery covering the inside of the box. It was definitely empty.

The desk beneath it was not.

Rachel had broken her own research protocol while unpacking her luggage and preparing for dinner. She'd opened each drawer just a crack. It was enough to determine all five were filled to capacity with documents and notebooks. Her heart skipped several beats at the thought of what might be contained within the antique mahogany furnishing.

Though it was midnight in London, she was still on New York time and thus not tired at all. She grabbed her camera and laptop and started her research.

First the outside.

A web of fine scarification crisscrossed the top, notably on the right-hand side. Most marks were shallow, the result of years of use and refurbishment. It had certainly been re-polished at some point in the past two hundred years, the scratches and nicks filled with wax and polish that had hardened generations ago. The camera flashed in the dull light of the room—two dozen closeup photos of nearly indecipherable words etched into the wood. *Reg. Serpent. Bright. Pav. Ruth. Mar. alto.*

The drawer fronts were free of mark and blemish.

Rachel leaned against the bed and checked the photos on the camera display. She smiled. The flash had been able to penetrate the layers of wax and polish. *Regiment. Serpentine. Brighton. Pavilion. Ruthven. Mary. Walton.*

The last photo held her attention. Walton?

She leaned close to the wood. Snapped another photo. Her name was etched into the mahogany. The *on* of Brighton, Pavilion, and Walton were identical. Polidori had written her name. She felt euphoric.

He must have been referring to the sea captain in Mary's novel. Still, she grinned.

Gripping her camera tight in her gloved hand, she lay on the bed, sinking into the mattress with the eiderdown blooming around her. Captain Robert Walton, from the opening chapters of *Frankenstein.* She'd read dozens of letters between Mary and Polidori outlining the evolution of the story into the full-length novel. Almost daily they had shared tidbits of their thoughts via ink.

Rachel shook her head. The connection might seem obvious, but she must not assume anything. It said *Walton.* Nothing more. She would have to find out why.

And the other words; what was their significance, that he took the time to etch them into his desk? She typed them into her spreadsheet.

The clock in the foyer downstairs struck one. A light rain was tapping against the panes of the three large windows and, outside, late-night revelers dashed along the sidewalks beneath umbrellas. Perhaps she should have gone out with Aubrey, to get to know her host. She pressed her cheek to the window and looked up at the sky. The clouds reflected the muted orange of London's streetlights as the rain increased to a torrent. She loosened the curtains and they fell across the glass, occluding light and sound from the world outside Polidori's room.

The left-hand desk drawer held thirty-six letters.

All were either fair copies or originals.

All were addressed to Mary Shelley or Doctor Polidori.

CHAPTER TWELVE

Mary Shelley
Albion House
Marlow
April 1817

Dearest Mary,
I offer you a reprieve from the horrors of your own wretch with some from my own occupation. As always it needs not be said that I value your thoughts on all matters and trust any advice you might dispense to me.
The foyer clock has recently struck one.
The elderly gentleman mentioned in my previous correspondence lies outstretched upon the table, the major arteries from both legs and arms hanging loose from where I sliced open the flesh. The sternum has been sawed and the ribs cracked. The heart lies flat within my left hand.
All are devoid of blood.
I was deep in consideration of this when my door flew open with a gusting breeze and the Bow Street Runner entered my basement, wet from rain.
"Excuse me, Doctor," he said. "I inspected the alley as requested and spoke to those within the vicinity."
I wiped my hands as Officer Hamilton opened his ledger and read his notes to me.
"Smith Court. One young lass—a three-penny upright—who, under questioning, admitted to accommodating the deceased just before his death."

"Does she have all her teeth?" I asked.

"She does. All are poorly and loose, but all are her own as far as I could tell. A pretty thing she is. Well-fed and intelligent. And adamant she and the gentleman had an arrangement and she had nothing to do with what happened after."

"Did she witness what happened? The animal that did this?" I waved toward the foot.

"Well, not exactly. They were embracing in goodbye when the gentleman screamed in apparent agony and twisted sideways, throwing her to the cobbles. Her view was occluded by his coattails, but her nostrils were filled with the unmistakable stench of charnel house decay as she glimpsed a low-crouching shadow in the darker reaches of the court. The gentleman yelled for her to run. And so she scuttled across the cobbles on hands and knees, overwhelmed by the hovering stink. She looked back in time to see the gentleman's flailing as he fell against the wall. She has no doubt she heard his skull crack, but she dared not stop until she reached the late-night crowds of Piccadilly Circus."

"No utterance from that which attacked him? No animal shriek or howl?"

Officer Hamilton cleared his throat in apparent discomfort. "Yes, Doctor. Amongst the screaming of her client and the deep grumbling of his attacker, she avows she heard the latter grunt the name Fairbank."

Officer Hamilton and I held each other's gaze, neither of us able to speak.

So, my Mary, I am certain you have already guessed my dilemma. The gentleman was killed where he was found. His vessels were devoid of blood, yet the scene of the crime contained little more than a smear. And further, if the lass's account is to be considered more than the imagination of a terrified soul, it is possible we are not looking for an animal, but a human. The worst of all creatures.

Best,

John

Postscript: I have made reservations at Rules for when you are in London next week—a booth in the main salon for Friday lunch. A private dining room upstairs for dinner that same day. We have much to discuss.

CHAPTER THIRTEEN

Rachel slid the letter carefully back into its envelope, placed it with the others in the drawer, and reclined into the depths of Polidori's wingback chair. She wondered whether the Archives of New Scotland Yard would contain cases from the Bow Street Runners. The Runners had kept the peace before the official police force was formed, but still there might be a chance. She made a note on her spreadsheet.

The rain was loud against the window panes. It was almost 3:00 AM. Almost 10:00 PM in New York.

The front door of 38 Great Pulteney Street creaked open and then closed with a loud *thunk* downstairs. Aubrey had returned. The air in the room stirred, and the temperature dropped.

He wasn't alone.

Rachel smiled as she heard uncertain, intoxicated footsteps, low voices and muffled giggles. Aubrey had had a good time; still was. Though they must both have been soaking wet. The hot water pipes in the wall rattled, followed by the dull pitch of flowing water.

Were these the sounds Polidori would have heard, living here with his father and siblings, Rachel wondered? There would have been no plumbing in the walls, but surely he'd have been aware of where each family member was and what they were doing? Or had he been alone in the townhome when he returned from Europe? Rachel was certain his father lived with him at the time but made a note to re-confirm.

Rachel hoped to find Polidori was not alone in his last years. That he'd known some kind of happiness. Some kind of love. Not only in his work, but personally.

She stood and peered out the window above the mahogany desk to gaze upon the deluged courtyard below. She guessed it looked the same as when Polidori had leaned against the same wall she was leaning against now. She imagined the warmth of his shoulder touching hers, his chest against her back, his cheeks ruddy from the cold. How she longed to truly know him, as closely as they both knew Mary. The yard, one story below, was slate-covered ground, whitewashed walls, and a wrought iron table and chairs. Urns at the edge contained topiaries of thyme, mint, and other herbs. A gas lantern reached out from the wall beside the kitchen door, flickering, sending stippled shadows amongst the raindrops and across the water-slicked flagstones.

The multi-paned bathroom window on the opposite side of the yard was steamed to translucency. Shadows and light within suggested a tender moment for her host and his companion. A naked, muscled back and buttocks—stark white—abruptly pressed against the fogged panes. Flesh and unruly hair, undoubtedly Aubrey's, wiped away streaks of condensation. Hands grasped him at the waist, urging him up until he appeared to be sitting upon the sill. The features of his companion were diffused and ambiguous within the mist. A lithe but toned body. Shaved head. Thick lips. A complexion to match Aubrey's, making them together appear as one surreal, affectionately writhing creature. Hands skimmed up the sides of Aubrey's torso, squeezing the V-shaped musculature about his shoulder blades, before the companion pressed face and lips into the crook of Aubrey's exposed neck, nuzzling the flesh, hard.

That's going to leave a mark, Rachel thought, and smiled.

She picked up her cell and sank into Polidori's bed. Adam would be in bed, too, ploughing through his latest book, *Anna Karenina,* no doubt. Rachel had never understood that book nor appreciated its heroine and had been almost glad when—

"Hey babe, you're up late. What's up?" Adam asked.

"I think, Mr. Walton, you need to tell me what you are wearing."

Adam snickered. "*Ma chérie d'amour*, you are well aware of what I don't wear in our bedroom."

The video icon flashed on the screen.

CHAPTER FOURTEEN

Officer Hamilton helped Polidori lift the body of the week's earlier victim onto the central butcher's block. He was younger than the elderly gentleman at his side, but taller, his bare feet hanging over the end of the table.

"Do you think they could be family?" Hamilton said.

Polidori gently pushed strands of blonde hair back from the younger's forehead.

"They do have similar facial features, particularly the nose and brow." He picked up his ledger and started to sketch. First the faces of the two deceased, then the wounds inflicted upon each. Whereas the elder was damaged about the calf and ankle, the younger had been mauled above the knee, chunks of muscle ripped loose from the inner thigh. Polidori squeezed the flesh of the intact leg. "By their clothing alone we know they are—or were—men of means. The lad was otherwise healthy with good muscle tone and complexion. No sign of vermin or pox. His type of athleticism indicates he was an avid equestrian. The softness of his hands, that he never worked a day in his life." The knuckles were swollen, bruised and split. "He put up a fight, but not for very long. By the grazed skin of his hip and buttocks, it appears he was dragged across the ground."

Hamilton made notes of his own. "And these?"

At both sides of the lad's waist, just above the hips, were deep scratches, some deep enough to expose the pink sinew of abdominal muscles beneath. Polidori pressed his hands to the flesh, fanning out his fingers to match the abrasions. Too broad for a hound, too grave for a human. "I cannot explain these. Fingernails would rip before they could cause this kind of damage; they would need to be as rigid as bone."

He stepped back, contemplating the two men. The way their bodies lay, the slight turning in of their knees and feet, the proportions of their legs, torsos, and skulls. The curves of their jaws, noses, and ears. The slight clench of their slender hands. Polidori held little doubt they were blood relations. One still possessed the beauty of youth, but soon enough both would be only dust.

Polidori leaned forward over the younger to reinspect the wound at the thigh for anything he might have missed. Intuitively he reached up and placed his hands upon the abdomen a second time. The tips of his fingers settled naturally into the grooves and pits of the lacerations. Directly before his face was the femoral artery, exposed and torn amongst ragged and ripped muscle. It was devoid of any remnant of blood.

Polidori looked up at Officer Hamilton. "Take me to where you found him."

The cabriolet rattled through the streets of Soho and into Mayfair, the horse's coat slick and shining from recent rain. Opulent hotels and townhomes, all much grander than any in Pulteney Street, loomed on either side. Polidori had attended functions in several of the homes of Mayfair, particularly surrounding Grosvenor Square. Played cards. Danced Quadrilles. Flirted with the women and men of high society. Met the one he'd once thought he loved, but now only despised. Perhaps feared. All his memories of Mayfair were bittersweet and mercifully ripped from the pages of the diaries he'd written as a much younger man.

The carriage pulled around the corner into Park Lane and jolted to a stop.

"You found the lad's body, late evening, in such a populated area? Surely the local residents would have known this strapping young man by sight, if not by reputation."

Hamilton jerked his chin toward Grosvenor Gate and the vast expanse of planetrees beyond. Polidori nodded.

Hyde Park.

The parkland was an inky blackness nestled between the lamplit streets of central London. Officer Hamilton unhooked a lantern from the carriage and led Polidori into the darkness. The trees and brush between Lover's Walk and the perimeter were dense and overgrown, opening into clearings lit only by the cloud-shrouded stars above. A

place where lovers of all persuasions were happy to become lost—
and found. Polidori felt unsettled, flushed, walking through this
familiar area of parkland so close to an officer of the Magistrates'
Court. "This is where you found the body?"

"Yes, against this tree." Hamilton held up the lantern.

The bark was marked by vertical scars. Polidori surmised they'd be
the same height as the lad's lacerations if he'd stood—been forced—
against the trunk. The ground between the exposed roots was
muddy—disturbed and pitted. He wondered at the lack of bloodstain,
even despite the rain of the past days. He stooped to touch the soil,
pinched his eyes shut, and sniffed his fingers.

Officer Hamilton cleared his throat. "I suspect the young man was
involved in an . . . an *unnatural* offense." He looked at his boots,
appearing uncertain. "It would be a strong coincidence, given the
elderly gentleman's occupation at the time of his death?"

"The *death* was unnatural. That is all," Polidori countered. "No
sign of blow or break to the body adequate to cause the lad's sudden
demise. Only the ravagement of the inner thigh." He glanced up at
the officer. "And the almost immediate immense loss of blood." *As if
it had been sucked from his flesh,* he dared not say. He pulled out his
pocket watch and squinted at it. "We should call into The Punchbowl
and the Running Horse. Those establishments . . ." He hesitated,
searching Hamilton's expression and unexpectedly finding a
gentleness and apprehension mirroring his own. Polidori rose to his
feet, his tension lessening. "Those establishments tend to be
frequented by others of the lad's means and possible inclinations."

The rain started to fall as their carriage rolled along the cobbles of
Park Lane and rattled into the depths of Mayfair. Polidori wiped the
condensation from the window as they came to a stop on Farm
Street, near Chesterfield Hill. The Punchbowl was a squat, cream-
colored building set amongst imposing townhomes. The ground floor
of the public house protruded onto the sidewalk—a black box with
dark windows, lined with gas lanterns and emblazoned with gold
lettering. Polidori placed his hand on the seat beside Officer
Hamilton's thigh. "Your uniform. Perhaps it would be best if you
stayed in the carriage."

Hamilton nodded. Polidori noted the color of his eyes, then quickly
pulled his hand back into his own pocket. The driver stepped out into
the pouring rain and pulled open both the public house door and

carriage door at the same time. Polidori dashed into The Punchbowl, sheened by the unavoidable precipitation.

In the lobby he shrugged off his frock coat and handed it to the doorman. He shook his head and ran his fingers through his hair, flicking the water to the floor. The meaty smell of roast game and gravy wafted down from the dining room upstairs. Straight ahead, in a light much too dim for conversation, cigar smoke hung beneath ancient rafters.

CHAPTER FIFTEEN

Rachel read and catalogued five more letters before she closed the drawer, put away her laptop, and crawled into bed. The details of the investigation had her intrigued, but she doubted they had any relevance to Polidori's death almost four years later. She sank into the feather mattress and stared up at the ceiling, crossed with broken shadows cast through the window by the courtyard lantern below. Two hundred years of dreams had been thrown across the same patterned plasterwork since Polidori had lain in this bed.

Alone, Rachel thought.

The rain was still heavy on the windowpanes, lulling her toward sleep. She bunched the pillow beneath her cheek and drew in a deep breath. At first, she thought of Adam, alone in their bed in New York. But then, as her thoughts mellowed with exhaustion, she sensed Polidori's warmth within the comfort of *his* bed, smelled the sweetness of his sweat, heard the gentle whisper of his measured breathing as he fell asleep beside her. She reached out in her haze to touch him, not wanting him to be alone. She skimmed her hand along his cleanly shaved jaw and reached up to twist around her finger the errant curl that flopped across his forehead.

"What happened to you?" she breathed into the pillow.

CHAPTER SIXTEEN

Mary Shelley
Albion House
Marlow
April 1817

My Mary,

Once again, forgive me for ceasing yesterday's letter without adequate conclusion. I was called to the Bow Street Magistrates' Court by Officer Hamilton. I shall tell you more on Friday.

For now allow me to continue where I left off. I stepped into The Punchbowl, shrugged off my frock coat and handed it to the doorman. He offered no towel, so I shook my head and combed my fingers through my hair so I might maintain some modicum of decency. The meaty smell of roast game and gravy wafted down from the dining room upstairs. Straight ahead, in a light much too dim for conversation, cigar smoke hung beneath ancient rafters.

Perhaps two dozen gentlemen sat within. I daresay most all have met our acquaintance at one gathering or another. The perfume of port was sweet, the cigars heady. The house manager confirmed I was familiar with the crowd, filled my glass, then personally selected and cut one of his very best cigars for me.

Those patrons who were not reading the broadsheets or playing cards shared banal gossip hardly worthy of the ink on this letter to you, my friend. I shared quiet words with those I knew well but made my way through the rooms as quickly as I politely could to determine the proclivity of those hidden within the crowd. A small parlor at the rear, lit only by the fireplace and the glow of cigars, proved promising. I shall not bore you with their dialogue though I myself consumed at least a third of my cigar in their company. At all times my attention was across their shoulders toward a young man in the corner. He was perhaps twenty-one—recently become a man. He was slumped in a wingback, his features drawn, his port unattended, his cigar extinguished and threatening to drop from his fingers. I excused myself from the fireside company and joined him in the wingback opposite his.

"I can see why any gentleman would choose this corner. If offers a splendid view of the room," I said. He lifted his red-rimmed, bloodshot eyes to mine. I daresay he had been weeping. I leaned toward him, took the cigar from him, and placed it in the ashtray. That brief touch of his fingers was cold and clammy. I shifted my wingback around so our conversation was hidden from those at the fire.

"I'm looking for a man," I whispered.

He was immediately startled and began to stand. "Do you want to get us both hanged?" He gulped before collecting his senses and quickly sitting back down.

"You misunderstand me, good sir." I pulled the case ledger from my waistcoat and opened it to the sketch of the deceased lad. "I'm looking for this man," I said. "Any information you might provide would be appreciated."

His eyes widened, and he drank down his full glass of port. He lifted the extinguished cigar to his lips and said, "Please." I leaned over that he might light his cigar from mine.

"You are acquainted?"

"Yes. I had met Master James Fairbank on several occasions over the last year. His family owns an estate somewhere in Sussex. Perhaps the countryside about Brighton. Though I know little more than that. He preferred his privacy, as do I."

Tears welled in his eyes, and his chin trembled.

"You can trust me," I said, and though he appeared no more than a year my junior, I added, "son."

We smoked our cigars in silence until they were spent.

"Did you see what happened?" I asked.

He nodded.

"I am assisting a Bow Street Runner in the investigation of Master Fairbank's demise, Master . . ." I waited.

"Aldridge," he supplied, his voice breaking.

"The Runner is waiting outside, Master Aldridge." He stiffened, and I grasped his hand. It was as soft as my own, starting to warm, his fingers sticky from the cigar. "As a gentleman, I assure you of our discretion regarding anything not immediately associated with the cause of death. Are you willing to come with us, to tell us what you know?"

Again, he nodded.

Best,

John

CHAPTER SEVENTEEN

Rachel jolted awake, the eiderdown on the floor—kicked there during the night—the room still dark from drawn curtains, the rain still heavy against the panes. She glanced at her cellphone. 6:00 PM. *Is that New York time or London time?* Had she slept right through the day? Two missed calls. She touched the callback icon.

"Hey, sleepyhead." Adam chuckled, the video bobbing and blurry as he climbed the stairs of their brownstone. "I guess the time change threw you for a loop."

"Yes. That and our, um, *talk* last night." She chuckled, too. "How's Henny?"

"Napping." The view flipped from Adam's face to Helen, fast asleep in her bed. It zoomed in close to the flutter of eyelash, the rose-colored lips holding tight to a thumb. "I can call you back when its dinnertime, or bathtime. Henny's and then later… mine."

Rachel's smile made her cheeks ache. "Deal. Love you, babe," she said.

The smell of bacon drifted up from the kitchen. She pulled on her dressing gown and slippers, hoping that other aroma was coffee.

Aubrey was in the galley, barefooted on the heated limestone tiles. A black silk robe with an embroidered dragon on it, sashed tight at his waist, enhanced his gym-built body. "It seems we both prefer a night schedule. Coffee?" he said.

Rachel accepted the mug. "Thanks. And it appears silk cravats run in the Polidori family."

Aubrey nudged the cravat a little higher on his neck. He didn't blush, but the gleam in his eyes intensified and the dimples in his cheek deepened. "You started your research last night, didn't you? I knew you wouldn't be able to wait."

"And, as usual, it has uncovered more questions than answers."

"The Fairbank case?"

"Yes, but please," Rachel said, "let me find my own way with the source material."

"I understand. Though allow me to offer one suggestion. The medical and personal journals in the middle drawer—read them in parallel with the letters. Each ledger and entry is dated and correlates with his letters to Mary."

Rachel walked over to the wrought iron French doors and peered out into the courtyard. The slate was submerged in an inch of rainwater that skimmed back and forth on the stone before swirling down the drain on the far side. "Is your friend still here?"

"Jess? No. Left before the sun came up. A creature of habit. And perhaps necessity. I hope we didn't disturb you." He flipped the eggs, and the toast jumped from the toaster.

Rachel caught the reflection of Aubrey in the rain-streaked windowpane. As he prepared the breakfast he appeared to study her every movement, reflect on her every word. It had been the same the previous evening before he'd left for Old Compton Street. She looked forward to discussing the Romantics and her research with him. But not yet. She had no doubt he knew as much of Mary Shelley as she did, and definitely more of his ancestor than she'd yet discovered from the letters, ledgers, and scraps of paper. The steam from her coffee fogged the window and obscured Aubrey's reflection, as her thoughts settled on the subjects of her research.

"Doctor Polidori loved Mary," she said.

"Yes, he did." Aubrey was beside her suddenly, his body hot in proximity. He wiped at the condensation on the glass to look up at the sky. His nails were strong, manicured, buffed. His robe sleeves were rolled up to his elbows, showing muscled forearms scattered with fine, dark hair. "Though love is a strange thing. At times, I think the romance of friendship can be much stronger, more enduring than that of intimate lovers. Of course, there was never anything sexual between them—Mary and John. It was trust. Respect. Its own kind of love." He gracefully brushed strands of hair from Rachel's face with the tips of his fingers. The familiarity felt natural. Irreproachable.

Rachel liked the way he thought.

They ate sitting at the kitchen counter, staring out at the rain. The bacon and eggs were good. The coffee strong.

"How is it you came to inherit this home?" she said.

"Doctor Polidori had four brothers and four sisters. He was the eldest of the sons, and the eldest son always inherits the estate."

"But he died. Without heir."

Aubrey held her gaze. Again, the intensity of his eyes darkened as he peered deep into her eyes. "I've made reservations at Rules for this Friday. A booth for lunch."

"Rules? Polidori mentioned taking Mary there in one of his letters. It still exists?"

"This is London, Rachel. Turn the corner and you'll travel from the twenty-first century back to the eighteenth. Sometimes farther. What day did he say he would take her there?"

"Friday." She narrowed her eyes. "But you knew that already."

His cheeky grin made him appear as roguish as she'd always thought of Doctor Polidori. "Two hundred years to the day. I'd already presumed your acceptance and ordered the same menu, down to the same vintage of bottled wine."

Rachel shivered, astonished that he'd go to such trouble and expense. The romance of the gesture.

"Then you must allow me to take you out for drinks and supper tonight. After I get a few more hours of research under my belt. Is The Punchbowl still open in Mayfair?"

He nodded. "And as sophisticated as ever."

CHAPTER EIGHTEEN

Doctor Polidori sat with Master Aldridge before his parlor fireplace in 38 Great Pulteney Street. Aldridge, a resident of Bath, was a refined young man, Polidori had learned, known and pursued by the mothers of all the available daughters in Somerset County. He'd much to offer, and Polidori assumed a Somerset maiden might yet secure his fortune. But not the totality of his heart, of that he was certain. Both men puffed on cigars and picked at a tray of cold meats and well-larded bread. Officer Hamilton stood by the mantle with his ledger.

"Master Fairbank and I were first introduced at The Punchbowl late last year."

"By whom?" Hamilton said.

"A mutual acquaintance, also a Fairbank in name. Possibly an elderly uncle, but other than the fact he plays poorly at cards I know nothing of him. Master Fairbank and I hit it off over The Punchbowl's roast venison, and ample tankards of their ale." He glanced at Officer Hamilton.

"Go on," Polidori said.

"We would often walk the grounds of Hyde Park. Sometimes we might circumnavigate the Serpentine Lake two or three times, stopping by the Keeper's Lodge to cut and light fresh cigars before continuing our constitutional. We'd share a flask of port and talk of the stars, the clouds crossing the night sky, the play of moon shadows upon the lawn."

Polidori had admired the same on several occasions—the consequence of living in a household of academics and poets. And certainly the result of the summer spent with Lord Byron and the Shelleys on Lake Geneva. He could look at nothing now without also observing the lyric, the romantic, the emotion that kept all nature unbridled. Even the bodies lying lifeless in his basement possessed a distinct type of poeticism. A rhythmic cadence that he would keep pressing his fingers and his mind to, until he understood its sentiment and message.

"Tell us of last Sunday evening."

"Master Fairbank arrived at The Punchbowl at around midnight. We cared not for venison, or beer, or cigars. Only to walk the parkland and enjoy each other's company. We strolled through Kensington Gardens, where we talked of dreams that could never come true."

Polidori's heart tightened.

"We were . . ." Master Aldridge stopped, distracted by the scratch of Hamilton's pencil on the page. "We were walking back toward Grosvenor Gate—a shortcut through the dense copse of trees sheltering the parkland from Park Lane." He abruptly choked on a sob. "We only stopped momentarily, in a clearing. And then it happened."

CHAPTER NINETEEN

The cab pulled up in front of The Punchbowl in the center of Mayfair.

"It looks just how I imagined it from Polidori's letter."

"The outside perhaps, but inside has been renovated at least a dozen times—Polidori wouldn't recognize it. He might know the layout of the private dining rooms upstairs, but even those are decked out with century-old antiques not even imagined until decades after his death. Despite their age they would all appear thoroughly modern, perhaps futuristic, to him."

Rachel had always been careful with dates in her research, but many things were beyond the breadth of her examination. There would always be some haziness as to what Polidori meant when he wrote *wingback* or *cabriolet*. They could have been current models to the day, or they could have been designs many years or decades old—perhaps even antiques at the time Polidori used them. All she knew for certain was the furniture in Polidori's room at 38 Great Pulteney Street was original, as were the wingbacks in the parlor— their leather worn to a sheen by countless evenings of reading, of conversation, of port and cigars.

Aubrey had confirmed the butcher's slab in the basement was also original, but she'd yet to venture down there, to confront what the letters and ledgers revealed in gruesome detail.

The sidewalk in front of the pub was crowded, men and women in suits, sipping sauvignon blanc or pints of beer. A few smoked cigarettes. Aubrey stepped up out of the cab, pushing his wallet back into his jacket pocket. He reached for Rachel's hand as she followed, then slipped his fingers between hers to lead her inside. His hand was warm and soft, his grasp friendly and pleasant as they made their way through the pub toward the bar.

"What do you feel like?" he asked.

"What are you having?"

"Fuller's London Porter."

"Is that a beer?"

Aubrey nodded. "And I can guarantee even Doctor Polidori was partial to a porter or two every now and then."

"Sounds good."

He ordered the beers and pushed a few pounds across the bar.

"I'll get the next round," Rachel insisted.

The pint glass was heavy and cold, the beer creamy with subtle undertones of chocolate and coffee.

Aubrey kept his hold on her hand, brushing his thumb gently over her fingers. Rachel assumed it was a subconscious action, affectionate perhaps, but innocent. And pleasant. He stood up on his toes to see over the crowd. "There's a table over there. Quick, head in that direction." He pointed and Rachel stepped blindly through the crowd toward the pub's front window where they found a high-top with two stools. Aubrey pulled one out for her, then sat upon the other.

They clinked glasses and took a sip of beer to celebrate gaining the table. "I've never read anything indicating Polidori drank beer," she said.

Aubrey shrugged. "It wasn't all port, gin, and madeira. Once he even secreted Mary into the Thompson Brothers' establishment to taste their ale." He leaned on the window sill, staring off into the crowd, face flushed and smile broad, as if recalling a happy memory.

Rachel smiled, too, dreaming of a life and all its vagaries from two centuries ago. They were quiet for a time, content with their own thoughts, watching the flow and ebb of the crowd and allowing the alcohol to mellow the evening.

Rachel leaned forward, her elbows on the table. "Tell me about gin with a tincture of arsenic. I read about it in one of Polidori's letters."

Aubrey took a steady draught of beer then licked the foam from his lips. "We need to consider London in the 1810s and '20s could be a very dangerous place. Poisons were available to anyone, even children, from any local merchant. They were a necessity for cleaning, making medicines, killing vermin, matters of everyday life.

Arsenic. Strychnine. Cyanide. There was no distribution protocol. They were also a way for someone seemingly powerless to exact revenge. A cook. A servant. An abused family member. A gambling partner who perchance had taken out insurance on your life." He chuckled. "Arsenic in particular was odorless and tasteless. Undetectable, at that time, both before and after death."

"But why would he knowingly drink it? Even such a small amount."

Again, Aubrey licked his lips, focused on the depths of his beer. Rachel couldn't help noticing how pink, how healthy, how wet his tongue was.

"Fortification. An experiment, if you will. To help the body build resistance."

"Against poisoning?"

"Exactly. Another beer?"

"Let me." Rachel swallowed her last gulp and headed through the crowd toward the bar. As she edged between the suits, she wondered if Doctor Polidori could have accidently overdosed. She doubted it, but it was a possibility. Or perhaps he hadn't built up the resistance he needed in time.

CHAPTER TWENTY

Polidori pushed his wingback closer to the parlor fire to ward off a sudden chill. Aldridge rose to stand before the blaze, gazing into its depths.

"Without warning, I was thrown from Master Fairbank, my tender grip wrenched from about my friend's waist by a great force. I landed awkwardly upon the ground, hitting my head, and for several moments I was stunned, breathless, my vision blurred. Then I heard Master Fairbank—James . . ." Aldridge stifled a sob that shook his entire body. His cheeks were flushed and wet. "James screamed. More of a gagging grunt, really, as if the very life were being sucked from him. He fell down upon me in the dark, his hands grappling to secure a hold upon my shoulders, but he was dragged away. I pushed myself up to follow, crawling upon my elbows along the damp grass and mud."

Polidori held tight to the arms of his chair, holding at bay his urge to give comfort until the account was finished.

"I had eaten very little that day, but still I vomited when a horrid stench met my nostrils, more putrid than the gutters and sewers that empty into the Thames. I found James sprawled over the roots of a tree, face white, eyelids fluttering, mouth gulping for air. For life. And then his features fixed tight, my face the last thing he would see upon this Earth, all beingness and lifeforce draining from him." Aldridge stared at his own reflection in the mirror above the fireplace, the grief on his face transforming to a subtle terror at the image of himself in the dim, firelit parlor. He reached up and touched his fingers to the glass.

"Go on," Polidori whispered gently.

"It . . . It was about his legs, a great bulk similar in size to James, but hunched and twisted, its torso muscular and strong but burdened by parts that appeared to be no more than rotted flesh. What I presume was its face was pressed to James's inner thigh. Its head jerked, its long hair in disarray as it . . . fed . . . upon him. And then, to my everlasting shame, I ran. Fear was much stronger than the need to protect the body of my dear, dead friend." Raw emotion overcame Master Aldridge, and he gripped the mantle, his legs buckling beneath him as he sobbed.

Doctor Polidori could bear it no longer. He rose and pulled Aldridge into a tight embrace as the younger wept against his shoulder. Polidori and Officer Hamilton stared at one another, wide-eyed.

CHAPTER TWENTY-ONE

Aubrey turned the key and pushed open the front door of 38 Great Pulteney Street with his foot. The clock in the hall chimed 4:15 AM. "Thanks again for the fish 'n' chips. I really enjoyed our evening together." He bowed with an intoxicated flourish and brushed his lips across the back of Rachel's hand. "A night cap, m'lady?" he asked, looking up at her.

She grinned. "Sure, why not. It's not like I can do any more research tonight."

In the kitchen, Aubrey shrugged off his bomber jacket and opened the top buttons of his dress shirt. He was sweating in the heat of the night, the white cotton clinging to the musculature beneath. The dark hair above his pecs was recently clipped.

"I have something you might enjoy." His smile was cheeky, just how Rachel had come to like it. He reached into the antique kitchen armoire and extracted two boxes. Both were stamped with ink with words Rachel recognized as Spanish, or perhaps Portuguese.

Aubrey carried them out to the courtyard's wrought iron table. The two of them sat, and Aubrey pried the boxes open. One held a squat bottle of port and two glasses; the other, cigars.

"Oh, I don't smoke," she said.

"I do only rarely, but these were Polidori's preferred brand, and this is a special occasion. You, here with me, in this house, researching and writing a biography that should have been published long ago. Celebrating a life immortalized after he dared write the unspoken."

Rachel chuckled. "I never expected to be tempted toward vice by a Polidori. Perhaps I'll have a few puffs of yours, if you don't mind.

Purely for research." She relaxed into the chair, her skin still tingling from the beer buzz. Through sleepy eyes she absently studied the line of Aubrey's jaw, the stubble upon his cheek, the way he pursed his lips as he opened the bottle of Porto. A drop of sweat slid down his neck to pool in the pleasant niche above his collar bone.

He pushed the cork off with his thumbs. It bounced across the table and disappeared behind the topiary of thyme.

"Salute." They clinked glasses. The port was rich and sweet.

Aubrey unwrapped a cigar and ran its length beneath his nostrils as he drew in a deep breath. Then he cut it, warmed it near the gas lantern flame, and lit it. He slumped into his chair, port glass in one hand, cigar in the other, held to his lips. Scented smoke escaped his mouth as he closed his eyes, thick lashes against ruddy cheeks. "Hello, old friend," he murmured.

"Did you do any research into the Fairbank case?" Rachel asked. "Apart from what's written in the letters and ledgers upstairs, I mean."

Aubrey scrunched up his face, eyes still closed. "What do you mean?"

"Did you look for any formal investigation papers from the Bow Street Runners?"

"I never saw the need to, I suppose. I had Polidori's papers. It didn't occur to me to confirm something I had no doubt was true."

Rachel thought his answer curious, at odds with how vested she thought him to be in the Romantics and his family's heritage.

He handed her the cigar. "Inhale slowly, just into your mouth. Savor the taste and aroma." He pulled his chair around the table to be at her side.

Rachel touched the cigar to her mouth, the sheen left by Aubrey's port-flavored lips wet and warm on hers. The smoke eddied, vanilla blending with the sweeter Porto. She was instantly reminded of the first time she'd opened Mary Shelley's document trunk, the heady aroma of port and cigars, of parchment. And again, when she'd opened Polidori's document box. *The empty box.* She giggled, the beer and port and cigar fully taking their toll. With no thought of consequence, she leaned into Aubrey's side, and he wrapped his arm across her shoulders.

"It's a good combination, isn't it?"

She nodded.

CHAPTER TWENTY-TWO

Polidori stood in his doorway as Officer Hamilton and Master Aldridge climbed up into a carriage. The first glint of day was emerging into the cloud-shrouded sky. A breeze crept down the street, remnants of night mist eddying in the doorways. Aldridge had a family town residence overlooking Berkeley Square Gardens in Mayfair, but he didn't know where either Fairbank, the younger or the elder, resided whilst in London. *Other than in my basement,* Polidori thought. It seemed odd Aldridge did not know Fairbank's address, given their closeness. He assumed the two of them would have appreciated any opportunity for privacy. Of course, one could expect very little privacy even inside a residence—of that, Polidori was acutely aware. Most likely the families of each lad were unaware the other existed, or wished not to know.

The clock in the hall chimed 4:30 AM. The house was quiet. The cook, parlor maid, and house maid would undoubtedly be awake and about their first chores, but they made no noise. Polidori scribbled a note and left it on the hall credenza for his valet not to wake him till early evening.

In his room he shucked off his boots and coat and loosened his cravat. He glanced out the desk window, down into the courtyard. The gas lantern cast fragmented shadows over the wrought iron table. The chairs sat side by side, a light mist swirling like the smoke of a savored cigar.

He needed a distraction from the horror of Aldridge's story. The horror that lay decaying in his basement. The horror his life had eddied into since . . .

He thumbed open the buttons of his vest and shirt and loosened the laces of his corset, throwing each across his dressing bench before sitting down at his desk with his document box. He flicked the latch and urged open the lid, cracking the wax seal confirming the security of his personal musings. The ledger inside contained page after page of his careful and thoughtful writing, much scribbled over until it could no longer be read. Only the last several pages were legible, the first discernable words being the title of his manuscript.

Ernestus Berchtold or The Modern Oedipus.

His written thoughts were his own, unencumbered by reality, which never seemed quite on his side. He was flawed, as were all men, but whenever he dipped his quill into ink, he felt he was giving some direction to his own course of destiny. And identity. It helped him make sense of the world.

He read through the pages of the incomplete story, sipping at his arsenic-tinctured flask of gin, adding a comma, then just as quickly scrubbing it from existence. He shook the flask, wondering how much was in it when he'd started. Then he took another deep draught and thrust it out of reach. He had been writing the novel for well over a year, the first words scrawled in the conservatory of Villa Diodati in the summer of 1816, as he'd listened to the rain falling on the glass surrounding him.

Piffle, Lord Byron had said when he'd peered over Polidori's shoulder. The doctor had muted his embarrassed anger until he'd once again been alone in the room. Then he'd ripped the offending pages from his ledger and thrown them into the fire.

"Piffle," Polidori whispered to himself. "My story is worth telling, too. I am no longer the lad you took advantage of. I have a will of my own and the words worthy to tell it." He stared at the blank page, but no more would come. Not yet.

He dug out his letter opener from a drawer and stabbed it into the mahogany, scraping and cutting until the word was complete: *Ruthven*. The name of his Vampyre, from his hastily scrawled manuscript, who bore no little resemblance to Lord Byron himself. Purely coincidental, he would say, should anyone ever ask. Fortunately, that story would never be published or read.

The clock downstairs chimed the hour, and he replaced the ledger into the box, dripped sealing wax onto the lip of the lid, and pressed his signet ring into it. After pulling on his nightgown and bed socks, he blew out the candle and crawled into his bed, drawing the heavy eiderdown up and over his head.

CHAPTER TWENTY-THREE

Rachel?

Rachel kicked the eiderdown from on top of her, half asleep, half awake, not remembering when or how she'd gone to bed.

Rachel?

Her eyelids fluttered as she inhaled the warm, sweet musk of sweat in the bed beside her.

Open the box, Rachel. Please open the box.

She tossed, throwing her arm across the bed, pulling the eiderdown over her chest. She darted a fleeting glance around the room. The curtains were drawn. She was alone in the dark.

She pulled the eiderdown up and over her head.

Please, Rachel.

She felt breath hot on her face, lips close to hers.

CHAPTER TWENTY-FOUR

Polidori's sleep had been restless. The heat in his room had been stifling. He needed to get out of the townhouse. Out into the streets to make sense of his thoughts.

The evening came quickly.

He stepped from his carriage onto the sidewalk at the Theatre Royal, Covent Garden. The night air was chilled, the cobbles shining from the early evening rain. Several dozen cabriolets and phaetons, their hoods up, stood in wait for the show to end. Valets and groomsmen attended their horses and ponies, the fresh, sweet scent of horse manure not unpleasant. Beggars and pickpockets lurked in alleyway shadows, hoping for a shiny penny or pocket watch from the well-to-do patrons, Polidori surmised. He kept a wary eye as he pulled a cigar from his pocket and lit it.

The monumental dome of St. Paul's Cathedral loomed in the dull night sky, wet and glistening.

"I shall walk back home, my good man," Polidori said to his valet. He tipped his hat, and the carriage pulled away.

Grimaldi was headlining tonight as Clown in another of his successful Harlequin pantomimes. Polidori and Lord Byron had once been introduced to Grimaldi, though he doubted Grimaldi would remember meeting anyone but Byron, who eclipsed anyone around him with his wit and condescension. He shuddered and pulled his frockcoat tight.

The doormen drew open the theatre doors, and the last of the audience wafted out into Bow Street, singing. Polidori glanced at the Magistrates' Court behind him, where the Bow Street Runners were stationed, wondering if Officer Hamilton had yet determined the city residence of the Fairbanks—or if they held a city property at all.

He puffed on his cigar as the theatre-goers passed by. Carriages filled and then rattled atop the cobbles toward late suppers, gentlemen's clubs, townhomes, and hotels. He walked across the street to join the remaining crowd, eager to follow the presumed track of the elderly Fairbank.

To somehow divine where he might have lived in this vast metropolis.

He followed a dwindling crowd down Long Acre toward Soho and arrived at Leicester Square without incident. Bright lanterns dangled from ropes hung between buildings and trees, illuminating the fashionably dressed as they sipped sherry by the central fountain.

The shrill call of a Runner's whistle echoed from the alleys to the north. Another pierced the night from the west—somewhere near Piccadilly. The whistles grew frantic, converging toward the heart of Soho. Polidori ran, wishing he'd brought his medical bag.

Running through alleys and passageways, he became turned around, the squalor of less favorable streetscapes and establishments quickly eroding his sensibilities of what London should be. He ran down a flagstoned passage, slim enough he had to scuttle sideways past some revelers, dumbfounded at seeing a gentleman in such haste. Suddenly he felt plunged hundreds of years into the past, surrounded by decayed Tudor homes and tilting shopfronts. The air was heavy with the smell of damp wood and wool. He pushed open a gate and stepped quickly over piles and puddles of excrement. Through another wooden gate and he skidded into Seven Dials, where seven lanes, each one seedier and more putrid than the last, fanned out from the intersection. Hundreds convened around the public houses—one on each of the seven corners—the stench of rancid beer and humanity less agreeable to him than that of the men lying in his basement. He became lost again in his haste, turning an ear toward the shrill whistles that continued unabated. No doubt he would soon find half a dozen Bow Street Runners hovering over another dead body in the descending London fog.

As he loped along another passage, he abruptly doubled over, pain reaching deep into his abdomen and knocking the breath from him. He leaned against a wall and knuckled his side to massage the ache. He was not a runner. He could box, but he could not run.

He looked around and determined he was perhaps half a block from

Charing Cross Road, in a desolate, convoluted space dominated by three large planetrees, their roots firm within a foot of what Polidori hoped was sludgy mud.

The whistles drew nearer.

The tree canopy obscured the foggy, sooty sky above so all Polidori could see was the spire of an unrecognized church looming high beyond the leaves. It started to drizzle. Then it poured. He huddled against the trunk of the biggest tree, his couture quickly saturated, his feet sinking into the mud almost to the top of his Wellingtons.

A movement of shadow, a deepening of the darkness caught his eye.

The familiar odor of formaldehyde cut his nostrils.

The shadow scuttled toward him, fast and low across the mud. Before Polidori could even think, it caught him about the waist and, with a resonating squelch, they landed in the mire. He was blinded by muck. The weight of the beast upon him and the strength of its grip around his torso filled him with terror that made him swing wild. It was as long as he was tall, with twisting, angry movements and sour breath hot on his face. He feared it was seeking the tender flesh of his neck, ready to draw the lifeblood running through his veins. He punched hard and heard the crack of bone. Again, and his fist sank into the thing's chest, caught between shattered ribs. With a fierce yell, he delivered a backhand with all the force he could muster. There was a resounding splintering sound. Its jaw perhaps. The thing leapt from him, a fleshless bone slapping heavily across Polidori's face. He blacked out only momentarily before jolting awake once more. His skull pulsed with a blinding ache.

The Runners' whistles shrilled, and Polidori wiped the mud from his eyes to see their upheld lanterns fragmenting light through the pouring rain. Officer Hamilton leaned down and gripped him by the forearm, pulling him to his feet and pressing his hand to his heart.

"Doctor!"

Polidori nodded. "I am okay. It got away?" he asked.

"It did. We've been on its course since Golden Square."

"You found a third body there?"

"No, sir. It appears however, *you* have found a third."

At their feet lay the body of a young man, his flesh decayed, his bones protruding, his tailoring impeccable but saturated in the grey-green ooze of a carcass long dead and buried.

Polidori and Officer Hamilton sniffed, diluted formaldehyde tickling their nostrils.

CHAPTER TWENTY-FIVE

Rachel's sleep had been restless. The heat had been stifling. She needed to get out of the townhouse. Out into the streets to make sense of her thoughts.

The evening came quickly.

She left 38 Great Pulteney Street and followed Polidori's course from Covent Garden at twilight. The squalor of the 1800s had been bulldozed or, more likely, detonated during the Blitz. Somehow, she made it to within a block of Seven Dials—possibly even along the same passageway he'd run that day. She followed each of the seven streets fanning out from the crossroads, each lined with theaters, restaurants, bars, and coffee shops. No sign of squalor anywhere.

Seven Dials was cordoned off from road traffic, the cobbles covered in rubber matting. A music stage blocked Monmouth Street, multicolored spotlights arcing around the intersection and up into the darkened sky. Several hundred millennials in headphones jumped up and down in a silent rave that swamped the crossroads. Many men were shirtless in the hot and sticky London evening, tank tops and T-shirts tied at their waists. Plastic beer cups were strewn everywhere, sneakered and bare feet crushing them in the joyful thump and hum of the otherwise silent celebration. The air was infused with sweat and beer and the sharp, fresh scent of ozone before the imminent rain. The beat pulsed along the veins at Rachel's temples—more a pressure inside her head than a sound at her ear. She wondered what Polidori would have thought of all this.

Her stomach rumbled.

She stepped off Upper St. Martin's Lane and into a tea shop away from the crowds. It was full of creative types sipping chai lattes and typing the next great English novel on their laptops. Rachel took a seat by the window, ordered a lemongrass tea and buttered toast and marmalade, and pulled up the photo of Polidori's letter to Mary on her phone. It had detailed his route, and his confusion. She reread the paragraphs following his entrance into Seven Dials.

Rain started to tap the glass beside her.

The ravers will be ecstatic, she thought. *Or electrocuted.*

"Is this seat taken?"

Rachel smiled at the newcomer and shook her head. She was about to return her gaze to her phone, but his eyes struck her. They were an intense green—a high contrast to the pale skin and neatly clipped copper hair. His thick brows matched the copper stubble along the defined edge of his jaw and around the curve of his lips. He smiled, revealing agreeably white teeth, his canines perhaps a little too pointed but not enough to diminish his appearance.

"Hi," he said, the word no more than a breath, before he sat beside her and opened a book on his lap.

Rachel gave him a covert sideways glance. His skin was stark white except for a scattering of freckles across the distinct lines of his cheeks and nose. His build was slight, but athletic. *Cute*, she thought. His loose-fitting white cotton shirt with the sleeves pushed up to his elbows revealed strong forearms covered in fine copper hair. *Yes, cute.*

He rested one hand upon his thigh, the other following the text of his book as he read. It was in Latin. Rachel squinted to read it upside down.

Disputatio Medica Inauguralis, Quaedam de Morbo, Oneirodynia Dicto, Complectens.

Rachel sipped her tea, mulling over the words. Her face paled and she almost choked.

She slowly turned her head toward him and found he was staring intently at her. His smile was crooked, his left canine pressed into his thick lower lip, now blood-red with the pressure.

"Are you following me?" she asked.

His smile broadened, and he was no longer cute. "Should I be?"

Rachel tucked a five-pound note under her saucer and charged out into the driving rain, toward the crowded rave. As she passed the coffee shop window where she'd just been sitting, she saw him inside, pulling on his jacket and shoving his book into a pocket. She quickened her step, her hair and clothes becoming quickly soaked, until she reached the throng of wet, semi-naked twenty-somethings packing Seven Dials into a tight, thudding mass. A flash of white skin and copper hair skated at the periphery of her vision, and she ran. She tripped on the steps at the intersection's central column, faltering sideways.

Firm, strong arms embraced her as she found her footing.

The green of his eyes, encircled by thick copper lashes, mesmerized her at such close quarters, with a depth she couldn't fathom. He smiled, his canines even more pronounced, and yet he was inexplicably, extraordinarily beautiful. Rachel felt as though the breath was being drawn from her lungs, the thoughts from her mind. She was thankful for the support of his grip as her legs felt weakened.

"Hi," he said again—that breath of a word.

He appeared to be studying her, savoring her face, his gaze skimming her lips, and the curve of her neck. He ran the backs of his fingers along the hollow below her jawline, slipped his hand around to cup the nape beneath her hair. Rachel sensed a strange, dulling euphoria, her head tilting back, baring her neck fully to him. The rain fell hard, soaking them both as he pulled her tight against the icy heat of his body and leaned down to place his open mouth upon her neck.

They were suddenly thrown sideways, down onto the mat-covered cobbles. Some of the crowd had stumbled and fallen inward toward the central column of Seven Dials.

Rachel blinked, awareness crashing in. She scuttled backward, crawling amongst the revelers as they recovered their balance and continued to dance. She squeezed through the undulating bodies to the other side and then ran toward Charing Cross. Once safely in a cab, she pulled out her phone to call Adam.

Instead she called Aubrey.

He was waiting in the portico of 38 Great Pulteney Street when the cab pulled up to the curb. He helped her out, wrapped a towel around her shoulders, and led her inside and up the stairs toward Polidori's room. They stopped on the landing.

"Could you have been mistaken?" he said.

"No, I'm certain. He was reading Polidori's medical thesis on somnambulism.”

“In Latin?”

“In Latin.”

“And that’s all you remember? He didn’t talk to you, or follow you?”

Rachel furrowed her brow, feeling as if there was something she’d forgotten. She shook her head. “No. As far as I know he’s still back in the café. I, um . . .”

Aubrey peered into her eyes, searching. He cupped her cheeks and turned her head from side to side, scrutinizing her neck.

“What?” Rachel asked, pulling the towel tight around her.

He shook his head. “As long as you’re all right. Best you get out of these wet clothes before you catch pneumonia. I took the prerogative of drawing you a bath.” He reached for her, but hesitated and withdrew his hand. “I’m sorry. I’ll be in the parlor if you’d like to talk afterwards.”

Rachel closed the door behind her and leaned into it, feeling like she needed to cry but couldn’t.

Polidori’s bath beckoned from beneath the windows, steaming. A glass of wine, blood-red, stood beside the claw-foot of the ancient tub.

CHAPTER TWENTY-SIX

"Forgive my impropriety, Doctor, but expediency is of the utmost concern." Officer Hamilton glanced at the valet stooping over the steaming, linen-lined bathtub. Then he turned his back to peer out the window at the night-shrouded Great Pulteney Street below.

"Certainly." Polidori shrugged off his muddy topcoat and let it fall to the floor. "My man's discretion is assured."

The valet poured in the final pail of hot water, stirred the tub with his hand to ensure it was temperate, then assisted Polidori with the removal of his ruined couture. The outer garments would need to be burned. The undergarments could perhaps be salvaged with a day of boiling. His pocket watch was secure in the vest's fob pocket and appeared sound.

"The body has been delivered to your basement," Hamilton said. "He appears similar in age to the young lad already in residence, but I will leave confirmation up to your autopsy. Despite the maturity of his decay, I did not observe any obvious mauling similar to that which the others suffered."

The valet unfastened Polidori's corset and placed it on the washstand with his undershirts. While the doctor sat bare-chested at this desk, the valet wiped the excessive mire from his Wellingtons and pulled them from his stockinged feet. The stench of the mud was decidedly distasteful.

"Perhaps we'd best dispose of everything," Polidori said to his valet. "Mrs. Hicks should not suffer washing and mending clothing I could not confidently wear again in pleasant company."

The valet nodded as he accepted Polidori's ruined stockings and pleated pantaloons, then bundled all into the discarded frockcoat and carried them out.

Polidori stepped into the bath, moaning involuntarily as he slipped into the soothing hot water. His right fist was bloody and swollen, his torso and arms rashed by blue-black bruising enflamed and painful to the touch. His hand shook as he washed the gravel from his wounded knuckles. Confident of the injury's cleanliness he rested his hands upon his abdomen beneath the water, leaning his head back and closing his eyes.

"Could you reiterate for the record how you came to be in the rectory garden of St. Giles-in-the-Fields?" Hamilton held his pencil poised over his ledger.

"Is that where we were?" Polidori sank farther into the tub. "I had been in Leicester Square, attempting to deduce the course of the elderly Fairbank from Covent Garden. And, perhaps, to guess the region of his residence. It was then I heard the whistles of your men. I followed them as best I could through the tangle of alleyways until final circumstance left me confounded and lost in that appalling space."

Hamilton nodded as he scrawled upon the page.

"At first, I saw my attacker as only a low shadow in the darkness. But then it slammed into my gut and hip, throwing me to the ground and gripping me around my chest. It was strong and agile." Polidori studied the open gash across his knuckles. "But I suspect its strength was out of desperation. Mightiness gained from terror, rather than musculature or physical size. I sensed more than anything that it was afraid. Of where it was. Of *what* it was."

Hamilton held his gaze. "What do you mean?"

The doctor was quiet for many minutes. Far too many for any reasonable conversation. "Have you ever been afraid, truly afraid for your life because of who you were?"

Hamilton swallowed, his jaw clenching. Polidori allowed the silence to linger, recognizing the emotions Hamilton was attempting to hide. Knowing they matched his own. The officer gave a single, almost imperceptible nod. "You talk like this beast is human." His voice cracked, as if his mouth were very dry.

"You forget, my dear Hamilton, I bore its weight intimately upon me. The possibility it might be human is not my greatest fear. My heart's dread is that it has forgotten it ever was."

Polidori flicked water from his hand and winced with pain. "Would you pass me a cigar? Thank you."

Hamilton knelt next to the tub, his wrists resting upon the rim, holding out a candle to light Polidori's cigar. As the flame flickered between them, his gaze was intent and not unpleasant. His smile slight but thoughtful. His eyes were an amiable emerald, his brows and slicked hair a handsome rust.

The men held each other's contemplation for longer than appropriate. And yet it felt right.

"Hello," Hamilton said, the word no more than a breath from his lips. He suddenly shook his head, stood and retreated. "Forgive my imprudence, Doctor Polidori," he muttered before returning to his ledger and pencil. He cleared his throat. "So, we are both looking not for a beast, but for a man?"

Smoke swirled from Polidori's nostrils, settling atop the bathwater. He stirred the vapors with his fingertips, mesmerized by the refraction of his own unguarded body beneath.

"As much as it pains me to confide it, yes."

CHAPTER TWENTY-SEVEN

Rachel checked her spreadsheet, confirming the date of the last letter against the next dated entry in the ledger. One letter remained before a several week gap in correspondence between Polidori and Mary, and she hoped the ledger would fill in the missing narrative.

The last sip of burgundy mellowed across her tongue just as there came a gentle knock on the door. She pulled her dressing gown tight and tied the sash at her waist. "Come in."

"I was hungry and thought you might be, too." Aubrey settled a tray on the desk. Cheese and onion toasties, the cheese gooey and still bubbling. Two small long-stemmed tulip glasses of Porto.

"You read my mind." Rachel pushed the ledger to the back of the desk and pulled off her gloves. "I wasn't really in the right frame of mind for work after . . ."

Aubrey was in his dressing gown, too. He toed off his slippers and sat on the end of the bed, pulling his feet up beneath him and balancing his plate on his knees. "How did you like your bath?"

"It was wonderful, thank you."

They said nothing for several moments, savoring the toasties and port, content in the quietness of each other's company. "I don't do it often, but when I do it reminds me of simpler times," he said, motioning toward the tub with his glass.

"Were times ever really simpler?"

Aubrey's face softened. "No. The . . . I believe the nineteen-twenties were good."

"For some."

Rachel licked her fingers then went to sit on the bed, tucking a pillow behind her to cushion against the wrought iron. Aubrey scooted back to join her, his dressing gown slipping open on the way. Beneath the silk he wore summer pajama shorts and a tank top—both powder-blue cotton printed with garlic bulbs with faces on them. He pulled at his top and smirked. "A joke present from Jess for my birthday last September. They said it was ironic."

"They?"

"Jess."

Rachel thought back to her only image of Jess. Light-skinned and sensuous behind the steamed glass of the bathroom window. She took a sip of port. "You've read Polidori's graduating thesis on somnambulism. What do you make of it?"

"It was relevant and important to his advancement at the time."

"It reveals more than that, I think." Rachel stared across the room at the document box. "He showed an extraordinary talent to complete the thesis and attain his medical degree at the age of nineteen. Still a child by Georgian standards. By current standards! He couldn't even practice his craft legally until his adulthood, two years later."

Aubrey nodded. "He had youthful promise, and that promise attracted the attention of Lord Byron."

"We both know it wasn't intellectual companionship Byron was courting."

"No indeed," he said.

"His thesis was also significant to the ghost story competition in the summer of 1816. Though the first sparks of competition were ignited by the tales of *Phantasmagoria*, it's been suggested by recent research that Mary's first waking dreams of her wretch actually occurred the night *prior* to their reading of that book."

"Ah. The evening Polidori and Mary discussed the subject of his thesis—somnambulism and wakefulness."

Rachel nodded.

"All right, I think I understand the relevance." Aubrey absently scratched at his chest, his tank top skewing sideways and revealing a platinum bar pierced through his nipple. "We should consider at this time Mary and Polidori deemed themselves subordinates to the literary genius of both Lord Byron and Percy Shelley. This isolated them to a degree, while they were staying at Villa Diodati, cementing a bond of friendship between them—a sibling-like affection. Indeed Polidori considered Mary's salutation to him of *brother* as being the most cherished complement of that ungenial summer. The intimacy of their conversations and combined knowledge might have indeed been the catalyst rather than *Phantasmagoria*. Mary was well versed in literature, romanticism, and the contemporary ideas of theology, and held a superior grasp of the modern sciences, particularly the controversial aspects of galvanism—animal magnetism. It was, however, Polidori who had a thorough understanding of the functioning of the body, its parts in relation to one another. His studies, and definitely his thesis, delved into the most recent theories of somnambulism. Of a person being aware, and unaware. Alive. Dead. The shadowy spectrum between the two extremes that were still so poorly understood."

"When is one alive, when is one dead. Awake, asleep. Aware, unaware." Rachel's thoughts trailed off like the steam still smudging the windows above the tub.

"There can be no doubt of the discussion's impact on both works born of the competition: Mary's *Frankenstein*, and Polidori's *Ernestus Berchtold*."

"And of course Polidori's *The Vampyre; A Tale*," Rachel added.

"Of course. All three are intimately connected to the thesis and its underlying implications."

Rachel considered the three narratives, her unfocused gaze drifting across the pleasant fullness of the powder-blue pajama shorts and down the gym-built curve of bare thighs and calves, coming to rest on the slender, masculine feet that leaned against her own.

"Mary was lucid during her dreams that occurred both when she slept and when she was supposedly awake, submerged in the deepest of thought," Rachel said. "And that awareness awakened the horror of her fiction."

"And perhaps that was the point of the thesis," Aubrey said. "One may be aware or unaware, whether awake or asleep."

"Whether alive or dead," Rachel whispered with a shudder.

Aubrey clinked his glass with hers. "The title of the thesis has also taken on new meaning since it was written."

"In what way?" she asked.

"*Disputatio Medica Inauguralis, Quaedam de Morbo, Oneirodynia Dicto, Complectens.* In modern medicine the term *oneirodynia* refers not to *somnambulism*, but to *nightmare*."

CHAPTER TWENTY-EIGHT

Mary Shelley
Albion House
Marlow
April 1817

Darling Mary,
It was in the early hours of the morning, still dark outside, that Officer Hamilton finished his questioning. Another conversation beckoned us, but it never began—neither of us possessing the fortitude or confidence required. I will open my heart to you at Rules, for I dare not arch ink across parchment of the demons that have tormented me since the summer within Lord Byron's, shall we say, accommodations.

I should have retreated to my bed, as the clock had just struck 4 AM. Instead I dressed and descended to the basement, where I lit the gas lanterns and cracked open the cellar windows and door to alleviate the thickening stench of my guests.

My new inhabitant lay on the central slab, his clothing and features camouflaged by the drying sludge from where he had been found. With my sleeves rolled up and my apron on, I wet a cloth to gently remove the mire from his eyelids and cheeks. The skin was fragile, and no matter how lightly I pressed to clean the filth, the putrefied flesh was prone to ripping. I thought it best to use only my wetted fingers, and that proved successful in reducing the damage to nil. His skin was soft—unusual for one who has expired. I poured two full ewers of water over his hair, running my fingers through until the water ran clear and a luster returned to what would have been an admirable coif. His face was pleasant once revealed, characterized by no inkling of pain of death.

Merely asleep. At rest. At peace.

I nudged his lips open, and they were fleshy and slightly rubbery to the touch. His teeth were his own, with some decay and chipping of the molars, only a few missing, but otherwise in good order. The canines appeared to have been filed down, and I thought this odd. Perhaps a hereditary anomaly his family thought best to eliminate. I extracted a coin lodged at the back of his throat—enough for a beggar to pay the ferryman for crossing the river of the dead. I pushed it back down, not wishing to deprive the lad of his passage.

But the coin presented a conundrum. The lad had been buried, but presumably not by his family. His couture and physicality, like that of the other lad, denoted wealth. However, the low denomination of the coin insinuated a pauper's burial, perhaps in a potter's field with familial relations left unawares. Hamilton confirmed no graves disturbed around St. Giles-in-the-Fields.

I washed the last of the mud from his ears, both decayed and heavily grooved, as if they had been dragged across gravel or the cruder cobbles of an alley.

It was then I was struck by his likeness.

I hurried to the other lad and pulled the shroud from his face. Then I opened my ledger to the pages of his autopsy, skimming down the list of measurements I had taken.

I had to be certain.

I stripped the new resident of his boots and couture, washing him with care, ensuring him the respect he deserved in his wretched state. Large sections of his torso had caved in, his chest had been punctured, and much flesh from his abdomen, legs, and arms had decayed away and been lost to the city or his original resting place. Further evidence he'd been dragged, an irreverent handling of the body after its death. And it was after—of that I had no doubt. The bones of his fingers and knuckles were exposed, the flesh worn. I took his measurements with care, double checking each length with a second ruler. Then I measured a third time with string, comparing directly against the first lad each length, thickness, and girth.

They were exactly the same.

I held no doubt they were twins.

Are twins.

Surely this fact will assist Officer Hamilton in his search for their identity.

Best,
John

Postscript: I shall meet you in the lobby of your London residence in Mivart's Hotel at twelve noon tomorrow. I know you will agree it is better to skirt all whispers of impropriety by meeting in a public arena, as 38 Great Pulteney Street is currently empty of my father and siblings, with their spending the spring and summer in the highlands. Alas, we are no longer on The Continent where men and women might entertain a friendship with one another without conjecture of impropriety.

I shall be so glad to meet with you again. It has been far too long, my beloved confidant.

CHAPTER TWENTY-NINE

Unable to sleep, to be unaware—*or be unaware she was aware*, she pondered with no little bewilderment—Rachel spent the remainder of the night going over her research. She reread Polidori's thesis on somnambulism, both the Latin version and her own English translation. It had taken her weeks to translate the paper back in the NYPL, but it was something she'd felt obliged to do before reading the translations by other scholars. Where the various English versions diverged, she went back to the original, confirming the etymology and history of each Latin word, and the English words evolving from each, and how they were used in other contemporary texts. She'd taken great pains in selecting the English words to convey Polidori's original concepts. As Aubrey had noted, the twenty-first century translation of *oneirodynia* was accepted as *nightmare*, but in the early 1800s its meaning had indeed been *somnambulism*. She'd written in her notes: *Oneirodynia. Somnambulism, Somnambular. Originally brought into use during the Georgian Era excitement over animal magnetism. Equivalent to somn(us)—sleep—and ambul(are)—to walk. Sleepwalking or night wandering. To be ambulatory while unaware.*

Rachel shuddered, recalling Polidori's hypothesis that one might be aware or unaware whether awake or asleep. Her thoughts spiraled down through reduced awareness, sleep, deepening comatoseness, toward death, but did not stop there. She shared Polidori's uncertainties on whether awareness ended with life, or if cognizance—of the environment, of loved ones, or of something much greater—continued on in some unfathomable way, even after death.

She drummed her fingers atop the words carved into the mahogany desk.

Regiment. Serpentine. Brighton. Pavilion. Ruthven. Mary. Walton.

Every word of her research had its own etymology, its own meaning to the one who wrote it on parchment or scarified it into furniture. Hindsight of historic events could reveal more of a letter from 1817 than the writer might have been comfortable with but one had to consider the events surrounding them at that time and contemporary understanding of those words when written.

Rachel drew back the curtains. It was almost 6:30 AM and the first streaks of sunrise should have been showing. Instead she saw only darkness rolling across the sky. Lightning flashed deep within the gut of the tumbling clouds. Thunder rattled the windowpanes. Windows that had survived two world wars and hundreds of years of industrial revolution and twentieth-century pollution. She doubted the sun would make an appearance at all today.

She pulled on her gloves and reached for the first of Polidori's ledgers. She had several hours of research to do before Aubrey's promised lunch at Rules, and she wanted to ensure the doctor and Mary were there with them at the same time.

CHAPTER THIRTY

Friday — April, 1817.

A miserable morning. No sign of the sun. Rain imminent.

Sitting in the basement with my . . . guests. Have reconfirmed all measurements of the two lads and sent a dispatch to Officer Hamilton. Included a sketch of their face—a face, among other things, that they share.

~~*I feel sorrow for their demise. It presses against my chest and makes breathing difficult. I dare not take too deep a breath in case it leads to sobbing I cannot control.*~~

~~*My unspoken conversation with Officer Hamilton last night has left me*~~

~~*Officer Hamilton has*~~

Leaning heavily against the wooden slab, my chin on my bandaged fist, I cannot help but closely study the upward arch of their naked feet, only inches from my face. Their soles are youthful and unblemished, soft to the touch without sign of corn, callous, or even the slightest labor beyond walking.

Much like my own.

How easily death comes to any of us.

As per my previous annotations, each foot measures thirteen inches in length. An inch longer than the royal twelve. Lucky for some, but not for these two. The toes are lengthy and straight, the consequence of bespoke bootmakers and cobblers. The toenails are thick and hard—the consequence of ready access to milk and cheese.

I dare not miss even the slightest clue, in case it assists the Bow Street Runners in reuniting them with their family. The intimacy of examination, of my profession, is not lost on me. For I need the familiarity. I need to understand. There must be more these bodies can tell me.

* * *

Polidori set his quill beside the inkwell and reached into his frock coat pocket to extract his flask. He took a deep draught, grimacing at the bitter taste of almonds. *Arsenic.* He had increased the percentage of the tincture—still minimal, less than a drastically diluted, precisely measured drop, but more than he had previously dared—determined to become immune to its effects. *Death.*

For hours he sat at the feet of his charges, deep in thought, contemplating the things they now would never do, that he had never done. And might never. He remained there, even after the lanterns had exhausted their oil and guttered, plunging the basement into almost absolute darkness. His vision adjusted to the shadows, the silhouettes around him somehow more comforting without the distraction of the flickering yellow light. The clock in the hall upstairs began to chime the tenth hour of morning. Daylight should have been apparent, but the heavy fog from the Thames was still so thick in Great Pulteney Street even the streetlamps couldn't penetrate it. A cool damp breeze eddied through the open basement door. He could taste London on his tongue.

He took another swig from his flask and again he grimaced, this time spitting the tincture onto the flagstones. He scribbled a note in the margin of his ledger to alter the formula. *Add sherry to make the solution palatable.* Then he crossed out *sherry* and wrote *brandy*.

With the last chime of the grandfather clock, he brightened, the heavy miasma that had been squeezing his heart letting go.

He felt his way along the bodies, pulling up the sheets to cover their ripeness but leaving their faces exposed so they seemed to be only asleep. He pulled the basement door closed and latched the heavy lock before climbing the stairs.

Another bath—his second within twenty-four hours. Then his valet dressed him in his new undergarments, corset and outerwear, and his favorite burgundy vest and frockcoat. It took three attempts to get the white silk cravat just so. Left alone in his room afterward, he stood before the looking glass and ruffled his hair, allowing the curls their own romantic freedom. It was part of an outward statement most modern young men shared, to relegate to the past the stuffy, uniform ways of their predecessors. He favored the curl atop his forehead, twisting it around his index finger before letting it spring wherever it might. He smiled for the first time in many days.

As he stepped out through the mist and up into the rented four-in-hand carriage, the morning fog began to swirl and eddy with the first drops of rain slicing through it. The carriage's valet offered him a blanket, closed the door, and climbed up onto the front bench. It would take perhaps twenty minutes to traverse the cobbled distance from Soho into Mayfair and Mivart's Hotel, where Mary kept her town residence. Polidori settled into the plushness of the carriage and pulled the blanket across his knees. The windows were obscured by condensation and fog, and the quiet tapping of raindrops quickly turned to almost deafening downpour. He chuckled, somehow relieved London was still London despite the horrors he had recently encountered.

He wondered how the valet and horses were faring, feeling certain they would be soaked. He pulled out his purse—black silk embroidered with a *Chinois* dragon, a treasured gift from Mary—to check he had adequate coin to compensate them for their trouble. The carriage slowed and turned, the high-pitched neigh of horses and the warning shouts of other valets loud and rambunctious at an intersection. Polidori assumed it must be Brook Street.

Lightning flashed, startling and blinding, its thunder instant and booming. Polidori jolted in his seat, unnerved but equally excited by the calamity of noise and light. Again, the torrent was lit bright—a second bolt—each raindrop seeming to explode as it hit the carriage. And again, simultaneous thunder, reverberating and tingling every cell of his body. He hadn't experienced such danger of electrocution since that odd night at Château de Chillon with Mary.

1816, Montreux, Switzerland. An extraordinary evening neither he nor Mary would ever forget. Could never forget. Strikes of lightning licking the turrets of the castle squatting in the shallows of Lake Geneva, adequate to galvanize even a cadaver back to life. A tumult lost on neither of them after the horrors they had uncovered around the affair of Doctor Frankenstein, the accumulation of dismembered bodies and the creation of something, of someone, beyond the realm of fiction.

He felt the rapid pump of his heart and the flow of blood through his veins, and he laughed out loud, feeling more alive than he had in a very long time. Another strike in the center of the street—light and sound synchronized, immediate and intense. Bewitching and exhilarating. He knew without doubt Mrs. Shelley would be relishing the excitement from within the luxury of Mivart's.

The four-in-hand pulled up to the curb near the corner of Brook Street and Davies Street. The hotel was an imposing four-level townhouse, a grand stone edifice, topped by a turned stone balustrade. Frequented mostly by wealthy country families, it was rumored European royalty kept permanent suites here for whenever an occasion or liaison required it. No fewer than a dozen doormen held umbrellas high in the downpour, creating a dry route from the four-in-hand, up the stairs, and into the extravagant lobby. Polidori suffered not even a drop of rain to dampen his coif.

"Such an entrance, Doctor Polidori. No less dramatic than Prometheus's casting from heaven." Mary was walking toward him across the Oriental rug covering the marble floor.

"Mrs. Shelley." He grasped her fingers, bowed deeply, and brushed his lips across the back of her hand. His face was flushed, his smile broad.

Mary slipped her hand around his elbow. "Come. We shall sit and allow the tempest to subside before we go to luncheon." She led him to a conservatory that jutted into the courtyard garden behind the hotel. Its glass walls and roof were awash with the weather, mirroring the potted palms, embroidered chairs, burr-walnut side tables, and shimmering candelabra. An embossed sterling silver tea caddy took pride of place in the middle of the room. "Tea?"

They took their seats as a raven-haired page poured a concoction imbued with the fragrance of violet.

"How does William—young Willmouse—fare?" Polidori asked.

"Almost fifteen months old and as high-spirited as his father. Despite the nursemaid and household staff, Percy shall have his hands full while I am in town."

"And the lyrical Bysshe himself—is his head still within the clouds?" Polidori said before taking a sip of tea.

Mary smiled, a puff of cheek and curve of mouth that had always made Polidori feel grateful when it was shared with him. "Percy's thoughts are still with the rugged climes of Chamonix in France. He talks of little else than the majesty of Mont Blanc. Well, that, interspersed with his notions on the nature of the human imagination and its relationship with the universe."

Polidori's eyes widened as he stifled a chuckle.

"I have no doubt it will have hatched into a poem by the afternoon of my return to Marlow."

Lightning streaked across the sky, a jagged, fluorescent bolt illuminating the rain. A marble statue was momentarily lit up in the garden outside—a Classic Greek male, nude amongst the foliage in a warrior stance. Leaning toward the feminine face of the Sphinx, to whisper in her ear, the warrior was imbued with a strength and physicality requiring no armor to protect himself from her malevolence. Polidori wished he could be so confident. Instead he kept himself closed off to the world—to keep safe from the intolerant laws of "civilized" society. The Sphinx's lion body was poised and ready to pounce from her rock, wings spread high.

The entire conservatory rattled with thunder.

"And your creatures, Mrs. Shelley. Have they yet fully escaped your waking dream?"

Mary chuckled. "It has become an epistolary nightmare. With each revision my creatures reveal more complex layers of their innermost dreams and fears. But they have taught me much I did not know I already knew. Concepts have expanded to propel the story farther than I had thought possible when I first began it back in Switzerland. Indeed, it is much changed since last summer's first draft."

"And its conclusion—has that been fully resolved in your mind?"

Mary placed her teacup carefully atop its saucer. She was silent for almost a full minute. "I sometimes wonder, does a story ever truly end? Is there ever an absolute resolution?"

Polidori nodded slowly. "And, further to the point, is an author responsible for exhausting all possibilities, answering all questions, before skipping to the next chapter or daring to write *THE END*?"

She locked her gaze on Polidori's face, but he knew her thoughts had turned inward. "No, I do not believe so," she said. "Both author and reader share a responsibility. An agreement to create a world and give it life. Whether the author offers a single sentence, a chapter, or a novel in its entirety, the reader—each individual reader—decides what happens between the words, and after they end. Miss Austen had no need to divulge every aspect of Elizabeth Bennet's and Mr. Darcy's life at Pemberley following her final page. She brought her story to a satisfying resolution, but nothing about it was absolute. Life went on. Flourished. Continued without needing to be written. Yet all readers, within their own hearts, know the unwritten words— what came after the last dash of Miss Austen's ink."

"Do you suppose what isn't written is more powerful than what is?" he muttered, almost to himself.

Mary glanced at his bandaged hand then returned her attention fully to his face. He could feel her attempting to read his mind, and he knew she could. "There is a time and a place for every word. Though some matters are best left unexplained. For now." She placed her hand gently upon his tightly clenched fist. "You've read the early drafts of *Frankenstein* and know well Victor never once mentions how he created his wretch. How he gave it life. Do you think he should?"

"I seem to recall there is also no mention of whether his wretch truly dies at the end." Polidori smiled thoughtfully. It felt good to be in his friend's company again. He had sorely missed her, had missed feeling happiness. He looked to the glass ceiling. The rain pummeled it unabated, the morning hour as dark as any moonless night.

"I daresay this storm will not let up. Let us see where the day and the luncheon take us."

CHAPTER THIRTY-ONE

Rachel sat on the carpeted bottom step in the front hall of 38 Great Pulteney Street. The ledger entry worried her that perhaps she'd find no adequate resolution to Polidori's life, merely gaps and open questions, leading to a final chapter of nothing but heartbreak. Empty of answers. Despite what she'd studied in the books, and the thesis, and the letters and ledger entries, she could not reconcile he'd just died broken and alone in the room at the top of the stairs.

A visitation from God, the coroner's report had read.

In the bed she now shared.

Do you suppose what isn't written is more powerful than what is?

How she hoped something had been written. Somewhere in this house. In his desk, or locked in the basement safe. Even something hinted at in the words carved into his desk. There had to be some scrap of paper, just one paragraph, one line that would suggest a satisfying conclusion to Polidori's story. A *happy* one. A lump welled in her throat.

Aubrey stepped lightly down the stairs and sat beside her.

"Did you get any sleep last night?" he asked.

"Neither me nor Doctor Polidori got a wink."

Aubrey chuckled, gentle and deep. He wrapped an arm around her shoulders and pulled her close. "Don't worry, Rachel. I know the answer is here. And I know in my heart that, because you're here, there will be an ending that will satisfy us both."

"Just don't tell me the answer is in the empty document box upstairs."

He laughed with a wink, then stood up, pulling her to her feet. "I trust you're hungry."

Rachel nodded. "Famished."

Aubrey checked his reflection in the hall mirror. Tweed slacks and jacket, black silk dress shirt, and black dress boots. He ran his fingers through his hair.

"Okay?" Rachel asked, waving a hand over her dress—the only dress she'd packed for the research trip.

"Perfect and beautiful in every way." Aubrey offered his arm and pulled open the front door.

The street outside came into sharp and abrupt clarity, a wall of heavy rain refracting streetlights into sparkles. Horns honked from the line of cars stuck behind a black taxi blocking the street in front of number 38. Lightning zigzagged across the sky, thunder rumbling in its wake.

"Dreadful day to go out," Rachel said.

"On the contrary." Aubrey opened an umbrella over their heads. "This is the perfect weather to go where the doctor and Mrs. Shelley went, exactly two hundred years ago today."

Rachel recalled Polidori's description of the weather in his ledger. It reminded her of her own experience in Montreux at the Château de Chillon during the research for Mary's bio. A tempestuous and electric event she still could not explain. "Yes, you're right."

They ran down the stairs and into the back of the cab.

"Rules, please," Aubrey said. "Thank you."

The cab turned down several one-way streets, avoiding congestion compounded by the weather, then pulled onto Regent Street, heading toward the Thames. The buildings lining the curve of the street were opulent, magnificent. Rachel wondered if Polidori's four-in-hand would have taken this route.

As if he could read her mind, Aubrey said, "Regent Street was not yet built in Polidori's time. This grand thoroughfare was completed perhaps a year or two after his, um, demise."

"Pardon me," Rachel said to the cabby. "Where is Mivart's Hotel compared to where we are now?"

"Mivart's? Blimey, how old is your guidebook, lassie," the cabby said with a ruddy smile. "Demolished afore my great-grandfather were born. Most probably no longer known as Mivart's when his father were born." Rachel leaned back into the seat, listening. "Mr. and Mrs. Claridge, who owned the hotel next door, bought it up. It would have been a decade or three afore the Great War that both hotels were razed and the current Claridge's was built. Takes up a whole Mayfair block, it does. Beautiful building. I once took the missus there for afternoon tea. A wonderful treat. I highly recommend it."

"Does anything of the original hotel remain? The statue in the garden? The warrior standing before the Sphinx."

The cabby shrugged, then banged his open hand hard against his horn, squinting to peer through the windshield. He flicked a knob on the console and the wipers sped up. Each sweeping arc revealed the London streets in front of them, grey and wet. In the distance, striding above the buildings on the far side of the river, the great London Ferris Wheel was pristine in its whiteness. It glistened in the rain, lit by powerful floodlights with a backdrop of turbulent clouds and incessant bolts of lightning.

Aubrey squeezed her hand. "What would you like to know about *Oedipus and the Sphinx?*"

"Is that what the statue was?" Rachel said, realizing its link to her research. Polidori's novel from the ghost story competition of 1816 would eventually be published under the title *Ernestus Berchtold: Or the Modern Oedipus*. She'd often thought he'd mimicked the title of Mary's work, *Frankenstein: Or the Modern Prometheus*, as an homage to his friend and a suggestion of both stories' unsettling beginnings in the Year without a Summer. Now she wasn't sure which had been given its title first, or whether one had influenced the other or vice versa. Or not at all.

"Is the statue still in Claridge's?"

"I don't think so." Aubrey shook his head. "At least, I haven't seen it. It might have been donated to the Victoria and Albert Museum. Or, indeed, it might have been destroyed during the Blitz." He shrugged.

"Doctor Polidori seemed enamored by it."

"Yes, I suppose that is the correct word," Aubrey said, tightening his grip on her hand. "Oedipus represents the flawed nature of humanity. But also, an individual's role in the course of their own destiny."

Rachel thought of her own course, toward an unknown destiny, sitting in a taxi cab thousands of miles from her husband and child, holding the hand of a handsome young man she'd only known a few days but felt like she'd known all along.

Aubrey wiped at the condensation on the window to peer out at the street. The line of his jaw was smooth, his hair unruly and charming. She pulled her hand from his and set it in her lap.

"If destiny always wins, though, then no action of the individual can be seen as flawed, as she has no choice. Every action, no matter what, can lead only along a path that's already been ordained."

Aubrey sank back into the plush leather seat and closed his eyes, his thick, dark eyelashes resting against the tops of his cheeks. "I believe it is our flaws that lead us to our destiny. Without them we would go nowhere, no need to strive, to better ourselves in any way. But by confronting our flaws, by letting them have their own way and, hopefully, by learning from them, our destinies are revealed." He opened his eyes, turned toward her and reached for her hand again. "Take care, Rachel. The Sphinx is beautiful. Mesmerizing. But also a ravenous monster that will clench tight and devour you if you cannot answer her riddles. We all must confront her at some point in our lives, in our own way. With or without flaws, with or without destiny, each of us must find the answers within ourselves before we can move on. Before we can determine our destiny and be truly happy with the life that is ours to live."

The cab circled Trafalgar Square and then turned from Charing Cross into the heart of Covent Garden.

"What was the riddle?"

Aubrey shifted in his seat. "Well, in Oedipus's case, it was this: 'Which creature is four-footed in the morning, two-footed in the afternoon, and three-footed in the evening?' "

Rachel smiled. "Yes, I've heard that one. The answer is *man*, who begins life on all fours, learns to walk on two, then in old age uses a walking stick and so has three."

"In the early eighteen hundreds, few were versed in Greek mythology or the tragedies of Sophocles. Fortunately, Doctor Polidori's training and travels had made him more astute than many of his fellows. He knew this riddle well and what it meant for his coming years."

"Years he'd never have," Rachel interjected.

Aubrey nodded. "It's all a matter of perspective. I think perhaps the second riddle of the Sphinx—Polidori's riddle—is more apropos of his faults. And his eventual destiny. 'There are two sisters. One gives birth to the other, and she in turn gives birth to the first. Who are the two sisters?' "

Rachel contemplated the riddle as the cab doglegged through the streets and lanes behind St. Martin-in-the-Fields.

"Neutralize the genders in the riddle," Aubrey suggested.

Still, Rachel could not guess the answer.

The cab pulled to a stop in front of the gold-painted columns and broad, red awnings of Rules.

CHAPTER THIRTY-TWO

"You seem pensive," Mary said in the privacy of the carriage.

He pulled his attention from the rain. "I was thinking of your words back in the conservatory. About what I have and have not written for *Ernestus Berchtold*."

"Oh, John! Surely you aren't pursuing that dreadful ghost story about the skull-headed lady!" They both burst out laughing.

"No, no," he said when his chuckling subsided. "The outline has changed much, and what you'll see through the keyhole of my ghost story will course shivers down even *your* spine."

"Well then, I am glad your novel is back on track. I always believed the original inspiration and underlying message needed to be written. Perhaps you will let me read a small portion while I am in town?" Polidori bowed his head, delighted. "I will also need to interrogate you for my own novel's benefit," Mary continued. "There is another murder I must commit to direct the dialogue toward the destiny of Frankenstein and his wretch."

Destiny, Polidori thought. *That word again.* It made his mind spiral in kind with the weather buffeting their carriage. He turned within its tight confines, unapologetic when his knee bumped his confidant's oyster-pink, ankle-length gown beneath the blanket they shared.

He took a breath and held it in his chest, afraid of what he was to say. Then he licked his lips and forced the words out. "There is a conversation you and I have never had. One I've not dared broach with even you, my dearest friend."

Mary's face softened and she placed her hand on his. And he knew she already knew. "John, know only that I love you as my dearest brother and I always will. Nothing can change that."

"But my . . ." His attention fell into the folds of the blanket, searching for the word. "My *flaw*."

"No," Mary chastised. "It is not a *flaw*. For who decides what are flaws in human nature other than bigoted people who dare not delve too deeply into their own hearts and inclinations."

"Remember the story of Oedipus. We all have our flaws. We cannot escape them nor our destiny."

"Ah, the catalyst—the statue back at Mivart's. I was wondering what you were looking at out in the garden. Tell me, what was Oedipus's flaw?"

Polidori pursed his lips. "He fulfilled the destiny foretold by the oracle. He killed his father and married his mother, both events burdened by an unnatural passion. An unnatural desire."

"But he was unaware of his familial relationship with them," Mary said. "From his point of view, he killed a man who threatened his life on the road to Thebes. He then saved Thebes from the Sphinx by correctly guessing her riddles. And he was made king and given the queen's hand in marriage. What was his flaw?"

"His flaw was that he did not know the truth behind his emotions and desires. His liaisons."

"Does that mean he should have stopped living, been untrue to his own nature? Deprived himself of all passions, all pleasure and pain, to prevent what could not be prevented? His unavoidable destiny within his tragic narrative?"

Doctor Polidori sank back into the seat cushion. "Then Oedipus's flaws, any of our flaws, are only the peculiarities of human nature as they relate to the greater scheme of things, whatever random happenstance surrounds us at a given moment."

"I think so. And perhaps it is not only *human* nature. God created Adam in His own image, His own likeness. He gave him life by sharing His own breath. Human nature is not a flaw. Every possible variation is, by default and definition, natural. Nothing short of divine. We are what He has made us. What He has allowed us to be. What we have dared to make ourselves before Him."

The carriage circled the broad open square in front of the royal stables and then turned from Charing Cross into the heart of Covent Garden.

"Do you think destiny might be changed, Mary?"

"Luckily, we are not penned in a Greek tragedy. Percy and I had this very discussion with regards to my creatures. They have made the story their own, brought it toward their own desired resolution. There is no doubt in my mind we each create our own destiny. No matter what *others* might guess or designate our flaws to be. I think, more than anything, we should embrace *who* we are, *what* we are, *while* we are. Celebrate it. We all have lives to live, and live them we must."

Polidori felt less confused and much heartened by his friend's words as the carriage dog-legged through the streets and lanes behind St. Martin-in-the-Fields. "Then perhaps this evening we shall speak openly on a matter close to my heart. My own complex, on which I would value your advice." His voice was a whisper, cracked by an ache too long suppressed.

Mary nodded, a caring smile crossing her lips as she gently wiped a tear from his lashes. The palm of her hand was warm against his cheek and he leaned into it, appreciating the tender touch he seldom received from any human being.

The cab pulled to a stop in front of the gold-painted columns and broad, red awnings of Rules.

CHAPTER THIRTY-THREE

Lightning lit up Maiden Lane, fluorescing the minutest details of the centuries-old thoroughfare. The broad red awnings of Rules appeared incandescent. Raindrops shimmered, frozen in the air for a single moment of blinding energy.

*   *   *

Rachel stepped from the cab and across the water-filled gutter to the protection beneath the restaurant's canopy. She slipped on the slick sidewalk, unnerved by the unexpected stumble and even more so when strong hands caught her and quickly turned her about. Aubrey pulled her in hard to the startling firmness and heat of his body.

*   *

The four-in-hand edged off the cobbles of Maiden Lane, its door opening beneath the restaurant's canopy. Polidori exited first and held out his arm. Mary placed her hand on his sleeve just as she slipped on the carriage's wet metal step. She pitched sideways, unnerved by the unexpected stumble, even more so when the doctor quickly grasped her by the waist and lifted her to the safety of the restaurant doorstep.

*

She reddened and glanced around, but the streetscape was obscured by the rain and lightning, the sidewalk devoid of people who, sensibly, were out of the weather.

"At least we didn't get wet," he said with that handsome, roguish smile.

The front door opened and a doorman, resplendent with gold buttons, welcomed them into the restaurant and motioned toward the maître d'hôtel. The inside was timeless. Plush golds and reds, ornate carpets, sparkling chandeliers and candelabra, crisp white tablecloths adorned with silverware and crystal worthy of royalty. Every inch of the gold-papered walls was covered in lavishly framed landscapes and portraits. Oil paintings, etchings, and cartoons. Kings. Queens. Ministers. Literary luminaries. Poets laureate. Celebrities of theatre, change, and creativity.

"Royals and their courtesans upstairs," he whispered discretely at her ear.

She smiled, enamored by the establishment's interior and those who had already been seated in the rich, red velvet booths. The maître d' escorted them to a booth in the rear of the main dining room. Handsome taxidermy, a mallard and a fox, perched upon the booth's ledges, and above it hung a gilt-framed oil painting of the Thames—fog-shrouded tall ships at the docks, almost invisible in the haze. Two gold-embossed blackamoors held lanterns high on either side.

"To your satisfaction, sir?"

He nodded, and they both slid onto the plush cushion.

The maître d' waved toward a line of footmen—matching one another in couture, coif, and upright manner. "All has been arranged as per your request, sir, madam." He bowed toward each of them. The first footman approached with a silver platter holding two cut crystal tulip glasses. "Bon appétit," the maître d' said as he placed the cocktails before them with gloved hands and returned to his post where he could survey all within his domain.

They clinked glasses and sipped, relaxing into the booth, allowing the quiet of friendship to settle between them. She was the first to join the subtle hum of the room's tête-à-tête.

"The three bodies in the basement have me intrigued."

"No doubt they would intrigue anyone. Well, anyone who knew they were there."

"All men of means, presumably of loving families. Families who would miss them."

"And yet, the lengthy absence of explanation for their residency."

"I will admit, the daily correspondence over their discovery, the mystery of it, invades my thoughts even in sleep. I'm not sure whether the details will help me finish my own work, and yet the slightest glimmer of hope in the back of my mind makes me think it might."

He nodded. "I understand. Appreciation for even the smallest detail gathered along the way might send things toppling toward a logical conclusion."

"The particulars of the autopsies, the two youngest being twins." Her thoughts turned inward, imagining the bodies on the slab, imagining their similarities, their differences. "Their differences," she said out loud.

He smiled and tapped his nose. "A-ha. Their sameness would, of course, assist the investigation, but their differences might offer just as much in determining their identities."

The cocktail glasses were removed. A champagne cork popped and a Crémant Blanc de Blancs was poured into the shallow coupe saucers—crystal upon stems of worked silver. Footmen with embossed silver trays and cloches presented the first course: *Duck rillettes with shallot chutney and walnut bread. Middle white pork terrine with cornichons and toast.*

"That one twin died before the other, possibly days or weeks before. And the manner of death." She shook her head, appalled. Amazed. "It is known when Master James Fairbank died, thanks to the testimony of Master Aldridge. What about studying the differences to determine when James's twin died?"

He raised his eyebrows, mulling it over as he nudged a thin slice of pork terrine onto a triangle of toast and bit into it. His lips and fingers were slick with grease. "A valid idea," he finally said before popping a cornichon into his mouth. "Elements of decay, structural integrity of the bodies, looseness of nails and hair, shrinkage of the skin, perhaps the weight of internal organs."

The champagne was crisp, the rillettes smooth and rich with the chutney.

"I wonder whether James knew of his twin's demise," she said, brow furrowed. "It doesn't seem as though Master Aldridge had any inklings of it."

"No, it seems not. Perhaps they were estranged, or on different personal journeys within the streets of London?"

"And the elder? One letter suggested he might also be familial."

"All families are different, and each of us handles grief, and death, in our own way."

Petite steamed steak and kidney pudding with oysters. A glass of Beaujolais.

Every table in the restaurant was occupied, mostly with patrons enjoying quiet conversation but one was engaged by a flamboyant group of young gentlemen. She glanced at her host.

"I've read that, since its doors first opened, Rules has appreciated a clientele of rakes and dandies, countered by persons of superior intelligence," she said. The portraits filling the walls seemed to confirm the theory.

"Perhaps that is why I've always liked it here. That and the wild game." He turned his attention from the table of men and smirked at her, his lips wet and red from the wine. "After all the letters you've read, how do you think the Fairbank case will end?"

"I still am unclear about the apparent familial element among the victims. Why has one bloodline been singled out? And the witnesses' descriptions, intimate in their details and yet almost nothing of value. Not to mention the manners of death. The exsanguination of the elder from the calf, and of James from the inner thigh. Such a low height of attack, and yet by not an animal but a human. A human who must have known his victims' identities and relationship. Who hunted them down through the metropolis, attacking at moments of sexual distraction, when all guard had been dropped."

Crown of pheasant with parsnip puree, sprout tops, and bread sauce. Bourgogne chardonnay. The first footman served the game and accoutrements onto warmed Wedgwood plates.

"I believe this is only the beginning. The method of slaying is unusual, more something found in *Phantasmagoria* than in the parks and alleys of London. Or anywhere. At any time. Even if the assailant is discovered, his or her reasoning—and method—would surely be beyond moral belief."

They both fell silent, intent on cutting the sweet meat from the bones.

"It was a man," he said. "To take down Master Fairbank in Hyde Park required strength proportionate to or greater than that of

Fairbank himself. But to also throw Master Aldridge to the ground—
a young man of equal size and fortitude—to the point of
disorientation and near unconsciousness."

"Yes, I remember reading that in the letters. The conversation with
Master Aldridge."

The remnants of pheasant disappeared. She held his gaze as he
sipped the last of his chardonnay.

"Which brings us to Officer Hamilton," she said.

He gave no indication of his thoughts. Instead he placed his empty
glass on the tablecloth, slender fingers grasping the stem, turning it
around and around.

*Cambridge burnt cream with sesame orange snap. Bordeaux
Sauternes.*

"Hamilton, my dear, is the topic of the evening meal in one of the
private dining rooms upstairs."

CHAPTER THIRTY-FOUR

It was still dark and raining heavily when Rachel turned the key in the front door of 38 Great Pulteney Street. Aubrey had stayed in the cab, headed for Old Compton Street and Jess. She on the other hand was ready for a hot steaming shower and a late-afternoon nap. After closing the door behind her with the loud clunk of the ancient latch, the howl of rain and wind dropped appreciably. She stopped in front of the hall mirror; her hair was disheveled by the wind but, thanks to wearing minimal makeup, her face was still clean and fresh.

Behind her reflection stood the basement door—dark paneled wood, almost invisible within the Georgian carpentry beneath the stair, except for its black metal knob and the light seeping through the cracks. She thought it odd that the light was on but shrugged it off and headed upstairs toward Polidori's room. The old house creaked with the weather, and somewhere a shutter rattled. Dust motes fell down the stairwell from the upper stories she hadn't explored yet. She'd no idea which room Aubrey slept in, or even what the other rooms were.

Feel free to come and go as you please. And nowhere in the house is off limits.

She kicked off her shoes at Polidori's door and walked around the landing. There was only one other room on this level, and she turned the knob and pushed open the heavy oak door. It creaked with the effort, as if it hadn't been unsealed in generations.

A dense network of cobwebs stretched across the room, from chandelier to wingback, bookshelf to mantle, window to carpet. Everything was covered in a thick layer of dust. At her feet, the dust and lint and layers of fallen webs crept up to her ankles. A shiver coursed down her spine.

The room was a study—possibly the office of Gaetano Polidori, the doctor's father, a scholar, translator, and writer in his own right. She looked around at the hefty wooden desk covered in writing instruments and papers, the cracked leather sofa before the soot-smudged fireplace, and the walls covered from baseboard to crown by shelves of books. Thousands of books. Above the mantle hung a replica of the painting of Doctor Polidori hanging in the National Portrait Gallery, and she furrowed her brow, surprised the artist had made a copy. The oil appeared burnished in the otherwise dim room. She wondered which was the original.

She stepped inside and reached for one of the books on the shelf. It all but disintegrated in her grip, the vellum sliding so the pages went askew and slipped to the floor. She blew the dust off the cover to reveal the gold embossed font etched across it.

Il Paradiso Perduto di John Milton.

Paradise Lost.

How often that title seemed close to her thoughts.

She retraced her steps, careful to make no further impact in the dust, then pulled the door until the latch clicked shut. She hesitated at the stairs rising to the next level. Every step, as far up as she could see in the dim lighting, was covered in that same thick dust. No sign of footprint—booted, slippered, or bare. No one had been up there in a very long time. She stared up into the pitch black where Aubrey's room must be.

A dull confusion muddled her thoughts. She was tired. She'd drunk too much at lunch, and she hadn't slept at all the previous night in favor of researching Polidori's writings and sketches. His odd scrawl in the margins, in both English and Italian. Sometimes Latin. She yawned.

Back in Polidori's room she undressed and pulled on her dressing gown then headed downstairs for a shower. On the way she passed the basement door again but, curiously, light was no longer seeping through the gaps. She needed to sleep.

As she sat on the shower's marble ledge with the water washing over her, the steam quickly fogged the full-length mirror and the window to the courtyard, even though she'd left the bathroom door ajar. She wished Aubrey was at home. She wanted to talk more about the letters and ledger entries, wanted to know more about what he thought. She remembered how she'd stumbled in front of Rules, the reassuring strength of his arms around her waist, the heat of his body against her. He was beyond pleasant, physically. He was intelligent. Generous. A gentle man. A gentleman. He was careful with his words, never speaking on anything she hadn't read yet in Doctor Polidori's own hand. She was on an uncertain journey with him—one he was already aware of, one she was yet to discover. She considered Polidori and Mary's conversation on passion. On destiny. And she wondered what hers was.

The hall clock struck four as she returned to Polidori's room, balancing a cup of chamomile tea. Her gaze fell upon the ledger on the desk, with her own note stuck to it: *Polidori and Mary's supper in a private dining room upstairs at Rules. The subject of Officer Hamilton.*

She took a careful sip of tea and pulled on her gloves. One last entry to determine how the evening supper at Rules played out before she fell into bed for a few hours. She opened the ledger, scanned the paragraphs she'd already read and then turned the page. Polidori had documented the menu—the same dishes she'd enjoyed with Aubrey, down to the last drop of Bordeaux Sauternes. Polidori and Mary had then spent the remainder of the afternoon beside the fire in Rules's salon, playing cards with other guests. Both had soon grown bored with the company and retired to secluded wingbacks where Polidori had smoked and Mary had recounted the time he sprained his ankle in Geneva by foolishly jumping over a hedgerow to assist her up a wet, grassy hill. Then the dinner gong had resounded from the restaurant's entry foyer.

And on the next page was . . .

"What?"

Rachel flipped the ledger pages back and forth, reconfirming the timeline. She gently flattened the volume upon the desk, pressing her gloved nail into the gutter of the book. One. Two. Three. Four torn edges of vellum. Pages had been cut from the ledger. She held the book upside down, thumbing through it to check for loose pages that might fall. None did.

What isn't written is more powerful than what is.

And more importantly, Rachel conceded, *what is written, then intentionally destroyed, is perhaps more powerful than what was never written at all.*

CHAPTER THIRTY-FIVE

Polidori pushed open the door of 38 Great Pulteney Street, his heart lighter after his whispered, tear-filled confidence with his one true friend over supper. He felt relief he had been understood. Not admonished. Not pitied. Just accepted. Loved.

He should have gone to bed, after two days without sleep. Instead he handed his frock coat to his man and went down to the basement. The lanterns were already lit, the smell of oil not so heavy as that of his guests. He pulled the sheets, exposing the full length of deathly white flesh to the insipid glow of the overhead lamps. The twins lay naked on the slab, their shoulders touching, their hands one upon the other in a loose familial hold.

He was certain he could determine how long Master James's twin had been dead, and he sat down to think. Per Master Aldridge's account, James had been dead five days.

His twin, for much longer.

Could Polidori assume the twins were duplicate in every way? Health? Wellbeing—both mental and physical? Could he assume their diets and activities were similar, if not the same?

At a glance, their unclothed bodies appeared identical, apart from the significant damage to the one found in the rectory garden of St. Giles-in-the-Fields.

Polidori penned a line down his ledger page, a column for each lad, to notate the intimate measurements he'd done of each twin. He had previously concentrated on similarities. He now needed to confront differences.

Polidori pulled the surgeon's trunk from beneath the table and raised its lid. Crouching, he removed all he would need—amputating knives and blades, artery forceps, bone nippers and screws, skull saws, catheters. Razors and scoops. Needles and thread.

He tied on his apron and took one last look at the mostly intact lads, not much younger than himself.

"Forgive me. Know that my actions are to assist you, to reunite you with your family."

First, he remeasured each twin, annotating the changes since his first evaluation. The longer-dead twin had shrunken further in stature and girth, even while at rest in the basement. Then he attempted to quantity muscle tone, pulling a tourniquet tight around calves, thighs, abdominals, pectorals, biceps, forearms, necks. He swore to measure them every day they lay unclaimed upon his table. Master James's twin had sustained damage across the abdomen, the flesh torn open, the skin and muscle at the hips scraped down to the bone. The injuries were a garish contrast to the remainder of undamaged skin with its downy wisps of blonde hair along the ridges and valleys of the abdomen. Polidori made an incision up the belly to the bottom of the sternum and peeled back the skin and muscle. The intestines and stomach were plump and glistening. He sliced along the length of the upper colon, and his eyes went wide.

The passage was full of congealed blood. Jelly-like and bright, blood red. Polidori blinked, astonished. Dumbfounded. He made a second incision in the small intestine, just below the stomach. It too was engorged, but with the yellowy liquid plasma that had separated from the fat red blood cells it would normally hold to.

Polidori's mouth hung open. He knew, without doubt, how the body functioned.

And how it did not.

He closed his eyes to think, but then his heart nearly burst when a hand grasped his wrist like a vise, tight, and cold. His arm was twisted backward at a painful angle and he was thrown to the floor, his head hitting the stone with a dull thud. At the same instant he glimpsed a bare arm swinging wildly above him, and the oil lantern was flung and shattered, flaming oil spreading across the flagstones. He recoiled from the heat, and a grunting groan emanated from where there should be none. From where it could not possibly.

The wretch rolled and flung itself from the slab down onto the quaking length of Polidori's prone body. The doctor flailed and punched in the flickering dimness, but the creature was as strong as he, perhaps stronger, writhing upon him, deflecting his blows. It kneed him in the abdomen and the groin, then slapped the back of its decayed hand across his face, its boney fingers clawing at his lips and cheek. The once-handsome visage of the dead twin was contorted in rage, its fragile skin ripping, its horrid mouth snapping and growling in an animalistic frenzy. Polidori's energy was quickly spent, his sight blurred by bloody saliva spat from the creature, his chest heaving as he gulped for air, the contents of his lunch and supper threatening to rise.

The beast grasped its hands together and raised them high, the bloody contents of its incised intestines spilling in disgusting clumps. In one disjointed jerk, it drove its fists down against Polidori's chest—cracking cartilage, disrupting his heartbeat. And then, it rose up off him, pulling itself awkwardly onto the edge of the table, pressing a rotting foot to Polidori's face, bare, broken toes against his eyeball, its breathing labored as it turned to its brother—cold and dead upon the butcher's slab. It let out a sob, a wretched howl that stung Polidori's own eyes—tears of grief, not terror, clouding his vision as he lay upon the floor. After a moment, it dropped its full, fetid weight upon Polidori's torso, then scuttled low across the floor and out the basement door, strong but cumbersome arms and legs bending at unnatural angles.

Polidori stared after it, his muscles aching from the fight, his blood pumping furiously through his veins.

CHAPTER THIRTY-SIX

Rachel slumped into the wingback in disbelief. She read the ledger entry a second time, but she still couldn't comprehend it. She set the book aside and powered down her laptop. She needed to sleep. And so she did.

*   *   *

She woke with a start at the chiming of the hall clock. Seven chimes, but she might have missed one or two. Or three. She reached for her phone, the eiderdown and sheets twisted around her legs. The screen flashed 10:00 PM. Rachel doubted her body clock would ever settle onto London time. She rolled over and pressed her face deep into the plump, duck-down pillow. Eventually she dragged herself from the bed's warmth and pulled aside the heavy curtains to peer out the window. The rain had stopped. The streetscape and evening sky were a dreary, dull grey, the road and sidewalk still wet, gutters still flowing and puddles reflecting the yellow glow of streetlamps. The moon was a meager silver blush behind the clouds. As dull as the night itself.

It was alive.

She turned around, let the curtains fall closed, and stared at the ledger where Polidori had written those implausible words exactly two hundred years before.

The floorboards creaked above. *Surely Aubrey in his room*, she thought.

A moment later, there came a gentle knock on her door. "Rachel?" Aubrey called through the heavy oak.

She chewed on her lip. *It was alive?*

"I thought I'd go over to Carnaby Street for a burger or something."

The ledger is fiction. She'd assumed it was fact from the beginning. She felt like a fool.

"Rachel?"

"Coming. I'll meet you downstairs in a few minutes."

"Okay."

The ledger is fiction.

She pulled on her gloves and thumbed through the pages she'd already completed, but the words scratched into the mahogany desktop caught her eye. *Regiment. Serpentine. Brighton. Pavilion. Ruthven. Mary. Walton.* She traced her surname with the tip of her forefinger.

She recalled her research for the Shelley biography. What had happened to Mary and Polidori in Montreux was also unbelievable. Unbelievable, yes. But it wasn't fiction. Cross-referencing with police files had proven it.

Before that project, she'd have thought the facts she unearthed preposterous. But the details of 1816—the Year Without a Summer, *Eighteen Hundred and Froze to Death*—were documented in diaries and broadsheets, letters and ledgers. Her research had been verified by scholars whose lives were dedicated to the Romantics. Why should she doubt 1817 would be any different?

There had to be a logical reason behind Polidori's words. The elegant copperplate of the main entries. The almost indecipherable scrawl in the margins. *Incredible.*

Rachel was no stranger to the incredible. Her husband and her daughter were testament to that.

Rachel and Aubrey settled into a hip burger joint in a laneway off the neon-lit Carnaby Street, both opting for a portobello burger and iced tea, sharing a plate of sweet potato fries.

She cleared her throat. "What were your first thoughts when James's twin attacked Polidori in the basement?" she asked, hoping to catch Aubrey off guard.

He licked salt off his thumb. "What was *your* first thought?"

"Disbelief."

"Valid. But we are talking the early eighteen hundreds. Death was an uncertain thing. Despite medicine and science, the line between life and death was nothing short of indistinct. A phenomenon that was guessed at, assumed. Hoped against, or for."

"But the lad had been dead for days—maybe even weeks! Parts of his body were decayed."

"And yet it was custom for people of that era to sit with their dead for at least a week to ensure they were dead. Even after burial, they kept a bell above the grave with a string attached to the deceased's finger. The cemetery watchman was there not only to stop grave robbers but to listen for bells." He reached for a fry. "And I assure you, that bell did ring. And often."

Rachel raised her eyebrows, wondering at his half smile, at the glint in his eye.

"I just realized I never asked you what you do for a living."

He sucked mushroom juice from the side his hand, rebalancing his burger. "I've been a hedge fund manager for the last few years. I like to try new things, stretch my knowledge and ability. Main office is in London City Centre, an upper floor of the Gherkin, but sometimes I'll spend several weeks at offices in Edinburgh. Recently I've been on sabbatical and, depending on how your research goes, may not go back."

Rachel's brow furrowed. "Why would my research effect your career?"

He made a noise of surprise and checked his watch. "Would you like to see where Polidori was buried? We can get there by midnight if we hurry. Maybe listen for that bell." That smile again.

It was about a forty-minute walk through Soho and Fitzrovia and into St. Pancras. There they passed the Gothic Revival St. Pancras Renaissance Hotel, with its curving redbrick façade and arches, pinnacles, and spires. The complexity and beauty was nothing short of incredible.

That word again, Rachel thought. It applied to a number of things she'd seen and read since arriving in London. Perhaps it was relevant to more truth than she'd thought. The point of her research was to determine what really happened. To find out whether the incredible was credible, or merely the fiction of an unhappy man soon to take his own life.

But she didn't believe that. Polidori had become someone she considered a close friend, in many ways. Someone she loved. She reached out for Polidori's hand—Aubrey Polidori's—as they continued along Pancras Road.

The scale of the buildings abruptly diminished, a stone wall with wrought iron pickets separating them from a park-like cemetery. Large trees provided thick canopy over the tombstoned gardens of St. Pancras Old Church. The gate was slightly ajar; Aubrey hefted his shoulder against it and it budged enough for them to sidle in. The grounds were dim and deserted, and Aubrey maintained a tight grip on Rachel's hand, which she was grateful for. Since Montreux, she'd kept a healthy distance from cemeteries. It seemed the sensible thing to do.

The light and cacophony of the city faded into the distance, the foremost sound the measured, staccato dripping of water from the tree canopy onto the deeply shadowed tombstones beneath.

"Are you scared?" Aubrey teased.

"Should I be?" she countered, comforted by his warmth at her side, his fingers intertwined with hers.

"This churchyard was considered remote during Polidori's time—the very outskirts of the city. A well known draw for body snatchers. Anyone laid to rest here was unlikely to stay very long."

They stopped under an old ash tree. Uncountable mossy tombstones tight together, front to back, radiated out from the tree like a sundial that never saw the sun. Those closest to the center had long been engulfed by the trunk, tilted by twisting roots.

"Is Polidori's body right here, among these?"

"Not anymore." Aubrey shivered, his grip tightening on her hand.

"Body snatchers?"

He was silent, and Rachel couldn't discern his features in the dark, his face a silhouette against the stippled light through the canopy. He wiped at his eyes.

"Are you all right?" she asked.

"Sure." The word cracked in his throat. He took a deep breath. "I need a drink, how about you? Old Compton Street?"

Rachel let go of Aubrey's hand and wrapped her arms around him. He was solid and willing in her embrace, his breath warm against her neck. He shuddered again and she felt the wetness of his tears on her cheek.

He pulled back, wiping his forearm across his face in the dark. "Ah, bollocks. I'm sorry, I seem to be getting sentimental in my old age. Silly, I know. He's only been dead for—what—a hundred and ninety-six years? C'mon, I'll take you to my favorite bar."

They caught a cab back into the heart of Soho.

Old Compton Street was still jumping well after midnight. Bars and clubs pulsed with music, patrons drank on the sidewalks in front of pubs. Police on horseback clopped down the center of the street. Aubrey and Rachel took a seat at a café table outside a white-tiled brasserie. A good place to people-watch. The waiter was tall and skinny, smart in black and white.

"May I?" Aubrey asked, motioning toward the drink menu. Rachel nodded. "Two Grey Goose martinis, straight up, with a twist. Thank you." When the waiter had gone, Aubrey reached across the table for Rachel's hand. "I apologize about that graveyard thing. For my sake, don't tell Jess. They'll never let me live it down."

"I promise, as long as you don't insinuate twenty-six is *old age* again."

The martinis arrived, along with a terracotta bowl of pork crackling and wasabi peanuts.

"Salute," they both said, clinking their glasses and taking a sip.

"Earlier today I came to a section missing from Polidori's ledger. Four pages. The evening supper with Mary at Rules."

He nodded. "Mm-hmm. I'm afraid you'll find several sections missing. Pages where he may have been, shall we say, too forthcoming about his feelings and thoughts. Matters that would've been deemed ungentlemanly at the time. Or, more to the point, illegal."

"So he tore them out?"

Aubrey peered into his martini glass, his face softening. "Polidori's sister and nephew *edited*"—he made air quotes with his fingers— "his documents after he was buried. For a man who wrote every day, kept exacting diaries of his work, and authored several novels and poems, there is a gerrymandered selection of material that no longer exists. Of note, you'll find no direct correspondence between Polidori and Hamilton, concerning either the investigation or any other matter. Of course, his family meant it out of love, wanting his memory and work to remain untarnished by . . . any ambiguities."

"His memory and their family name," Rachel added.

"That, too."

Rachel pondered the groups of men and women walking along Old Compton Street, many of them hand in hand, no hint of Georgian

London suppression of their open displays of affection.

"How do you know about the missing letters if they aren't there?"

"You will come across fragments of notes from Polidori's sister and nephew as you work through the collection. You'll also notice some letters from Polidori aren't in his hand. His sister made clean copies to preserve what she deemed was important information. But you'll recognize the gaps in the narrative, select words and observations omitted from the final reproductions. I've no doubt you'll be able to read between the lines."

They sat till well past two, people-watching and sipping martinis, then espressos, his hand never far from hers. Finally they walked home to 38 Great Pulteney Street.

At the entrance to Polidori's room, Rachel hesitated. "Where is your bedroom?"

Aubrey bit his lip. "Oh. Well. Would you like to come up, to . . . to see it?"

She held his gaze for much longer than she should have. "I wondered about the dust on the stairs. It doesn't look like anyone's been up there for decades."

A tired glimmer of that cheeky smile at the corner of his lips. "You've discovered another of my vices, I'm afraid. I clean only what I use." He walked over to the wall and nudged the wooden paneling. "A service stair runs the full height of the building. Not as wide as the main stair, and much less to clean whenever I do get around to it."

Rachel smiled. "Good night. My turn to cook breakfast in the morning."

CHAPTER THIRTY-SEVEN

Rachel leaned against the washing machine in the alcove between the kitchen and bathroom. The smell of percolated coffee drifted from the galley. A bowl of pancake batter was ready for the griddle, her whites were in the washer, and her colors were in the dryer. On her laptop, she scrolled through all the photos she'd taken since starting her research.

She glanced up when Aubrey stepped into the kitchen, eyes sleepy and hair tousled with errant curls, wearing the black silk robe with the dragon. Its tongue curled below his abdomen.

"Morning," he said.

"Blueberry pancakes ready when you are," she replied.

"Sounds great." He walked into the bathroom and doused a washcloth with hot water before pressing it to his face. Then he came back out, whipping the contents of a shaving mug.

"You photograph everything?" he asked, pointing a cream-laden shaving brush at her laptop screen.

"All original source material, yes. My editor likes to triple check everything, to ensure I haven't left out what she calls the 'sexy bits' of research.

"Hmmm," Aubrey said, brushing the cream along his jawline as he squinted at the screen. "*Serpentine.* Do you know what it refers to?"

"I'm thinking the Serpentine Lake in Hyde Park."

"Yes, but why do you think he cut it into the desk?" He ran the brush back and forth across his cheeks and around the fullness of his lips until his morning shadow was completely covered. "I have my own thoughts. They're kind of melancholy, I'm afraid."

Rachel thought over her research. Everything she knew of Polidori and Mary. "It's where Percy Shelley's first wife, Harriet, drowned herself . . . where she committed suicide, thinking her lover had left her while she was pregnant, though he'd actually been deployed abroad as a Lieutenant Colonel. An unfortunate case of undelivered letters."

Aubrey nodded. He stepped back into the bathroom, angling his face in the mirror and drawing the razor over one cheek, then the other, in swift, unhesitant strokes.

Rachel considered Polidori, alone in his room, contemplating his own innermost feelings, real enough for him to pull a knife from his pocket and dig them into the mahogany. She hadn't thought of the emotion behind each of the words. Words that obviously meant something to him. She clicked through the photos again. *Serpentine* was jagged, the *S* deep and broad, the inner space of the *e*'s scratched out of the woodgrain altogether. *Pavilion* appeared to be stabbed in a frenzy, the wood splintered and broken around each letter. *Mary* was carefully carved, perhaps lovingly, exact in the fullness and curving sweep of each letter. Almost as neat as the calligraphy of his letters to her. *Walton* was similar—great care had been taken to make it elegant.

"What do you think of *Walton*? Does he mention it in any of his other writing?" Rachel looked up from the laptop just as Aubrey stepped behind the glass shower screen. Steam rapidly obscured the glass.

"Perhaps it'll become clear when you answer the Sphinx's second riddle."

There are two sisters. One gives birth to the other, and she in turn gives birth to the first. Who are the two sisters? She blinked, still clueless.

He leaned around the screen; condensation wiped from the glass where his body pressed against it. "Were you able to find the investigations from the Bow Street Runners?" he asked. "As confirmation, I mean? Perhaps to read in tandem with the ledger and letters."

"I was going to go into the Magistrates' Court on Bow Street this afternoon."

He sloshed about in the shower, his fogged silhouette bending and turning as he soaped and scrubbed himself down. Rachel wondered that they'd fallen into such easy rapport that his casualness didn't unsettle her in the least. A seductive bond she'd never expected from anyone but a lover.

"Did you already try online? I'm certain I read that the Old Bailey—that's the Central Criminal Court of England and Wales—that they've published all their criminal investigations and court cases online. Hundreds of years' worth, as a resource to anyone requiring it."

Rachel minimized the photo viewer on her laptop, clicked the search engine, and typed in *Bow Street Runners Old Bailey Research*.

And there it was. Hundreds of thousands of records dating from the mid-seventeenth century up until the early twentieth century. Categorized. Indexed. Searchable. She brought her laptop into the kitchen and settled on a stool at the counter looking out into the courtyard. She clicked through several pages, familiarizing herself with the site's search capabilities, then typed in *Bow Street Runners.* Page after page of results surfaced. She'd need to be specific enough to limit the volume, but not too tight she might miss something relevant.

Aubrey padded barefoot out of the bathroom, a towel wrapped around his waist and another across his shoulders. Water beaded on his skin, glistening in damp hair. He poured two cups of coffee and sat down beside her.

"You found it. Do you think it will have what you need?" He took a gulp of coffee, his attention on the screen. "Try Officer Hamilton."

Bow Street Runner Officer Hamilton.

Over three hundred results.

Bow Street Runner Officer Hamilton Fairbank

Thirty-five results.

Rachel glanced sideways at Aubrey as he toweled his hair dry. "Do you mind waiting a bit longer for those pancakes?"

He grinned. "Be my guest. I'd like to see the officer's side of the story, myself."

She clicked on the first document. It was handwritten in a barely legible scrawl, heavily slanted and uneven. The ink was splotchy and smudged in spots, as if the page had gotten wet. Written across the top of the lined page, in a different hand, a darker ink: ***FAIRBANK CASE***.

Document BSR-OCH-01 ***FAIRBANK CASE.***

April 1817: 1:20 AM. Several Bow Street Runners converged on the Mayfair end of Hyde Park after report of death screams. The body of a youth was found a score of yards from Grosvenor Gate amongst the foliage. Well-to-do young man. Well dressed. Thigh mutilated. We undertook a search. No hounds found in vicinity. Two officers presented to bear-baiting arena on South Thames. No bears missing. Body taken to Doctor John Polidori for examination.
—Officer Hamilton

Document BSR-OCH-02 ***FAIRBANK CASE.***
April 1817: Doctor Polidori unable to determine type or size of animal due to the flesh being extensively ripped rather than bitten. No identifying papers or marks on the body. Door knock search for family underway in immediate vicinity to ascertain missing person. Doctor Polidori has promised a sketch of the victim's face, if identity not immediately determined.
—Officer Hamilton

Document BSR-OCH-03 ***FAIRBANK CASE.***
April 1817: A second body. Smith Court. Elderly gentleman. Well-to-do. Leg ravagement. Same animal suspected. Doctor Polidori brought to the scene. Death apparently by head strike against wall. Decayed human tooth found lodged in wound.
—Officer Hamilton

Aubrey chuckled. "He certainly is concise. Not as entertaining or descriptive as Polidori's letters."

"It does answer one question, though. What happened was real."

They read Hamilton's reports up to the point Rachel had reached in her research, briefly hesitating on Officer Hamilton's interview of Doctor Polidori in his bath. The entire interrogation had been distilled down to seven words.

Document BSR-OCH-06 ***FAIRBANK CASE.***
April 1817: We are both looking for a man.
—Officer Hamilton

Rachel's and Aubrey's thoughts were their own on what it didn't say. And what it did.

CHAPTER THIRTY-EIGHT

Polidori reclined in his wingback before the parlor fire, robed in a tufted-silk lounge suit and dressing gown, his slippered feet upon a footstool to appreciate the fire's full warmth. He gulped a broth Mrs. Hicks had demanded he eat. The matronly woman stood over him to supervise. Mary sat upright in the wingback opposite, silent and smiling intently at Officer Hamilton who was likewise silent, hunkered down on the wooden bench beside the fire. His head was bent low, his pencil poised above his ledger. His shock of rust-colored hair fell across his emerald eyes. He didn't catch Mary's smile, as he was intent on Polidori's lips appreciably slurping the soup. Finally satisfied, Mrs. Hicks returned to the kitchen with the empty bowl, the heavy aroma of boiled chicken, leeks, and pepper lingering behind.

"Surely he was never dead," Mary whispered.

"No," Polidori muttered, wincing at the pain of a cut in his lip. His voice was nasal from the cold he'd caught laying on the basement floor, semi-unconscious, in a draft from the open door.

"He certainly seemed dead when we found him in the rectory garden of St. Giles-in-the-Fields. Decayed. And yet, we must have been wrong." Officer Hamilton stood and stretched his legs, straightening the jacket of his well cut uniform. He pushed his hair back from his forehead, but almost immediately it flopped forward again as he leaned against the mantle. "We cannot ignore that he lay for days on your slab. Without sustenance. Without tending to his wounds. Without movement or sign of life. Your claim makes absolutely no sense, Doctor." In the mirror over the fireplace the two held one another's gaze in reflection. The officer smiled gently, then blushed and paced over to the front windows.

"If he were alive, he would have bled when I cut into him. But he did not. He was *dead*. Of that I have no doubt." Polidori shifted awkwardly in the wingback, grimacing.

"Could he have been *partly* dead?" Mary asked. "We have seen soldiers return from war in France and the Kingdom of the Netherlands with missing limbs, but also with *lifeless* limbs they were unable to move. Limbs that could be pricked and cut with no response. I recall gruesome stories in the broadsheets after Waterloo—men half dead in the mud, their limbs rotting, needing to be excised. Yet the soldiers lived."

A fire log collapsed with a crack. Sparks fluttered.

Polidori steepled his fingers, index fingers tapping his lips. "Perhaps. But no, I am certain he was—*is*—dead. I poked and prodded both lads for days. I would have recognized even the slightest sign of life. I could not have missed it." He shook his head and made to rise from the chair, but fell cumbersomely against the upholstery. Officer Hamilton raced to his side, his ledger and pencil discarded upon the floor. He gripped Polidori, formality relinquished to necessity, as he settled the doctor back into the wingback. His hand lingered upon Polidori's shoulder.

"Still," Mary continued, "if it was a weakness, or an apathy, that had settled over his body, is that any different from a death of sorts? If only the mind lives, but all other functionality and temperament of the flesh ceases? Waiting for the spark to return . . ."

Polidori chuckled. "I am afraid, my Mary, your thoughts run parallel to your own Doctor Frankenstein. They are indeed only, what did you call it, science fiction?"

Polidori reached for his shoulder to place his hand upon the officer's, closing his eyes and enjoying the subtle warmth, appreciated more than that of the fire.

"Would you like a sherry, or a cigar to temper the pain?" Mary asked with tenderness. Polidori nodded, and she rang the bell.

The doctor's valet answered, opening the parlor credenza to select three sherry glasses and a cedar box of cigars and smoking accoutrements. Officer Hamilton declined on both counts but assisted Polidori with the cutting and lighting. "Doctor Polidori," he said, holding the flame to the doctor's cigar, "could we assume the brain might be alive while the remainder of the flesh is dead?"

"Perhaps, but when flesh is deprived of life, especially for many days as is the case here, to the point of rot, it does not suddenly reanimate. And not with the strength and agility to take down a living person. At least not without some outside intervention. Some futuristic medical treatment, or"—he glanced at Mary and they shared a knowing smile—"science fiction."

"Have you read *Phantasmagoria*?" Officer Hamilton asked, resuming his place on the bench beside the fireplace, his back against the wall. His teeth appeared bright in the flickering light, strands of his hair seemingly aflame.

Polidori and Mary stiffened, memories resurfacing from that ungenial summer of 1816—the incessant rain, and Lord Byron's reading of that work of horror in the parlor of Villa Diodati on the shores of Lake Geneva.

"You read German?" Mary asked.

"Enough to get by, though I am more adept at French and Italian. My uncle is a magistrate at Bow Street—he's mentoring me until I start university for a degree in law. He and my aunt chaperoned me on a grand tour within weeks of Napoleon's defeat in 1815, both adamant I witness history first hand. We spent most of our time in Bavaria, on the outskirts of Ingolstadt, as my uncle is partial to the food and wine along the Danube, but our tour took us as far as the Jewel of the Nile."

Polidori raised his eyebrows. "Egypt. You must have wonderful stories. When the horrid situation at hand is finalized, I would appreciate your company by my fire to speak intimately on more civilized matters."

Officer Hamilton glanced at Mary. She was sipping her sherry, admiring the intricate detail of the doily on the arm of her wingback.

"But back to *Phantasmagoria*," Hamilton said.

Mary stood and paced behind her wingback. "The folklore and legends of Eastern Europe, of people who were thought dead, but not. Do you think it possible?"

"Medically, one is either dead or alive, are they not?" Hamilton asked. "Though the spectrum between the two may be unclear, in the end we ascertain it is either one or the other."

Mary placed her half-full sherry glass on the sideboard.

"Neither full, nor empty," she said.

"Which correlates with my thesis, Mrs. Shelley" Polidori

countered. "There is something of life, down through the spectrum, with less and less verve until there is none. But when it is gone, when it is dead, then life is no more."

Officer Hamilton rubbed at his knee. "Actually, I would gratefully accept your hospitality of a cigar, Doctor Polidori, if I may." He cut and lit it then hunkered back down onto the bench facing his host. He took a puff and closed his eyes. Only the crack of the fire interrupted the silence. Hamilton stretched his legs out over the carpet, the edge of his boot coming to rest beside Polidori's wingback. He plucked the cigar from between his teeth. "But who truly understands death, beyond the dead man, the theologist, or the poet?" He blushed, seemingly remembering he was speaking to the latter. "Your thesis, Doctor. Could the point of physical death be in the middle of the spectrum, rather than at the bottom of it?"

Mary rested her folded arms atop her wingback. "Ah, like those mythical beings who exist below the threshold of death. The vrykolakas of Greece. The moroi of Romania. The incubus and succubus of ancient history. The vampyres of the underworld who drag their rotted carcasses from the grave to feed off the living. No doubt the realm of folklore, and nightmares. Something *Phantasmagoria* illustrated in horrifying detail."

Once more, and for quite some time, the lick and pop of flame was the only sound in the hushed parlor.

CHAPTER THIRTY-NINE

Rachel exulted in the brief glint of sunshine slanting into the courtyard of 38 Great Pulteney Street. Though Aubrey had gone for his run over an hour ago, the flagstoned space still smelled of the coffee and blueberry pancakes they'd shared for breakfast. She bookmarked the Old Bailey website and closed the browser down, wanting no distractions as she outlined the next chapters of the Polidori biography up to her current point of research. The document was already over one hundred thousand words, researched and honed during the last four years, but she knew Margie, her editor and friend, would excise at least five thousand—maybe ten—to polish it for publication. Rachel thought of it as friendly fire, but she still took care to highlight her darlings, hoping most of them would make the final draft.

Her phone pinged with a text from Aubrey.

Heaven tonight?

Rachel smiled.

Well, that sounds ambitious, even for you, she texted back.

LOL. It's a club. Dress casual, with flats, and expect to get foamed. 1:00 AM?

She checked the time and giggled. Thirteen hours.

LOL, OK.

She drained the last of her third cup of coffee and headed up to Polidori's room, forgetting her outlining, intent on digging forward in her research.

CHAPTER FORTY

"What you are proposing is fantasy."

"And yet you know with certainty the twin was dead. *Is* dead."

"Yes." Polidori's cigar was burning down close to his fingers. He held it to his lips, drawing in the last of its muskiness then allowing its smoke to drift from the side of his mouth. "Perhaps it is best you inspect my basement, Officer Hamilton. Ensure the door is bolted." He hesitated. "But also please secure our two remaining victims. You will find cord in the cupboard, adequate to tie them down. If what you surmise is correct, then James's twin will be back, and he might not be the only one stirred from death."

Mary reached over and grasped Polidori's hand as Hamilton slipped out the door. "You believe what we read in *Phantasmagoria* is real?"

"What legend doesn't contain some inner core of reality, Mrs. Shelley. The seed may be scant, but it is always there. Your Frankenstein is testament to that."

Mary shuddered, and he knew she must be recalling the horrors they'd witnessed on the shores of Lake Geneva.

The clock struck, but neither dared count the number of chimes.

"Vampyres?" she asked.

He heaved a sigh. "Crawling from the grave to feed on the lives of those most familiar—their families."

Mrs. Shelley's face flushed.

Polidori rubbing the ache in his knees and calves. "No more than corpses, rotting, uncouth and vile, their thoughts narcissistic, wishing only for something they cannot have and willing to wrestle it from those who still possess it."

He made to stand, leaning heavily against the wingback. Mary rose with him.

"I shall have my man secure a cabriolet for you, Mrs. Shelley. It is best you are in Mayfair at this time."

The shrill whistle of a Bow Street Runner echoed from the street in front of the townhome. Mary ran to the window and peered between the curtains.

"Officer Hamilton, no doubt," Polidori said. "Summoning backup to guard my basement guests. It is going to be a long night." He made his way over to Mrs. Shelley's side.

Officer Hamilton stood in the middle of Great Pulteney Street, a light mist swirling about him, the cobbles glistening beneath his boots.

"I like him," Mary said.

"So do I," Polidori replied.

CHAPTER FORTY-ONE

Rachel sat at the mahogany desk, laptop open, ledger in hand.

Saturday evening, April, 1817.
I walked Mrs. Shelley out to her cabriolet. She promised to return by mid-morning to ensure I am well looked after during my recuperation.
"How can this possibly be real—this talk of demons, of vampyres?" she asked as we said our goodbyes under the portico.
I recalled something she had said on the shore of Lake Geneva last summer. "We are asleep until we are awake, unaware until aware. There have always been stories, and we assume their creatures live only within the words of a book, a song, a myth. We dare not view our own world through the same lens, lest we discover the types of creatures we actually share it with."
Mary conceded, and I believe it was right then we accepted our revised reality.
The staff retired, but I returned to sit upon the parlor footstool before the fire, gazing at the embers, lost in my thoughts. Then I felt a comforting hand once more upon my shoulder. Officer Hamilton assisted me up to my room. Of that I am thankful. The pain in my chest was such he had to carry me the full rise of the stair, nudge the door open with his boot, and deposit me in the wingback at my desk.

A single line had been scissored from the page.

> *He returned to the basement to keep watch over my guests, whom I wished with all my heart would remain dead. He assured me, before he left my presence, that two additional officers were keeping watch from the doorstep across the street.*
>
> *I sat a while, lowering the lantern flame, trying to push the world from my thoughts but needing a distraction. I broke the sealing wax on the box upon my desk and pulled my* Ernestus Berchtold *manuscript into my lap.*
>
> *I took several swigs of the tincture from my flask. It was much better tasting with the brandy as a base for the diluted drops of arsenic. It also complemented the previous sherry and cigar in tempering my pain.*
>
> *I opened the book to its last pages, skimmed through my words, then picked up my pen and dipped it into the inkwell. A favored line was daring to be declared in ink. It holds close to my circumstance since returning from Switzerland, and I trust it will soon relinquish its power over me. "There was yet a weight upon my heart I could not explain; my dreams always terminated unhappily, and sleep, that refuge common to all misery, was to me like the waking hours of others."*

Rachel pulled out her paperback copy of *Ernestus Berchtold: Or the Modern Oedipus* and found exactly where he was up to in his writing. It was word for word, unchanged from the first draft. A line below it caught her attention. *"We could not understand the decrees of fate, lulled by the peace and apparent happiness around us, we were unconscious of what was in future,—we remained,—and I am what you see—a spectre amongst the living."*

The words wrenched at Rachel's heart, because she knew they were truth. His truth. She wondered whether any author ever really strayed far from their own insecurities, their own questions about life and death, happiness and sadness. Existence. Who was it that said writing was easy; you just sit down and open a vein?

Ernestus Berchtold was received as agreeably scandalous when it was eventually published. The public delighted in the horror, but Rachel was painfully aware the narrator's temperament was Polidori's—his feelings, open and raw, printed in plain view without the literary world realizing.

> *I wrote until my eyes tired and my inspiration was no more. I had the energy only to seal the manuscript within its box and crawl into bed, still wearing my lounge suit and dressing gown, too pained even to toe the slippers from my feet.*

> *Sunday morning, April, 1817.*
> *Church bells rang in the distance, but I had no motivation to seek them out. My man helped me to wash the night from my skin, and to dress. I was feeling much better and was adamant I'd not spend my day secluded in the suite as Mrs. Hicks's patient. She has, no doubt, already sent a letter to my father in the Highlands reporting on my situation, and he'll soon return home. He loves me, as I do him. However, I would prefer he enjoy the approaching summer as he'd intended. I shall send my own letter this evening, assuring him of my stamina.*

> *It took me ten minutes to hobble down the stair. Nonetheless I found my feet once I reached the parlor.*

> *I requested Officer Hamilton be fetched from the basement. He was reticent to come upstairs after a night spent in solitude with the dead, but he dutifully obliged when prompted by Mrs. Hicks, who none doubt is the true commander of 38 Great Pulteney Street. He sat beside me, appreciable of the fire's warmth as well as the tea and crumpets to break his fast. His eyes were red-rimmed from sleeplessness, his jaw handsomely covered in morning stubble as rust as the thatch upon his head.*

> *"They are still dead, I suppose?" I said.*

> *He nodded as he bit into his crumpet, honey*

sheening his lips.

"How is it one in the missing twin's state might move freely about the city, crawling, decaying, naked?" I said.

"It was night when he escaped. Smears of flesh and blood were noted on your stair outside before the evening rain washed them away. I suspect he finds shelter in the alleys. The urchins who cruise those same passages wear little more than what they've stolen from street laundries and clotheslines. Likewise, our lad could easily secure clothing, if he had a bother to. At any rate, he might take refuge in plain sight. None with any sense in this city would dare disturb a heap of arms, legs, and rags in the corner of a putrid alley without risking the slash of a knife."

We had barely finished our tea when Mrs. Shelley came to call. What she had to say astounded us both.

Rachel reached for her laptop and clicked to the Old Bailey web archives.

Document BSR-OCH-10 ***FAIRBANK CASE.***
April 1817: Backup directed to 38 Great Pulteney Street. ~~It is surmised the second lad is not dead, or rather is not alive but is~~ Two Bow Street Runners positioned in the street. I took up guard in the basement after securing the corpses. It is feared the murderer will return to further desecrate the bodies. No disturbance during the night. Intelligence received the following morning indicating the possible identity of all three parties.
—Officer Hamilton

CHAPTER FORTY-TWO

The kettle whistled and Rachel picked it up to pour boiling water into the tea pot.

"Brilliant," Aubrey said, entering the kitchen in his running gear, a brown paper bag in his hand. "Hot meat pies for a late lunch. Steak and cracked pepper, with lashings of tomato sauce. Sorry, ketchup. I know, I know. We'll go vegan tonight to make up for all our evil eating ways."

They settled in the courtyard, slivers of afternoon sunlight reflecting off the upper windows down onto the flagstones. Aubrey toed off his runners then hit the bottom of the bottle, sloshing ketchup over his pie. Rachel followed his lead. "Twinings and Heinz," he said pointing at the tea and sauce. "Both 'by appointment to Her Majesty the Queen.' Can't get any more British than this. And the pies are from Fleet Street. The place where Mrs. Lovett's Pie Emporium supposedly stood. Surely you've seen that Sondheim musical. Mmmm, pies filled with choice cuts of corpse." He smirked, then added, "Don't worry, eating a bit of poet never hurt anyone."

"Nor a bit of hedge fund manager," she replied, returning his grin. "How far did you run?" she asked before biting into the savory pastry.

"A touch over forty-two."

"Miles?" she said, flabbergasted.

"Kilometers," he said. "About twenty-six miles."

"You ran a marathon while I was up in Polidori's room slouched in his wingback?"

He shrugged. "These skinny legs are pretty fast."

His legs were lean and muscular in floppy running shorts. His forest-green tank top was darkened with sweat, and his hair was glistening. He stretched one leg under the table, pulled the other up onto his knee, then sloshed more sauce onto his pie.

"How's Polidori doing?"

"It appears Mary has discovered who the victims are."

"She always was rather astute. We still on for tonight? Jess is eager to meet you."

"Sure. I'll probably hit the mattress for an hour or two before we go."

He wiped the back of his hand across his lips. "I'll wake you up at midnight, if you like. Before the final strike of the hall clock."

Rachel peered at him over the top of her pie, secure in both her hands. "Is it the same clock?'

Aubrey nodded. "And it hasn't missed a single tick, or tock."

CHAPTER FORTY-THREE

Officer Hamilton rose from the wingback and offered it to Mrs. Shelley.

"There's a chill in the air, London still shrouded in fog," she said, accepting a cup of tea. "Was the evening eventful in Great Pulteney Street after I retired to Mayfair?"

"As you see, Mrs. Shelley," Polidori said, "we have both survived the night. No sign of our fiend. Those below remain secure, unhindered in their repose."

"As above, so below," she said, glancing sideways at Hamilton hunkered down on the wooden bench. His legs were far too long to be comfortable on such low furniture. "Are you mending from your skirmish, Doctor Polidori? I'm grateful to see the rose has returned to your cheeks."

He grinned at the minute up-twitch of her right brow—a surreptitious language that had evolved between them during the summer with the commandingly verbose Lord Byron. "Yes, though I will need a gentle constitutional to stretch the ache from my legs and back."

"It would be my pleasure to escort you, if I might. I am told the trees and flowering shrubbery in Kensington Gardens are particularly lovely at the moment."

He tilted his head in agreement.

"My own evening at Mivart's was quite lucrative toward our investigation," Mrs. Shelley said.

Hamilton stood from the bench. "What can you possibly mean, Mrs. Shelley?"

Polidori relaxed into the wingback, unsurprised at his friend's aptitude for discovery.

"The cabriolet deposited me in Brook Street coincident with a grand, luxurious chariot pulled by a team of four horses. Though it was pristinely polished, I noted the undercarriage was caked in mud, the consequence of a substantial journey. The horses were fresh, undoubtedly acquired just outside London for the grand entrance into Mayfair.

"As I stepped down from the cabriolet, I could see clearly through the chariot's window. Two matrons in matching herringbone tweed travelling cloaks were seated within. Rigid and severe in manner, they stared straight ahead with no animation at having arrived at what I presumed was their destination. I stood back as they entered Mivart's and followed close behind.

"Mr. Mivart summoned me as I entered the lobby, and said, 'Mrs. Shelley, may I introduce you to Lady Fairbank, of the Sussex Fairbanks, and her sister, Lady Field.' We made our introductions and agreed to meet for a light supper and tête-à-tête after they had settled into their suites.

"They appeared refreshed when they arrived in the parlor for tea and sandwiches. Lady Fairbank caught Mr. Mivart's attention, and the chamomile was quickly replaced by a fortified wine.

" 'I have read all of your husband's poems,' Lady Fairbank said. 'I have often wondered what it would be like to be married to a poet, but then I recall my own dear husband—God rest his soul in heaven—and I realize I already have the perfect marriage.' She selected a watercress and egg salad sandwich. 'Is Mr. Shelley with you here in London?'

" 'No,' I said. 'He has remained in Marlow, too ensconced in his latest poem to join me.'

"Lady Field seemed pleased. 'You're a woman of the world, much like your mother,' she said.

" 'Did you know her?' I asked, a lump catching in my throat.

" 'Of course, my dear,' Lady Field replied. 'I championed Mrs. Wollstonecraft's work, *A Vindication of the Rights of Woman*. And I have seen to it all my daughters have been educated as well as my sons. All show such promise. Though beyond obtaining a wealthy and sensible husband I do not know how they shall use their knowledge.'

"Lady Fairbank petted her sister's hand. 'Do not fret, my dear. Men tend to die young and your girls' skills will be paramount in keeping the estates together for their own sons.' Then she asked me, 'Mrs. Shelley, are you still acquainted with Lord Byron? Such a ghastly and tormented affair, though I expect most writers are damaged in some way. How was it he described himself, *a strange mélange of good and evil*?'

" 'He has his demons,' I said.

" 'His novel, *The Prisoner of Chillon,* was thrilling,' Lady Field interjected.

" 'Still,' Lady Fairbank said, 'just be thankful you are not a writer, Mrs. Shelley. I would not wish that sort of torture upon anyone.'

"I dared not tell her of the manuscript secured in my suite two floors above. 'What of your own family, Lady Fairbank?' I asked, conjecturing they might be one and the same as your basement guests, Doctor Polidori.

" 'Seven handsome sons,' she said proudly. 'The youngest are twins.'

"I took a sip of sherry. 'Are any of them in London?' I asked.

" 'They had better be if they know their worth,' she said. 'The twins are not yet married. As it is the social season and they are prime to be wed, I have spent the last months organizing tomorrow evening's ball, here in Mivart's grand salon. You are welcome to attend, Mrs. Shelley.'

" 'Thank you. It would be my pleasure,' I said. And then, I do not know what made me say it, but I added, 'When did you last hear from your boys? And their uncle?'

"She furrowed her brow. 'Did I mention the twins were accompanied by my brother-in-law? Well, the man is desolate in his letter writing. The boys are less sporadic. I received correspondence a week ago from one, two weeks ago from the other. Both shall be in attendance tomorrow evening.'

"I did not take the conversation any further, thinking it wise I retired from their company."

Officer Hamilton had taken to pacing back and forth beside the fire.

Polidori was gingerly dabbing at his cut lip. "There is little doubt, if any, you have successfully connected the pieces of our puzzle, Mrs. Shelley."

"I will confer with the magistrate on how best to proceed," Officer Hamilton said. "Though I do agree with you, we cannot yet advise

Lady Fairbank of the deaths of her sons and brother-in-law, on the small chance we could be mistaken. And then there is the delicate matter of the missing twin. We must, by circumstance, be discrete."

They fell into a silence among the crack of the fire and the ticking of the clock.

"We should attend the ball," Mary said at last. "If Lady Fairbank's twins arrive unscathed, then our search continues."

"And if they do not show?" Hamilton said.

Polidori strummed his fingers on his thigh. They all knew what it meant if the twins did not show.

CHAPTER FORTY-FOUR

Polidori and Hamilton stepped up through the gauntlet of valets and doormen and into the main lobby of Mivart's Hotel. The doctor was resplendent in a dark blue frockcoat and vest, fitted chamois pantaloons, and polished knee-length Wellington boots. A sapphire pin secured his signature white silk cravat. The officer was equally splendid in his regimental dress uniform, his chest regaled with a silver Waterloo victory medal hanging from a crimson ribbon with blue trim. A bas-relief of the personified *Victory* was prominent from the medallion, seated on a plinth underscored by the word *Waterloo*. Polidori could not have been prouder to walk at his side.

Mary greeted them at the foot of the lobby stair, vibrant in a gown of coquelicot-colored gauze over a white satin slip, a frosted Italian frivolité adorning her hair. She hooked arms with both men and they proceeded into the grand salon.

Inside, a dozen white columns bore aloft a second-story balcony high above the polished wooden floor. Early arrived guests held close to the walls, admiring the spectacle and eyeing the competition. Young couples in the center of the room danced the opening bows and skips of a quadrille. The ceiling held a fantastic mural depicting the Celtic Queen Boudica leading the charge against legions of the Roman Empire. Chandeliers hung from chains wrapped in burgundy velvet, candles flickering, giving life to the battle that raged above them.

"As above, so below," Polidori said, repeating Mary's comment of that morning.

They strolled the full circumference of the salon to the strains of Rossini's "La Cenerentola," conversing with friends and acquaintances alike.

"An excellent interpretation of the Cinderella theme," Officer Hamilton said as they passed the orchestra—a pianoforte, harp, flute, and three violins.

Mary held tight to Polidori's arm and whispered in his ear. "You haven't told him you were thrown out of La Scala Opera House in Milan, have you?"

He stifled a deep chuckle. "Do not fret, Mrs. Shelley. I shall ensure you are present when at last my depravity is divulged. I would not wish to devoid you of any merriment."

Mrs. Shelley accepted a glass of champagne and they settled into a niche by the courtyard doors, where they were afforded a view of the entire room.

Several quadrilles ensued, partners passing one to the other, twirling with furtive glances and appropriate blushing. Already, two fine looking couples had sidled into the hotel garden, lanterns low, mothers and sisters observing from behind chiffon-draped French doors.

"You have attracted attention, Doctor Polidori," Mary said.

He scanned the room, his forehead creased.

"The lass in the jonquil-colored slip. An old fashioned hue, but still one of my personal favorites. Note her fan," Mary said.

The lass held the fan, hand-painted with daffodils, at her heart, then touched it to her forehead. Her heart again, then her mouth. Her heart, her right arm.

"P—O—L," Mary translated. "You may assume the rest of the conversation by the depth of her blush."

Polidori followed the young maiden's line of sight to a matron standing staunchly by the orchestra on the far side of the salon. Copious nodding followed each of her signals. The matron suddenly turned toward the doctor and locked her eyes on his. He blushed and turned away.

"Clearly it is time to withdraw to the parlor for a cigar," he said.

Mrs. Shelley shook her head, grasping his hand and indicating the salon's main entrance. There stood Lady Fairbank and Lady Field, both visions in white Grecian gowns, laurel wreaths of silver, diamond, and emerald encircling their crowns. "Lady Fairbank on the left," Mary said.

It took an hour for the hostesses to circle the salon. In the meantime, Polidori took great care to avoid eye contact with the jonquil-gowned maid and the undoubted matriarch of her family.

"Mrs. Shelley, I am pleased you accepted my invitation."

Mary curtsied. "Lady Fairbank, Lady Field, may I introduce to you Doctor John William Polidori, son of Gaetano Polidori, and Officer Craig Hamilton, nephew of Justice Hamilton of the Bow Street Magistrates' Court." Both men bowed.

Lady Fairbank lifted the officer's medal with her fingertips to admire its mint and inscription. "They call you the Immortals," she said, then glanced first at the officer's face and then at the doctor's.

Hamilton cleared his throat. "Yes, my lady. I am thankful to have survived the mud of Waterloo, but also grateful to those who did not."

"Are your sons arrived, Lady Fairbank?" Mrs. Shelley asked. "We would be honored to make their acquaintance."

Both ladies stiffened.

"We expect them any moment," Lady Field said. "Such a beautiful selection of girls," she added, peering around the room.

A valet arrived with a tray of champagne saucers. Both Polidori and Hamilton declined.

Lady Fairbank raised her eyebrows. "The champagne is the very best in London."

"I do not drink while I am working, Lady Fairbank," Polidori said.

"Ah, then, as I suspected, neither of you are competition against my own boys for tonight's game." She smiled knowingly at her sister. "Tell me, Doctor. Are you resident to St. Bartholomew's Hospital?"

"No, my lady. I am currently under commission to the Bow Street Magistrates' Court. Assisting in their investigations."

She glanced from the doctor to the officer, her gaze lingering on their glassless hands. "I see." She turned quickly toward the entrance, scanning faces, her hand beginning to shake. She handed her champagne to her sister, clearly agitated. "I think it best we go out to the courtyard for some fresh air."

CHAPTER FORTY-FIVE

Rachel stepped out of the lounge bar entrance of the Sherlock Holmes with two gin and tonics. Aubrey had scored a table on the sidewalk while she was inside, directly under the etching of Sir Arthur Conan Doyle on the pub's front window. The table was lit from above by old fashioned gas lanterns, the light spilling across the brick Northumberland Street. It had been cordoned off from road traffic. *A good idea*, Rachel thought. The midnight crowd had been reveling for several hours.

"How long have you known Jess?" she asked after taking a sip.

Aubrey was slow to answer, his brow knitting. "A long time," he finally said. "We've been through a lot together. They are an old soul; one I came to love and respect many years ago."

Rachel nodded, still adjusting to the pronoun usage, uncertain what to expect as she'd only seen Jess as an ambiguous silhouette through the fogged bathroom window.

"You'll meet my closest friends tonight. Jess, Taylor and Peyton, Harley and Dakota. Taylor and Peyton are a couple—always have been, always will be. Harley and Dakota are on and off—mostly off, unless they meet an occasion, or a third, that appeals to them both. Jess likens them to hunters, but their hearts are in the right place.

"And you and Jess, are you a couple?" Rachel asked.

Aubrey swirled his gin and tonic, then reached in for the slice of lime and bit the flesh from the rind. He licked his thumb and finger. "We have a bond," he said. "But we are not tangled by a relationship beyond *élan vital* and an acceptance of our history. We're fluid in our thoughts and our liaisons." He stood up and drained his glass, looking appealing in stretch denim jeans, white Nikes, and a lycra T-shirt. He reached out his hand to help her up and Rachel gladly accepted it. There was something reassuring about his grip, something hopeful about his description of his relationship with Jess. "C'mon, let's go to Heaven."

They took the passage beside the Sherlock Holmes, then across and up a side street and along another passage before entering a dented, black metal door. Rachel thought they must be entering Charing Cross Station, but she'd gotten turned around. They approached a second metal door and Aubrey shook hands with a bouncer twice his size. The doorman slipped whatever Aubrey had given him into his pocket and nudged the door open with his foot. Another tight passage, this one with red brick walls arching over in a barrel vault. Suddenly they were in a cavernous and very loud pulsing gallery. Arcs of pure white light swung urgently to the DJ's beat, then diffused into scattered pinpoints, highlighting the crowd, their hands in the air, whooping and jumping and dancing. Strobe lights flashed over denim, latex, leather, rubber, and copious amounts of exposed flesh in a staccato of raw, still images burning into Rachel's mind. Neon lights highlighted the length of the bar, high-end liquors being mixed by at least two dozen bar staff—fresh-faced men sporting 'man buns,' tattoos, and close-clipped beards; gorgeous women who personified the 'London look' with blood-red lipstick and adrenalin-pumping lashes.

"Polidori! Over here!" called a man in a black leather kilt, laced Highland boots, and little else.

Aubrey led Rachel around the crowd and into a barrel vaulted side room. The music was muted by the heavy brick masonry and thick curtains to converse without shouting. The man who had called Aubrey now guarded a table and tufted banquette. He and the similarly kilted man next to him were powerfully built, their bare chests as smooth as their jawlines. They held tight to each other's shoulders, their smiles wide and bright.

"They're dentists," Aubrey whispered close to Rachel's ear.

Both men grabbed him in a double bear hug, lifting him up off the ground, unabashedly kissing their friend on the cheek.

"Peyton and Taylor McKee-McNamara, meet Rachel Walton," Aubrey said.

"Pleased to meet you, lassie," Peyton said.

"Lassie," Taylor echoed with a nod, indicating for Rachel to take a seat. He slid onto the banquette beside her, his pleasant male scent and affable chuckle putting her at ease.

"The others here yet?" Aubrey asked, taking a seat on Rachel's other side.

"Still too early for Jess. The others are in the scrum at the bar."

Harley and Dakota approached the table with two ice buckets filled with bottles of water and beer. Harley looked like a nerdy Abercrombie & Fitch model with oversized Clark Kent glasses. Dakota was perhaps five-foot-two, amiably chubby and exuberantly pretty in a red polka-dotted, fifties-style dress. Her porcelain skin was a sharp contrast to Harley's sub-Saharan complexion. Rachel liked them instantly. As Dakota slipped her hand up the back of Harley's untucked shirt, Rachel surmised the couple were currently *on*.

"So, Polidori, we finally get to see who is taking you away from us," Dakota said.

He gave her a side-eye, then smiled, almost sadly. Rachel thought he must be tired. It was 1:00 AM, after all.

"I'm invested in Rachel's research and writing, as you know. But I assure you, you and I will rekindle our daily café gossips up in Carnaby Lane," he said.

Dakota nodded, appeased.

"Aubrey tells me you're both dentists," Rachel said to Peyton and Taylor. "Is your practice here in the city?"

Taylor glanced at Aubrey, looking confused, until his husband placed a hand on his shoulder and leaned in. "We have two clinics. One up here on Portobello Road, Notting Hill—another down in Brighton. We split our time between the two. Of course, Polidori is one of our mainstay clients." He grinned at Aubrey. "He had terrible teeth before he met us."

"Oi, they weren't that bad," Aubrey complained. "At least they're all my own."

Peyton's laugh was booming. "Yes, yes. Amazing what a little straightening and filing can do." He pulled at Taylor's arm. "Come on, babe. I need to dance."

"You two go ahead, too," Harley said with a nod to Aubrey and Rachel. "We'll look after the table." He grabbed a bottle of beer and took a swig.

Soon they were among the throng, and Rachel was glad to stretch and twist and jump to the beat after a week of rolling days into nights slouched over her laptop. She could feel herself loosening up, muscles warming in the heat of the crowd, her mind free of the details of her research. Aubrey writhed beside her, his movement easy and sensory, his steps more structured than most. Gregarious. The tender touch of his hands and fingertips to hers. The music segued from beat to beat, unbounded euphoria lifting the room as the DJ spun ABBA's "Dancing Queen." Rachel and Aubrey grabbed hold of each other and sang at the top of their lungs. Rachel was blinded by her own jubilant tears as the last notes rang through her heart and Aubrey held her in a gentle swaying embrace. They were drenched in sweat. Hot and happy.

He leaned close to her ear and cupped his hands around his mouth. "Men's room! Meet you back at the table!"

She nodded and made her way through the crowd, feet falling to the beat of "If I Could Turn Back Time." Slick bodies pulsed and pushed her this way and that. She laughed when she realized she was deeper into the center of the crowd. Suddenly, muscled arms embraced her from behind. She squirmed, but the hold tightened, painfully, her captor pressing in hard against her back. His lips and tongue were wet on her neck. She was forcibly spun about, confronted by a freckled, bare torso. She looked up, confused, into the intense green eyes of the guy from the café in Seven Dials. She was sure of it—that same copper hair. Then she was dizzy, falling into those green eyes, mesmerized, small flecks of brown swirling past her, the depths of the iris narcotic.

"Miss me?" he mouthed against the din of the music and the crowd. His breath was rancid.

He smiled, his mouth contorting, exposing canines that looked sharp and inhuman. In her haze, she watched his face jerk abruptly toward her neck, but then he jolted to a stop just inches from her flesh, saliva spattering across her skin. He released his grip on her, his arms falling limp at his sides. Rachel stepped back, lightheaded, and blinked to clear her vision—to see fingers clenched tight around her attacker's neck. The green-eyed man's knees buckled, and he cowed, nodding, as if he were ashamed. He was pushed roughly, and he ducked and hurried away through the crowd.

"You okay?"

Rachel nodded, her breathing heavy.

Her savior was fine of face with New Romance-style eyeliner and close-cropped bleach blonde hair. Leather pants and a sheer top accentuated an athletic build. Beneath the gauze shirt, Rachel discerned faded horizontal scarring, just above the hard, flat stomach, almost invisible in the shadow of muscular pectorals. She knew scars well. The kind that would heal and disappear. The kind that never would. The kind that allowed someone to be true to their authentic gender identity.

She was led through the crowd to the drop of curtains separating the two rooms. "You sure you're okay?" The voice was tender. Comforting.

Rachel nodded again, holding her hand to her heart to calm her breathing. "Thank you," she said. "Do you know who he was?"

"Yes, I know who he was. And I know who he is now. He's a dick. Has been for some time. Forget him, Rachel. He won't bother you again."

Rachel cocked her head. "You know who I am?"

The pleasant smile set her at ease. "I'm Jess. I've been waiting to meet you for years."

"Years?" Rachel said, laughing. Uncertain. "I mean, it's great to finally meet you, too." She held out her hand, but Jess pulled her into an embrace.

"I really appreciate what you're going to do. With the research, I mean. We both do."

Aubrey slipped his arms around both their shoulders and pressed in close to kiss Jess on the lips. "Well, I see you two have met."

CHAPTER FORTY-SIX

Lady Fairbank crumpled against the Sphinx's marble pedestal in the garden of Mivart's. She quickly regained her composure, stiffening her back and lifting her chin, but still her hand shook, the paper sketch pressed against her breast.

"You drew this portrait, Doctor Polidori?" she said.

"Yes, my lady," he said softly.

She touched her brow. "Tell me, did he have a small scar, just here?"

"No, not this one. The second young man who fled from my basement possessed the scar."

She looked again at the sketch, seemingly losing herself in it. "James," she whispered, touching her fingertips to the vellum. "And my husband's brother—he also lies upon your slab, dead?"

"There does appear to be a strong familial similarity between the elderly decedent and Master James." He motioned toward the picture.

She nodded. "Then it will be him. The male Fairbank brow and nose are regrettable and unmistakable." She turned toward Lady Field, who was sobbing on a bench amongst the shrubbery. Mrs. Shelley was holding her hand. "Stop your whimpering, foolish woman," Lady Fairbank snapped. "I am trying to make sense of this matter." She returned her attention to Hamilton and Polidori. "You say James's twin, Andrew, was likewise confirmed dead. But also, that he has fled from your residence."

Polidori nodded.

"What kind of doctor are you?" Lady Field wailed. "Either he is dead or he is not!"

"Quiet," Lady Fairbank said before urging Polidori and Hamilton to follow her around the courtyard to the opposite side of the statues. They stopped beneath the wings of the Sphinx, the light and music from the grand salon mottled by the overhanging foliage. "You may think it strange, but I have witnessed this before."

"How so, Lady Fairbank?" Officer Hamilton asked, wide-eyed.

She drew in breath, but then hesitated, chewing on her lip. She was staring past them, her eye movements rapid. Polidori knew the object of her view. It was the marble of Oedipus, fully exposed to interpretation from this position. No fig leaf to protect delicate dispositions. The Lady did not blush or seem concerned by the nude masculine form.

"I need you both to swear," she said at last, her words firm and measured. "Swear upon your own and your family's graves you will never speak of this. I will assist you in finding Andrew and then bring their bodies back to Sussex. But these fatalities of the Fairbank family must never be spoken of again." She squinted up at the Sphinx before locking her gaze once more on the officer and doctor. "No matter what you might see or hear."

"Any and all relevant accounts must be recorded in the investigation report," Hamilton said, alarm in his voice.

"That may very well be. But none outside of your official channels need be told of these deaths. Swear to it."

Polidori and Hamilton exchanged glances.

"Swear to it," she repeated, her voice devoid of emotion. "Not a word to anyone."

"I swear," Hamilton said. "Once the investigation is resolved to the satisfaction of the magistrate, I shall never again speak to anyone of these incidents."

"Swear your oath, Doctor Polidori."

Polidori saw no harm in the lady's request. She was no doubt shocked by the news, and he would offer a sedative if she so desired. He bowed his head. "You have my undying word, my lady."

CHAPTER FORTY-SEVEN

Harley collapsed onto the banquette, exhausted from several sets on the dancefloor.

"Who's next?" Dakota shrieked. "Polidori." She pulled at his arm.

He'd just sat down, drenched in sweat from dancing with Jess and Rachel. "Okay, okay," he said, after guzzling a bottle of water. He stood and peeled off his saturated top, the clipped hair on his chest matted with perspiration. His lowcut jeans, much lower than Rachel had realized, hung inches below his hips without a belt. But with the curve of his butt, there was no way they were going to fall down.

After Aubrey and Dakota disappeared into what had devolved to look like the first circles of Dante's hell, Jess grabbed two water bottles and beckoned Rachel to follow. They pulled back the curtain and headed through the tight brick corridor.

"Jess," the bouncer at the back door said with a nod as they passed.

"Won't the others wonder where we are?" Rachel asked.

"They'll find us—we know each other well enough," Jess said.

It was warm outside, but Rachel shivered after the heat of Heaven. Jess slipped an arm across her shoulders, leading her around the block and along a darkened alley. They sat down on some shadowed concrete steps with a view through an arched pedestrian tunnel that ran under Charing Cross Station. The underground passageway was pitch black, echoes of late-night revelry bouncing along the bricks.

Jess took a swig of water and leaned back into the shadows.

"You don't know how it ends yet, do you?" Jess said.

"I'm almost through Doctor Polidori's desk. I haven't yet ventured into the basement. Have you read the documents?"

"A handful. You know—a lazy Saturday, a winter night in front of the fire, Indian takeaway and a bottle of red. Always interesting to ruminate on the past."

"So, you know how it ends?"

There was a hesitant silence Rachel wasn't able to read with Jess's face in the shadows.

"Have you heard of *ellipsism*, Rachel?" Jess touched her on the arm. Their fingernails were trimmed short, a slim wedding band encircling the ring finger.

"Do you mean ellipsis, the omission of words?"

"I suspect both words share the same etymology. Something to do with leaving out, or falling short," Jess said. "Ellipsism is an obscure type of sorrow, that you'll never know how everything turns out. Hundreds of thousands of years of human history, development, culture stretching from our past into the distant future. And yet we're only here for such a short time and will not be privy to the end result. To what will occur in those last moments of time."

Rachel nodded, her mind aching with the concept.

"I guess what I'm trying to say is you don't need to be there right at the end to make your life—your moment in time—worth it. Sometimes there's more value in a short, well-lived life than a long, drawn-out existence just for existence's sake. To find out what happens."

"I don't understand," Rachel said.

"You will," Jess replied. "When you reach the end of Polidori's story."

The two of them sipped their waters in the dark. Jess twisted the band of gold around their finger. "He's seductive, isn't he?" they said quietly.

"Who?" Rachel asked. When Jess didn't respond, she said, "Yes, he is."

"It's in his nature. It's never meant with malice or egotism. He truly is a gentleman, in every way I've ever known him. But take care with his heart, Rachel. Despite his exuberance and confidence, his heart's been broken more times than he deserves."

Rachel nodded. "Is that a wedding ring?" she asked.

Jess paused their fidgeting. "It is. I was married. For about three hours, before Polidori and another valued friend helped me realize the error of my ways. I wear it as a reminder."

Raucous singing echoed from the other end of the pedestrian

tunnel—A bunch of silhouettes, but there was no doubt who they were. Two slender men leaned heavily against one another, holding each other up, plodding slowly through the dark. Beside them, two kilted titans balanced the smallest of the group high upon their shoulders, all singing some indiscernible anthem, some alcohol-fueled mashup of at least two Queen songs, the reverberation as discordant and off-key as it could be.

"A reminder of what?" Rachel asked.

Jess stood and pulled her to her feet. "The evil, my friend. The evil around us."

CHAPTER FORTY-EIGHT

Mary Shelley
Albion House
Marlow
May 1817

Darling Mary,
You've been gone only a day from London and already
there is much to tell you. With the oath we three swore to
Lady Fairbank, I feel you ought to be apprised of the
developing details we are obliged to keep secure.
I know I am assured in your confidence.
Lady Fairbank directed us to the terrace of her brother-in-
law, Lord Wayne Fairbank., at number 8A, Park Crescent,
overlooking eight acres of private gardens. It is central to a
grand arc of magnificent terraces, half of which are still
under construction, all of which are beyond comparison to
anything else south of Marylebone Road. In itself, number 8A
is twenty rooms strong.
Lady Fairbank provided us the key, and as soon as we
opened the doors we knew Master Andrew Fairbank was in
residence by the stench that assaulted our senses. Officer
Hamilton and myself had come to investigate alone, foolishly.
Hamilton, a pistol secure at his hip, pulled out his nightstick,
and I selected a cane from the hall stand. If I am to be honest,
I had not the slightest inkling how we might stop a man who
was already dead.
The main foyer was a diagonal chessboard of black and

white marble tiles. An imposing oval-shaped stair held to the walls, climbing the full height of the four-story home. A stained-glass ceiling, centered on the stairwell, was translucent in the afternoon light. I pushed open the double doors of the parlor, which appeared large enough to accommodate a recital for three dozen. All the furnishings within had been destroyed.

"Is there no valet, no servants?" I enquired of the officer. He shrugged, as surprised as I.

Settees in the French style were overturned, their wooden legs splintered. Cushions were torn. Silk curtains were pulled from the windows, their delicate brocade and pompoms ripped from the fabric. Perhaps most disheartening was the obliterated antique harpsichord. It must have been repeatedly borne upon by some great force. Some great anger.

Next we searched the dining room, which had been spared destruction. We latched its doors so it might remain so.

Officer Hamilton raised a finger to his lips and pointed up. I heard the hollow sound of wood on wood and followed his lead up the stair. I held tight to the curved, ebony banister, not wanting to be set off balance should the fiend come barreling down the tread. A gilt-framed oil painting of the twins hung at the second floor landing. They were as handsome on canvas as in death, with two wolfhounds huddling at their boots, peering up at Master Andrew, the one with the scar. The one inside number 8A just then. The wolfhounds' demeanor was not of devotion, but of fear. In life as in death, I surmised.

For a second time, we heard the scrape of wood above our heads, and so continued our ascent. The stained glass ceiling threw colors upon the walls—blood reds, pinks, and mauves. The top floor foyer was awash with bleeding, intermingling hues.

"The stench is strongest down this corridor," I whispered. Officer Hamilton followed at my back, so close our frockcoats were no more than a thread apart.

Bits of flesh were smeared along the rumpled hall rugs. I indicated where Andrew must have lain a while—cashmere carpet and wooden floor planks stained by seeping fluid.

Hamilton edged past me to peer through a door, slightly ajar. "Bedroom," he mouthed.

Then he abruptly threw himself against me, pushing me to the wall behind him, as Andrew came hurtling out of the room on all fours and slammed into Hamilton's legs.

It was then, to my horror, I realized we were dealing not with Andrew. Not with a man who, on the slightest glimmer of hope, might have been reasoned with. We were dealing with a creature that could no longer be classified as human.

Hamilton was yanked forcibly to the floor, his skull thudding against the wood with a horrendous crack, and the creature jerked him into the bedroom and batted the door shut.

I threw my weight into the door, but the solid oak would not budge. I heard the snap and snarl of the creature inside, the repetitive thud of its bulk against the door and I feared for the life of my . . . of my dear friend. I drove my shoulder into the door and this time it slid open several inches. Through the gap, I spied Hamilton's limp body and, to my dread, the naked, torn, and muddy form of the creature spasming atop him.

I screamed words I would never put to ink. I struck my bandaged hand against the oak, and the wound split and blood seeped through the cloth. I laid my weight to the door again, and again, until I could thrust my arm through the gap, pressing and squeezing my whole body after it.

Hamilton lay on his back, body twisted oddly, eyes staring blankly—dead or dazed, I did not know. The creature was upon him, unclothed and uncouth. It had ripped the belts and buckles from the officer's waistcoat, torn his undershirt, and rent four deep scratches across his exposed chest. It wrenched at his protective military corsetry, and at the buttoned collar of his cape with its teeth, trying to reach the tender flesh of his neck.

I kicked the creature in the side of its chest and heard the crack of bone. It contorted sideways and clamped the ankle of my boot in its mouth, teeth puncturing the thick leather until they pressed into the skin of my leg. It punched its tattered fist against my kneecap, which popped audibly, and I tumbled to the floor, breathless from the pain. Then it crawled upon me, pinning me down, its weight significant from bloating, its foul breath heaving as it leaned what was left of its face close to mine. The eyes were yellow and dead, thread-like worms slithering in the vitreous fluid. It skimmed its face against mine and a rancid tongue licked sweat from my jaw.

My thoughts were rampant in the creature's horrific embrace, my heart beating rapid, my breathing shallow and fast. In my mind's eye I reviewed every part of its damaged physicality, attempting to determine its Achilles' heel. It did not breathe. Its veins did not pulse. Its heart did not beat. I doubted any brain function, as its actions were only primal.

And yet it was able to seek out family in this vast metropolis—ties stronger than any other.

My faculties were fading, lungs and body and brain starving from lack of oxygen as the creature's grip about my neck tightened. I started to gag. I knew I was on the verge of unconsciousness, most possibly death, when some heavy item of furniture crashed upon the creature's head and shoulders. Hamilton. He threw himself onto its back, slipped an arm around its neck, and bent the rotten head back at an impossible angle, struggling to choke it in his hold.

The creature heaved up off the floor, pulling myself and Hamilton with it, splintering through the solid oak door and into a heap in the corridor. Despite its stature no greater than ours, its strength seemed unbounded as we fought to stop its crawling escape down the hall. We were dragged by sheer brute force, our bodies thudding against the walls as we delivered blow after blow upon its torso and head. The blood that splattered belonged only to myself and Hamilton. Our actions seemed little more than futile.

Still I racked my knowledge for a way to neutralize it. And then I thought of you, Mary, and our conversations last summer. About animal magnetism, and whether electricity might define life, bring life back, maintain life—even if only on a cellular level. Perhaps even the smallest spark is capable of keeping a body animated. I imagined where that spark might be, in a body otherwise deceased. And I thought with confidence, it must be in the heart. That organ so intimately associated with our emotions of love, of sadness. Life. Death. An association inexplicable but undeniable.

I gripped the creature and with all my might delivered a solid blow to its chest, directly upon the ribs protecting the heart.

The creature convulsed—its first pained response to any of our efforts. With its damaged lungs and punctured throat, ripped cheek and swollen tongue, it screamed, a gargling, wet, and sorrowful scream emanating from where I wouldn't have thought it possible. It lurched and, without recourse, the three of us tumbled down the stairs.

The treads were awash with crimson-mottled light from the stained-glass ceiling as we fell one upon the other. Our legs and arms tangled in the brawling descent, Hamilton's arm breaking beneath our weight. We crashed through the ebony balustrade two stories down. I managed to grab hold of one of the balusters but Hamilton and the creature fell to the marble tiles below.

I stumbled down the last curve of the stair, favoring my damaged knee, just as Hamilton loosed his pistol and shot the creature point blank in the face. Its cheek exploded, but it countered with a backhand to the officer's head, resulting in a gruesome crunch of bones—Hamilton's or the creature's, I had no way of knowing. Without hesitation, I grabbed a shattered splinter of ebony from the broken balustrade and stabbed it into the creature's chest. The stake slid through its ribs and into its heart.

The creature dropped.

Dead.

All animation gone.

I slumped beside Officer Hamilton and pulled him tight to my side, my cheek against his, bloody and smudged by tears. And I will admit, I sobbed when I detected the steady rhythm of his breathing, and his hand clasped mine.

Best,
John

CHAPTER FORTY-NINE

Rachel grimaced and set the toast with its black, sticky spread back onto the plate. Reluctantly she swallowed the bite, and shuddered. "That is disgusting," she said, eager for a sip of tea.

Aubrey chuckled and reached for the discarded toast.

"So, as I was saying," she said, pointing to a document on her phone, "the Fairbank case ledger confirms the Bow Street Runners found the staff of 8A Park Crescent dead in the basement, kitchen, and service quarters. No specifics on their manner of death. Only that they were."

"And do you believe this fantastic tale?" Aubrey asked.

"How can I not? Not only is it detailed in Polidori's writings, it's registered in official magistrate documentation."

"But do *you* believe it?" he asked through a mouthful of toast.

She leaned back in the wrought iron chair and peered up at the sky. They were just having breakfast but it was already twilight, the early evening darkness spreading. "I have to. Everything correlates. I even searched the Old Bailey Online for other mentions of what Doctor Polidori explicitly labeled as a *vampyre*. There was one other case that specifically used that word, but it was decades later. Interestingly, it was also a case of a sexual matter. Similar in nature to the original two deaths in the Fairbank case."

Aubrey poured more tea. "This type of occurrence, while uncommon, was not unknown. Stories had abounded for centuries, across the continent and beyond. But back then their understanding of *vampyre* was not the modern interpretation we have now. There was no Dracula or Lestat or Louis. No Edward or Angel or Spike. No gentlemanly seduction. There was only the poor wretched creature,

146

crawling from its grave to avenge itself of the imagined wrongs inflicted upon it. To suck the life force from those it held most dear. And anyone else it might have come across."

She nodded absently, thinking about the extensive bibliography she was going to need for this. Every index would need to be double checked. Every letter and ledger entry categorized, with certified copies, if not originals, placed on file at the British Library.

Aubrey chewed another mouthful of toast, his lips curving into an enigmatic smile, his gaze upon her. Intent. Tender. Allusive. *Seductive.*

*   *   *

She propped herself against the pillows on Polidori's bed, the eiderdown pulled up over her lap to ward off the evening chill, her master spreadsheet and document open on the laptop. With gloved hands, she turned the pages of the ledger.

Polidori had spent the summer and autumn recuperating under the care of his father and Mrs. Hicks in a rented estate on the shores of Loch Lomond in Scotland. There was little to no mention of Officer Hamilton in the remaining pages, other than that he was alive. In one section, to Rachel's horror, twelve straight pages had been carefully cut from the binding. The loss made her heart ache. Not just for them but for history. She could hardly believe there was not a single letter of correspondence between them. If only to acknowledge the bond created by that last horrific event. She'd thought there would have been letters weekly, if not daily. Perhaps she was wrong. Perhaps she'd misinterpreted their words and actions, her own romantic notions blurring the truth. She made a mental note to ensure the final biography adhere strictly to the facts, devoid of her personal views. Her hopes.

The letters between Polidori and Mrs. Shelley continued at a clip of one per week, sometimes two. Many as short as one sentence: Polidori describing a rugged valley he'd come across on his constitutional along the lake. Mary seeking advice on synonyms for *feel*, *life*, and *will*. The Shelleys' plans to return to the continent the following year, to visit the splendor of the Amalfi Coast, the ruins of Rome, the rugged beauty of Cinque Terre. One of Polidori's letters was alternate opening pages for *Ernestus Berchtold*. Rachel checked it against the final printing. She much preferred his ultimate choice and, a few letters later, Mary agreed with her. There was a tentative but joyous letter from Mary on the day Percy delivered her completed manuscript to the publishers, and an equally enthusiastic response from Polidori, congratulating her on the achievement.

Rachel had often wondered what the two of them would think of her prying into their world. Relishing their every word. Slipping forward and backward in time within their writings, and watching how their points of view would change. Interpreting their actions and seeing how they would impact future events. Knowing their losses before they themselves knew. And grieving with them when they, too, came to know.

According to the Old Bailey Online, Officer Hamilton's next case was in late autumn, the first flakes of snow powdering his crime scenes. No further instances of vampyrism after the Fairbank Case had resolved. His reports had become lyrical, more descriptive. Eloquent. Perhaps the effect of regularly conversing with poets and authors. His notes on squalor, pickpockets, prostitution, and murder were now so well articulated they reminded Rachel of Charles Dickens's imagery and stories. Classic novels that Dickens wouldn't write or publish for another two decades. Rachel found it hard to grasp what it would be like to live in a world without Oliver Twist, David Copperfield, and Miss Havisham. She wondered if Officer Hamilton had lived to enjoy Dickens's books. She knew Doctor Polidori had not.

Her thoughts suddenly veered toward the creations of authors and artists she adored—ones who came long after both Polidori and Hamilton were no more than dust. They would never read Brontë, Melville, or Dostoyevsky. No Dickinson, Carroll, or Twain. They would never experience the pure joy of Rachmaninov, Gershwin, Sondheim, or Lloyd Webber. No Elvis! They'd never experience the excitement of Fred and Ginger dancing across the silver screen, or the Man of Steel flying through the clouds, or the Rebel Alliance defeating the Galactic Empire. They would never know what it was like to sit in their parlors, like the rest of the world, and witness on their television screens mankind's first steps upon the moon.

An unexpected sob escaped her.

Ellipsism.

A sorrow that no longer seemed so obscure.

What was she going to miss?

She pulled on her slippers and went downstairs to shake the torment from her thoughts. The hall clock would soon strike 1:00 AM. Aubrey was in the parlor, asleep in the wingback, his dressing gown unsashed and loose about him, his legs stretched out onto the ottoman. *His pajamas must be in the wash*, Rachel thought. A book lay open on his naked thigh: Stephen King's *Salem's Lot*. She stared for much longer than a moment, astonished by the feelings she'd developed for this man in such a short time. Friendship. Love. Something more? She didn't know.

His lashes fluttered and he opened his eyes. "Hello," he whispered, his voice soft and sleepy. A vibrato between childlike and manlike. "What time is it?"

"Cup of tea time," Rachel said. "I'll be back in a few minutes."

"Sorry about that," he said when she returned with the cups and steaming teapot upon a tray.

"Nonsense. It's your home. And it's the middle of the night. What was it Polidori said of Lady Fairbank regarding her view of Oedipus?"

"That she was as well-accustomed as he to the strengths and weaknesses of men." He chuckled as he tightened his sash. "Still." He let the word linger.

The tea was hot and sweet, just how Rachel liked it. She kicked off her slippers and placed her feet up on the ottoman beside Aubrey's.

"What are your thoughts on the future?" she asked.

"Mine, or just in general?"

Rachel had been thinking in general, of mankind as a whole. "Yours," she said, suddenly more interested in him than unfathomable events that might occur after her lifetime.

"I prefer to live in the moment, unencumbered by unknown possibilities. It's useless to worry about things that haven't yet happened."

"But surely you plan ahead."

He crossed his ankles and pulled at the hem of his gown. "Of course, I plan ahead to avert danger or misfortune as best I can. But mostly I plan for moments of happiness. Fulfillment. Resolution."

"Resolution?"

He stared into the fireplace. Real logs had been replaced by artificial ones. The small flame of the gas pilot light glowed in the depths of shadow. "Yes, resolution. I expect within the next week or so I will resolve a matter that's been weighing on my mind."

"There's nothing wrong is there?"

"No, Rachel. On the contrary it will be a moment of joy. Of understanding and solace."

Rachel felt it would be intrusive to push the matter further. It seemed more personal than she'd earned the right to know. Yet. She wondered if perhaps he was going to ask Jess to marry him, and felt both happy and sad at the idea.

"I really like Jess." She was silent for a while, taking care with her words. "Did you know them before? Before the change, I mean."

Aubrey nodded. "Yes. Long before we knew physical change was possible. Fundamentally, Jess is the exact same person I fell in love with when we first met. Kind. Loving. Strong. Reassuringly dominant when moments require." He knocked his foot against hers and winked. "Some would say dangerous, but that makes any relationship extra delicious. Don't you think?"

Rachel smiled, recalling the danger of her first months with Adam. Danger that still existed on the periphery of their lives. Biding time. She wondered what was dangerous to Aubrey. "Jess said something about 'the evil around us.' As if it were something specific and tangible. Immediate."

Aubrey pulled his leg up to massage the swell of his calf. Childhood scars dented the flesh beneath the layer of fine, dark hair.

"We all live in the same world, Rachel. Whether dangers are known or unknown, commonplace or fantastical, it should be apparent to anyone that there is evil around us. Some might have the good fortune to live their lives in peace and never encounter it. But those without that good fortune, well . . . I suppose they just need to be ready."

Ready for what? Rachel thought.

CHAPTER FIFTY

Polidori took a swig from his flask as he scratched out a letter to Mary in the club lounge on the second floor of Brooks's in St. James's Street. Boar heads and stag heads—one a twenty-pointer—adorned the walls amongst paintings of fox hunts, sea battles, and man's best friend. Normally the gentlemen, and a few requisite dandies, would be reading the broadsheets, huddled in quiet conversations or card games, or hovering over the billiard table. But tonight the wingbacks and card tables were empty, the library nooks deserted. The billiard table was dormant save for the club feline, Duchess Angela, stretching luxuriously and licking her paws.

The men, tonight, were all crowded around a mantle at the far end of the room, under a cloud of smoke, listening to the reading of a newly acquired novel.

> *You should see them, Mary. Their eyes are agog. Their cigar puffing is frantic. I cannot help but giggle at each indecorous shriek. Already sherries and ports have been replenished several times over and it is not even supper.*

A panting huff arose, an awkward intake of breath twenty-seven men strong, followed by an intolerable moment of silence as even the orator stood dumbfounded. Polidori had to stifle a chuckle.

> *Your wretch has just made his entrance. Expressions have glazed over. Complexions have gone ashen. One poor fellow has retired to his wingback, his shaking hand attempting to relight his cigar. To my knowledge, a woman has never*

stepped within these sanctified walls. But you, my dear, have walked right in and taken up residence with your parchment and ink.

Brava to you. If only they knew.

The dinner gong sounded and the crowd disbanded in a commotion. Most retired to the main dining room in hushed dialog. A few settled in to resume their card games. Two dandies took up residence on the chaise near Polidori, just out of view. Polidori lit a cigar and leaned back to listen to their conversation.

"I read the novel in its entirety last night," said one, "Without one wink of sleep. I expect tonight shall be sleepless as well, as I cannot stop thinking about Doctor Frankenstein and his wretch."

"Surely Mr. Percy Shelley is the author. He wrote the introduction about the ghost story competition on the shores of Lake Geneva two summers ago. He mentions only that he, Lord Byron, and Mrs. Shelley were there. The prose is unlike Byron's and, well, a woman could not possibly possess such a horrific imagination."

Polidori drew on his cigar, savoring its taste before puffing out rings. He glanced sideways, able to see only the legs of the dandies on the chaise, their trousers scandalously tight fitting. He knew their type well. Harmless 'macaronis.' Good for a jovial tête-à-tête and perhaps a light after-supper respite.

"What do you suppose was the relevance of Mr. Shelley's reference to Doctor Erasmus Darwin in the introduction?"

"Survival of the fittest. The struggle for existence. Perhaps to place the story within the context of man's theorized evolution. Or to suggest scientific advances that might forward such evolution."

"Shocking," the other whispered. "Do you suppose fiction could advance a theory? Impact the course of nature?"

"I do. Consider that transfusions have been fictional for centuries. Calf blood, dog blood, water, wine, beer, opium. We've now seen it skip from the pages of fiction into the pages of medical thesis, and only recently into reality by successful transfusion of human blood, to prolong life! I believe imagination, even the most fanciful fiction, is the vanguard to our unknown future."

"Then any author should take care what they publish. For it may lead to future reality!"

Take care, Polidori thought and he was reminded of the Vampyre tale he had written and then discarded in Switzerland after the summer of 1816. He was irresponsible to scrawl those unguarded words and emotions on parchment, and was thankful they would never see the lamp light of a publisher, or the ink roller of a printer's press. *There is no need for worry. No need at all*, he told himself. *None*. He rose and approached the mantle, to get away from the conversation. He puffed on his cigar, studying the oil painting above the fireplace. Horses galloping across hillock and vale. The foxhounds running before them. He smiled at the fox that had gone to ground amongst the brambles with his mate. *The hounds will not catch them*, he thought.

Someone behind him cleared their throat. By its timbre he knew it to be one of the dandies.

"Doctor Polidori, forgive our intrusion. It is rumored you were at Villa Diodati with Lord Byron and the Shelleys during the competition."

He bowed his head. The dandies had the same face—bright-eyed with rouged cheeks in the French fashion. They reminded him of a time when he was happy to stroll hand-in-hand along the cobbled streets, sit at the café tables, and dance with Lord Byron within the taverns of Geneva's medieval Vieille Ville.

"Would you please confirm the author of *Frankenstein: Or the Modern Prometheus*? I have a wager with my companion here that it was penned by Mr. Shelley. He suspects it may have been authored by Mrs. Shelley, due to its dedication to her father, Mr. Godwin."

"What does the title page state?" Polidori said.

"The title, a quote from *Paradise Lost*, and the publisher details. Nothing more."

"Anonymous, then," he said. "Why do you think that might be?"

"Pardon me for interrupting, Doctor," said the evening manager of Brooks's as he approached.

"Gentlemen," Polidori excused himself.

"Your guest has arrived and is being escorted to your reserved private dining suite."

"Thank you. I shall be along momentarily." He checked his fob watch. "We shall play cards for a few hours, then require supper at 10 PM."

"As you wish, Doctor."

Polidori gathered his writing papers and placed them folded into the inside breast pocket of his vest. He waved to the dandies as he took his leave.

"Beware, for the author of *Frankenstein* is fearless, and therefore powerful."

CHAPTER FIFTY-ONE

The sun hadn't risen yet. Hours ago Rachel had heard Aubrey climbing the creaking stairs to his bedroom, but she'd continued her research and heard nothing since. She closed her laptop, checked the charge on her phone and then headed out, down Great Pulteney Street toward the Thames. The cobbles were dry and the night sky clear. No stars, but the edge of the uppermost eves caught a glint of predawn moonlight.

She felt unusually empty, but still she thought she knew in her gut where her research was leading, where her time within 38 Great Pulteney Street might end. She imagined Aubrey alone in his bed. Warm and naked beneath a thick eiderdown. The gentle measure of his breathing, the flutter of his eyelashes as he slept.

She stopped and leaned against the stone balustrade at the river's embankment.

To be honest, she was oblivious to the final resolution—of either research or relationship.

But she knew Aubrey would be there to help her resolve both.

And she knew he'd known it long before he'd mailed her the empty document box.

She shook her head in uncertainty.

A warm wind swept down the Thames, almost as fast as the churning current flowing beneath the arches of Westminster Bridge downstream. The London Eye stood dormant. From the distance came the hum of early morning traffic, the hiss of lorry brakes, the deep, reverberating horns of ships and barges downriver. In the sky, just lightening toward the palest of blue, was a flock of gulls. They screeched high overhead, a cloud of velvety-black silhouettes that ebbed and flowed over the Houses of Parliament, splitting into two to pass on either side of the Gothic Elizabeth Tower holding Big Ben, then merging again before heading north of the city. *No, not gulls, she realized.*

What did she know?

She knew it would soon be light and she was exhausted. She had no desire to see the sun, only to crawl into the warmth of Polidori's bed and welcome the comforting embrace of darkness.

CHAPTER FIFTY-TWO

Polidori woke with a start, the horrifying nightmare consuming his fragmented sleep sucked from his mind toward oblivion, before slamming harshly back through the darkness to smother him. He lifted his face from the top of his desk, rolling his shoulders to stretch out a kink as his gaze settled once more on the letter from Lord Byron with its single loathsome line.

>*You foolish, stupid man. What have you done? Only God can help us now. —Byron*

The envelope contained pages ripped from *The New Monthly Magazine,* 1 April 1819 issue. The story commenced on page three, where even the most careless reader could not miss it:

The VAMPYRE; A Tale.

Polidori was at a loss how the manuscript had found its way from the Swiss countryside to a London printing house—something he had never intended. Uncertainty and fear clouded his mind as he recalled the words of the dandies at Brooks's regarding fiction, as fantastical as it might be, influencing reality. But beyond even their simple, innocent musing was the recollection of Lord Byron's horror when he'd forcibly discarded the fragment of his own vampyre story, begun during the competition of 1816. He had shared the scant passage of evil with Polidori before tossing it into the fire with words of warning. Byron knew without writing more than a few paragraphs the effect the tale could have if completed. And, despite his overbearing arrogance, Polidori conceded the lord had been correct in destroying it. Polidori also recognized without doubt it was his own conceit, his wish to show his talents as a writer, bolstered by an all-consuming anger that had urged him to weave his own fantastic tale from the seed. Perhaps it was to somehow make sense of Byron's abandonment. The ungenial summer when Polidori was not yet a man, still legally a boy, only twenty, that Byron had consumed his vitality then discarded him as no more than a transient plaything.

Polidori slumped in the wingback, the pages from Lord Byron held in a trembling grip. "Surely none of it could come true. My words are too fantastical for reality."

Officer Hamilton stumbled through the door with wide and frightened eyes. Polidori's valet followed close behind.

"Doctor Polidori, we are required immediately at Kensington Palace."

"What? What's happened?" he said.

"There's been an attack. Far worse and of higher consequence than the Fairbank Case. But with a similarity…."

Polidori glanced at the magazine page in his hand, the word VAMPYRE pronounced and horrid. He felt bile surge up from his stomach, threatening to choke him. He swallowed hard. Hamilton and the valet assisted him in dressing. His head ached but he forged on when the officer grabbed him by the arm and led him down the stair.

"A carriage will only delay us," the officer said as he barreled out the front door of 38 Great Pulteney Street. He swung up onto his horse, yanking Polidori onto the rump behind him, and kneed the animal into a full gallop. Polidori's thighs were hard to the back of the officer's, hands gripping tight to his medical bag and Hamilton's belted waist. They dashed down Great Windmill Street, through the confusion of the new Piccadilly Circus into the heart of St James's, then along the length of Pall Mall, and beneath the canopy of Green Park. They were soon at full stride along the southern greens of Hyde Park and Kensington Gardens. Polidori was breathless, panting with the exertion of the ride, but Hamilton held his whistle between his teeth, blowing it continuously for the full twenty-minute journey to the palace. The king's mounted guard, two dozen in full regalia, paralleled their gallop through the gardens and into the courtyard. There, their horse was led away and Polidori and Hamilton were marched—at a run—into the lobby of Apartment 1.

CHAPTER FIFTY-THREE

Rachel triple-checked Polidori's desk drawers to ensure she hadn't missed anything. She pulled the drawers out completely and reached into the gaping cabinetry, fingertips searching blindly within the shadows. Nothing. She pulled the desk away from the wall; no compartments hidden in the back. She slid underneath it on her back, and stopped short. On the bottom of the thick mahogany apron at the back was another word carved into the wood. She traced it with her finger.

Hamilton.

The letters were careful and etched with what Rachel thought was loving intention. Like *Mary*, and like *Walton*. She reached for her camera and took a picture, its outline as crisp as the day it had been dug into the wood. She lay there under the desk a full hour, knowing her subject had lain there two centuries before. It was quiet and safe beneath the mahogany, with just her thoughts. And his. She stirred only when she'd built up her bravery to finally confront the basement and what it might contain.

Down in the front hall, she opened the wall panel and found the Bakelite switch inside. It was large and hard to shift, and when it finally thudded to what she assumed was the *on* position, the basement stair light crackled and fizzed for a full minute before sparking to its meager glow. The basement's brick walls were crisscrossed by water pipes and electric cables that appeared to have been added sometime in the nineteen-fifties—maybe the forties or thirties—and not touched since.

She looked up the dim service staircase, toward the upper floors. She hadn't seen Aubrey yet this evening. He might have gone out for a run. Or to meet Jess. She wondered if she should go up, rather than down. She went down.

The basement ran the full depth of the townhouse. The main area at the front of the house was surrounded by wooden benches and glass-doored cabinetry. Most were empty, but some held vials and jars of dark, murky liquids suspending indiscernible specimens. She recognized tubes and flasks reminiscent of her own school days in chemistry. At the back of the space sat an ornate safe as tall as she was. A door and a set of windows, long painted shut, delineated the front of the basement. She peered through the dirty glass into the lightwell, the outside stair long gone. Light shone down from the street lamps of Great Pulteney Street.

And in the middle of the room was a wood-block butcher's slab, six feet square. The size of a king size bed, big enough to hold the Fairbank twins, side by side. She knew their most intimate measurements and could imagine them lying there, naked and dead. Well, naked. One dead. Both dead?

A shiver slid down her spine.

She went to the safe and entered the code Aubrey had given her when she'd first arrived: 1-8-2-4. The safe's well-greased door swung wide to reveal its scant contents. A leather-bound ledger, seventy or so pages thick. Atop it lay a medallion and a large bundle of letters, tied together with a navy blue silk. Possibly a cravat. She recognized the medal from Polidori's writings. Hamilton's Waterloo victory medal, its ribbon torn.

The safe's remaining shelves were empty, though curiously one held a rectangular imprint, where motes of ancient dust had settled around something she knew instinctively was the empty document box. The one Aubrey had recently dispatched to her in New York. She wondered if that box had once contained the ledger, letters, and victory medal now stacked on the shelf. They would certainly have fit.

She lifted the small pile of artifacts with her fingertips and held them to her chest. Her heartbeat quickened with the hope of what they might surrender. And the reasons why they might have been secured in the safe instead of the desk upstairs.

CHAPTER FIFTY-FOUR

A guardsman escorted them at speed through several interconnecting rooms, all dim with the early hour.

"Hold here," the guardsman whispered before stepping into the next room, closing the door quietly but securely behind him.

The bookshelves of the salon in which they stood held a vast number of volumes, as well as clocks. Polidori counted thirty-six clocks of varying times, scattered at regular intervals among the books. They ticked, none in unison, creating a dull arhythmical clacking that reverberated within the increasingly pained center of Polidori's skull. A servant entered and lit the lamps, kindled the fire. Polidori bit at his lower lip, nervous about what he would find here, thankful for the warmth and discrete pressure of Officer Hamilton's shoulder against his own. He checked his own fob watch. 3:25 AM.

You foolish, stupid man. What have you done? Only God can help us now.

He thought back to Lord Byron's letter, but this time not with scorn. What *had* he done? He replayed the scenes of his novel, horror for horror, suddenly uncertain whether his foray into ink upon vellum might have unleashed something that had never before existed. Just like those dandies on the chaise at Brooks's were discussing. He spied a pile of volumes of Descartes and recalled a lesson from his school days: *I think, therefore I am*. In that case, he pondered, *I wrote, therefore it is*. Polidori shivered. Surely it was his imagination run rampant. Perhaps too high a dosage of arsenic in his flask. Or not nearly enough for the good of mankind.

The fire flared to life and he was immediately hot, perspiration slicking his brow, his hands. Every inch of him. He stepped away from the officer.

Above the stack of Descartes sat a nest of twigs with a small red bird in it, stirring from its sleep with the lighting of the salon. Amongst the ticking of the clocks Polidori now discerned soft, high-pitched tweeting sounds and noticed nests were as frequent as clocks. Songbirds awoke with the false dawn of artificial light. Some took flight, coming to rest upon wingback and mantle, with a chorus of song incongruous to the darkness of Polidori's thoughts. For a moment he was mesmerized. It dampened his dread, but then the door opened and he was beckoned to enter.

"His Royal Highness, Prince Augustus Frederick, Duke of Sussex," the guardsman said, "has requested the audience with you alone, Doctor Polidori. Officer Hamilton shall await you here in the salon."

The sixth son of King George III stood by the mantle in his dressing gown and slippers. His hair was unkempt, swishing around a bald spot, unattended since being awakened. His features were careworn, his eyes dark and puffed, red-rimmed from worry. Polidori bowed.

"My son and daughter, Augustus Frederick and Augusta Emma, are currently in residence for the season." His voice was dry and cracked. "They attended a ball last evening at the Banqueting House in Whitehall. Per the staff they returned here to Kensington Palace before midnight. Spirits were high and it was not until about two hours ago"—he glanced at the nearest clock— "that the household was awakened by their screams."

"Your Royal Highness, have the royal physicians attended to your children?"

"They have. And given them both sleeping draughts to see them through the night. However, it seems to me you might provide answers our own doctors cannot." He narrowed his eyes. He appeared exhausted. "I read your manuscript," he muttered. "I thought it fiction, but now I know it is not. Come. You will see my offspring as they were found, and I trust your oath will afford us every confidence in this matter."

Polidori bowed again, then followed the prince to Augusta Emma's suite. It was well lit and grandly appointed with floral pink papered walls and a four-poster bed with silk taffeta curtains drawn. Two doctors stood at the bedside, their expressions somewhere been disapproval and uncertainty. A woman sat on a bench in the corner, her back hunched as she read aloud from the King James Bible. The verses sounded hollow.

"Leviticus seventeen, verse ten. 'And whatsoever man there be of the house of Israel, or of the strangers that sojourn among you, that eateth any manner of blood; I will even set my face against that soul that eateth blood, and will cut him off from among his people.' Verse eleven. 'For the life of the flesh is in the blood: and I have given it to you upon the altar to make an atonement for your souls: for it is the blood that maketh an atonement for the soul.' "

The suite smelled heavy with the saltiness of dried blood. Polidori approached the bed, then pulled the curtains behind him so he was alone with the girl. A lantern lit the privacy of the bed. Augusta Emma was perhaps eighteen. Her hair had come loose from her sleeping bun, dark curls cast over the pillows. She was pretty, but her cheeks held no color, nor even her lip. There was a stillness about her and yet, when he placed his ear to her mouth and his fingertips to her wrist, it was evident she was alive. Her nightgown had been torn from her torso. Her neck and breast were covered in dried blood, and upon her throat was the reason the prince had thought to have him summoned.

The marks of teeth, undoubtedly human, were imprinted in the thin flesh, the upper canines having penetrated the skin and opened a vein. Blood had since coagulated in the punctures, the wounds sealed. Viscous globules of blood-flecked saliva speckled the surrounding flesh. He touched a speck of it, then dared to test it with the tip of his tongue. An essence of garlic.

He pressed a sheet of paper to the wound to trace its outline as best he could. Again, he checked Augusta Emma's breathing and pulse, assuring himself of her slumber, then pulled open the curtain. He gestured for the physicians to join him by the elaborately draped window, and he placed his hands upon their backs to draw them close.

He lowered his head and whispered, "Have you confirmed her virtue is intact?"

"It is," the elder doctor said. "Though the saliva apparent at her neck was also noted in quantity at her virginity."

Polidori's brow furrowed. "Was she bleeding?" he mouthed discretely.

"Per the lady in waiting, her time of month was just ended and she'd ceased wearing her crimson petticoats yesterday morning."

"And is there any indication of how the assailant was able to enter the room?"

"None advised by the king's guard."

There were the double entrance doors to the suite and no others. The window drapes billowed and Polidori nudged them aside. The sash was open and he leaned out over the sill—two stories above the internal courtyard, guards stationed around its perimeter. No ledge. No ladder. No rope. No way to enter the maiden's room.

"Take me to the prince's son."

The woman reading *Leviticus* pulled at Polidori's frockcoat from her bench. "Doctor? May I wash my lady, now."

He nodded and helped her to her feet. Her hand trembled in his grip, and he noted the terror creasing her features. *This is my fault*, he thought without hesitation.

Augustus Frederick's room was directly across the second floor lobby. The prince and medical entourage stayed outside as Polidori entered alone.

The four-poster bed dominated the room. A valet slumbered on a small cot, stirring but not waking as Polidori pulled back the royal's bed curtains. Augustus Frederick was only a few months senior to Polidori, but remarkably more powerful of build. He spasmed fitfully in his drugged sleep, the blankets kicked to the foot of the mattress. A bed sock missing. His nightgown was intact, but bloody around the torso. Polidori leaned over him, loosing the ribbon at the neck and tugging the cotton down to expose the top of his bulky, hairless chest.

Augustus Frederick's neck was thick with ropey muscles, covered with indentations marking unsuccessful attempts to bite through the flesh. Dark crimson bruising bloomed where the blood had been pulled close to the surface by intense suction. Polidori caressed the darkest welt, a thin skim of blood still beading where it had been drawn through the skin. Bite marks and tooth punctures at and above the unshaven jawline were evidence of frenzy, of failed satisfaction, or conceivably an all-encompassing lust, a need to consume by any means that which was desired.

Polidori found the deepest punctures upon the left side of the neck. Sharp canines had eventually secured their hold and plunged through flesh to rupture the thick pulsing vein beneath the muscle. As with his sister, copious amounts of blood-flecked saliva coated his neck and face. The blood had clotted, the wounds sealed. Polidori made tracings of the bruises and bite marks and, after close inspection, determined more than one mouth had benefited from Augustus Frederick's blood.

The victim's hands were larger than Polidori's, handsome and well muscled, floppy in his drugged state. Bruising was beginning. The thumb and small finger of the right hand, though unbent, were broken—gone unnoticed by the physicians. He bound them to ensure no further injury. Then he skimmed the side of his hand along the line of each rib. All were intact. He was leaning far over to study the broken veins crazing the victim's cheeks when Augustus Frederick suddenly seized him by the neck, clapping Polidori's forehead hard against his own.

"You've come back for more, fiend? A taste for my blood, my life, my seed. An incubus sniffing the trail of the succubus who came before him?"

Polidori gasped as the grip on his neck tightened. "You misunderstand, Augustus. I am a doctor, come to tend your wounds."

"You do not deceive me." His breath was sour and hot in Polidori's face, the spittle rancid. "I see you for what you are. Sneaking into my bed chamber at the darkest hour to enact your vile urges. You wretch. You damnation upon mankind. You abomination, you pox who disobeys God's law."

"No." Polidori choked on a sudden anger. He had been addressed in this fashion before, had witnessed the same dressing down of men and women he'd felt kindred with. It had once elicited his shame, even terror, but since the summer of 1816 all he'd felt was anger. Rage at the supposed superiority and piety of his tormentors. "I am a man, like any other, wanting to love and be loved. That is all," he said through gritted teeth. Augustus Frederick's gaze was intense, sparked by a palpable hatred and disgust, bravado Polidori had grown bored of long ago.

Augustus Frederick threw him off, himself rolling from the bed and hitting the floor with his face, unconscious. Polidori gasped for breath as the valet stumbled across the room to help him to his feet.

"It was naught but delirium," Polidori said. "Nothing I've not heard before."

CHAPTER FIFTY-FIVE

Rachel set down Polidori's ledger and leaned against the slab, her own anger surfacing for the times her friends had been assaulted and ridiculed. By the "devout." By the "pure." By the falsehearted.

The front door of 38 Great Pulteney Street thudded shut and she heard footsteps on the floorboards above. "Rachel?" Aubrey called.

"Down here!" she yelled, but he must not have heard her, as his steps creaked toward the kitchen.

She looked over Polidori's ledger entry for the incident in Kensington Palace. It was difficult to read where he'd scrawled the verse of Leviticus 17 diagonally across the original text, crossed it out, then rewritten it below. She searched online for source material documenting the palace and its residents throughout the Georgian period, confirming the lodging of Prince Augustus Frederick and his family, right down to the science books, clocks, and singing birds. She could find no mention of the *incident*, or of vampyres, but curiously she found several annotations about the younger Augustus Frederick's nocturnal spasms, weakness, and clumsiness of the limbs. Afflictions he'd never recover from.

"Vampyres," she murmured just as Aubrey came down the steps with two mugs of cocoa, the rich aroma drifting before him.

"Ah, you're finally at the interesting bit," he said, his smile flashing as he handed her a mug and jumped up to sit on the slab.

"Every piece of the puzzle has its need for the whole to be complete," Rachel said, climbing up beside him. "I wondered if you had an original copy of *The Vampyre; A Tale*. Anything in Doctor Polidori's hand."

"Anything I don't have here has been archived at the British

Library, where I'm certain you've already seen them."

Rachel nodded.

"And once your research here is complete, I'll be sending the remainder of the documentation to the library as well, including Polidori's wingback and desk, as part of the bequest."

"I think you mean *donation*. A bequest is when someone has died and left it in their will."

"Ah, right." He drained his mug then lay back upon the slab, a balled fist behind his head.

"Do you really think Polidori's story ignited vampyrism as we now know it, in Georgian London? The vampyre as a gentleman, I mean." She lay down beside him, propped up on her elbow to sip her cocoa.

Aubrey licked the remnants of cocoa foam from his lips, his eyes narrowing as he scrutinized her, before his attention drifted up toward the beams and floorboards overhead. "I have no doubt his writing highlighted the existence of vampyres in their modern incarnation, exposing them to the light so to speak. But whether it had a direct hand in their evolution from decaying corpse to seductive aristocracy, who can say? Times were changing in Georgian England. Rapidly. The sciences in particular were in immense flux, combatting theological thought. The discipline of biology itself began to split, with conflicting theories on zoology, geology, botany, anthropology, and evolutionary biology. Thousands of new life forms were being discovered—some that could be named by any kindergartener today. But some that have sunk back into total obscurity."

Rachel lay down fully on the slab beside him, staring at the unlit lightbulb above. She reached up and gave the lampshade a tap to send it swinging back and forth. "Okay then. Let's assume that these creatures didn't suddenly come into existence, but rather *awareness* of them evolved, due to the publication of Polidori's story."

"Now you've got it," Aubrey said.

"So where is the rest of the confirming documentation?"

Aubrey rolled to face her, resting his cheek on the bulge of his bicep. "Vampyrism is documented in the Bible. You have seen it noted in The Old Bailey Online. And thousands of *nonfiction* books on their kind have been published since Polidori's story. An Internet search will bring up hundreds of instances of the most blatant vampyrical crimes right up through this century. And that's just on the English sites. You can find professorial theses on the number of vampyres currently living in England, as well as the details of donors who willingly supply them blood."

Rachel rubbed her forehead, incredulous despite her years of research. "So the evidence has always been there, just pushed below public awareness."

"Which is exactly the concept *you* first surfaced in *Fire on the Water*, with Mary's thought process and the creation of her wretch."

"But Polidori's ledger depicts abuse. Violation. Probable intent to murder."

"Yes, it does. The publication of his novel fueled an increased awareness, an extremely dangerous situation, an instability of the previous status quo. But, as you will see, not only did it cause an escalation of slaughter due to the flux, it also resulted in other deaths being correctly attributed for the first time. No longer were these creatures hidden in the night. No longer could the deaths of their victims be erroneously designated as 'a visitation by God.' "

"I still don't get how such brazen crimes could be wiped from history to the point people now think of it only as fiction."

"In the case of vampyrism, fiction is a calculated blurring of reality. Muddying the waters to hide those who walk amongst us in plain sight. Fiction is an intentional construct to place the existence of vampyres in the realm of entertainment instead of fact."

"So you're saying I can treat Anne Rice's novels as mere camouflage for reality?"

"Well. Some works are closer to reality than others. Booklovers need only *think* they're reading fiction for the paradigm to work. Whether they are or not is another element entirely."

They held each other's gaze, Rachel thinking, Aubrey watching her think.

Her laptop clicked into sleep mode, its blue light shutting off, sending them into darkness. They heard only their own relaxed breathing. They felt only the heat from each other's bodies on the slab.

CHAPTER FIFTY-SIX

Hamilton pulled on the reins, his horse slowing to a clop in the dark of Hyde Park, just beyond the cusp of lamplight from Carriage Drive. Polidori sat behind him, a hand holding secure about the officer's waist.

"You're quiet, John," Hamilton said over his shoulder.

"I cannot help but feel responsible."

The mount came to a standstill on the gravel, the silence of the park surrounding them.

"I understand. Neither the Bow Street Runners nor the magistrates who oversee us have any knowledge of such an occurrence in the history of our force. And the similarities to your novella have been noted." He nudged the horse with his knees and guided him into the park. "I spent the hour with the captain of the guard while you were occupied. They have found no evidence of the interloper's breach of the palace grounds. No foreign horse or carriage within the courtyards or surrounding lanes, no scuffing of the gravel recently groomed by the parkers. The guards saw nothing. The staff saw nothing. All blissfully unaware until the screaming began."

"Was Augustus Frederick's window also open when the guards discovered him?"

"It was. His valet was adamant it had been closed when Augustus had retired—a standing order from his master who distains fresh air. A fear of the pox—or worse—drifting upon the night breeze."

"But surely no one could enter a window at such a height," Polidori said.

"The captain of the guard pointed out the casements to me from the central yard. The lanterns around the lower stories send those higher up into darkness, partially illuminated by the moon. They made good to confirm all doors to the roof ramparts were locked from within. All were found secured by padlocks that only the keeper of the house has keys to. The captain also conducted brief interviews of the king's grandchildren immediately after the attack, whilst the doctors were being fetched from St. Bartholomew's."

"What did he determine?" Polidori said.

"Augusta Emma was the most forthcoming, though her statement was scattered due to her terror. She'd at first thought it a dream—one she'd never dreamt before nor had any notion of."

"Yes, of course. A young lady would have no concept of such matters."

"She claimed a man of exceptional beauty, his eyes mesmerizing, was with her in her chamber," Hamilton continued. "She was reportedly paralyzed by his splendor. Enamored by his tenderness as he extolled her virtues and joined her in her bed. He licked the perspiration from her, and his mouth settled upon her throat, pleasure tormenting her as he drew upon her life. Through her haze she glimpsed a second apparition at the window drapery, but that vision became dim as she succumbed to a blinding, numbing delight. The two figures retreated from her chamber, she does not know how, and for a time she was still captivated by the dream, only coming to her senses when the pain at her neck became agonizing and she discovered the wetness of bloody bedsheets."

"Did she recognize the assailant?"

"That is the intriguing part." Hamilton stopped their mount under a canopy of oak, placed his hand on Polidori's knee, and turned to observe him. In the mottled moonlight, Hamilton's freckles shone, making his eyes glint a deeper emerald. "Though she described the apparition as handsome, she was reminded of a gentleman who'd attended the ball at the Banqueting House in Whitehall. That guest, however, was far from handsome. Though the form and outline of his face may have been pleasing, they were eclipsed by his deathly pallor. Augusta Emma and her companions observed him and noted the grey deadness of his eyes, which moved from object to object without apparent recognition. He conversed only with mothers and daughters known to be virtuous, ignoring any women who might engage in flirtation. Gossip circulated that his peculiarities and winning tongue made him engaging. He approached Augusta Emma while she was unattended by her company, speaking only when no one else was near enough to hear his soft mumbling, and never making eye contact with her. Eventually she was relieved by her brother, Augustus Frederick, who accompanied the gentleman up to the gallery where other men were smoking and surveying the bounty below."

"Did she say the gentleman's name?"

"No. They were never formally introduced. All very odd, and ungentlemanly."

"Agreed. And Augustus Frederick's account?"

"He recalls nothing. Neither from his bed chamber, nor from the ball."

"Nothing?" Polidori raised an eyebrow, considering the reception Polidori himself received in Augustus's chamber.

"Nothing. The palace guard has increased security at Kensington Palace—all the palaces—and the Bow Street Runners have been tasked with obtaining any intelligence that might be found on the streets of London in gossip or whispers. We are also to obtain a guest list from last evening's ball with a view to interviewing any who might possess information on the matter. The promised bounty for valid information could keep the Bow Street Runners operational for a year, perhaps two or three. It might be enough even to secure a permanent force to police the streets."

The high-pitched trill of a Bow Street Runner's whistle cut through the park. Hamilton urged his horse into a gallop. More whistles screeched, near the first. Polidori thought they must be at the northern rim of the Serpentine, in the center of the parkland. They rounded the eastern end of the lake, then headed west along the water's edge.

"Cease!" Officer Hamilton yelled, standing in the stirrups. Ahead, Polidori could make out two men fighting, one of them a Bow Street Runner in uniform and cap. The other, clothed in a dark frockcoat, swung his fist and jettisoned the runner out into the water—much further than Polidori would have thought a blow could send a man. The aggressor shifted amongst the shadows and was instantly lost to sight.

Their mount halted on the graveled walk. "There are two in the water," Polidori yelled as they dismounted.

They waded out into the lake, Hamilton toward the Bow Street

Runner, Polidori toward the other who was floating face down. The doctor struggled as the bottom of the Serpentine unexpectedly dropped beneath him, and he swallowed a sizeable amount of stagnant water. His Wellingtons filled with slush, his pantaloons and vest heavy and restricting with the saturation. He paddled toward the body, hoping he was not too late. He grasped the man by his coat collar and reversed direction, kicking and gulping more of the Serpentine in his panic. He made his way slowly back toward the upheld lanterns of the officers now gathered at the water's edge. They waded in and yanked Polidori to his feet, relieving him of his burden and carrying the man up onto a grassy embankment. Officer Hamilton made land at the same time, hauling the other officer, unconscious from the blow, across the gravel path and onto the grass as well.

"This one is dead," an officer called, crouched over the man Polidori had brought back to shore. "A gaping wound in his neck."

The others stood around their colleague, retrieved from the water. Polidori staggered over to determine how he might help, finding Officer Hamilton shaking the unconscious man, frantic and frightened. "It's Smith!" he bellowed.

"Help me take off his coat," Polidori ordered, tearing at the belts and buckles. "Now give me two dry coats. Hurry."

He wrapped the coats around Officer Smith, then dragged him so his head was positioned lower down the embankment. He opened Smith's lips and dug his fingers down his throat, flicking out a putrid sludge. Then he grabbed Hamilton's hand and placed it on Smith's bloated abdomen. "Push here after each of my breaths." Polidori pressed his mouth to Smith's. Three breaths, three pushes sending water belching out of the runner before Polidori balled his fists high above his head and struck them down with unapologetic force against Smith's heart. Ribs audibly cracked, and the Bow Street Runners fell back, shocked. But Smith convulsed, retching mud, water, and his supper over himself and Polidori. The doctor pulled him up into his lap, thumbing vomit from the man's lips and holding him close.

Finally a wagon arrived and Smith was lifted into it. Polidori climbed into the rear, numb and wet, and Hamilton trotted at the fore as Officer Smith rested within the comforting warmth of his fellow Bow Street Runners.

And there in the center of the wagon lay the bloated carcass of

Master Aldridge. No longer grieving the loss of the Fairbank lad. No longer to steal the heart of a Somerset maiden without totally giving his own. Just dead. Bite marks and lacerations covered his throat and face, half of the neck muscularity ripped from his spine in an unimaginable frenzy.

CHAPTER FIFTY-SEVEN

Polidori sat on his basement step, staring at but unwilling to approach Master Aldridge's body. This was the first on his slab he had known by name, by life, by shared cigar, port, and tête-à-tête. Without even touching the cadaver, he knew there would be not a single drop of blood within its heart, within its veins. *His* heart; *his* veins. Attacked by a beast of vile creation. *My own creation*, he could not help thinking.

The sucking and consumption of blood. Gross exsanguination. Loss of blood adequate to cause death. But this was much more. The total and utter depletion of blood from a body dying in its attacker's arms as he drained it. Polidori attempted to imagine the stance, the tight grip to keep the victim from collapse, the sensuality of mouth and tongue upon flesh, the piercing of skin, the plunge into virginal warmth. The sweetness of that last drop when there was no more to be drunk. Would the monster be aware when the plumpness of the heart was exhausted, spasming and collapsing with no more left to pump?

Master Aldridge was slight in comparison to Polidori. Perhaps ten pints of blood, and just over a minute for it to circulate his entire system. Would the creature that penetrated the jugular have allowed the blood to squirt into his mouth without tempering its speed? *Perhaps one and a half minutes to drink it*. Or would he have savored it one mouthful at a time? Four ounces per mouthful. Twenty Imperial ounces to a pint. Fifty mouthfuls. Conceivably he might have taken up to two to three hours to consume Master Aldridge's life. An intimate coupling affecting life and death that made Polidori's heartbeat erratic. He shuddered.

The basement door scraped open, a cold wind swirling in to embrace him, to chill the sodden clothes still cloaking him. Officer Hamilton sat on the step beside him, soaked and smelling of the Serpentine—a pungent odor of carp.

"Officer Smith is in recovery, though the whack you gave his ribs will remind him of the night for months to come. He and the Bow Street Runners offer you their utmost thanks."

Polidori bowed his head.

"That was the first I saw you doctor the living."

"It seems something I seldom do these days." He took the flask from his coat pocket. He intended to take a sip but involuntarily took a mouthful, the tincture burning across his tongue and down into his gut. *Forty-nine mouthfuls to go*, he thought.

"May I?" Hamilton asked, reaching for the flask.

"No!" Polidori yelled, startling even himself. "I'm sorry—I—Forgive my rudeness. Let me fetch something better for our taste and to warm the chill from these clothes." He climbed the stair and returned with a jug. "From the Highlands above Loch Lomond. *Aqua Vitae*, the water of life."

Officer Hamilton smirked. "Contraband? I won't tell the magistrate if you won't." He took a swig and almost immediately a ruddiness flushed his cheeks.

Polidori brought the jug to his lips, taking only a taste.

Hamilton stood, touching the doctor on the shoulder. "Get some sleep, my friend," he said. "I shall return tomorrow with direction from the magistrate."

CHAPTER FIFTY-EIGHT

Dr. John Polidori
38 Great Pulteney Street
Soho
London, England
May 1819

Darling John,
Word of your novel has reached us here in Italy. Everyone we have met is ecstatic with the horror you've created. Such a creature! Such a scandal!

Already there is talk of enacting it on the stage, much to Lord Byron's chagrin. He is upset people believe he is the author, even more so that you named your vampyre Lord Ruthven, a name he's despised since Lady Caroline Lamb published Glenarvon, *her Ruthven no less than a thinly disguised caricature of Byron. A bit of revenge after their notorious liaison.*

How delightful!

At a dinner party last evening, I was advised by a correspondent of Herr Beethoven that the composer himself was captivated by your prose and the horror of your imagination.

Well done to you, my dearest brother.
Best,
Mary
250 Riviera di Chiaia
Naples, Italy

Post Script: We have rented a most beautiful apartment overlooking the Royal Gardens with a view beyond Naples Bay to the Isle of Capri. But as always, Naples is a paradise inhabited by devils. I shall confide my thoughts on our time here in another letter.

PPS: There is talk of an escalating situation in London. Please advise at once of your safe carriage. Love, M.

CHAPTER FIFTY-NINE

Aubrey basked in the moonlit courtyard, his face tilted toward the glow, eyes closed, fingers entwined on his belly, agreeably full from Rachel's bolognaise. He appeared younger in the radiance, his skin illuminated.

"Cup o' tea?" Rachel called from the kitchen in her best English accent.

He smirked without opening his eyes. "Sounds good."

The kettle whistled and then she plunked the pot in the center of the table to steep.

"So, what's happening?" he asked.

"Master Aldridge is on the slab."

"Pre or post autopsy?"

"Pre."

Aubrey leaned forward and turned the teapot three times with his finger. "An old trick I learned from my nana," he said. "It's the third one that does it."

It was Rachel's turn to smile.

"Why do you think the royal family was targeted for that first vampyre attack?" Aubrey asked. "You don't get any higher profile than that."

"It might have had something to do with the 'blue blood' concept," she said. "European nobility has long been known for the profound blue appearance of their veins and skin. Whether you attribute that to highly selective inbreeding or otherwise, there *is* a specific blood type for the royals—mostly O negative. Only five percent of the world's population is O negative. If you take into consideration specific antigens confirmed in royal blood, specific immunities, you're looking at zero-point-one percent of the population. Pretty unique."

"What about Master Aldridge? There's no indication in the documents he was of royal blood."

Rachel poured the tea. "No. But bloodlines tend to disseminate, either through marriage, dalliance, or otherwise. The Empire is old—bloodlines and family names have intermingled for centuries. Maybe even millennia. Even the lowliest commoner could have at least a drop of royal blood in their veins. The upper class, in this case Master Aldridge's family, would have had more opportunity to, shall we say, *mingle* with royal bloodlines. But there's another reason royal and aristocratic blood might have been ... tastier?" She laughed, and Aubrey did, too.

"Silver spoons," he said. "Right? There was something on the Discovery Channel."

"Spoons, goblets, and plates to be precise. An emblem of wealth and one the royals and the upper class used to show their status. Also a potent antibacterial that leached into their bodies and bloodstreams with daily use. The upper echelons of Europe were toxic with it—but in a good way."

"And a vampyre might desire it for its antibacterial effects."

Rachel sipped her tea, then furrowed her brow. "Wait. Don't vampyres have a weakness to silver?"

"I believe that's North American folklore. More applicable to the legend of werewolves than vampyres. Again, all part of the misrepresentation and mystification through fiction."

Rachel slumped in her chair, smiling. "How is it you know so much about vampyres of the Romantic era? Something largely irrelevant for the last two hundred years."

"Because I'm a Polidori," he said. "Encumbered by ... by the misplaced judgment of my ancestor. And because perhaps vampyres are not *totally* irrelevant."

Despite what she'd discovered in her research, and what they'd previously discussed, Rachel still thought his words eccentric. Beguiling. She'd come to accept the strange occurrences in the early 1800s, whether as vampyrical or, more likely, as a way for the Romantics to explain away the medically unexplainable, the psychiatrically insane, definitely the criminal, and possibly the highly drugged. That didn't mean she was ready to enter *The Twilight Zone*.

On the contrary, she was very aware Doctor Polidori was on a daily dose, miniscule as it might be, of arsenic. Other references noted prussic acid and cyanide. Any or all could have affected his observations and recollection of events.

On the other hand, there were Officer Hamilton's reports which, though scant in detail, did corroborate Polidori's notes.

Her cell phone rang with a number and country code she didn't recognize.

"Hello?" she said.

"*Bonjour Mademoiselle*, pardon, *Madame* Walton."

She recognized Detective Gendarme Baertschi's voice immediately. A high-ranking detective in Interpol, he had investigated the murders in Montreux, Switzerland, when she was there researching the Shelley bio. What he'd unearthed had shattered her life, then sutured it into something she never could have imagined. Mary Shelley's wretch revealed. Her husband, Adam, laid bare.

Rachel's mind tumbled with uncertainty.

"I'm in a town car parked in front of 38 Great Pulteney Street," Detective Baertschi said. "I'd appreciate your joining me for a conversation, immediately. And *madame*"—he hesitated— "please say nothing to the gentleman you are with. Not a word."

He hung up.

CHAPTER SIXTY

Polidori sliced the scalpel down the center of Master Aldridge's belly from sternum to pubic bone. The body was sparse of hair, with softening muscle tone, grey in pallor. The stomach was plump with venison and vegetables. The arteries, veins, and heart were empty, as expected. By the third hour of the autopsy Polidori was sewing his incisions back together. Not with the thick needle and coarse twine of previous autopsies, but with a fine needle and cotton thread from his own sewing kit. The loops were close and tight, the interconnecting knots tenderly secured below the line of the flesh. The neck was harder to reconstruct, with torn musculature splayed out. However, the underlying muscle and sinew was intact. Polidori twisted it back into shape, molding it around the spine and under the jaw, sewing it together with care. The mark of the vampyre stood prominent between the rips, both upper and lower incisors having penetrated the flesh. Polidori compared its shape and size to the tracings he'd done at Kensington Palace. It matched the marks on Augusta Emma's throat and corresponded to the larger print on Augustus Frederick's. He wondered whether the smaller marks on Augustus Frederick's neck might have been of female origin.

Polidori took his time to dress Master Aldridge. Based on his measurements of the corpse, he procured bespoke couture from the high-end shops of Savile Row. New Wellington Boots, buffed to a shine. There was nothing he could do about the deathly sallowness of the face, but he took care to arrange Master Aldridge's coif and white silk cravat—one from his own collection.

I don't even know his given name, Polidori thought, remiss at his inattentiveness. Renewed guilt overcame him. How could he not feel responsible?

He scattered dried perfumed flowers and strong-smelling herbs across the chest then wrapped the shroud tight, swaddling the young man as if he were his own brother. Then he tied a length of string to the index finger and flicked the bell at the other end. A high, hollow ring.

His burial in the yard of St. Martin-in-the-Fields was attended by a priest, a gravedigger, Polidori, and Officer Hamilton.

"I alerted the staff of the gentleman's family residence. I was denied entry and advised the family had disowned their son, refusing to acknowledge his death or his life. His indiscretion. His shame and his love," Hamilton said. He pulled a half sovereign from his pocket and handed it to the priest. "Thomas Aldridge was his name."

And though there was no tombstone to write it on, it was a name chiseled close to Polidori's heart.

CHAPTER SIXTY-ONE

"*Madame*," Detective Gendarme Baertschi greeted Rachel as she stepped into the back of the town car.

"How did you know I was here?" she asked.

His face softened and he appeared almost apologetic. "The circumstance of your family, of your husband and daughter, are of continued interest to Interpol—I'm certain you understand why that is. At most we keep a cursory check on your whereabouts as part of the ongoing Montreux investigation. But that is not the reason I'm here." He stroked the length of his nose with the tip of his ring finger. She recalled a wedding band, but it was no longer there.

With Detective Baertschi, Rachel knew she was better off saying nothing to avoid being misunderstood. Or caught in a lie. Again.

"Your recent online search activity was flagged by Interpol computers. Though I personally was not surprised, given the nature of your work and preoccupation with the Romantics. It was only a matter of time before you once again landed within my area of responsibility."

"What are you talking about?" Rachel said.

He cleared his throat and locked his eyes on hers. "There are people, *madame*, who believe they are something they are not. Perhaps they are enamored by their forefathers, or the romance of history, or the desire to be more than simply human." He settled into the plush leather, watching her for a reaction, but she remained expressionless. "Sometimes imagination is a good thing," he went on. "Other times, it is not. On occasion, it can even be dangerous. It can cause misfortune. It can kill."

Rachel shook her head, her brow furrowing. "Okay, what are you alluding to? What do you want me to tell you, and why didn't you want me to let Aubrey know? Please, just tell me."

"It is the subject of your research, *Madame*."

"Doctor John William Polidori," she said.

"Vampyres," he said.

Interpol was interested in her research on vampyres. Interpol. Vampyres. Her mind stuck on those two words, not knowing how they could relate to one another.

"Of course," Baertschi continued, "vampyres are not real. Not in the sense we know them in *histoires d'horreur* fiction. But there are some people delusional enough to believe they are vampyres, and to carry out their lives by moonlight, and to partake of a diet of—"

"Okay, some people are crazy. I get that."

"And some people kill, *madame*." He pulled out his phone and scrolled through the photo gallery. "Do you know this gentleman?"

Rachel's heart sank. She'd been here before during the Montreux investigation. And it hadn't turned out well. At least not for the person in the photo.

The image was of a cute young guy, caught off guard by the flash of the camera. Intense green eyes. Freckles scattered across nose and cheeks. Thick copper brows and clipped hair. Copper stubble accentuating his attractive jaw and mouth.

She knew her expression had already answered the detective. She dared not tell anything but the truth. "Yes. I saw him in a café in Seven Dials a few days after I arrived in London. And I saw him again at Heaven—a nightclub. He frightened me, but I didn't know who he was. Has he killed someone?" Rachel thought of Jess, their assurance that the copper-headed guy wouldn't trouble her again, and Aubrey's later inference that Jess was dangerous. Deliciously so. "Has he been killed?"

"We would like to talk to him. That is all you need to know. But is there something else you'd like to say on that matter?"

She shook her head.

He narrowed his eyes and pressed his lips tight. "And what do you know of"—he glanced at his phone—"Mr. Aubrey Polidori?"

Rachel felt flustered by the questioning and by her own indefinite feelings for her host. By what she was willing to admit to the Detective. And to herself. "Well, um, this is his family home. He's a descendent of Doctor John Polidori. He's, ah, a hedge fund manager at some company in the Gherkin. I, ah, oh I don't know! What do you want me to tell you? He's a nice guy."

"He's a nice guy," the detective echoed softly. "We've only just started our research on him, but so far we can't find any record of his birth. No record of title for this building."

She was increasingly exasperated, angered the detective was now questioning someone she had come to trust, had come to . . . It wasn't as though she loved Aubrey—or did she? Did she love him? She didn't really know him. Not really. And yet she felt like she'd always known him. Had always loved him. The idea seemed outrageous, and yet she couldn't think of another word to describe her bond with him.

She balled her fists. "Aubrey Polidori is a good man. A gentleman. In every way I've ever known him," she said, realizing she'd echoed Jess's words from that night in the alley outside Heaven.

"Are you sleeping with him?"

"That's enough!" she shouted, reaching for the door handle.

Detective Baertschi extended his hand, his card between his fingers. "You can reach me via London Interpol for the next month, and you now have my cell number. Don't wait until it is too late, *madame*. Not like last time."

Rachel accepted the card. She wanted to rip it to pieces in front of his face, but she didn't.

CHAPTER SIXTY-TWO

Polidori supped with Officer Hamilton at Brooks's, both somber but finding solace in each other's quiet company. When the club lounge clock struck one, the doctor took his leave. Instead of taking a carriage home to Soho, he walked a circuitous route south, through St. James's Park, past the Houses of Parliament, ending up on Westminster Bridge. The River Thames churned below, dark and forbidding. Most of the city lights had been extinguished, but fires blazed along the hazy riverbank, highlighting shanties, barges, and tented rafts. He listened to the murmur of late-night conversations, muted laughter. Muted life. He should have kept to the bridge and upper embankment, but instead he descended the stairs to walk amongst the hovels and feel the warmth of companionship—of acceptance. All seemed to be in good spirits and for that he was glad.

Somehow, he knew these Londoners would not be targeted by the evil he had let loose upon the city from his inkwell. *An aristocratic fiend preying upon high society. Sucking from them both blood and vitality. Seducing them toward undead oblivion.*

A shiver coursed down his spine, and he turned up the collar of his frockcoat and climbed back up the stairs to the cobbled streets. Aside from one lone horse and wagon, the streets of London were deserted. The spire of St. Martin-in-the-Fields shone ahead, a shaft of moonlight striking it just so. He was drawn to it, with more to say to Master Aldridge, more to apologize for, the sod not yet settled upon his grave. No sooner had Polidori pushed open the iron gate of the cemetery than he heard it.

The hollow ring of a bell.

Adrenaline sluiced through his veins and he sprinted amongst the gravestones. His boots crunched on the gravel paths, loud within the quiet of the yard. He stopped to get his bearings, listening for the direction of the ring, then ran again. Then halted again. The bell echoed from granite slab and angel, was muffled by moss-covered tree and demon. It was like a delusion, swirling along the strokes and serifs of the epitaphs chiseled into marble.

He stood for a moment in the shadow of a tomb. The bell had stopped. He was out of breath and his ears ached to hear it again, to give him direction, but there was only silence. He imagined the poor wretch, buried beneath earth, perhaps not knowing they were six feet down in hallowed ground. A sob threatened to escape, but he quashed it to listen. He closed his eyes to focus. The smell of death was subtle but evident, with the deceased piled one upon the other in family graves, some less than a foot beneath the surface. And then he heard it again.

A single strike. Hollow. And he knew where it was. Who it was.

He lumbered across grass and gravel, leaped between headstones and trees to the darkest part of the yard, under the shadow of the church spire. He pulled off his frockcoat and threw it aside, dropping to his knees to claw back freshly laid sod. He dug, frantic, ripping his fingernails and scraping his skin on rocks and shattered remnants of bone. The bell hung right next to his face, from a string slung over a branch above and pulled taut into the ground. One last time chime, and the bell was tugged straight off its perch.

"Dear God!" Polidori shouted as he shoveled more dirt with his hands, with no real awareness of what he might find at the other end of the string. Finally, he uncovered the shroud, the features of the tortured face beneath evident in the folds—mouth wide, gasping, attempting to breathe through the soil-clad layers of cotton. Polidori tore the shroud from Master Aldridge's face, and the young man took a heaving breath. "Dear God, dear God," the Doctor whispered as he went on digging, excavating his friend from the grave.

Aldridge spasmed, his gasps loud and grieving. Polidori freed his torso and thrust his arms under Aldridge's pits, hauling him wholly out into the open air. Aldridge looked around at the graveyard, and screamed.

Polidori pulled him into a tight embrace, and Aldridge quaked, pressing his face to the doctor's breast, his sobbing raw and uninhibited. Interminable minutes passed before his distress quieted into soft weeping. The doctor spoke tender words at his ear—words neither man would ever wish to remember, but which brought them some semblance of comfort. Soon the graveyard was still once again, save for the loud beating of the hearts within their chests.

CHAPTER SIXTY-THREE

Mary Shelley
250 Riviera di Chiaia
Naples, Italy
May 1819

My precious confidant,
All logic fails me, and so I simply must state the occurrences of early yesterday morning through last evening without edit. I have not slept since my previous quickly dashed letter to you. Please forgive me the weariness of my words.

The morning was overcast and threatening as only a London sky can be when myself and Master Aldridge arrived at my home from St. Martin-in-the-Fields. He was exhausted and so I laid him in my bed. Meanwhile, I stood by the window to watch over him, bewildered beyond the capacity of my knowledge.

I remained at the window for hours, the curtains drawn, the room dark, my breathing slow and paced in measure with Master Aldridge's as he slumbered. It was late afternoon when I joined my staff to apprise them of my feeble guest. My valet and I were climbing the stair with pails of hot water for the bath when the young master's ungodly screams pierced the household. We raced to my room and found him sobbing in his distress.

"No more darkness, no more darkness," he cried.
I flung open the curtains, but the windows offered little in

the way of light as the sun stayed hidden behind thick dark clouds. My valet lit candles and lanterns, cracked windows, and filled the bath. I pulled Aldridge into my arms to comfort him.

"No more darkness," I murmured. "Master Aldridge, Thomas, my staff and myself are here at your service. Please," I said, motioning toward the bath. "Make yourself comfortable as you regain your strength. We shall take our leave to give you privacy. If you need anything, just . . ." I glanced at the bell on the bedside table. "I shall return to your company shortly."

"Please, Doctor. I cannot be alone."

"Of course." I nodded.

My valet left, and I took a seat at the desk, with my back to my guest. I documented the previous evening in my ledger, dubious at the words I was writing even as I wrote them— words no one could possibly believe. Words even I could scarcely believe. He'd been dead, Mary. Dead and sliced open on my autopsy table. His abdomen splayed, his ribs cracked, and me, exploring the inner workings of his body. I'd held his heart in my hand, the arteries severed and hanging limp.

"Master Aldridge," I said without turning. "After you have bathed and broken your fast, I think it best we commit to my office downstairs for a physical review of your wellbeing. To determine the extent of any injuries from, um, events."

Water dripped as he stood from the bathwater without a word.

I trembled at the thought of his nakedness behind me, wishing to glance upon him, to see whether the vast damage of the attack, and the later suturing of his flesh by my own hand, had been a fabrication of a dream. A nightmare. A somnambulation I'd believed to be fact but was not.

And yet, I knew for certain he'd been in the ground. I had pulled him from the ground. I pressed my fingers to my temples, a migraine threatening. I almost welcomed its approach. At least as an understandable, explainable pain.

I turned as he was pulling on his undergarments. His body was not as I recalled it. His flesh showed barely blemish or scar of youthful enterprise. Lithe musculature was intact with no hint of gross disfigurement. I squinted, concentrating on the groove down the center of his abdomen from sternum to groin. There was, perhaps, the remnant of a scar, though it might have been a trick of the candlelight, or a thin trail of hair. But even across his chest, the sparse growth of hair seemed to part and curl in a way I could believe was caused by my scalpel and bone saws. I could not believe my own eyes. My own memory of events.

I approached him, indicating with my hand toward his neck.

"May I?" I asked.

He nodded.

The flesh of his neck was warm and supple. The muscles from shoulder to spine were sinewy and strong. Intact. The flesh was smooth. Youthful. Unblemished. Undead. No sign of the vampyre's mark. The more I stared at the skin of his throat, the more translucent it appeared. Drops of bathwater sparkled. The pulse of his jugular was mesmerizing, the skin tinging a darker blue along its thin length with each beat. I caressed it with my fingertips, drawn closer and closer. Enamored by its pulsing life.

Thomas's lips were at my ear. "Would you like to taste it?" he whispered.

I cannot tell you what overcame me. But though I did not answer him aloud, within my mind I thought, "Yes."

The soft knock at the door pulled me from my reverie and I jerked away from Master Aldridge, horrified.

"Enter," I said as I strode to the desk.

Officer Hamilton came in, his eyes raw, evidence of his own sleepless night. The color drained from his face when he saw Aldridge, and then I knew I had not dreamed the entire ordeal. As Thomas dressed. I sensed the machinations of the officer's mind as he surveyed the scene, scrutinized the half-naked man he'd last seen being lowered into the ground.

We left Master Aldridge in the parlor under the matronly rule of Mrs. Hicks, who no doubt would ensure he ate every last drop of porridge and heavily larded toast. Hamilton and I retreated to my father's study, both lost for words.

"I don't wish to impose, but is it too early for a cigar?" he

eventually asked.

"Not at all." In truth, I was glad of his request.

We both puffed on our succor, tangibly thinking through the last forty-eight hours.

"Your novel was real," he said. "That cannot be disputed."

"Creatures I wish with all my heart that should not exist in either fiction or reality. And yet they do." My thoughts eddied between the dreaded concepts of my novel and the days and nights spent in the company of Lord Byron. "These beings are the ultimate incarnation of narcissism. The unrestrained self-worth and awareness, seduction, and sexuality. They steal vitality, consume life, suppress and violate dreams, discard the ambitions and lives of those not of their kind."

Hamilton was aghast. "Yet Master Aldridge lives on," he countered.

"That he does. I cannot explain it. Unless the syndrome incumbent upon the original predator is easily spread."

"Do you mean, like a plague?"

"Perhaps."

"Has he said anything that would assist our investigation?"

I shook my head as I settled on the settee opposite the mantle. Hamilton sat beside me and we stared into space. Above the fire my own oil-painted visage stared at me or, more to the point, ignored me to gaze off frame. The same distant thought. The same distant horror. And shame. Whether Byron, or Ruthven, or some unknown entity currently lurking parks, parlors, and bedchambers. I felt sick to my stomach and had to close my eyes. To relegate my own likeness to obscurity.

Officer Hamilton wrapped his arm around my shoulders and I welcomed the warmth and strength. He is the friend I need at this time. That I have needed for a long time. His presence and sensible thoughts and conversation have been of great comfort and joy. I am glad you met him before departing for the continent.

Mrs. Hicks delivered Master Aldridge to us in the study along with a tray of tea and sandwiches. She raised her eyebrow at me and I knew it best I and Hamilton start eating before she left our company. "Mrs. Bent shall be up shortly to make the fire. We hadn't expected you to use your father's study in his absence," she said on her way out. Again, with the raised eyebrow you and I both know so well.

Officer Hamilton extracted the case ledger from his satchel. "Master Aldridge, do you recall the last evening you were in Hyde Park?"

"I do."

"If you please," the officer said, setting down his half-eaten sandwich to pick up his pencil.

"I spent the majority of the evening at The Punchbowl. Dinner, cards, port and cigars. May I?" he said, motioning toward the cigar box.

I assisted his lighting then returned to my supper.

"It was perhaps two in the morning when he entered the establishment," Aldridge continued. "His cheeks were flushed by the cold night air and much ruddier than I recalled. I was astounded by his vitality, uncertain of my previous recollection and dread, so thrilled to see him, yet confused when by all accounts I'd thought it impossible. But there he was, and that was all I cared for. I knew my memory must merely have been a nightmare. A waking dream. He warmed his hands by the fire, his gut with a glass of sherry, his thoughts with one of the house's best cigars. Still, he was . . . he was very cold whenever I touched him in conversation. He said he had supped already, so we ventured out into the park for a nighttime constitutional. Our conversation was moonlit and we slipped easily into silent acquaintance, words no longer adequate to convey our thoughts as we stood on the embankment of the Serpentine." His face fell. "I have no memory beyond that point, up until the all-encompassing pressure and terror of being shrouded beneath the earth."

I nodded slowly. "You know who this man was," I said. "We need to be apprised of his identity, as he may be tangled in a similar circumstance that occurred nearby."

"I cannot tell you, for I swore an oath."

Hamilton stood, appalled. "But this man killed you, desecrated your slain body."

Master Aldridge also stood, to appraise his reflection in the study mirror. "He clearly did no such thing. For I am here, very much alive." He lifted his chin to view the length of his neck. "Excuse me, gentlemen. Might I utilize the convenience of your night stool, Doctor?"

He left the study and crossed the lobby to my suite, leaving both doors partially open behind him.

"Do you believe his story?" I asked.

"What is there to disbelieve, other than every logical fact that occurred while he was presumably unaware?" Officer Hamilton said.

A cold night breeze suddenly blew into the study, and immediately we held no doubt as to its source. We ran to my suite, and found the window sash was fully up, the curtains billowing. No sign of Aldridge. We leant out the casing to view Great Pulteney Street. I had my doubts he could have jumped to the cobbles without impaling himself on the wrought iron fence or, at the very least, spraining his ankle. Still, he was gone.

My incredulity has only compounded.

Your dearest friend,
John

CHAPTER SIXTY-FOUR

Rachel replaced the letter in the pile on the desk and pulled off her gloves. The sash of the closest window was open about a foot and, though she couldn't push it any higher, she was able to squeeze her head and shoulders through the gap. The early evening air was blustery and cool on her face, carrying the echo of revelry from nearby restaurants and pubs. She agreed with Polidori's observation that the chances were minimal of surviving the drop without at least some damage. Even sliding across the eve of the portico would require extreme dexterity. She certainly would not attempt it. She pulled on her coat and took her laptop downstairs.

Aubrey was sitting at the kitchen counter reading his book. "Hey," he said.

"Hey," Rachel replied, her thoughts still lost in the letters and ledger entries. In Detective Gendarme Baertschi's visit.

"The documents are getting pretty profound, aren't they," he said.

She nodded, now thinking more of the Detective than the papers. "Do you drive, Aubrey?"

"Of course. Would you like to go for a ride somewhere? We can hire a car."

"So, you have a driver's license?"

A quizzical look crossed his face. He lifted his butt off the stool and pulled his wallet from his back pocket. He flipped open the leather and pulled out the card, slid it across the counter.

1. POLIDORI
2. AUBREY JOHN WILLIAM
3. 7-9-1995 LONDON

Rachel picked it up and tilted it, noting the security holograph and raised surface pattern. It looked real enough to her. What did she know? She was thoughtful of the birth date then flicked her attention to the photo.

"Well, I'm glad to see you take a bad picture like the rest of us."

"Oi, it's not that horrible," he said with a grin, grabbing it back. "So what've you got planned?"

"Thought I'd work down here for a while. A bit closer to the living." She set up her laptop out in the courtyard as Aubrey continued reading his book in the kitchen. His face was animated as he read, the miniscule movement of his mouth, the glide of his eyes back and forth with each line, the slight raise of an eyebrow, the lick of his lower lip. He gasped.

"Don't you just love the bad guys?" he said without taking his attention from the page.

Rachel wasn't sure whether he was talking to her or himself, so she let it slide to concentrate on her own research. She clicked on the search engine.

Vampyre. London. England. Current news.

She hadn't expected to find anything. Had hoped she wouldn't find anything. But there it was, the half-page headline on *The Daily Sun Tattler* website. *Death in Heaven.*

The sidebar linked to another article titled *Aliens at Heathrow Airport.* It seemed a dubious page for news, but she read it anyway.

> *Couple found dead in Heaven nightclub. A confidential source confirms the bodies of a bartender and a female patron were discovered in a liquor storeroom located in the basement of the club. "I had trouble opening the door," our informer said. "Finally, I budged it. A shelf had been knocked down, tens of thousands of dollars of high-end liquor bottles were smashed across the floor, and the fumes were overbearing. I flicked on the light and saw two people sprawled over the tiles in the back of the store, almost naked. I recognized Deon, one our bar guys, from his dreads and tattoos. He has this snake inked onto his arm, with its fangs sunk into an apple. Kind of cool. It*

was supposed to be his night off. And I guess it was. His jeans and boxers were down around his ankles, his shirt and singlet still tangled around his wrist. Otherwise he was butt naked. His body was bent at a really strange angle, like his back had been broken or something. There was a young lass beside him, her blouse open and her skirt pushed up. She had massive amounts of hair and it was all disheveled. She was still wearing her stilettos. I couldn't see her face because her head was kind of under Deon's back. I could see her neck though. And Deon's. Both were heavily bruised a dark purple-blue. And there were bite marks. Definitely bite marks. Like Deon and this lass had sunk their teeth into each other a bit too deep. Like a sexy vampyre thing. You know, like domination or choking or something. I took some photos with my phone then called 999.

The nightclub management and Scotland Yard have refused comment on the matter. Images after the hyperlink and paywall.

Rachel glanced over the screen toward Aubrey, her gaze unfocused. Death by passion? Could two people bite each other's necks at the same time? She subconsciously tilted her head, imagining Aubrey biting her neck as she bit his. Her cheeks flamed, but still she couldn't see how it would be physically possible. Not so the canines could pierce the jugular, sealing the wound to secure every drop of blood.

She skimmed the article again. No mention of blood or manner of death. No explanation for the possible broken back. No indication the liquor shelf had fallen on top of them or was brought down in a struggle. Surely the informer would have mentioned the copious amounts of blood Rachel imagined must surely belong to such a scene.

She started a new search. *Heaven. Nightclub. Death.* She hesitated. *Murder.* She clicked the first link.

Cloud Network News: Murder on the Dancefloor—Part II. Several fragments of video footage from

*Heaven nightclub have been edited together and
released by Scotland Yard, along with a £10,000
reward to anyone offering details leading to an arrest
in this matter. The images begin with Mr. Deon
O'Reilly and Ms. (name not released at time of
publication) on the dancefloor. The suspected person
of interest enters frame at 0:46. Warning: Adult
content—nudity, explicit sex scenes. Warning:
Lighting effects—stroboscopic.*

Rachel clicked the play button. The video was in color. No sound, but her imagination filled in the audio. The camera was tight on a section of dancefloor she recognized nearest the bar. At least thirty people in frame were writhing and jumping wildly. Angles of light and splashes of deep shadow swooped across the crowd. A blue circle superimposed on the image highlighted the victims. The video became grainy as it zoomed in on them. A third shirtless person joined their circle. They seemed to welcome him, slipping their arms across his shoulders and around his waist as they all danced in a close huddle. Their movements against each other were intimate, uninhibited, sexual. They kissed openly and passionately. A flash of light emphasized the trio. Deon with his dreadlocks. The woman with her luxurious mane of dark hair. The third with his pallid skin and copper trim. Despite the grainy image, Rachel recognized him immediately.

She paused the video on his face. The frozen image was distorted and horrific. He might have been laughing, or exulting in a moment of joy. His eyes were closed, his mouth opened wide. *Happy*, Rachel thought. She couldn't discern his teeth, but she knew them from the café in Seven Dials. The curiously sharp canines, and the red of his lower lip where his teeth pressed into it. Each recollection of him made his canines longer. Sharper. More dangerous. Fangs rather than teeth. She pushed the false vision from her thoughts and clicked play.

A second camera angle showed the trio walking down the same corridor Rachel had walked along, first with Aubrey, then with Jess. The three were still tangled up in each other, unfastening buttons, unbuckling belts, unzipping flies as they descended a stair. A third camera caught them outside what Rachel presumed was the liquor storeroom. Deon's pants were down his thighs, his shirt mostly off as he unlocked the door. The copper-haired man had nudged off his shoes and was kicking loose his crumpled blue jeans and briefs from his feet. He yanked Deon hard against him, his hand splayed across the barman's taut stomach, and his mouth brushing against the woman's lips. This camera's video was clear and close. In the U.S. it would have been intentionally blurred. Or not shown at all. But not here. The image was potent and mesmerizing, graphic and carnal. The woman delighting. The men flushed. It was nothing short of pornographic.

Rachel gasped, recalling Detective Baertschi's warning. Interpol's online search engines. She slammed the laptop shut, her heart pounding. Would he know she'd seen the video? That she'd recognized the copper-haired man? Of course he would. He could read her better than she could lie.

"Are you all right, Rachel?" Aubrey asked, running out into the yard.

"Nothing. It's nothing," she said, shaking her head.

His face softened. "You need a break from the research. The body count tends to pile up during the last years of Polidori's writings. Some of those events are still enough to turn my stomach whenever I reminisce." He checked his watch. "Would you like to come to the gym with me? Get out of your head for a while? I have a guest pass you can use."

CHAPTER SIXTY-FIVE

Polidori waited an hour in the office of the captain of the guard, checking and rechecking the fresh supplies he'd bought at the apothecary on the way to Kensington Palace. At noon he was called to Apartment 1. A valet led him through the clock-chiming, bird-caroling salons, up the stair and into Augustus Frederick's suite. The curtains were open wide, sunlight streaming in, but the window sashes were firmly secured. The air was stale with the smell of sweat and unwashed masculinity. Augustus Frederick stood at the window with his back to Polidori—greasy, shaggy hair, a dirty quilted dressing gown, silk slippers, bare hairless calves and forearms.

"You have returned, Doctor. Do you require an apology?" he said without turning from the window.

"Not at all, sir. I came to determine your health, to ensure no continued ill effects from that evening's occurrence." He remained at the door until invited further into the room.

"Very well then. Do as you must."

Polidori inspected Augustus Frederick's hands. They were warm and rough to the touch. The bruising had diminished, the cuts healing well. The broken finger and thumb were still secured by the original bandaging, now dirty and frayed. Polidori unwound the fabric, then took care to wash the hand and fingers with alcohol and cloth. Augustus Frederick's hand trembled.

"Please tell me if I cause you any pain," Polidori said. He felt gently along the length of the broken appendages, then tightly wound them with fresh bandages. "It is best if these remain secure for a week or so. You will know when they feel adequate to be unbound. Please, sir, if you would have a seat." Polidori indicated for his patient to sit upon the sill.

The scars left by the attack were prominent, pink and puckered amongst the dark bristles of his unshaven neck and jaw. Polidori ran his thumb across the scars on the cheek and just below the lips. The bottom lip remained bruised and swollen. He urged it back and noted the rip of flesh inside. "This cut may take longer to heal, but there is no sign of infection." The nicks and cuts on Augustus Frederick's neck were healing, with the exception of the deep punctures on the side, which were inflamed and raw, gaping wounds filled with pus. "Have the palace doctors attended to this at all?" He glanced up, noting the sheen of tears brimming in Augustus Frederick's eyes. "You are assured of my discretion, sir. In all matters."

"I refused to see them. I was ashamed that . . . that I had been . . ."

For a moment neither man said a word as they held each other's gaze. "I understand," Polidori said. And he did.

He opened his bag and indicated for Augustus Frederick to lay upon the bed. Sitting at his side, Polidori extracted a jar from his bag. "This will decrease the swelling and promote the movement and cleaning of the blood in this area." He selected a leech from the jar and placed its front sucker upon one of the puncture wounds, holding it there until it secured a hold of the flesh. He placed another on the second puncture. The area of inflammation was a mouth shaped oval of teeth marks, perhaps four inches by three, hard to the touch. Thinking of Master Aldridge and the events following his demise, Polidori thought it best to place several more leeches across the bulge to remove any accumulated toxins, possible residue from the bite.

"The bloodletting shall take about thirty minutes. Though once the leeches drop you may continue to bleed freely for up to ten hours. I would prefer to stay with you until completion." He checked his fob watch. "Around midnight. Or I can direct your valet to attend you during this time."

Polidori made to rise, but Augustus Frederick gripped him by the wrist. Polidori sat back down, and Augustus Frederic loosened his grip but did not let go.

Again, there was silence. Not uncomfortable, but beckoning to be filled. Polidori nudged one of the leeches to ensure it was secure. "I suspect this wound was made by the same fiend that attacked your sister. It is similar in measurement and mark of teeth." He pressed his fingertips against the flesh beneath the swelling to better feel the pulse. The pad of his thumb fell naturally to Augustus's cheek, on the cusp of his lip. "Augusta Emma was able to describe him, and it would assist our investigation if you could corroborate her statement. Again, sir, you have my utmost discretion in this matter."

Augustus Frederick nodded and closed his eyes. A tear gathered in his lashes, and his grip on Polidori's wrist shifted, firm but placid. "It was a man, perhaps a year or two younger than ourselves. His couture and manner were gentlemanly. A nobleman. Clean of face with hair straight and blonde. Though I have always found other men to be particularly ugly and brutish compared to the fairer sex, I felt an unusual allure to this fiend as he crept across my bed covers. His eyes were a blue I had never seen before. His skin so soft I thought it possible only in a fair maiden. He spoke to me, but I could not tell you what he said, for I saw only the parting of his lips, the strands of saliva that stretched from tongue to teeth as he leaned over me and pressed his mouth to my neck. I felt no pain with the connection, merely an intensely pleasant, wet heat pressing within me. A lightheadedness. A pulsing euphoria unfamiliar to me."

The leeches were growing plump with blood. One by one they released their grip and Polidori placed them back into the jar. He held a cloth to Augustus Frederick's throat to stem the bleeding. "Had you seen him prior to his appearance in your chamber?"

Frederick grunted. "I don't believe so, but I'd hardly know. Who notices the features of any man, save one's own father or our king?"

"And the second fiend who attacked you?"

Augustus Frederick chuckled, and it was the first time Polidori had seen him without a scowl. "A waif of the night. Voluptuous of figure and temperament. A more beautiful creature I have seldom seen. She crawled over me, licking along the lengths of my body, her hair falling like a curtain as she mirrored her companion's actions about my neck. She kissed me with a passion, a frenzy that excited me. Even as she bit into my face, my lips, my chin, I felt only exultation. A need for her to bite deeper, to rip the very flesh from my body to satisfy our communion."

"This waif—might she have been at the Banqueting House ball?"

Augustus Frederick opened his eyes. "She was," he said, surprised at the realization. "I saw her from the balcony. The gentleman I was smoking with pointed her out to me. She was standing alone, not appearing part of any congregation. A beautiful object in every way."

"Did you approach her, sir? Were you introduced?"

Augustus shook his head. "By the time I descended from the balcony and found a member of the Committee of Arrangements to make me a formal introduction, she had gone. A Cinderella without the opportunity of a lost slipper."

Polidori pressed a clean cloth against Augustus Frederick's throat. "The gentleman who brought this maiden to your attention. Was he known to you? Can you tell me his name?"

"Unfortunately not. He had been bothering Augusta Emma, and so I distracted him into conversation for her sake. He was dead of eye, his dialog momentarily witty but otherwise forgettable, with only his notice of young beauty on the floor below us opportune and to my liking. I can tell you nothing of his posture, countenance, or circumstance."

CHAPTER SIXTY-SIX

An hourlong trail hike above the cliffs of Dover was pleasant and distracting. White clouds tumbling above the waves of the English Channel. Gulls riding the updraft beyond the bluff. The intermittent whistle of a train in the distance and the bellow of cattle nearby. No cadavers. No vampyres.

The screen on the elliptical flashed, the bucolic scenery replaced by digits alternating between Metric and Imperial. Five miles. Four-hundred calories burned. Rachel pumped the treads for a few more minutes to push the burn up, her legs and arms aching, her mind clear and alert. Then she stepped from the machine and headed toward the locker rooms, sweating through the tank top she'd borrowed from Aubrey, XXL and baggy, with *Knowledge is stronger than memory* emblazoned across the front.

She stepped into the dry sauna and joined the handful of people already relaxing inside—some naked, some not. It was all the same to Rachel. She spread out her towel on the middle tier and leaned back against the spruce wall to enjoy the heat.

"They found another last night. The fourth person attacked in just over a week."

Rachel's ears pricked.

"In the courtyard of some high-end hotel in Temple Court, under the gaze of a topiary dragon. The staff thought she'd drunk too much and fallen from her nine-inch heels. Wasn't until the concierge carried her into the lobby that he realized her scarf was red because it was saturated in blood. His suit was smeared with it."

"Yeah, I saw they interviewed him on the news. Decent sort of chap. Still wearing his uniform jacket with the right breast just absolutely soaked. He said the bleeding was from her neck, like a love bite gone too deep, the damage raw and puckering. That's what he said. He was able to stem the flow until medics arrived. Said she awoke in his arms all delirious and, like, lifted her neck to him. She begged for more, grabbing him to pull his face and mouth to the wound on her throat. He was horrified—had to yank himself away—and then she fell into a fit. At least, that's what he said."

"Why'd she do that?"

"Must've been mad."

"Drugs, I reckon."

"Yeah, she was prob'ly balling with some bad blow."

One of the guys snickered. "Beam me up Scotty!"

"Did she die?" Rachel asked pointedly, wanting to quell their cheerfulness. She realized how American she sounded amongst the local accents.

"Ah, no. She's been institutionalized, though," a woman said. "Too much for the poor dear."

A ladle of water was thrown onto the rocks, steam pluming up the walls and across the ceiling.

"Somebody said there were four," Rachel said. "I heard about the two at Heaven. Who was the fourth?"

A guy on the top tier, naked and shining with perspiration, dropped down to the lowest level and tucked his towel around his waist. He skimmed the sweat from his arms and chest, then poured his water bottle over his face. "The fourth is actually the first," he said.

It sounded like a riddle. But Rachel knew exactly what he meant.

"There was one of those silent raves in Seven Dials. Millennial nonsense. Monmouth Street and the other lanes were closed to traffic around the dial. It's been on the news for days. How've you missed it?"

"What happened?" Rachel asked, thinking it was better she didn't know.

"Initially there was confusion, the sound extinguished from the headphones of those dancing to the beat in the rain, as security rushed into the middle of the crowd. There was a young girl, around your age, sprawled across the steps of the central column. She was dead. Mouthfuls of flesh had been torn from both sides of her neck. The news said her jugular and carotid arteries had been severed, blood spray saturating those nearest. Panic shattered the crowd, sending them in all directions. There was no way in the chaos to determine the beast that had done it to her." Three of the occupants hurriedly left the sauna. Then a fourth. "The coroner and detectives agreed it was an unbridled attack fueled by intense rage. Intense psychosis. Drug induced or otherwise."

"Do they have any idea who did it? Any video or photos of the crowd?"

"Not that I've seen. I don't think Scotland Yard or Interpol have released any."

"Interpol?" Rachel said.

"Yeah. Not sure why they're involved."

Rachel knew why. At least, she thought she did.

She left the sauna, collected her phone from the locker room, and went to cool off by the indoor pool. The room smelled of chlorine and echoed with the splash and sluice of water, the bounce of the diving board at the far end. The moon, soon to be full, shone through the clerestory windows above. Aubrey was swimming, his stroke easy and methodical. Untiring. He rarely needed to lift his head for breath. She didn't know how anyone could do pool circuits for over an hour. She thought it too claustrophobic to have her face underwater for such a time. She needed to get out of her head, not stuck further into it with only the black line at the bottom of the pool as distraction. Guidance.

She wondered how many laps he'd done.

She wondered if the copper-haired man had killed the woman in Seven Dials. And the two at Heaven. If he'd attacked the one in Temple Court. She pinched the bridge of her nose, to block the imagined scenes of slaughter. *Imagined*, she reminded herself. There was no indication the copper-haired man had been involved at Temple Court. Even for the murders at Heaven, there was no visual evidence or direct statement he'd been the attacker. Sex was not murder. And Seven Dials was just a coincidence to her meanderings through the city. And her initial sighting of him.

He's just a dick, Jess had said. Maybe that was all he was. Not a murderer. And not a psychotic one at that. Just a dick.

She flicked on her phone and searched: *SEVEN DIALS MURDER*.

"Hey, how was the workout?" Aubrey called from the pool edge. He lifted himself from the water—dripping, his red Speedos clinging—and plodded over to join her on the bleachers.

Rachel couldn't breathe. She turned her phone off the instant the photo flashed across the screen—the girl in Seven Dials, before she was killed. She looked the same age as Rachel. The same skin tones. The same jawline and brow. The same hair color and style. She could have been Rachel's sister. She could have been Rachel.

"Ah, good," she said, trying to hide her shortness of breath.

He sat down beside her, brushing water from his chest and thighs.

"How many laps did you do?" she asked.

"Hundred and twenty. A bit slow tonight. Easy to get lost in your thoughts underwater."

Rachel's eyes went wide. She knew she wouldn't be able to do even ten laps. Realistically seven or eight before her arms turned to jelly. But Aubrey wasn't even huffing. She didn't know anyone as fit, except her husband, who she couldn't in fairness compare to any other man. Except Aubrey. Physically they were very different. Adam was twice Aubrey's size. But both were muscular, beautiful, intelligent men in their own way. Both beguiling. Both easy to love.

Aubrey was leaning forward, muscles flexing as he shook the water from his thick, curling shag of dark hair. Like most Englishmen, his skin had hardly seen the sun. He had called his pale white complexion his "moon tan." Nevertheless, the pallor of skin accentuated the tone of muscles beneath and left no doubt to his health and vitality. His physicality. His sexuality.

It was after 3:00 AM and Carnaby Lane was still buzzing by the time they'd showered, changed, and headed toward home. They stopped in a courtyard restaurant for avocado toast and kelp smoothies. Aubrey's idea. But Rachel could barely taste her food, her thoughts so muddled by the recent murders. A reflection of her research.

Aubrey had said barely a word since the gym. She'd said none at all. He reached across the table and squeezed her hand. "What's on your mind?"

Rachel looked up from her smoothie. His curls were wild and untamed from the hard water of the gym shower, and she smiled. Without a thought, she reached over and wound the curl just above his forehead around her finger. His gaze was intense beneath her hand, his attention holding fast to her face, clearly attempting to read her. She let the curl spring back and dropped her hand to his cheek. His stubble was soft, his skin warm. He closed his eyes and leaned into her touch until a slow and extravagant yawn stretched his face away from her. It ended in a sleepy smile, and he slouched into his chair. Rachel sank into the cushions of hers, content with the food in her belly and the one she was sharing it with. Her worries slowly dissipated within the calming silence, gradually submerging into that part of her mind where she stored all ridiculous, illogical ideas. Coincidence. Conjecture. Nothing more. Nothing less. Nothing to be afraid of. And yet . . .

CHAPTER SIXTY-SEVEN

Rachel took a sip of her tea and settled back against her bed pillows with her laptop.

Wednesday late evening, May, 1819.

The guest list of the Banqueting House ball was distributed amongst a dozen Bow Street Runners, with Officer Hamilton taking charge of those family names between G and J. He has already interviewed several well-to-do families of Hanover Square, Queen Square, and Wimpole Street. This evening he recruited my assistance with his interviews, in case I might notice something he might not. His request was fortuitous, as I was able to contribute in a small way during an hour or three at a grand family home on the corner of Upper Grosvenor Street and Park Lane, Mayfair.

The Griffith family were in the city for the season, their main estate spreading across several valleys in the Lake District of Cumbria. We were welcomed into the parlor by His Lordship. A room decorated with simple but elegant furniture and chandeliers. Muralled walls depicted the sublimity of their native landscape. His Lordship had not attended the ball, preferring to stay within the confines of his study on that evening.

"My books are much better company than any dandy with an eye for one of my daughters," he said. "I trust my wife's judgment. And only when a man—

young or old, alive or dead to any degree—has fulfilled her requisites do I care to see their shadow cast upon the threshold of my library." He passed the conversation to his wife and promptly left the room, presumably to return to his aforementioned books.

Lady Griffith was a tall and commanding woman. Handsome in a way. I was instantly reminded of our own Mrs. Hicks.

"Please take a seat," she said. "Before we start the interview into this horrid circumstance, please apprise me on whether either of you young gentlemen are married or, preferably, in need of a wife."

I glanced sideways at Hamilton.

"Neither, my lady," he said, which evoked a perplexed look from our hostess. "Would you please advise us whether you noted anything unusual regarding any of the male or female attendees at the ball that evening?"

"It is good you came to me, Officer Hamilton. I have a good eye and am able to read a gentleman better than most. Tell me, are you of the Islington Field Hamiltons?"

"I am, my lady. Now if you would be so kind, my question."

She smiled and rang a small bronze bell beside her. Immediately, four young ladies, undoubtedly her daughters, were ushered into the room by a valet. They took their seats around the parlor without a word, their gaze as intent as their mother's upon Hamilton and myself.

"Most of the men at the ball I have known of for years, either by sight or familial reputation. Some are scoundrels. Others would benefit from a year or two in the military. I dare say at least five had no right to be at the ball. I am certain you can agree less than a thousand pounds a year is not adequate fortune to entice any respectful lady or her family. There were perhaps seven or nine who could have benefited by dancing with any of my daughters." She walked over

to place her hand on the shoulder of the daughter sitting upon the piano bench. "Kathleen is rather handsome, don't you think, Doctor Polidori?"

I felt obliged to nod and immediately regretted it as the girl, perhaps nineteen, began to play the piano. Her gown was full and flowing with a silver thread patterning the bodice. A garland of flowers circled her neck.

"Were there any gentleman you were not acquainted with?" Hamilton asked.

"Only one. He was an odd spectacle. Pallid of skin and lifeless of eye. But of course, fortune outweighs misfortune, and so I made my enquiries about him. Lady Danswan informed me he was from the highlands, Lady Moore that his family owned most of Cornwall. Another said Sussex. Another, Nottingham. It was all very confusing, and no one seemed to agree. I watched him and could have sworn he never spoke at all, but as I followed more closely in his wake, I was assured his conversation was witty—an illumination. And yet none could tell me his name or circumstance. Or fortune."

She stood a moment behind her second daughter, deep in thought as she studied the line of Hamilton's uniform. She cleared her throat, drawing Hamilton's attention from his ledger to look upon her and the daughter in her clutches.

"It was the subject of some conversation that he held his ground a good while up on the balcony with the king's grandson." A flash of distaste crinkled her nose. "An extremely fine-looking royal," she continued, contrary to her countenance. "One I would welcome to call son."

The first daughter's tune came to an end, and she began pulling at the garland around her neck. I was initially uncertain but the more I studied the length below her jaw the more I was aware of a slight discoloration in the skin. Lady Griffith noticed my attention and seemed pleased.

"Would you mind, my lady, if I spoke to your eldest, alone?"

"Of course, Doctor Polidori." She almost ran to the double doors leading into the drawing room, motioning for her daughter to make haste. "Come quickly, Kathleen."

Hamilton furrowed his brow but made no move to counter my request. Lady Griffith placed her hand on my shoulder as I passed her. "She is intelligent. She's read most of her father's library, including your own father's Italian translation of Milton. She is rather attractive, don't you think? You might even say pretty." She pursed her lips tight together as she closed the doors behind us.

Kathleen stood with her back to a large picture window, the streetlamps of Park Lane sparkling in the evening drizzle behind her. I did think she was pretty. Her hair fell in ringlets to her waist, her lips a soft pink against the starkness of her skin. Her feminine curves were reminiscent of the sculpted caryatids, Botticelli angels, and foreign-tongued maidens I had encountered on my own grand tour of Europe as a young man—searching for myself in all the mistaken but exciting places of youth.

"You have no eye for me," she said.

"I do not," I said honestly.

She approached and put her hand upon my breast. I could feel its coldness through the material of my frock coat. "I know what you are here for," she said, pulling the wreath from her neck.

Flowers and loose petals fell to the floor. She licked her fingers and wiped them down the length of her neck, smearing white face powder from the skin to reveal the bruising beneath.

"Your heartbeat has quickened," she said. She tilted her chin, the veins from her collarbone to her jawline pulsing just under the skin, in time with the pulse of blood through my own veins. I could see no sign of puncture or bite, only the bruise of a paramour.

"Who gave you this mark?" I asked.

She smiled and ran her hand across my breast, up over my cravat, and against the flesh of my neck. I could feel the warmth being sucked from me by her bleak touch. She appeared enamored, her gaze drifting slowly over my face, my hair, before settling on my eyes.

"Who gave you this mark?" I repeated.

"Someone as beautiful as you. Someone who would give us both everlasting life, with merely the caress of his lips upon our skin, the tangling of our bloodlines, the feeding of our souls."

A chill coursed through my entirety, emanating from her touch along the measurement of every vein and artery twisting through even the most intimate dimensions of my body. I felt as though the breath was being pulled from my lungs, the thoughts from my mind. I stepped away from her, heat immediately returning as my blood began to flow once more within me.

"Will you tell me his name?" I asked.

"I swore an oath, but you already know his name," she said.

Rachel pressed her fingers to her eyes, stifling a yawn as she checked the date of the next ledger entry and compared it to the following letter and case annotation on the Old Bailey Online website.

Document BSR-OCH-13 ***KENSINGTON CASE.***
May 1819: 7:00 PM. Griffith family townhome. 93 Park Lane, Mayfair. Lord Griffith did not attend the ball in question. Lady Griffith supplied cursory description of person of interest commensurate to annotations 10a, 10b, 11, and 12. No further descriptive details adequate to identify suspect by name. Polidori attended interview. 8:15 PM he escorted first daughter Kathleen Griffith into adjacent room for questioning. 9:50 PM he returned to the

parlor. Full report to be submitted by 8:00 AM with findings of his interrogation.
  —Officer Hamilton

Polidori's suite fell into a subdued darkness as Rachel closed the laptop and then her eyelids. She could feel the cloud-dimmed moonlight shining through the open windows and across her face. The same moon that had shone upon the doctor two hundred years ago. Despite her exhaustion, her mind refused to slow, instead rattling on with thoughts of the fantastic and the horrific. Of the darkness and the light. Of what was real and what was merely romantic.

She wondered whether she should contact Detective Baertschi.

CHAPTER SIXTY-EIGHT

The drizzle had turned to a subtle mist, in no way deterring Polidori and Hamilton from walking the distance from Mayfair back to Great Pulteney Street. A brief time of shared company on the damp, empty streets of London. "We cannot force her to break an oath. Personal integrity is of a higher value than either life or death itself. And in this case, no one has actually died," Polidori said.

"Yet," Hamilton replied. "I'm confused. Do you suspect Miss Griffith was the waif in the royal bedchambers, the one who sucked upon Augustus Frederick's flesh?"

"I do."

"So, she is a vampyre?"

Polidori hesitated. "I do not believe so. At least not yet. I have no doubt she was enamored by the one who lead the attack and who actually drew upon the royal blood of both Augusta Emma and Augustus Frederick. But I believe Miss Griffith's actions were driven by infatuation, an intoxication of the being who so brazenly bared his naked soul and revealed his true nature in her presence."

"And from what you told me of her behavior during your interview, she is still inebriated by this demon." They slowed to a stop and glanced up and down the deserted street before holding to each other's gaze. "I can understand her intoxication with another," Hamilton said, gently brushing the back of his hand against Polidori's. The clop of hooves and the rattle of a wagon echoed ahead of them as a night soil cart turned the corner. They pulled away from each other and recommenced their stride toward Soho. "Did she say how they entered the bedchambers?"

"She refused to comment on her time with him. Her oath."

They were silent for many blocks, both deep in their own thoughts. "When, or how, does someone become a vampyre?" Hamilton wondered aloud as they reached the demolition surrounding the proposed Regent Street. A swathe of houses had been torn down northward toward Oxford Circus and eastward toward Piccadilly Circus.

"Perhaps it happens only with complete exsanguination. The drainage of every last drop of blood from the body to the point of a deceptive death, as with Master Aldridge. Or it might be caused by the intermingling of blood, of any bodily fluid between the vampyre and his prey. The object of his seduction." They crossed the construction zone into Soho.

"Do you suspect either of the king's grandchildren might turn?" Hamilton said.

"I do not know. It is best to continue monitoring their wellbeing for a time. As it is, Miss Griffith's."

They were at the corner of Great Pulteney Street when Polidori placed a hand against Hamilton's chest. "Would you be able to secure access to Montagu House at this hour?"

"The British Museum?"

"Specifically the basement levels holding the National Library collection."

They reached the museum steps just after the night watchman of Bloomsbury Square Garden called the midnight hour. The streets were dark and uninhabited, the earliest of morning mist creeping along lane and alley to puddle at their boots. The keys to Montagu House clanked as the librarian turned one in a rusted escutcheon. The librarian, sparse of hair and good humor, and much older than Polidori thought feasible, escorted them through a wood-paneled foyer and down into the basement.

"Have you any works on Eastern European folklore, my good man?" Polidori said as they followed the elder down tighter and dustier corridors. "Explicitly, the rising of the dead. The undertaking of their expiry."

They were led by lantern light along passages lined with ancient tomes of leather and vellum. Stones covered in cuneiform and glyph. Marbles chiseled with Latin and Greek. Totems of myth and unspoken antiquity. The librarian left them in a corner, cold blockwork cutting an angle against sagging wooden shelves, the aisle barely wide enough for their shoulders. There were four- or five-score of books on the ledges indicated by a bent and gnarled finger. A marble of Minerva, the Goddess of Wisdom, half-draped by a dust-covered canvas, monitored their quest.

"What exactly are we looking for?" Hamilton asked.

"We will know when we find it," Polidori said.

Side by side they leaned into the stonework, holding books up to catch the lamp light. Flicking through page after page for any relevant word or phrase.

"Do you think it a disease? A virus that could infect many?" Hamilton said.

Polidori scanned a page written in Latin. "I know only that this city is borne upon the bodies of millions. We must be ready for any eventuality. Is vampyrism inflicted upon only the living, or the recently deceased? Or can it spread even to those who have been relegated beneath the sod for months, years, or indeed generations?"

Hamilton looked horrified. "Surely your imagination has run rampant, John. We have seen only Master Aldridge return from the dead, his demise and grave both fresh."

"Have we? What of the one who turned him?"

"We know that gentleman only as well as a shadow in Hyde Park."

"And yet Miss Griffith was certain I already knew his name."

Hamilton pulled another book from the shelf to pursue its table of contents and index. "What of Lord Ruthven, your own fictional vampyre? Even I have heard the rumors you based his character upon Lord Byron."

Polidori stretched uncomfortably in the confined space then reached for another book. "Byron is in Italy and unlikely to return to this island. He has naught to do with any of this. Though he does have a certain aptitude for consuming the vitality of those around him, a witty domination that enamors him to the submissive. Only he seizes power with words and condescension, not the draining of blood. Sadly what was only intended as a metaphor has somehow become reality on the streets of London."

"Here, have a look at this," Hamilton said. Polidori leaned in as the officer read the words aloud.

A paling of the heart may incur the wrath of death.
Awaiting the afflicted, Hell's descendent circling wreath.

"This harks of Master Andrew Fairbank," Hamilton said. "Your strike of the shattered baluster through his heart."

"Sheer luck it was the correct action to end him."

"And your knowledge of anatomy, the scientific, and the romantic." Hamilton ran his finger down the page. "Do you think the same . . . method . . . might apply to this more seductive and gentlemanly incarnation?"

"Perhaps."

Hamilton continued to read.

> *But heed, my friend, the course you wish that death to take.*
> *For love may break the downward spiral by driving in the*
> *stake.*

Hamilton turned the page to reveal an engraving plate bearing a scene from Dante's *Inferno*. Polidori recognized the eighth circle of hell spiraling toward the darkest depths of Hades. *Seducers. Counterfeiters. Deceivers. Two pale shadows, naked and biting. Teeth of one set upon the neck of the other.* A place to be feared, avoided at all costs. He shuddered with the recollection of the cantos that had been driven into him by his father at an early age, both in English and Italian. The horror had never left him, had made him always strive to be a man of good intention. Of noble purpose. The flicker of lamplight did nothing to hide the worry on their faces as they continued their search.

"Master Aldridge also swore an oath," Hamilton said. "There is no doubt he, too, knew his antagonist."

"Your thoughts mirror my own. The aggressor might have been welcomed."

"Do you surmise the other Fairbank twin is still alive?" Hamilton said.

"Perhaps not as dead as we believed. Aldridge would willingly have gone with him, so enamored with him in life as in death. He would have sworn an oath without question. Such a love has trapped many a soul." Polidori cleared his throat and stared into Hamilton's eyes, to distract himself from exhumed thoughts of Villa Diodati and the seduction there that had left him spent and numb.

CHAPTER SIXTY-NINE

Rachel stepped into the town car and buckled in as it started south down Great Pulteney Street.

"I'm glad you contacted me, *Madame* Walton," Detective Gendarme Baertschi said.

"Why didn't you tell me there was a murder when I mentioned seeing that man in Seven Dials?" she asked.

"There is much I cannot tell you. Surely you understand my reasons for discretion."

Rachel reluctantly nodded. "Okay. I've seen him twice. At Heaven he called me by my name. He knows who I am."

"And how could that be?"

"I don't know. You're the detective. Do you think he killed those people?"

"It doesn't matter what I think. Only what the facts relate."

The pressure in Rachel's head increased with her exasperation. "All right then. What do the facts relate? The ones you *can* tell me."

"You confirmed the gentleman in question was in Seven Dials on the night of the first murder. The video footage confirms he was at the night club with the next two victims. The same night you were also in attendance."

"How do you know it was the same night I was there?"

He narrowed his eyes but stayed silent. The car circled Trafalgar Square and headed down Whitehall, stopping at a traffic light before the Banqueting House, a building she'd never entered but felt she knew well from her research.

"Do you think I'm in danger?" she asked as they continued past Downing Street.

"We have no evidence he is the killer. Frankly, *you* are equally suspect, because you were also in those locations."

Rachel pulled back from the detective, her eyes wide. "But he was having sex with them." Even as she said it, she knew the statement was ludicrous and not evidence of guilt.

The detective pressed his finger to his ear.

"Sir?" the driver asked, his finger also at his ear.

"Yes, head straight there," Baertschi said. "I'm sorry for the inconvenience, *madame*. There is an—ah—an incident we must attend to. You will need to find your own way back to your residence once we have stopped."

The driver opened his window and stretched to place a police light up on the roof of the car. Immediately the lights flashed red and blue, arcing out on either side of the car, a siren cutting the night air. Rachel was thrust back against the seat as they increased speed. The town car careened left at Parliament Square, past the statue of Winston Churchill, cars and double-decker buses pulling over to make way. They thumped over a median strip to drive along the center line of Westminster Bridge to the southern side of the river. Police sedans and military-looking Humvees swung in beside them. Rachel held tight to her seatbelt. Still she was thrown against the door as they rounded left, the wrong way down a one-way street. Pedestrians pressed themselves against the facades of imposing nineteenth century buildings, their eyes wide. Another corner and the giant London Eye loomed above them. They lurched to a stop at the water's edge and Detective Gendarme Baertschi stepped out without a word.

Rachel sat a moment, her cheek to the cool glass of the window, her gaze on the driver as he swiveled the rearview mirror. There was a quiet thud as the door unlocked. "If you would, *madame*," he said. She was no longer needed. At least not tonight.

Thousands of tourists milled along the boardwalk, staring up at the twenty-seven story Ferris wheel. Police urged them back, dark-clothed military with semi-automatic carbines at their waists running up onto the platform at the base of the wheel. As one observation pod reached the bottom, the doors released and twenty or so were rushed out by the authorities.

"Please descend the platform immediately!"

"What's going on?" someone asked.

"Look up there, man," someone else replied, pointing skyward. "See? Three pods down from the top."

Rachel held up her hand to shield her eyes from the reflected glare of searchlights trained upon the immense circle of white powder-coated framework. Thirty-two capsules were spread evenly around the structure, each an elegant metal-and-glass pod filled with tourists. But one pod was different. She couldn't see through many of the glass panes. Instead of being transparent, they were opaque against the evening sky.

Hundreds trained their cell phone cameras on the wheel. "See here," said the guy beside her as he nudged his mate. His phone screen showed a news alert—a journalist and the wheel behind her. Rachel craned her neck and noted the cameras and the journalist on the roof of a nearby satellite truck. The time delay between life and the screen was several seconds.

"Oi, Roger," the guy said. "Some bloke was live streaming on the internet while it was all going down."

The screen cut from the reporter to the inside of one of the observation pods. A dozen young men, square headed, square shouldered, and square toothed. They looked like a cricket team in grass-stained whites. The amateur video panned around the capsule, zooming in on smiling faces, then out to the brilliant night sights of the city. The Shard. The Houses of Parliament. Bridge after twinkling bridge along the river. Up and over at the other capsules in their wake. Then the screen abruptly tilted sideways as if the one holding the phone camera had been knocked off balance by the rocking of the capsule.

Someone or something crashed feet first through the overhead hatch.

Slivers of glass scattered.

An immediate brawl with fists flying and feet kicking.

The device recording an indelible staccato of jerking, erratic imagery.

The spray of blood.

A blur of unrecognizable speed and movement amongst the men. Inhuman in its pace.

An extreme close up of an open mouth, sharp and bloody teeth sinking into flesh.

Then eyes wide and terrified.

The phone was flung the full length of the pod, rolling with its trajectory. It recorded the arc and splatter of blood across the windows, as the men collapsed one by one, spasming, clutching at their throats, holding onto the last pulses of life as blood spurted between their fingers. The phone crashed to the floor, half the screen obscured and dripping toward total blackout.

Only one remained standing in the capsule, dressed unlike the others. Slim blue jeans and jacket stained red. Copper hair. He wiped at his mouth with the back of his hand then dropped to his knees to press his face into the crook of a prone neck, his body quivering. Shuddering. Exulting, as he fed.

The screen went black, the drip of what was undoubtedly blood covering the last of the pixels. The recording time flashed red in the bottom corner. Ten minutes ago.

Rachel realized she was clenching the bicep of the guy holding the phone. They looked at each other, then turned to watch the final descent of the bloody pod down toward the platform. As it glided to a graceful standstill at the bottom of the wheel, two score of officers sighted their weapons upon it. The blood-smeared doors opened automatically, and an officer tossed in a smoke grenade.

No one came out.

The gathered crowd was dead silent.

Authorities in full-body armor rushed into the smoke-filled pod. They pulled the men out onto the platform one by one, gripping limp hands, skidding lifeless bodies over the rough metal surface.

"Clear," one of the officers yelled.

"Clear," confirmed another.

Medics ran onto the platform to tend the wounded. But Rachel knew they were all already dead.

The top hatch was obliterated, but Rachel couldn't understand what happened to the assailant in the slim jeans. He couldn't have escaped the pod without notice. Even if he'd climbed out of the hatch, he'd be visible on the structure of the wheel. He'd been captured on the recording, but he wasn't there.

He wasn't there.

Rachel shook her head and focused on the bodies laid across the platform. Eleven in all, the men looked to be only eighteen or nineteen years of age. And very dead. Eleven body bags. Eleven ambulances. She retreated away from the crowd into the architectural greenery of the Jubilee Gardens, paralyzed by the glimpse she'd gotten into three of the vans that had pulled onto the grass to take away the dead. Each contained a single body and two police officers, weapons trained upon the cadaver. The body bags were unzipped at the top, the wrists of the dead cuffed to the metal gurney beneath them.

CHAPTER SEVENTY

"There are eleven in all," Officer Hamilton said. "We have touched nothing, thinking it best to leave it for the magistrates' and your own good judgment."

The cabriolet pulled to the curb on Park Lane. Bow Street Runners had cordoned off the intersection into Upper Grosvenor Street and stood the perimeter of the handsome townhome.

"Is Miss Kathleen Griffith amongst the eleven?" Polidori asked.

"She is."

The entrance lobby showed no hint of the horror that lay waiting beyond. The ornate furnishings and floor rugs were undisturbed, the candelabra at the first turn of the broad, carpeted stair offered nothing but a reassuring glow. All was still, dampened only by the wind that drifted in behind them. A runner closed the front door, leaving Hamilton and Polidori alone in the mansion with the eleven corpses. The officer lifted his chin toward a double door opposite the parlor and Polidori followed him into Lord Griffith's library. A fire still burned beneath the mantle, its flickering light casting shadows across the wingbacks and bookshelves. A desk was littered with paperwork a foot high. Neat stacks of bills and ledgers. Sealed letters. Lord Griffith sat in his chair, mouth agape, eyes wide. He appeared an elderly gentleman who had died a quiet death surrounded by his books. No sign of struggle. The only apparent abnormality was the two neat puncture wounds swelling within the abundant wrinkles of his neck—bluish puckers in the stark pallor of flesh. Not a drop of blood evident. A cushion on his lap held the weight of his arm, his hand resting on the pages of the King James Bible, open to Ecclesiastes 9:11.

I returned, and saw under the sun, that the race is not to the swift, nor the battle to the strong, neither yet bread to the wise, nor yet riches to men of understanding, nor yet favour to men of skill; but time and chance happeneth to them all.

For man also knoweth not his time: as the fishes that are taken in an evil net, and as the birds that are caught in the snare; so are the sons of men snared in an evil time, when it falleth suddenly upon them.

Polidori pulled the wingback away from the desk and scripture to kneel before the lord. He ran his hands down the clothed lengths of the elder's arms and legs, ensuring no damage. Then he loosened the buttons of the waistcoat and undershirts to brush his palms across the fleshy belly, chest, and around the waist to the lower back. No sign of any gross trauma. Crouching, he closed Lord Griffith's eyes, then sniffed at the cavity of the open mouth. He touched his finger to the still-wet inner lip, glancing at Officer Hamilton before pressing his fingertip to his own tongue.

"No odor or residual taste of poison," he said, almost apologetically, as he nudged the mouth shut. He pulled at the neck, stretching the wrinkles away from the tooth punctures. The holes were clean and dry, the paper-thin skin bloodless and white. "A full autopsy is in order, but it seems apparent exsanguination killed him dead, in kind with the attacks we have seen." He rebuttoned the clothing, tucking the shirt tails into the top of the pantaloons. He took care to adjust the cravat, evening the folds, slipping the embroidered length behind the lapel of the forest-green waistcoat.

"The rest of the family is in the dining room. I assume Lord Griffith preferred his books to an evening meal with his wife, daughters, and their guests."

"Guests?" Polidori arched a brow.

The dining room was decorated to impress. The sideboard held a banquette of silver bowls and platters filled to capacity with goose, duck, lamb, vegetables, pottage, and gravy—uncarved, unstirred, cold to the touch. The gravy floated a skin at least three hours old. Along the center of the dining table was a decorative sugar sculpture, perhaps eight feet in length. Granulated white figurines of Aphrodite, Eros, Hymen, Pan, and Hermes seduced their way over the tablecloth, leaving no doubt as to the desired outcome of the gathering.

The table was set for ten, but occupied by only five. Lord Griffith's chair sat empty at one end, save for a sumptuously folded napkin. Lady Griffith was at the other, her face pressed flat upon the blue and white Willow Pattern of her plate. Her arms splayed across the pristine table cloth, Pan's sweet, masculine endowment gripped and broken in her last moments. Polidori touched the inside of her wrist, placed his ear before her lips. No beat, no breath. He pulled back the ruffles of her collar and the ringlets of hair to expose the marks of the vampyre. Not a smear or drop of blood remained. By the pallor of her skin, Polidori supposed exsanguination had been complete. He gently lifted her chin, and her expression held awe, a joy so sheer it appeared she'd welcomed her fate with open arms.

Polidori stepped to the opposite end of the dining table to survey the rest of the party. The four daughters wore Grecian gowns in kind with the carved-sugar gods. White flowing silk with a hint of classic embroidery showcased their subtle and not-so-subtle virtues. Each bore the mark of the vampyre on her neck, their skin as pale as their gowns. Polidori confirmed each was indeed dead—by traditional definition—then sat upon an empty chair beside Kathleen. Unlike the others, her neck and lips were covered in the dried residue of saliva, the remnants of a paramour. Of a lust for more than the blood running through her veins. She, like her siblings, held an expression of exultation. Unbridled ecstasy.

Four chairs were empty.

"You said there were guests," Polidori said, "and by the evocative centerpiece and abundant décolletage I surmise they were gentlemen that fit the requirements of the lady of the house. Did they escape and raise the alarm?"

Officer Hamilton started to speak, but a quiet sob distracted him, cut short by an urgent intake of breath. The officer pulled his pistol from his belt and crept to the rear of the room, pressing his ear to a muraled panel. From behind the wood came a high-pitched whimper followed by unabashed sobbing—a woman, terrified.

"Come out, lassie. I'm an officer of the law. You've nothing to fear now. Not from us."

Polidori noted a spyhole drilled into the brushwork of the muraled wall. There was a dull click as one panel creaked open, revealing a pantry of sorts and a serving girl cowering on the floor. Hamilton stooped and offered her his hand. Immediately she threw herself into his arms and sobbed upon his shoulder. He lifted her up and carried her into the parlor, where he lowered her onto the settee and cuddled her to still her fear. Polidori followed, opening his bag for a sedative. He thought better and instead poured a sherry and held it to her lips. She gulped it down.

"Everyone is dead, both upstairs and down," she cried.

Polidori caught Hamilton's gaze. The officer nodded and mouthed, "Eleven."

The girl quieted with the sherry, back stiff, chin raised.

"Breathe slowly, my dear," Polidori said, refilling her glass. "In, and out. In, and out." Her gaze was fixed upon the family portrait above the mantle, her eyes and nose dripping unchecked. Polidori offered her his handkerchief, but when she did not respond he gently wiped her cheeks and nose.

"I saw it all," she said, her chin quivering. "The four gentlemen arrived as expected at five o'clock, sharing a grand carriage we seldom see the likes of, even in Mayfair. 'Lord Wayne Fairbank,' Lady Griffith said with a curtsy."

Polidori noted as Hamilton's face drained of color, as deathly white as the cadavers reclining in the dining room and library. He knew his own pallor must be just as bleak.

"A mature gentleman, perhaps in his late forties, greying at the temples but still with all his own hair, and beautiful teeth. Quite debonair. He smiled and Lady Griffith almost swooned, patting her hand against her heart. Then he said, 'May I introduce to you my sister's sons, Masters James and Andrew Fairbank.' His voice was pleasant, almost mesmerizing."

Bile surged from Polidori's gut, and he clapped his hand over his mouth. He felt drowned with confusion, the memory of the three cadavers in his basement, their flesh cut, their organs removed, measured, weighed, and replaced. Their skin sutured with care. The elderly uncle had indeed been handsome even in death, in kind with the rugged looks of his nephews, the wrinkles about his eyes reflecting a life well lived. Sweat beaded on Polidori's forehead and saturated his shirt. It dripped down between the muscles of his breast.

And I killed Andrew with the stake, he thought. *Putrid, stinking, undead Andrew. How . . .* Polidori measured his breathing, wishing another sherry glass was within reach. After the events at 8A Park Crescent the twins and their uncle were assuredly beyond any capacity for life, their rotting remains relinquished to Lady Fairbank, taken far from London, and buried deep in hallowed ground.

Surely that was the end of it. But clearly it was not.

"I thought the Fairbank boys must be twins. Both were tall, broad of shoulder, with blond hair. They appeared almost identical, thought Master Andrew seemed slightly dead of eye, his movement not so languid as his brother's, as if he were pained by injuries, or perhaps regaining his strength after a long sickness or incapacity. 'My lady,' they said in unison, each bowing and taking one of Lady Griffith's hands to kiss. 'Men of good manners and good fortune,' she said. 'I am certain I have seen you, young Andrew, on a previous occasion. Were you at the Banqueting House Ball?' She narrowed her eyes, a thing she does when she has already decided upon the only correct response. 'I was,' he replied. 'Though if I had seen you, my lady, I would have swept you around the dancefloor, impressing you with more than the prominence of my pocketbook.' Lady Griffith giggled, as though she were a maiden herself, then smiled at the fourth young gentleman.

"Lord Fairbank said, 'Master Thomas Aldridge, a gentleman of Bath and an *acquaintance* of our family.' Master Aldridge bowed and kissed her hand. Then Lady Griffith said, 'Four fine gentlemen, and all in my parlor at the same moment. I know of your family, Master Aldridge. Good stock, yes, very fine.' She led them into the parlor, and I offered them the very best from the Griffith cellars. The maidens of the house filed into the room, and Lady Griffith indicated where everyone should sit—Kathleen with Andrew, Lydia with James, Justine with Thomas, and Penelope with the elderly Fairbank. 'Penelope will be excellent company for your good self, Lord Fairbank,' she said. 'Though Pene is my youngest, she is well versed in literature and the more astute disciplines of running a household. Benefits even to a bachelor such as yourself.' Lord Fairbank bowed his head, stiffening slightly when Pene, likely more than thirty years his junior, sat beside him.

"Three decanters of much-needed wine were consumed with subdued conversation. Of course, Lady Griffith extolled the virtues of each of her daughters, though I noted Kathleen and Andrew seemed already to have an accord. They entwined their hands and fingers to the ecstatic side glances of Lady Griffith. 'My husband shall not be joining us for dinner,' Lady Griffith said as she opened the doors to the dining room. 'Though if any of you fine gentlemen feel disposed to ask the question *any* maiden and their mother wants asked, I would be pleased to show you the most expedient route to the library.' She eyed each of the Fairbanks and Master Aldridge, but none seemed yet inclined.

"I retreated to the pantry and kept my eye to the spyhole, awaiting a sign from Lady Griffith to serve the next course of wine. Lord Fairbank held out Lady Griffith's dining chair then bowed low beside her, talking quietly at her ear. She appeared hopeful, enamored, by whatever he was saying. She smiled up at him, more sweetly than I had ever seen her, with a spark in her eyes and the worry lines smoothing from her brow. Her age appeared to drop from her countenance as she flushed a deep crimson. I have no doubt she was bewitched by his words, his gaze, the closeness of his lips to hers.

Then the four men stood behind the chairs of her four daughters and bowed to place their lips close to the ears of each maiden. I was entranced by their intimate gesture. Kathleen, Lydia, Justine, and Penelope—at almost the same instant—took on the joyful, glazed look of women in love, a delight that slackened their lips and closed their eyes. Each arched her neck under the amorous gaze of her companion. Even I found myself closing my eyes, arching my neck, my lower lip dropping to accept a gentleman's subtlest of secrets. When next I opened my eyes, each of the gentlemen had his lips to the neck of a maiden. I felt a heat rising within myself, but this turned to dread when the girls began convulsing in their seats, the men gripping them by the shoulders as they drew the life from the girls I have known since nappies.

"I was frozen in terror, a scream choking me. The sound of the sucking, a strange and urgent slurping and swallowing, the color draining from the four girls in the unwholesome grip of our guests. All the while Lady Griffith's gaze drifted idly across her daughters, some type of somnambulism that horrified me more than anything else I had seen. When Penelope slumped in her seat, Lord Fairbank turned his attention to his hostess, his tongue and teeth thickly coated in virginal blood. Then he lunged toward her, the flesh of her neck audibly popping and ripping as he thrust his fangs into it. His tongue flicked from his mouth as he drank, back and forth, allowing nothing to escape his hunger. My lady's eyes rolled back, a euphoria I have seen only upon my husband's face during our most intimate of moments. After two or three minutes, Lord Fairbank let her fall onto her plate. Then he left through the parlor toward my master's library. The other three ran from the dining room and down the service stairs, to pursue those I once called family."

CHAPTER SEVENTY-ONE

Despite the horror of the scene at the London Eye, Rachel felt disturbingly unperturbed. Perhaps it was the awfulness of her research, her own experience in recent years, or the numbing themes she and everyone else had been subjected to on the news, in the cinema, in literature. She dawdled, deep in thought, on her way through the city among the supper and theatre crowds who were clueless about what had happened. They were happy, excited, their plans for the night full of fast or fine food, perhaps dancing or a stroll or a show, their blood enhanced by intoxicants legal or illegal. But what impressed her the most was they were alive. She was alive. And what she'd witnessed was not specifically directed at her. She'd been knocked from her own egocentric viewpoint. Of course it was horrendous, but it wasn't about her, or her research. There were similarities in the manner of attack, something intrinsic related to her subject matter, but as Aubrey had said, it had been ongoing for centuries. Millenia. Even Baertschi appeared composed, business as usual, treating the evening's events as part of an investigation he'd long been pursuing. Long before she'd arrived in England.

A shimmer of guilt startled her, that within a year she might publish a work furthering what Doctor Polidori's seminal novel had evoked two hundred years previous. She stopped in the middle of Leicester Square, surrounded by thousands of revelers, wondering if she were really so narcissistic to think her work could blur the thin line between night and day as Polidori's seemed to in Georgian London.

And there it was—the answer to the Sphinx's second riddle.

Two sisters. One gives birth to the other and she, in turn, gives birth to the first. Who are the two sisters?

"Night and Day," she murmured. But what was it Aubrey had suggested? He'd said to neutralize the genders in the riddle. *What the hell did he mean by that?* she wondered. *One begets the other. Polidori begot the modern vampyre? The vampyre begot him?* It didn't make sense to her.

She hurried toward Soho. In the front hall of number 38 she heard voices from inside the parlor. "Are you sure she's the one?" It was Peyton's charming burr. Rachel hesitated but then she pushed open the double doors. "I'll miss you, my *bragh* friend," the Scot said. He released his embrace of Aubrey, and the two men stepped apart as Rachel entered.

"Ah, I wondered where you were. Everyone's out back," Aubrey said. He ducked his head and walked quickly from the room.

Rachel furrowed her brow. "Is he okay?"

"Oh, aye, lass." He placed a hand, massive and gentle, on her shoulder and pulled her to his side. "It is as it is."

"Oh." Her mild confusion deepened. "Are you leaving? You told Aubrey you'd miss him, so I just—"

"I hope you like pizza," Peyton said, leading her from the parlor. "Hubby makes the best. He's a wee bit heavy on the garlic but don't worry, the pizza's not deep fried."

Taylor had control of the kitchen. A pizza was already in the oven, the smell of roasted garlic lifting the room, with two more half assembled pies on the counter. Smoked salmon, prawns, and dill. Aubrey, Harley, and Dakota were out in the courtyard beneath the smoky plume of Polidori's favorite cigars. Rachel accepted a freshly cut cigar and a tequila, neat, after what she'd seen earlier. Aubrey hunkered down on the flagstones, holding a long wooden cigar match. The flame flickered between them. Their gazes locked on one another and she accepted their relationship had grown to much more than an unexpected tenderness.

Taylor slid the first pizza onto the table. Despite her hunger, Rachel leaned back into the chair to savor the tequila and cigar, to listen to the music drifting from the overhead speakers. The smooth silence between Nina Simone's vocals pulled her into a pleasant space, away from thoughts of the London Eye and the horror of her research. Harley and Dakota slow danced in the corner of the courtyard, less intent on their folded slices of pizza than the four-step that kept their bodies glued together. Aubrey puffed on his cigar, staring into the empty space between the topiary. Now and then he glanced to the sky, pitch black with no sign of stars. Rachel wondered what he was thinking as his tongue flicked out to wet the pleasant pink of his lips. The crease in his brow suggested his reflections were heartfelt, intense. Important.

She reached for a slice of pizza and caught his reflection in the bathroom window, and she realized he'd been studying her in reflection the entire time. Rachel stared back, not shying from his intensity. Welcoming it.

He took a deep breath and nodded, like he'd made up his mind about something. He turned and walked over to stand behind her chair. Then, with careful and slow deliberation, he leaned down so his lips were at her ear.

His breath was warm and heavy with the sexy earthiness of Don Julio 1942 and Polidori's cigar.

"I know what's happening," he said. "Tomorrow evening I'll introduce you to the Spaniard."

CHAPTER SEVENTY-TWO

Polidori was hesitant to cut into the tender flesh of the young Kathleen Griffith on his slab. His grip trembled and the scalpel clattered to the floor. He didn't bother picking it up.

He knew she was dead, but he also knew the vampyre's mark meant her death might not be permanent. Perhaps it was best to wait.

After all, he'd seen the three Fairbank men in various levels of postmortem decay. Andrew Fairbank had been beyond putrid, his flesh ripped and rotted and much of it missing, smearing the cobbles of London streets as he'd sought out his family members. And yet, far beyond his grave, his body had become revitalized, the muscle and sinew renewed. From witness descriptions of him at the Banqueting House and now at the Griffith residence, there was little doubt of his increasing stamina and physical wellbeing. An ungodly resurrection. And if he still held even a portion of the strength and vitality he had displayed as a rotten corpse brawling down the stair of number 8A Park Crescent . . .

Polidori shuddered. Indeed, Lord Fairbank—given the Griffith servant's description of him—not only lived but held an increased youthfulness and potency as well.

Polidori wondered whether Master Aldridge's strength had likewise increased. A new breed of vampyre. A gentleman of the highest caliber and physical ability. A danger indistinguishable amongst the gentry.

He cast his gaze along the curve and dip of Miss Kathleen Griffith's nakedness. She was undoubtedly beautiful. Both in life and in death. Perhaps even more so now, her flesh like unblemished porcelain without the blood coursing beneath. She was cool and smooth beneath the touch of his hand. This was not the first woman Polidori had disrobed. Granted, all had been dead, but there was an unusualness about Kathleen's form he could not rationalize.

Should he forgo the autopsy and recommend burial?

But if she had been turned, as he suspected, she would be traumatized when she awoke beneath the sod. What if no one heard the ringing of her bell? Surely that would make Polidori more of a monster than the vampyre himself. Conversely, he could not continue to hold her in his basement, allowing her to rot past the point of respectability and morality for no valid medical or scientific reasoning. Nothing beyond supposition.

There was a hollow tap at the outside basement door, and Polidori flicked open the latch.

"Kensington Palace is demanding a full debrief before sunrise. We have five hours," Officer Hamilton said, carrying a shrouded body over his shoulder. "Penelope," he added, shrugging her down into his arms to lay her gently on the slab beside her sister. "Oh!" He stumbled backward, eyes wide as he took in the full length of Kathleen. His face flushed, seemingly mesmerized by the voluptuous curvature and dimple of flesh.

"What is it?" Polidori asked, certain it was not the nudity alone.

"Well, you see," the officer said, pulling back the shroud from Penelope's face. "All the others on Park Lane look like *this*."

Though she was perhaps three or four years the younger, the proclivity of decay had left Penelope's face sunken and grey, her flesh slack. The two sisters were incomparable. One exquisite in death. The other rapidly dissolving toward sludge.

"What on Earth?" Polidori mumbled. Then, "You say the others are in this state?"

Hamilton nodded.

Polidori looked from one to the other, recalling Mary's recommendation at Rules. *Differences.* "How is Miss Kathleen Griffith different from the rest of her family?" he said, conceding he would have to autopsy all of them.

"Do you mean physically?" Hamilton asked.

"Perhaps, but as we have stepped far from the realms of science and medical autopsy, I welcome any suggestion. Any at all."

"She is the eldest."

"Yes."

"You suspected her of being the waif accompanying the vampyre during the raid at Kensington Palace. And the servant noticed a certain . . . *intercourse* . . . between Kathleen and Andrew during the gathering at the Griffith residence."

Polidori nodded. "And just as Master James Fairbank turned Master Aldridge, perhaps Master Andrew has now exsanguinated Miss Kathleen for the same reason."

"But what of the others?" Hamilton said.

"No more than sustenance. Nourishment through the theft of life. The stealing of *élan vital.*"

"But how could the exact same act lead to two different outcomes? There must be something more in the case of Master Aldridge and Miss Kathleen. Some primary underlying factor."

"Primary," Polidori repeated as he began to pace the floor. "Or primal."

CHAPTER SEVENTY-THREE

"Love," Rachel muttered into the lonely darkness of Polidori's suite. "If not love, then lust and all the variations of need, want, adoration, and fancy in between. It was the Age of Romance after all." In a way, it still was. She tossed and turned, pushing the bulky eiderdown to the foot of the mattress, flicking off the sheets so she lay naked on Polidori's bed.

In kind with the girls in his basement.

She'd retired long before Aubrey, laying alone in Polidori's bed, the mellow vocals of Nina Simone still casting a spell on the shadows of the townhome until eventually the others left and she recognized his footsteps creaking up the stair. He had hesitated on the landing outside her door.

There was no lock, nor would she have latched it if there were.

She'd held her breath, imagining his hand upon the doorknob.

Perhaps he'd enter and whisper more of the Spaniard. Perhaps he would . . .

When his steps had continued on, she'd reflected on her research, on him, on his life. On her own. Now, only twelve feet above her—twice the depth of a grave—Aubrey lay in his own bed. Naked and alone. Asleep, or awake.

"Love," she said again out loud. A word with so many definitions, with as much power to cause grief as happiness. Could it also be instrumental in immortality? In ensuring its beginning, its continuance, its... *what*?

She crawled from the bed and crossed the room, careful to sidestep the floorboards that creaked. Her laptop filled the room with its dull blue light as she clicked on the search engine and typed *Aubrey*

Polidori.

She surfed, thoughtful with each reference, each image that appeared, assembling the scant pieces of the puzzle that made up her host.

Only a handful of images surfaced, pulled from social media, and from an old article on the descendants of John Polidori. One image in particular caught her eye.

Aubrey in his brown leather bomber jacket, no rips or tears as it showed now. He was smiling somberly in front of an old fashioned biplane, his arms around the shoulders of two others similarly dressed. A Zeppelin hovered in the air behind them. She guessed the photo was somewhat recent, an old-timey airshow souvenir that had been artificially aged in sepia tones. A stamped imprint smudged the bottom. *Salisbury Plain. Royal Flying Corps. Item 1260.* The photo was hyperlinked to an article on a 1916 Great War air battle she'd never heard of. *Because of the biplane*, she thought.

When sunlight glanced through the slim gaps between the drapes, she closed her laptop and slid into the warmth of the bed, her thoughts drowsy, her conclusions hazy. Her deductions *Romantic*.

"It is as it is," Peyton had said earlier that evening, when she'd asked about Aubrey.

Yes, perhaps it is, she now thought as she drifted into a wakeful dreaming.

CHAPTER SEVENTY-FOUR

Polidori sipped from his flask and checked his fob watch. Less than an hour before Hamilton and he were due at Kensington Palace.

Two women lay dead in his basement. Nine others in the grand home in Mayfair. He held no doubt at least one would rise to continue the killing. He pulled on a fresh jacket and coat and descended the stair from his bedroom at speed, hesitating only momentarily at the hall stand to see the package he'd ripped open earlier—the first printing of *Ernestus Berchtold: Or the Modern Oedipus*. There was also a letter from Mary. He placed the unopened envelope in his breast pocket.

Outside, he nodded to the Bow Street Runner stationed in the shadows of early morning beside 38 Great Pulteney Street and climbed up into the cabriolet with Officer Hamilton.

"We have one guarding your porch and another the basement. Katherine has been bound to the bench," Hamilton said. "Penelope has also been secured, as have those in Mayfair. I'm only just comprehending why the rich nail their deceased's coffins shut. And why they lock the doors to their family tombs." He pulled a blanket across both their knees, then reached up to thumb an errant lash from Polidori's cheek. "This will have resolution, John. Whatever the answer, you and I will find it."

At the palace, they stood in the room filled with books, clocks, and birdsong for almost a full hour, in silence with Justice Hamilton of the Bow Street Magistrates' Court, and the captain of the royal guard. Finally, His Royal Highness the Duke of Sussex and his son, Augustus Frederick, joined them.

"Justice, Doctor, Officer," the duke said with a slight incline of his head.

The three guests bowed.

"Your Royal Highness," the justice said as he stepped forward and handed a thick dossier to the king's son. "Investigation has suggested the matter in Mayfair is indeed related to recent occurrences here at the palace. All members of the Griffith family, and all but one of their staff, are dead."

"A sorry matter indeed," the duke said. "A good fellow, Lord Griffith. Though we never met his wife and daughters, we have enjoyed several evenings discussing science with the good sir—in this very room, in fact. We are happy to ensure their carriage back to their estate in Cumbria."

"That won't be necessary, Your Royal Highness. Those matters are already being attended to," Justice Hamilton said.

Augustus Frederick stood behind his father, his body pudgy and stiff, his attention on the doctor and the officer. Polidori noted his hand was free of bandages. His jaw was also cleanly bladed, the multitude of scars almost invisible amongst his brusque features. A broad, black cravat was tied high about his neck. Though he was in no mood to smile, Polidori felt an inkling of wonder that the royal— who adamantly denied noticing the features of any man save his own father or the king—seemed absorbed by the countenances of both Officer Hamilton and himself.

"Keep me apprised, Justice Hamilton. We must see these fiends caught and hanged within short order." The royals turned and departed, leaving the captain of the guard to usher them out of Apartment 1.

Polidori sat waiting in the cabriolet as Officer Hamilton conversed at a distance with his uncle. He pulled Mary's letter from his pocket, broke the seal and held the parchment up to the cabriolet's lantern. It was a single line. A line with the power to break his heart. Mary's young babe, William—Willmouse—was dead. An anger immediately rose within him. That an innocent could so easily die without recourse. And yet he was dealing with men who so blatantly stole life from others, had died themselves but once again lived without consequence to continue killing. The concept infuriated him. He read the line a second and a third time with no recognition of how he could possibly console his beloved friend. His beloved confidant. He placed the letter back in his breast pocket, against the erratic beating of his heart.

"Was she one of them?" asked a gruff voice.

Polidori turned, startled. Augustus Frederick peered into the carriage window, his heavy arm resting on the sill. "The woman who attacked me. Was she one of the eleven?"

"I believe she was. A lass by the name of Kathleen," Polidori said, composing himself.

"I need to see her, to confirm with my own eyes."

"Forgive me, sir, but I do not believe that would be appropriate."

Augustus narrowed his eyes and motioned toward Officer Hamilton. "The officer and yourself." He held his gaze steady, allowing silence to linger within the stink of his breath. "Rumors start somehow. Especially within a palace. It would be a shame to see you both hanged without burden to prove the truth of any unnatural affection."

Polidori went rigid, forcing his face to remain slack with no indication of his inner thoughts. "It would not be appropriate," he said through gritted teeth.

"Captain of the guard!" Augustus Frederick bellowed across the yard. The captain came running, his boots crunching on the gravel.

"Yes, sir?"

Augustus stared at Polidori, but the doctor did not flinch. Augustus grunted and turned to the captain.

"Fetch me a horse. I will be with the doctor until sunup."

CHAPTER SEVENTY-FIVE

"How exactly will the Spaniard help my research into the Romantics? Or is he more relevant to the subject of vampyres?" Rachel said. Twilight was rapidly diminishing into the orange night-light of London as she and Aubrey trod the streets of Soho toward Leicester Square. She was acutely aware of his easy movement beside her, the tautness of the T-shirt around his torso, whenever his arm inadvertently brushed against her own as they made their way through the crowds.

Aubrey chuckled. "The Spaniard isn't a person, Rachel. It's a pub—a good place for Scotch eggs, and you can't beat their roast leg of lamb. It should take about thirty minutes on the tube to Hampstead, then another twenty walking through the village and around Hampstead Heath. Or we can taxi from the station if you like."

"Oh, okay," Rachel said slowly. "I mean, it sounds great, but . . . how is it relevant? You made it sound like it was of the *utmost* importance."

"It is," he said. "I'm remiss we hadn't visited earlier in alignment with your research. The inn and its beer garden are hundreds of years old. Frequented by poets, authors, and highway robbers before even Byron and Polidori clinked beer glasses within its oak-paneled rooms, or under the canopy of its trees. But it's probably best known for its mention in Bram Stoker's *Dracula*—written almost eighty years after Polidori's *Vampyre* for reasons you're now aware of. Van Helsing and his torch bearers set off from the Spaniard to kill the vampyre. Fictionally, it's where every good staking venture should start."

They caught the Northern line from Leicester Square and were soon in Hampstead. Rachel thought it a lovely village. They dawdled to gaze through store windows and check out the menus in front of restaurants before falling into an easy step to climb Heath Street.

Aubrey's cell phone chimed and he smiled. "Jess is already there."

At the top of the hill, they turned onto Spaniards Road, tunneled by green, leafy trees. A respite from the glass, concrete, and stone of the city. Though the sky was dark, streetlamps lit the trees in a magical way. Just beyond the trees was Hampstead Heath—nearly eight hundred acres of rolling hills and vales. Open parkland and dense woodland. Streams and ponds. Foxes, deer, woodpeckers, and kingfishers. Bats.

The inn loomed out of the darkness ahead of them. Three levels of cream-colored brickwork with dark shuttered windows and a gas lantern swinging in the evening breeze above the portico. Over the inn sign, two swords crossed, pointing upward, in readiness for battle. *THE SPANIARDS INN. 1585AD.*

The inside of the pub was packed with an incongruous clientele in silk suits and little black dresses, cut sharp against the dark wood-paneled walls and ancient planked floor. Martinis and gin and tonics. The clean scent of expensive aftershave on freshly shaved jawlines. Ties, Rolexes, and the polish of wingtips. Rumpled gloves, diamonds, and stilettos. Rachel felt underdressed as she and Aubrey slid through the crowd, catching covert glances at her from beneath manicured brows and over the rims of cocktail glasses. Every single person was ludicrously beautiful. Not one wrinkle or blemish.

She sighed in relief when Aubrey led her past the bar and out the back door into the beer garden. It was just as crowded under the canopy of trees and overgrown trellises, but at least they were a jeans and T-shirt crowd.

"What was all that about? Was everybody staring at us?" she asked.

He shrugged. "I'll go grab some beers. See if you can find Jess."

She walked down a long candlelit arbor, patrons drinking and eating, talking and laughing loud. *The roast lamb does look good*, she thought. She squinted in the dimness, studying face after face to ensure she didn't pass Jess by mistake. Despite the casual dress of the crowd, she was struck again by the attractiveness of each face as it inevitably turned and glanced at her—every single one. Just a glance, and yet she felt as though they summed her up instantly. As she moved through the crowd, conversations halted, heads leaned together to whisper.

She became hyper aware of those around her, considerations growing that these people all knew each other. And knew she was . . . Was what? She was second guessing herself. She stopped as a single thought struck her. *These people know I'm not one of them.*

A punishingly good-looking man held her in his gaze much longer than any other. Then he smiled and nodded, as if he recognized her. Like he knew why she was there and was happy she was. Rachel had visited small towns before—the unknown stranger sparking interest and gossip. But this felt different.

She came out the other end of the arbor, noticing Aubrey at the outside bar, in conversation with a couple squashed against him in the crowd. Their intimate proximity didn't seem to bother him. He laughed jovially as he waited to be served.

She couldn't get to him—the sea of people was impenetrable in that direction. Instead she sidestepped around the end of the arbor, down the flank of a picket fence that separated the beer garden from the car park. The moon shone full and white, reflecting off the hoods of Range Rovers, BMWs, and Jags luxuriating in the dappled shadows of hundred-year-old trees.

"Come with me," someone said, just as a hand slapped firmly over her mouth. A filthy, salty stench. Another arm crushed across her chest. Adrenaline instantly pumped through Rachel's veins, and she squirmed against the tight grip but couldn't wrench free.

"You can't trust them. None of that lot."

She was lifted from her feet, her weight seemingly inconsequential, and carried swiftly through the parking lot. A moment ago she'd been surrounded by hundreds of people. Dipped into a shadow for less than a breath, and yet it was just long enough to be taken.

"Leeches." His voice was deep and bitter, and sprayed a bloody spittle along the forearm and hand pressed to her face. They crossed Spaniards Road at an impossible pace, a streetlamp momentarily glinting off the copper hair curling down the length of the pallid, muscled forearm. And suddenly they were entering the dark, dense wood.

Oh my God, oh my God.

Rachel kicked her legs wild but couldn't make contact. He carried her down a brambled ravine and up the other side without effort or pause. Finally, her foot made purchase against her assailant's leg, and left her in throbbing, bruising pain. Blinded by ache and angry tears, she reached up behind her head, swinging her fists toward his unseen face, all without effect. Branches and twigs slapped across their path, obscuring any view beyond a few feet, and great trees rose around them even the moon could not penetrate.

He shifted his hold and threw her forward, headfirst, through the foliage. She felt as though she was falling, and a sapling branch smacked her chest as she tumbled, knocking the breath from her. Through tears her view was disoriented, dizzy and confused. The ground looked dozens of feet down, like he'd tossed her over a gully. Then suddenly his grip was on her again, jerking her against the hardness of his body, her chest to his, and she saw his face. His clipper-short copper hair.

It was him.

His features were warped by brooding anger, almost hatred, turning down the sides of his mouth. The fangs of fairytale, of nightmare, of cinematic and literary horror pressed into his lower lip. Blood smeared his mouth and copper-stubbled chin.

This couldn't be happening. It was unreal.

Impossible.

He peered down at her, his hold tight and his legs wrapped around hers, pulling her into the disconcerting coldness of his groin. Faster and faster, leaves and branches no more than a blur all around them. Above. Beside. Below.

"They won't find you," he said. Bloody saliva dripped from his mouth, his lower lip torn by the razor edge of his fang. "I'll give you life. Forever, Rachel. I promise."

The canopy of vegetation fell away behind them and Rachel realized they were seventy or eighty feet above the ground. *Are we flying?* The idea made her head ache, and she questioned whether she was even awake. She held on to him instinctively, as she began to feel the fall. The ground approached fast, and she thought they would crash. But then everything slowed. Her captor's legs loosened from around her own and his feet landed gracefully upon the grass of Hampstead Heath.

The moon shone down and he lifted his face to it, exulting in the light, his skin translucent, fine veins just below the surface pulsing with blood. He sneered, baring blood-tarnished teeth, both upper and lower canines like pointed fangs. But his incisors were changing, too—lengthening, sharpening, the gums pulling back to fully allow an unhindered depth of penetrating damage.

And yet somehow Rachel found him extraordinarily alluring, beyond beautiful, in the cold celestial light.

He lowered his gaze to her, and his green eyes were astonishing in contrast to his sallow, freckled skin. "We've been waiting for you a long time. But I won't allow you to do it, Rachel. I couldn't bear the loss. Not again."

"I don't understand," she said, surprised by how meek and submissive she sounded.

He swayed his head slowly from side to side, swiping his tongue over the tip of each of his fangs, drawing gossamer strings of blood-stained saliva across the foul-smelling cavity. "Of course you do. Leave it, and I will give you what all mortals seek." He caressed her cheek with the backs of his fingers and she felt herself numbing, enamored by his magnificence, falling into the depths of his eyes, her head heavy and drooping sideways, exposing the length of her neck to his desire. And to hers.

"Let her go."

The voice was strong and commanding, and she knew who it was.

"Let her go." This time the tone was soothing, friendly. Almost loving.

The grip around her loosened and Rachel fell to the grass, groggy and immobile. Then Jess stepped down into the moonlight. Not from the left or the right, just down into it.

Jess placed a hand on the copper-haired man's shoulder and leaned in to hug him.

"Baertschi will be here shortly. He'll give you the assistance you need, old friend."

Sensation returned to Rachel's body, and she pulled her legs and arms in close on the wet grass. *Detective Gendarme Baertschi?* She pushed up onto her hands and knees, the dulling euphoria crumbling away to be replaced by an ache of confusion.

The copper-haired man expelled a single sob, then appeared to check himself, straightening to his full height, his musculature noticeably tensing beneath denim and cotton as he pulled away from Jess. "No," he said without emotion.

He moved in an almost imperceptible blur, and Jess was catapulted up and away into the darkness. But almost instantly Jess was back, crashing into him and sending them both sprawling over the grass toward the trees. The crack of fist against jaw, elbow against cheek, head against chest, echoed around Rachel, and she staggered to her feet. They blurred past her at incomprehensible speed in the opposite direction, the thud of flesh upon flesh leaving no doubt each was causing major damage to the other. Rachel wavered, her perception indefinite and bewildered within the blueshift and redshift of movement forth and back. The velocity of action baffled her concept of what could possibly be real.

Jess abruptly crashed to the ground beside her, as if thrown from a great height, with a horrific cracking of spine and ribcage. The copper-haired man lay clutching his stomach several hundred feet away. His movement was slow and unbalanced, but he was regaining his foothold. Rising. His attention on Rachel.

Jess looked up at her, shocked blue eyes determined behind the sheen of tear. "Run," Jess mouthed, before the eyes darkened, like candles blown out.

Rachel turned and ran.

CHAPTER SEVENTY-SIX

As their carriage pulled up to 38 Great Pulteney Street, Officer Hamilton was the first to notice the Bow Street Runner missing from his station on the stoop. Hamilton and Polidori leapt from the carriage, then leaned over the wrought iron fencing to peer down into the basement air well. The officer blew his whistle—three loud, sharp warbles into the darkness—before he threw the signal to the carriage valet.

"Keep sounding the alarm until the runners arrive," he said. "Otherwise we'll surely be dead before the sun rises."

Augustus Frederick pulled his horse to. "What is the meaning of this?"

"Sir, unless you have a pistol, I suggest you leave immediately," Hamilton said, but Augustus Frederick dismounted and followed them down the iron steps, the dull ring of metal beneath their boots.

A runner lay at the bottom, his neck broken and ripped open, no spray nor ooze of blood evident. They bounded over him and slammed their shoulders against the soot-covered basement door until it shattered, shards of glass and splintered wood littering the basement flagstones.

Hamilton stumbled on the lip of the threshold and went down. Polidori and Augustus Frederick tumbled over him, the three of them sprawled across the floor.

*   *   *

Rachel tripped crossing a bog, faltering to the ground into a thorny thatch of undergrowth. She'd no idea how far or in which direction she'd run. She lay silent a moment, catching her breath, listening to the wood. The movement of branches in the breeze above. The remote hoot of an owl. The creep of creatures best left unimagined.

In the far-off distance she thought she heard a whistle. But the city was nothing more than a quiet orange glow at the edge of the sky. She carefully lumbered through the thickening brush, barely daring to breathe, bypassing the open lawns where she might be seen from a distance. She could see a stately home standing just beyond a lake, above a swathe of groomed meadow. Forsaken and dark.

"Rachel!" called the copper-haired man. His voice held a cold anger that sent her heart beating erratically. At least she now knew which direction he was coming from, and which way to run.

Away.

*   *   *

Augustus Frederick scuttled from on top of the heap, pulling his pistol from his belt as he threw himself against the wall. Polidori rolled in the opposite direction, yanking Hamilton with him, shaking him into groggy consciousness and wiping blood from his cut brow.

Andrew Fairbank stood beside the naked cadaver of Miss Kathleen Griffith, aware but unconcerned by their ungraceful entrance, taking care to unknot the ropes at Kathleen's ankles and wrists.

"I'm glad you chose to forego the autopsy, Doctor Polidori." He ran his finger down between her breasts, stopping at the lowest of her ribs. "Of course, the turning would have eventually smoothed over all the damage, but such a process I would not wish upon even the darkest of souls. Some cannot handle it—their mind and all cognizance of who they once were, who they could be, irreparably wounded by the experience." He stretched his neck from one side to the other, his spine audibly cracking. He sneered with the pleasure, baring blood-smeared fangs.

Hamilton rose to his feet. "Where is the other runner?" he said, aiming his pistol.

"What do I care?" Andrew answered.

Augustus Frederick's eyes were wide, mesmerized. "What is your meaning, sir? Miss Griffith is obviously dead."

"Is she?" Andrew grinned, his teeth splendid and horrific in the lantern light. "You might say the same of me, both now *and* when I explored your soul within your bed sheets. When I sank my teeth in and sucked the life force from you, and you exulted in the pleasure it gave us both."

Augustus Frederick's pistol issued a loud blast and the spark of gunpowder. Fairbank lurched as the shot hit his shoulder but seemed otherwise unruffled. Augustus charged him with an angry, guttural yell, barely reaching striking distance when Andrew threw him to the ground with a single flick of his arm. The crack of Augustus's skull was dull upon the flagstones.

Polidori raced over, crouching to check Augustus's breathing and pulse. The rhythm of blood along the vein remained sound.

"How long?" he asked Andrew, lifting his chin toward Kathleen.

"The awakening takes time. The turning even longer. But time is . . . something we have in unlimited abundance."

"Why Kathleen, and not him?" he asked, motioning toward the unconscious Augustus. "Why not her?" Penelope, on the other side of the slab.

"We all know *the one* when we meet them. Love, above lust, is far superior to any base requirement for continued survival. One must consume. Whether blood, food, flesh, or love. But love above all else. As I am certain you understand." He glanced at Officer Hamilton, still gripping his pistol, his features intensified in the wavering lantern light. "And when the one finally crosses our path, Doctor, I assure you nothing can alter the course of their destiny. Not without significant and dire consequences."

*   *   *

Rachel reached a clearing, the moon bathing it through the break in the canopy. Ancient gravestones, barely more than moss-covered slabs, slanted this way and that among unkempt grass. She hesitated at a stone almost as tall as she, its epitaph obscured by a spongy layer of moss, the earth beneath it sunken and soggy.

And then she heard a bell. One solitary fluttering jingle, unmistakable in its clarity. And meaning.

Dread devoured her, years of research and reality crumbling into dust. She cried out and instantly regretted it. She heard him alter his course, pushing through the wood in her direction.

Screaming her name with a penetrating loathing.

An intense and unambiguous hatred.

* * *

The basement standoff was broken by the warbling echoes of the runner's whistle from the street outside. In between the shrieking blasts, Polidori heard subtle noises emanating from the darkened passage beneath the townhome's service rooms. A sensual sucking and swallowing. He caught Hamilton's gaze and motioned toward it. The officer tilted the lantern above to cast the light into the passage.

Masters Thomas Aldridge and James Fairbank held the missing runner between them, their faces nuzzled into either side of his neck. Seducing, embracing, consuming the man's vitality.

"Cease!" Hamilton yelled. "Cease!" He ran toward them, pulling out his second pistol, aiming and firing both. The two vampyres were thrown further into the passage, and the runner crumpled to the ground, his face pallid.

There was a blur in the dark, a shifting of focus, more a dropping of air pressure than actually seeing, before Polidori recognized Aldridge and Fairbank were upon Hamilton.

He hadn't even seen the officer fall. He was simply on the ground, beneath the bulks of the two vampyres as they ripped at his uniform jacket, animalistic with a frenetic snap and snarl. Their mouths were dirty and bloody, lips and gums retracted, teeth exposed, eager for more.

Hamilton's neck was stretched, exposed, but as yet untouched, and Polidori dared not hesitate. He threw himself into the fray, hoping only to delay until backup arrived, but willing to do damage he had sworn himself against when becoming a doctor.

* * *

Rachel had no choice. She made a break for it, running across the open heath and toward the orange glow of London in the distance. She glanced over her shoulder just as he stepped from the wood out into the meadow behind her. She faltered as a distortion of shadow struck from the treetops and landed directly in his path, flinging him several hundred feet in the opposite direction. Rachel blinked, fast, the involuntary action of panic freezing staccato images in between the blur of movement. Jess's silhouette.

Their clash appeared an illusion, not quite on the ground, but above it.

In the distance, the whir of a helicopter cut through the night sky. It was circling the northern end of Hampstead Heath. The location of the Spaniards Inn. Hundreds of bats lifted from the northern wood, a great swath of darkness rising, shifting, arcing across the heath. They converged and headed directly toward Rachel and the open ground where Jess and the copper-haired man fought.

As the bats eclipsed the moonlight, the man let out an almighty bellow of grief. Of anger and hatred. His anguish tore at Rachel's heart and blinded her with terrified tears. She wiped at her eyes as she ran, her heartbeat inconsistent as she realized the copper-haired man was hurtling after her up the slope. Not running. Hurtling. Several feet above the ground. His face contorted by rage. Jess held to him, their efforts ineffective in anything but possibly slowing the speed of his approach. Much faster than Rachel could ever run.

*   *   *

Andrew remained at Kathleen's side, caressing her flesh, ignoring the four brawling upon the flagstones.

Polidori yelled when Aldridge clamped his teeth around his forearm, fangs and incisors sinking into his flesh to the gumline. Polidori thrust Aldridge back and slammed his head repeatedly into the floor until his bite loosened.

Master Aldridge and Master James were strong, but nowhere near as strong as Andrew had been as a corpse, or presumably now as a gentleman. They were superior to mortals in speed and agility but, though they seemed immune to gross pain or damage or death, they had no idea how to fight. How to gain the best of their adversary by any means other than seduction or brute force. Their combat was without knowledge of pain points, of how to gain the upper hand and bring a fight to resolution.

Polidori took care to avoid their gazes, to prevent a seduction from taking hold. Instead, as the four of them brawled across the floor, he looked to Hamilton. They both were panting heavy, energy draining rapidly, when Hamilton nodded toward the shattered remnants of the basement door. Polidori understood. It would buy them time. Just as it had at the foot of the grand staircase at 8A Park Crescent.

He grabbed a shattered wooden mullion, broken from the doorframe, and thrust it into Master Aldridge's chest. The stake slid in cleanly without hindrance, and there was an audible pop and rip as the heart was breached, split open within the chest. Aldridge staggered and gazed dumbfounded down at the wooden stake as Polidori twisted it further into him. The light in his eye dimmed and he spasmed.

Then he combusted.

One instant mote of brilliant, licking flame—orange, yellow, and black. Scorching. And then a dense, dark detonation of ashes that exploded throughout the basement with an explicit malevolence.

The three remaining on the floor scuttled away from the flareup on hands and knees, all as astonished as the one who had ceased to exist. Polidori pushed himself to the wall, shaking, his hand burnt and unsteady, still gripping the stake. He stared at the broken shard of wood.

Oak.

The king of all trees.

The holy tree of Europe.

The Tree of Life. Of folklore. Of Pagan ritual. Of druids. Of wisdom.

The protector and guardian of the virtuous.

Polidori scrambled to his feet, launching himself through the cloud of ash until he reached the slab. He grasped for Miss Griffith and pulled her naked body across the table and up against his chest. Then he clenched his fist tight around the end of the stake and held it high above Miss Kathleen Griffith's breast.

Andrew stood wide-eyed, looking uncertain. As if he'd never known fear, and now he did.

"You cannot kill her. You're . . . you're a doctor," he said.

"She's already dead, sir. And by my oath I swore not only to prolong life, but to relieve needless suffering. To ensure dignity in my handling of those in my charge, both in life and in death."

He thrust the stake into Kathleen's heart. A vivid purple flame coursed over her voluptuous curves and dips before her body disintegrated, the shapeliness lost as ashes collapsed down onto the slab. Polidori shivered as an intense and pure evil lifted from the dust then abruptly evaporated.

A ripple of color blurred through the basement haze, and Andrew and James were gone.

* * *

Rachel was ready to collapse. The ache in her legs, the pain in her lungs almost unbearable. She struggled up the steepening incline of the heath, aware of the enraged creature closing in behind her.

A flash of Aubrey, on the periphery of her vision. Running, legs and arms pumping, and then he was at her side. In a single fluid motion, he lifted her up into his arms and cradled her tight to his chest without slowing. She curled up, feeling irrationally secure against his solidity. His T-shirt was soaked with perspiration, his body flushed and hot, his chest rising and falling rapidly as he gulped for air. His heartbeat was strong against hers. Just as urgent. Perhaps as terrified. But still reassuring.

They made it to the top of the hill, and the wide expanse of London City opened up in front of them. The moon cast its light on the cityscape, enhancing the twinkle of distant lights. The striking silhouettes of the Shard, the Gherkin and the London Ferris Wheel dramatic amongst the hundreds of skyscrapers. The sky appeared broader from here, and the stars sharper as they continued to rise. But Rachel was more aware of the glimmer in Aubrey's eyes as he touched his forehead to hers. An indistinct and unfathomable depth of chestnut she was coming to understand. Their breathing was heavy, the brush of lips upon one another's unintentional but not objectionable.

Still they rose, the heath rapidly falling away beneath them, the air around them still. Quiet.

"I thought I'd lost you, Rachel. I'm so sorry," he said, as his breathing slipped into an easier rhythm. He loosed her legs but reassured his grip around her torso, his hands and fingers spread across her back, her feet supported on the tops of his.

She recognized herself reflected in his gaze, then closed her eyes and nuzzled her nose alongside his, fingers loosely gripping the curls at the back of his head.

"Are we safe?" she said, lips still so close that each word intimately strengthened their connection.

"Yes. He can't make it up this high," he said. "He doesn't have the capacity—physical or mental."

"And Jess?"

He chuckled as he rubbed her back. "Jess is stronger than any of us. An old soul. Indestructible with all they've gone through."

Still they rose. Nothing about them bar moonlight reflecting off wisps of vapor.

His body was beginning to cool, to soften as he relaxed. His grip was supple, the pressure of his length against hers pleasant. A subtle flexing of his musculature, a shift in the wind and the arcing movement of stars beyond his unruly curls caused her to look down.

They were several thousands of feet above Hampstead Heath, airplane high. The tallest building on the skyline lay far, far below. And yet she was unafraid in his arms. She knew without question she was safe. A dozen military-looking helicopters circled below them. Searchlights targeted a grassy swath of parkland, illuminating several vehicles at the edge of the light.

"Detective Gendarme Baertschi," Aubrey said.

"You know him?"

"We all know *of* him. And I'm certain he knows of most of us."

"You all," she repeated slowly. She wanted to ask him what he meant. She knew what he meant. "Is that a good thing?" she said instead.

"In cases like this it is. Baertschi and Interpol will know how to handle . . . him."

"Will they kill him?"

Aubrey flinched, then chuckled, perhaps tinged by sorrow. "Rachel, I'm afraid you're stuck in the eighteen hundreds. We've come a long way since then. Certainly, it was the only handling at the time, but we're a lot more organized now, less barbaric. No need for vigilantism. Our kind are also not as evil as once perceived. As once we may have been. As some of us most definitely were."

"But he killed all those people. Seven Dials, in the club, and on the London Eye."

"Did he?" Aubrey looked thoughtful. "He has his problems, and he has for a long time. His turning was filled with horror and anguish that's never subsided. But this time . . . his guilt or innocence must be determined by the appropriate authorities."

"And that's where Baertschi comes in?" She winced with the ache in her head.

He nodded, then pulled her tighter against him, massaging the muscles of her neck. "Does that help?" he said.

"Yes," she said.

He pressed his lips into her hair. "We're almost there, Rachel."

She snuggled against him as she wondered.

Where?

CHAPTER SEVENTY-SEVEN

Hamilton lay asleep in Polidori's bed. The doctor pressed his hand to the officer's sweat-beaded forehead, then pulled the sheets and blanket down to expose the torso to the cool night air breezing through the open windows. His face, chest, and arms were bruised with savage bites. Polidori had dabbed each with iodine, sutured and bandaged the deepest punctures. He had lost little blood, but his naked flesh was flushed red with fever, his rust-colored body hair tending toward golden where it crept from his chest to eddy down his stomach.

"The fever should break by dawn, but I advise he rest as long as possible," Polidori said.

Mrs. Hicks folded the discarded eiderdown and placed it on the trunk at the end of the bed. "Soup is simmering on the kitchen fire. I won't be sleeping a wink tonight, so best you call whenever the officer requires it. Or whenever *you* do, Doctor Polidori."

He slumped at his desk, his attention sinking toward the unanswered letter from Mary.

The housekeeper placed her plump hand on his shoulder and he leaned in to her side. She stroked his hair with a gentleness he had missed, and he wished his own mother was still alive to confide in. "Don't stay up too late writing, John. You need your sleep, too." She gazed over at the sleeping officer. "This bedstead was certainly large enough for the strapping bulks of you and your brother, God rest his soul. I think it's time it be shared again, don't you?"

Polidori pressed his lips to Mrs. Hicks's hand. After she had quietly closed the door behind her, he pulled paper from his document box and dipped his quill.

Mary Shelley
65 Via Sestina, Roma, Italy

My Mary, My darling, darling sister,
I am devastated to read of the death of your beloved babe,
young William. Beautiful Willmouse. My heart is broken and
I can only hope my words may bring you some comfort at this
horrid time

He ripped the parchment and cast it to the floor, then reached for
another. For almost an hour, the time passed by Hamilton's gentle
snore and the chiming of the downstairs clock, he stared at the blank
page, before finally dipping his quill once more.

Master William Shelley
65 Via Sestina, Roma, Italy

Dearest Willmouse,
Allow me, young sir, to share something even I am still
learning. And that is the importance of each and every one of
us.
Through the fall of angels, we find ourselves in lives that
are transient at most. Whether Adam or Methuselah, Solomon
or Willmouse. Whether we live mere moments, hours, years,
or centuries. We each have a life, and because it is ours, it
has meaning and relevance.
Some might foolishly squander the time allotted them;
others might rejoice in the simplicities and complexities it
allows. Whether shared with others of like or unlike mind,
with words or songs, thoughts or dreams, all lives are beset
by the vast spectrum of the passions. The best. The worst. And
every hunger in between that makes us who we are.
But there is one passion our Creator gave us above all. The
propensity to love and be loved. Without regard to doctrine,
birth, race, or kind, we each have within us the spark that
joins us to all others. That allows us to know, to long, to feel,
to rejoice in our own and another's existence.
None should pine for immortality, when all that is needed is

already within reach.

Right here. Right now.

We must merely allow ourselves and all others to grasp it without hinderance or rebuttal.

And by sharing that love, by accepting that love, we openly commit to the importance of one another and He who has allowed us this brief opportunity to be ourselves.

To be true to ourselves.

And Him.

You sir, our beautiful Willmouse, have always been and will always be loved.

You are important and unquestionable.

And therefore immortal.

With all my love,
John William Polidori

CHAPTER SEVENTY-EIGHT

Rachel brushed at her eyes as she reread Polidori's letter to Mary. It reminded her of something Jess had said, on the steps outside Heaven. *"Hundreds of thousands of years of human history . . . And yet we're only here for such a short time."* It reminded her of the quiet conversations she'd shared with Aubrey in the parlor, the kitchen, the courtyard. Over port and cigars. With nothing but words bringing them closer together. She sank into the wing of the chair, a shiver running through her.

The vast spectrum of the passions. The best. The worst.

"He's seductive, isn't he?" Jess had said.

She recognized Jess's voice in the courtyard below her window. She hadn't heard the front door's usual creaking salutation and presumed there was no longer a need for the pretense of using a front door—when you didn't need to.

She knew who they were, now. What they were. At least she thought she did. But she didn't know when or how their story started. When or how Doctor Polidori's story ended. And how the two threads must surely be related, even if by nothing more than bloodline. At least in Aubrey's case. Or maybe just blood.

She wanted to complete Polidori's story before delving into the intrigue of Aubrey's. And though the fact of his reality certainly boggled her mind, it didn't scare her. On the contrary, his strength and sensitivity, his genuineness in all their moments together, the sincerity of his words and actions had already proven his true nature. His amiable touch no matter the communication. His unchecked chuckle at anything even remotely funny. The soft and subtle curve of his mouth whenever she caught him staring at her.

She secured the clean copy of Polidori's letter and closed down her laptop.

When she reached the kitchen, she peaked around the doorway. Her host was sitting on the counter, with Jess held tight between his legs. A passionate embrace, kisses intermingled with whispered words and deep giggles. Neither showed any indication of the previous evening's events.

Rachel cleared her throat as she entered. "Hi."

They turned to her, smiling.

"I wanted to thank you for what you did on the heath last night, Jess," she said.

Jess held out an arm and pulled her into the embrace. "Consider it repayment. Well overdue."

For what? Rachel was about to ask, but then she caught sight of Jess's ring finger, and the wedding ring wasn't on it. She wondered if tonight was the night Aubrey had alluded to—perhaps there'd been a proposal. Then she spotted the simple gold band on Aubrey's pinky, and it made her smile, wondering who might have asked who. And what.

She'd decided some time ago that Jess and Aubrey were well suited, both physically and mentally. They were agreeable and strong on all accounts, with a collective lure enhanced by Jess's fine bone structure in contrast with Aubrey's roguish features. If they'd formalized their bond, she was happy for them. But even if it remained open and fluid, she doubted they would ever be far from each other's conscience.

"I'll get my jacket and we'll be off, then," Aubrey said, leaving the kitchen and running up the stairs.

Jess's face softened into a perceptive smile as Rachel looked down the corridor after him.

"What do you have planned for tonight?" Rachel asked.

"Oh, I expect we'll just wander and talk most of the evening. Perhaps enjoy a martini or two. Probably have dinner at our favorite French brasserie in St. Christopher's Place, before coming back here when words are inadequate. Then . . . then Heaven."

Rachel's mind swam with a multitude of questions, knowing she was not even scratching the surface of Jess and Aubrey's existence. Clueless how to even start asking them.

"I have a request of you," Jess said, rubbing their ringless finger, voice dropping to a whisper. "He's a strong man. But even strong men need to cry sometimes. Grief, or happiness, or both at once. If Polidori needs someone when I'm not here . . ."

"What do you mean?" Rachel asked, when Jess went quiet.

"Okay, baby, let's go!" Aubrey called from the front door.

"The Sphinx's second riddle," Jess whispered. "One begets the other. From what I've observed, only twilight separates the two. But twilight isn't a beginning or an end, it's the journey between. A journey not without strong emotion. Or hunger."

"*What?*" Rachel whispered, her mind spinning, unable to make sense of a single word. But then Jess squeezed her hand and mouthed, *Goodbye*.

* * *

Rachel was shaken from a dead sleep by the alarming sound of shattering glass. She fumbled in the darkness for her phone. The screen flashed 3:28 AM and then the battery died. The air felt electric. Dry, with a fluctuating pressure. Still the terrible noise of breaking glass was loud and reverberating from above. From Aubrey's room. A window? A mirror? She pulled on her dressing gown and ran out onto the landing, groping the wall for the panel to the service stair.

Her sight refused to adjust to the dark, so she searched for the first step with her bare foot. There was no handrail, so she pressed her palms to the wall on either side, treading slowly and carefully up through the pitch black, stairs creaking. She closed her eyes, her other senses somehow more attuned. Twenty steps up and no more. She leaned into the wall for a panel like the one she'd entered, but nothing budged. She ran her hand blindly over the carpentry and felt a small protruding metal plate that swung sideways. A key hole. She knelt down and peered through it.

An intense brightness from within blinded her, diffusing an ambiguous image of silhouettes inside. But then the light abruptly extinguished, and the sound of fragmenting glass ceased. 38 Great Pulteney Street instantly plunged into the silent depths of the dead of night. Rachel blinked, her sight slowly adjusting to the remaining dim light seeping through the keyhole.

Aubrey stood alone in the middle of his suite, his back to her, naked and still. The curves, bulges, and smooth lengths of

263

musculature were delineated by shadow and the cool white moonlight pouring in through the windows overlooking Great Pulteney Street. The windows were intact, no sign of broken glass. He just stood there, his face in his hands, his shoulders trembling.

"Aubrey, are you okay?" she called through the key hole, tapping gently on the wall. There was a deep intake of breath and he crumpled, down on his haunches, all his weight on the balls of his feet. His sobs became loud and raw.

"Aubrey! Aubrey, I'm coming in. Okay?" Rachel pushed her shoulder into the wall. The wood splintered and the panel hinged open. She crawled quickly across the floor until she was at Aubrey's side, fragmented memories of Jess flashing through her mind. Memories she didn't recognize. Memories that weren't hers.

The bedsheets were awry with the lingering scent of passion, but no sign of Jess. She pulled Aubrey into her arms, his flesh cool and goosebumped, his body hair erect. His cheek was cold and moist against hers, and he shivered and sobbed as she held him close.

"Jess is gone," he eventually said in a broken whisper. His lips were wet against her neck, brushing her skin as he spoke. "It was time, but still I . . ." He tensed and pulled away from her, rolling back onto his buttocks. The intensity and depth of his gaze vacillated. "You should leave. I don't know if I can . . ."

She grasped his trembling hand, his chest heaving. He thumbed tears from his face, and Rachel felt drawn to his naked vulnerability, so handsome on a man powerful enough to show it. His gaze drifted over her face and hair, down the length of her neck to the lapels of her dressing gown then back to her eyes. She could sense him trying to search within her, delving deep to understand her, to know her as best he could. And as the depth of chestnut flared in intensity, she felt a barrier shatter. She could hear his thoughts. She knew them.

You should leave.

"No," she said.

The resonating complexity of his gaze was not what mesmerized her. It was what she recognized behind his eyes that drew her to him. And she knew it was her choice, what would happen next. What had to happen if she were to truly know him—and his kind—as well as she needed to. Wanted to.

He nodded.

Then he rose up onto his knees, leaned forward to bring his lips to her ear. She shivered.

Are you certain?

Yes.

He placed his hand on the small of her back. Stretching his neck with several bone-cracking pops he turned his face toward the moonlight, delighting in its glow as the fullness of his lips drew back and his canines sharpened and lengthened.

He didn't stand and pull her from the floor. He simply lifted and she rose with him. He tugged at the sash of her gown and it fell to somewhere beneath them. They touched only each other, his body now firm and warm, the bedroom seeming to roll gently around them, no sense of up or down, right or wrong, just the intimate suggestion that this was the way it should be.

Aubrey closed his eyes and tilted his head, his mouth at her neck. His tongue scorched as he licked her skin, flicking and rolling along the length of vein grown plump with arousal. His lips sealed against her and he gently sank his fangs into her flesh, breaching the vein beneath.

Rachel was seized by an ecstasy, an immediate awareness of every vein, every artery and capillary throughout her body and the blood coursing through them. He drew on her in concert with the beat of her heart, sucking her life as its chambers emptied and he swallowed hard. She reveled in the stretching and contracting beat, the opening and closing, the gush of blood between atrium and ventricle. The euphoria of oxygenation and knowing she was feeding him, her tender and intimate companion.

Aubrey's breathing became deep and frantic with the feeding, escalating until he suddenly exulted in their bond. He arched his back, breaking the seal between them, his sweat-slicked flesh skimming upon her, his musculature spasming and clenching repetitively in rapid, unrestrained succession and gratification. When the urgency of his movement quelled into a shivering tremble, he collapsed against her, the rolling of the suite subtly altering around them, a revolution oblique to any recognition of gravity.

Oh, my God, Rachel, I never knew how I hungered until I tasted you.

He touched his forehead to hers, closed his eyes, and kissed her. Her own blood tasted warm and salty within the kiss. His tongue was soft and affectionate. They rolled and he thrust into her again. This time to draw in dissonance to the beat of her heart. She felt the blood suctioned back along the artery from her brain, making her giddy. Her entire body lightened, aching and electric, the rhythm of her heart matching Aubrey's, every muscle relaxing and contracting in growing intensity with the unhalting cadence of his.

*   *   *

Rachel jolted awake, drenched in perspiration, her nerves alive and tender, her fingers and toes trembling.

She was alone in Doctor Polidori's suite, in the warmth of his bed. The house was silent and still. Staring up into the darkness, she slowed her breathing until her body settled, then swept her hand over the eiderdown to find her dressing gown. It wasn't there. She pulled herself across the bed and reached for her phone on the side table. It wasn't there. Frustrated, she stumbled through the room to flick on the light switch. The electrified wall sconces with their mock candles flared. Her dressing gown wasn't on the bed or under it. Her phone lay on the desk, its battery dead. She plugged it in, and it flashed 3:28 AM.

The exact time of her dream was disconcerting, but also a relief. It was just a dream. She pressed her fingers to her neck. No blood. No wound. No indentation. Just a dream. Still, the way she felt, the stirring warmth in her body was real.

She pulled on Aubrey's tank top, the frayed hem falling to mid-thigh, and sat down to work. To take her mind off the dream.

I never knew how I hungered until I tasted you.

Twelve letters left to be studied and twenty-three unread pages in Polidori's ledger, one with a dragon sketched the full height of the sheet, rendering the words beneath difficult to decipher. She checked her research parameters in the Old Bailey Online search engine. Only a handful remained to reference Officer Hamilton and the Bow Street Runners. She was closing in on all 38 Great Pulteney Street could give her. The best she could do while her thoughts were so scattered was to photograph the last of Polidori's writings and upload them to the cloud drive she shared with her editor. She made some cursory annotations of dates on her spreadsheet but left room to fill in the other details once she'd read and understood each reference.

She wondered what Aubrey tasted like.

She wondered if Adam was awake and whether she should call him, but her phone charge was still too low.

She yawned and scanned the next page of the ledger. Polidori had summarized the major proceedings of the Fairbank case. The elements that might indicate whether a cadaver, no matter how rotted or dismembered, might not actually be dead. The process, as he understood it, that resulted in the awakening and turning, as opposed to decomposing. And finally, how to kill one who had turned, returning him or her to the natural course of death. Beneath a particularly large splotch of ink, he referenced the tome Hamilton had read aloud in the basement of the British Museum.

> *A paling of the heart may incur the wrath of death.*
> *Awaiting the afflicted, Hell's descendent circling wreath.*
>
> *But heed, my friend, the course you wish that death to take.*
> *For love may break the downward spiral by driving in the stake.*

She understood the allusion to Dante's *Inferno* and the downward spiral of circles toward the depths of hell. The research even suggested the predestined ring specifically for those who had been turned and stolen the lives of others—the Eighth Circle with its seducers, counterfeiters, and deceivers. But Dante's divine comedy was just that. A comedy. A literary device to ridicule fictional, historical, and contemporary figures, the pompous and self-righteous. Despite the suggestion of staking, and Polidori's attestation that oak had the desired effect, Rachel saw the reference as a quaint reasoning toward the destiny earned by one's own actions in life.

And yet she shuddered, recalling the staking and combustion of Thomas Aldridge and Kathleen Griffith, and knowing despite her better judgment they were scorched directly into the brimstone and hellfire of the Eighth Circle.

The smell of coffee wafted through the courtyard window.

4:52 AM.

She went downstairs to find Aubrey sitting at the kitchen counter in his pajama shorts. His hair was disheveled, his eyes bright and bloodshot, his skin flushed.

"Sorry if I woke you. Too wired to sleep," he said, wiping his lips with the side of his hand. "I'll probably spend the day in bed, curtains drawn, catching up on sleep and finishing my book. I'd like to finish it before, well, you know how librarians can get with overdue hardbacks."

Rachel poured a mug of coffee and sat beside him.

"We should talk, huh?" he said.

She bit her lip, disconcerted by sensations and scattered images from her dream. She glanced at his naked shoulder, recognizing the rake of fingernails across the flesh. She instinctively checked her nails. "Yeah, we should," she said. "You start." She stared at the crema swirl atop her coffee.

"I expect you've reached the gap in the timeline."

Rachel looked up. "What?"

"The yearlong gap in Polidori's writings."

She had noticed the gap when sequencing the dates of the remaining data. There were several documents before the break still to be read, but she was ready to see where this conversation was heading. The further away from her dream the better. *It was just a dream*, she reassured herself.

"The letters and ledgers were destroyed, of course," Aubrey said.

"Of course," Rachel echoed.

"But there have been family conversations and you may at least be able to build up evidence of locations during this time from other sources."

"Such as?"

"The University of Edinburgh." Aubrey took a sip of coffee, his gaze unfocusing.

"That's where Polidori received his Doctor of Medicine."

Aubrey nodded. "And also where he returned to study law." He smiled and his eyes narrowed on Rachel.

"Officer Hamilton was mentoring at the Bow Street Magistrates' Court until he started university. Do you think they were in Scotland together the whole year?" she said.

"It seems plausible. Where else to study law? And what better place to escape the strictures of Mother England than within spitting distance of the Scottish Highlands and their freedom?"

Rachel could only hope it was true. She'd need to expand her research, but just the thought they might have spent some time in happiness before Polidori's demise buoyed her spirits. "But what about the Fairbank case? They haven't secured either Andrew or James."

"Ah, so you're not quite up to the research gap, then." He chuckled and drained his mug. "You'll find out in short order. Both disappeared without trace after the incident downstairs. Not another sign of them or their kind in the environs of London. The case remained open but unresolved. And that, my beautiful friend, brings us to this." He stretched along the counter to retrieve an envelope. "Jess left this for us."

The envelope was massive, eight inches by twelve, made from a pulp rich with blue and gold threads of silk. Inside was an embossed card. Opulent and intriguing.

"A masquerade of sorts," Aubrey said. "A reenactment by a historical society or some such. Could be fun, and Jess thought it might provide new insight for your research into Georgian England. The embellished pseudonyms were Jess's idea. A bit of a lark to put us into the right state of mind."

PLEASURE BALL
While we live, let us LIVE.
Lady Rachel Walton
Doctor John William Polidori
Are requested to attend the BALL,
at THE PAVILION, on Friday,
at 7 o'clock PM
BRIGHTON

CHAPTER SEVENTY-NINE

The four-in-hand rolled through the streets of Brighton, the cobbles slicked by early evening rain. Clouds, hovering above the village's pebbled beach, were bruised by purple internal flashes of lightning, fluxed with the rumble of thunder.

Aubrey sat stiffly in Wellington boots, vest, frockcoat, and pantaloons. "I'd forgotten how uncomfortable these blasted corsets are. And it's hardly offset by the Georgian fashion of going commando." He poked at his side. "Did you need to pull the ties so tight?"

Rachel smirked. "Authenticity. Still, you do look wonderful. Reminiscent of Mary's words to Polidori at Chillon. 'Do you think I'd have allowed you to escort me had I not known you would eclipse all other gentlemen in the room?' " She reached over and straightened his white silk cravat.

He tipped his hat. "And you, my lady, are exquisite. A natural beauty."

Rachel felt relaxed but excited in a Georgian-era gown of gold silk and gauze. Ruffled at the sleeve, multiple layers enhanced her bust and cascaded from a high-waisted ribbon to her ankles. She admired the matching silk slippers. "I'm surprised you had these just lying around. They're museum quality."

"Mrs. Shelley would've approved of your attire, perhaps even procured similar for her own wardrobe," he said.

The carriage jolted onto the gravel drive winding through the Pavilion's Romantic-era garden of mature trees. Elm, maple, holly, plane, palm, and ash. Oak. Beneath the trees sloped a picturesque landscape of shrubbery dotting hand-clipped lawns. Gas lanterns and open fires highlighted the foliage, like the garden itself was daring its guests to wander shadowed paths toward unknown circumstance.

Lightning flashed, and the accompanying thunder was deep and cracking. As the carriage bounced along, Rachel caught glimpses of King George IV's Royal Pavilion and could hardly believe this lavish affair existed by the English seaside. A vast array of ribbed, perforated, onion-shaped domes were interspersed with thin minarets. Persian and Indian architecture combined with a Georgian affinity for the Gothic. Rachel thought it whimsical and bizarre. Extraordinary.

The air was electric, fat drops of rain beginning to fall. Lightning licked haphazardly around the Pavilion's central dome to strike its spire.

"We should hurry inside before the downpour," she said. The carriage slowed to a stop behind several others.

"Polidori!" someone yelled from among the trees, where men in Georgian military dress uniforms lit the shadows with the glow of their cigars.

"I'll be just a moment, Lady Walton. Meet you inside the lobby?"

Rachel accepted his hand to step down onto the gravel. "Doctor Polidori," she said with a nod, slipping into character for the masquerade. Half a dozen automobiles and horse-drawn carriages lined the circular drive, guests in elegant 1820's fashion hurrying to beat the inclement weather. She gathered up her gown and followed their lead, rounding between Ferraris and Aston Martins, between carriages and horses, bypassing valets bowing their heads. She reached the Pavilion's entrance and stepped inside.

The ceiling appeared like the underside of an ornate umbrella, its rim festooned with fanciful bells. The connecting lobby was decorated in the Chinois style, with painted birds flying across the panels of paper lanterns, muraled dragons curling their scaled lengths over garish green walls. A gilt-framed canvas leaned on an easel, its lavish text welcoming guests to the ball at the king's summer residence, with a watercolor depicting couples dancing a Quadrille. Elegant calligraphy below announced the assumed date of the masquerade.

Friday, August 24th, 1821.

The date of Doctor Polidori's death.

Rachel was knocked to the ground in a blinding flash. Thunder was immediate, loud and all encompassing. A rush of energy enveloped her, an aliveness she hadn't experienced since the close lightning strike atop the parapets of Château de Chillon in Switzerland. The ceiling bells chimed, discordant and piercing, as the entire lobby structure shook. Bird flew, dragons writhed, their stares intense and accusatory as she attempted to regain her composure. She felt foggy, not quite certain where or when she was.

"Lady Walton?" Doctor Polidori ran across the carpet and kneeled to offer his arm. "Are you all right, my lady? Have you been hurt in the fall?"

Rachel looked up. Polidori appeared different from this angle, with a pleasant softness about his features. "Thank you, Doctor Polidori." She grasped his forearm and allowed him to assist her to her feet. "An unexpected shock with the storm's proximity, that is all. No damage done." She smoothed her gloved hands down the length of her gown.

"Are you certain? I would understand if you wished to return to the residence to recuperate."

She shook her head, charmed by his tenderness. "I'm fine. Really."

He grinned, and perhaps his teeth were a little less straight than she recalled. Even so, he still would eclipse all the other men at the ball.

"Mrs. Shelley confided that she considered you fearless," he said. "She admires you, and your research. Perhaps it is her writer's consciousness of worlds both real and imagined. At any rate, I'm glad you accepted my offer to accompany me tonight in her stead." He offered his arm. "Shall we see where the evening takes us?"

"Always a pleasure, Doctor Polidori." Rachel slipped her arm along his to rest glove on glove as they stepped into a gallery that ran the length of the pavilion and continued the Chinese theme. Flamboyant pink walls muraled with sticks of blue bamboo. Double height ceilings with extravagant crown molding. Hundreds of decorative bells and at least sixteen more dragons flourishing throughout the décor. Two grand stairs rose to the upper level, of golden metal fashioned as bamboo.

A valet at the doors of the Grand Saloon struck his staff against the floor three times. "Lady Rachel Walton and Doctor John William Polidori," he announced. "Doctor Polidori as personal guest of the king, for private services rendered to the royal family." Polidori bowed his head as the other guests clapped politely.

They accepted saucers of champagne and strolled the circumference of the circular saloon. Sumptuous red silk drapes with gold brocade dropped almost two dozen feet framing French doors almost as tall. More bells. More dragons. A crystal chandelier dominated the center of the sky-painted dome.

"Doctor Polidori, I didn't expect to see you here," said a hearty woman in white. Her features were pleasant, pulled taut by civil restraint. "And with a lady, no less. Where is your military friend?" She craned her neck to peer around the room in unmistakable distain.

Polidori bowed. "My lady, may I introduce to you Lady Rachel Walton. Lady Walton, Lady Fairbank of the Sussex Fairbanks."

Rachel flinched, surprised at the research the historical society must have done for the evening's authenticity.

"Walton? Somerset or Lancashire?" Lady Fairbank asked.

"Warwickshire," Rachel said when she recalled her family history. "Currently resident in New York City."

Lady Fairbank appeared bewildered, unsuccessfully concealing the upturn of her nose by sipping champagne. She appeared to think better of her fast judgment. "Married?"

"Yes, my husband is in America." Rachel glanced sideways at Polidori.

"Well, I am certain the good doctor is the perfect chaperone under his and your circumstance. A gentleman who can keep his word. His oath." With a measured, cold temperament, she held his gaze. "A pity you didn't arrive earlier. One of my youngest sons was married this afternoon in the gardens. An elegant affair sanctioned by the king himself. A handsome couple." She glanced over Rachel's shoulder, arched her brow and beckoned with her hand.

"Lady Walton, Doctor Polidori, may I introduce my sister, Lady Field, and my newly acquired daughter-in-law, Lady Jessica Fairbank, née Duval."

Rachel turned to greet the newcomers and felt as though her heart had stopped. "Jess!" she said, all pretense of propriety dropped.

Lady Jessica Fairbank curtsied and grasped Rachel's hand. "Well, that is a strange salutation indeed. And a man's name, no less. But do you know, Lady Walton, I like it." The words were said with a generous smile. They, no, *she* was voluptuous and feminine in her wedding gown, a loose oyster-white silk with gold embroidery at the neck and hemline. Her hair was antique gold, falling about her shoulders. A garland of olive leaves circled her head and another her wrist. And the simple gold wedding band decorated her finger. Rachel peeked at Polidori's pinky. No ring.

"Have we met previously, Lady Jessica?" Polidori asked.

"We've not been formally introduced, Doctor Polidori. Though you might have seen me at the Mivart's Ball a few seasons ago. A jonquil-colored gown. A fan I painted myself with daffodils. Did you notice me?"

She seemed to crave his answer more than a new bride should, but Rachel suddenly understood where her research and tonight were leading her. "Which one of Lady Fairbank's sons did you marry today?" Rachel asked.

"Why, the most handsome twin of course. Master Andrew Fairbank," Lady Jessica said.

All color dropped from Polidori's face. In sharp contrast to his diminished pallor was the adamant glare from Lady Fairbank, and Rachel was immediately struck by the image of the doctor's first discarded fragments of *Ernestus Berchtold* and his skull-headed lady. A horror best kept behind locked doors. Lady Fairbank forcibly gripped Polidori's upper arm, and he recoiled at her familiarity and contradiction to all decorum. "Remember your oath. It remains paramount," she said. "Break it and you will regret it. That is my oath to you."

He stood stoic and unresponsive, though Rachel detected a fleeting uptick of his brow.

The valet's staff struck the floor. "Officer Craig Hamilton Esquire, Lawyer of the Bow Street Magistrates' Court. A personal guest of the king, for private services rendered to the royal family."

Rachel craned her neck but couldn't see Hamilton through the crowd. Polidori turned a shoulder to Lady Fairbank, his skin flushing, his eyes sparkling. "I believe it is time to dance," he said. He urged Rachel and Jessica to follow as he headed toward the saloon entrance. There he hooked arms with Officer Hamilton and guided him through a crowded gallery toward the music room. Rachel could see only the backs of their heads as she and Lady Jessica walked in their wake.

"What, not even a sip of champagne or fortified wine to loosen my limbs before a jig?" Hamilton said jovially, seeming pleased to have Polidori on his arm in such a brazen fashion. The doctor leaned close to the officer as they walked swiftly toward those taking positions for the Quadrille. From behind them, Rachel noted the urgent whispers, saw how Hamilton's spine stiffened and his attention flicked around the room. He reached for his belt, and Rachel guessed he was wishing he'd brought his pistols. Not an ordinary accoutrement for a pleasure ball, but one she too wished he'd brought. She was no longer attempting to wrest any logical reasoning behind where she was. *When she was.* Accepting only that "*it is as it is.*"

"He's assertive. A trait to be admired in a man," Jess said, linking her arm with Rachel's as they followed the men.

"How long have you known Andrew? I mean—um—Master Andrew Fairbank?" Rachel asked.

"I've been acquainted with Master Fairbank a few weeks. As long as it takes to know any man."

Rachel was starkly aware of how long she'd known Aubrey Polidori. Less than two weeks. Thirteen days. And yet she *did* know him, as well as she knew Doctor Polidori, she was certain of it. She was just as certain Jess did *not* know Andrew. Did not know who he was, or what he was capable of.

Was she just as blind where Aubrey was concerned?

The music room was large and improbably spectacular. A whimsy that dramatically defied all sense and sensibility with myriad brash colors, styles, and textures; a massive dome that appeared covered in tens of thousands of gold-leafed shells; nine lotus-shaped chandeliers; and hundreds of painted and sculpted snakes and dragons, teeth bared, swooping and flying.

And there were bells. Hundreds of bells, ready to ring for those dancing below.

They fell into line for the *Le Pantalon* of the Quadrille. Doctor Polidori gripped Rachel's hand, his touch warm and welcome. Rachel glanced diagonally at Jess, her ample décolletage, much fuller than Rachel's own, free of bitemarks or powder-covered bruises. *The wedding not yet consummated, the bride unaware of what her new husband will take from her.*

Officer Hamilton turned and reached for Jess's hand for the first steps of the dance, taking his position directly before Rachel. He was as handsome as she had imagined him to be from Polidori's descriptions. The freckled face, the cleanly bladed jawline, the rust-colored trim of his hair, the penetrating emerald of his eyes.

Rachel felt her heart break. Felt the tears threatening and the blood halting in her veins. She took a slow breath, forcing herself to remain calm. To not run. To not collapse with the heaviness of emotion.

It was him. At Seven Dials. At Heaven. On the heath. In her nightmares. Here.

Friday, August 24th, 1821.

Tonight the gentle man gripping her hand would die, either by heartbreak or by his own hand. And tonight the man opposite her would suffer a fate she could not fully comprehend. One that would torment him for centuries. Destiny. Immutable. Absolute.

Strains of harpsichord, violin, and flute filled the room, and the men circled round to bow before their partners.

"Please follow my lead in all things tonight, Lady Walton," Polidori whispered. "I fear our every action may be vital."

Rachel nodded.

She and Jess stepped forward to grasp the hands of one another's partners. A shiver coursed through her as she touched Officer Hamilton's. But he gave her hand a gentle squeeze, and the instant they locked eyes, her fear dissipated and she knew she could trust him. For now.

They reversed the turn and again she and Hamilton gripped hands for an instant during the pass. They caught each other's gaze a second time, his attention drawn from scanning the surrounding crowd to see only her. An uncertainty rippled over his features.

She returned to Polidori, who bowed and raised his arm for her to twirl beneath. "I must assume Mary has confided in you, or at the very least you've a heightened awareness about you," he said as they pressed palms and stepped around one other. She nodded. "Whatever the course of events this evening, may I entrust Lady Jessica Fairbank's welfare to you?"

"Yes, Doctor Polidori. I will do everything in my power to ensure Jess's welfare," she said. And she knew she would, no matter what she might need to do. The music swelled and with her grip tight on his, she stepped forward and grasped Jess's hand, the latter mirroring her action so that the four of them were linked. Bound together by more than a Quadrille.

Another step and she turned a single time beneath Officer Hamilton's upheld hand, her attention cast from the security of her immediate group, through the gallery and Grand Saloon and into another gallery. Her gaze landed upon two men entering through a large double door. Twins. Blonde and straight of hair, they stood six inches taller than the crowd. She knew them by Polidori's description and sketch. She knew them by their most intimate of measurement.

She faltered, tripping over her slippers, but both Hamilton and Polidori caught her before she could fall. "Thank you, kind sirs. Perhaps some fresh air?" she said. They retired from the dance, out through French doors to a gothic arched portico. The gardens beyond column and lattice were shrouded in heavy rain. "They're here, at the far end, past the main saloon," she said.

Lady Jessica furrowed her brow.

"Your husband and his twin," Rachel added.

"Is something wrong?" Lady Jessica asked.

Polidori and Hamilton walked along the portico, their hands upon one another's backs, their heads close in quiet tête-à-tête. "Lady Walton, Lady Fairbank," Polidori said. "We will locate our military associates in the crowd. It would be best if you remained inside. Far from the shadows. Lady Walton." He bowed and kissed her hand. Then he took Lady Jessica's hand and brushed it with his lips. "I did notice you, my lady. How could I not?" His voice and demeanor were tender and affectionate. "Please stay with Rachel—with Lady Walton. You can trust her." He strode into the ball with Officer Hamilton.

"What is going on?" Lady Jessica said.

Rachel bit her lip. "How well do you know your new husband, really?"

"Does it matter? Society has rules and we live our lives by them."

Rachel closed her eyes, to put herself into the frame of mind of an early nineteenth century bride. She couldn't do it. Refused to do it. She needed to talk to Jess as she would anyone of the twenty-first century. As an adult with a will and a journey of their own.

"Jess, living by society rules doesn't work when society is driven by a bigoted patriarchy obsessed with its own agenda and self-importance." They walked into the Pavilion, and a valet offered them champagne. Rachel was reticent to accept it, but then thought the saucer might fortify her for the evening to come. The Quadrille had reached its finale, where moments of friendly pat-a-cake were interspersed with the ladies hooking arms, circling to the clapping hands of the men. Then the roles were reversed, the men exuberant in turning about with linked arms in the uninhibited joy of the dance. Rachel wished all of life could be so simple and interchangeable.

"Surely there is nothing *I* can do to change society," Jess said.

Rachel urged her into an alcove, the menacing visage of dragons looming close. She took several moments to gather her thoughts, considering who Jess would become—who she was. "I think the best we can do is begin with ourselves. We must be true to ourselves, our dreams and our desires. Our knowledge of who we truly are." She thought of Polidori and all he had been through. "To do otherwise is a farce. A masquerade that placates the arrogant and how they demand things to be. It is no less than submissively baring our neck to the vampyre—blindly allowing the domination that robs us and the world of our vitality."

Jess stood very still, quiet within the noise of the ball, subtle emotions playing her features. "Do you see me?" she asked, her voice the softest whisper.

Rachel nodded. "And I admire what I see. The strength it will take to be yourself in a world that is far from kind."

Jess's eyes shimmered. "How can you know this—this shame I dare not admit even to myself?"

Rachel stared into her champagne, watched the bubbles rising. "Because being yourself is nothing to be ashamed of, Jess. All that matters is that you know who you are. And are true to yourself."

A shotgun blasted in the adjacent room, an echoing boom followed by shattering glass, the shouts and screams of men and women, and the ringing of hundreds of ceiling bells. Panicked guests ran into the gallery, champagne and propriety discarded. Rachel and Jess were caught in the flow to be swept into the main dragon-green corridor. The crowd unceremoniously clamored in the confines of the space, attempting to escape the commotion, forcing Rachel and Jess to the southern end of the hall. The door at their backs suddenly broke open and the two of them were thrown into a vast banqueting room.

James and Andrew Fairbank stood at the head of a table large enough to hold two dozen, laden with candelabra, centerpieces, and uncountable variations of cuisine. Within the curve of a dome perhaps fifty feet high, an immense dragon, wings spread wide, swooped above them all, clutching in its claws a stupendous chandelier. A dozen soldiers in the blood-red of military dress stood around the room with sabers, pistols, and shotguns drawn toward the twins. Polidori and Hamilton stood at the far side of the room.

The Fairbanks seemed unconcerned by the room or events, but then Master Andrew Fairbank spied his new bride and stiffened. In such close quarters, Rachel felt her senses begin to dull, the allure of James and Andrew dampening any fear. Their stature and beauty seemed to embrace her. Seemed to call her to admire them, worship them, succumb to them.

"Rachel!" Polidori yelled across the room. It was enough to break her from her stupor.

Four heartbeats was all it took. The pressure and temperature of the banqueting room abruptly dropped, and a blur of movement torqued up and around the space, no dependence on floor, wall, ceiling, or gravity. Soldier after soldier was hurled to the ground or flung against wall or furnishing. The twist and rip of flesh was resounding. A shotgun blasted again and the stupendous chandelier swung with the breakage of chain and crystal. The dragon careened beneath the dome, its bared teeth horrific and deadly. The vast dining table screeched askew across the floor as the legendary serpent plunged into it, splintering it against the outer wall, pitching Polidori and Hamilton amongst the curtains and shattering them through glass doors out into the garden.

For the briefest of seconds, Rachel knew she was the only one still alive within the room. Soldiers lay dead on the wooden planks, and Jess was gone. Only the swing of the pantry door gave indication of where anyone might have escaped to. Rachel ran toward it, and then Polidori and Hamilton were two strides behind her.

The Pavilion's great kitchen was in disarray, deserted of all downstairs staff, pots boiling, meat simmering, shelves of copperware cast to the floor in haste. One of four cast-iron columns fashioned as palm trees had been bent in the fury of the twins' escape, its canopy of metal fronds strewn across the workbenches to garnish platters of rabbit, fish, and swan. Splintered doors and balustrade led them through the service corridors and down into the Pavilion's basement, where the mouth of a tunnel was cut into the stone foundation. They ran into the lantern-lit dimness, Hamilton at the fore. Damp and down-sloping, the floor a mire of squelching mud beneath their boots and slippers.

As they made their way, stumbling into each other, gripping arms and shoulders in support, Rachel thought inexplicably of Oedipus and the Sphinx. She wondered if destiny could be changed. Could answering the Sphinx's questions alter a determined course? Or would it only ensure its rapid approach.

Wind and rain churned before them.

The tunnel opened onto Brighton Beach, the pebbles slippery beneath their feet, and mounds of tangled fishing nets defining their course toward the foaming surge. The sky was black and purple, streaked by lightning, blurred by rain. Lanterns atop the road embankment were long-extinguished by the torrential storm, rendering obscure the rocky gradient of beach down to the waterline. Tall-masted colliers were moored, dark and forbidding, out in the deeper water.

"Do you see them?" Rachel shouted over the torrent and roar of waves crashing along the beach. She spied a splintered shaft of wood in Polidori's hand, possibly from the devastated banqueting table. She hoped it was oak.

"No," he called back. "I—"

Master James Fairbank descended from the darkness, his couture sodden, his rain-splashed face twisted with emotion. "You killed the one I loved," he said to Polidori. "Drove a stake through his heart and no less through my own."

Polidori tightened his grip, his attention fixed on James, who levitated three dozen feet above them.

"Tell me, Doctor Polidori, do you love the woman at your side? Or is it the man, or both?" James said.

Polidori glanced from one to the other, Hamilton giving an almost imperceptible nod. Rachel was abruptly wrenched into the air, James's arm tight around her rib cage, her head pushed awkwardly back to expose her neck. "Answer! So I might inflict the pain you have borne upon me!" he screamed. He jerked with an angry sob, baring his teeth above the curve of her flesh. "The truth, Doctor! And then I will gladly offer myself to execution from this pain."

Rachel winced with the twist of her spine.

"You are aware of my passion as much as I," Polidori yelled. "A love that holds more importance to me than my own life."

Lightning struck, and with the crack of thunder Rachel was thrown down onto the rocks and James yanked Hamilton and Polidori up into the air, out over the waves.

Rachel strained to see, lightning illuminating a horror she could not bear. Both men were held secure in Fairbank's superior grip, apparently unable to free their arms. James sank his teeth into the officer's neck, ripping at the flesh, tearing muscle, sinew, vein, and artery, his cheeks and face bloody as he fed. But beyond that, higher in the sky and further out to sea, the brilliance of electrical charge highlighted Master Andrew Fairbank and his bride. She was limp, her arms and legs dangling, Andrew's face buried in her décolletage and then about her neck, feeding on the vitality of virginal blood. He arched his back in self-exultation, then discarded her, dropping the exsanguinated cadaver into the ocean.

In the same instant James was finished with Officer Hamilton and cast him into the roiling waves with spine and neck clearly broken, the meager threads of flesh above his shoulders barely holding his skull secure. At James's momentary distraction, Polidori freed one arm and held the oak shard high.

An intense flash strobed the sky, Master James Fairbank extinguished from existence.

But no sooner had the light subsided and a thick ash plumed than Andrew grabbed Polidori mid-fall, sinking his teeth into the doctor's neck and sucking the life from him as they plummeted toward the water. Andrew's body shuddered as he drank, tangibly consuming deep drafts of Doctor Polidori's blood with each physical spasm of his body.

They hit the water at speed and there was an instantaneous explosive flare and evaporation. Both of water and of Andrew Fairbank. Lightning incandesced, highlighting a dense, malignant cloud diffusing above the waves. It swirled, sparked and blazed, a horrendous guttural agony echoing within its malevolence, before it collapsed in upon itself and vaporized.

CHAPTER EIGHTY

Rachel shuddered awake from the somnambulism, pushing through the twilight to recognize she was back where she should be. *When she should be.*

She nestled, stunned and unblinking, against Polidori's side, the gentle motion of the high-speed Thameslink rail reassuring as it shot through the English countryside toward London. Rain hazed the nightscape outside, blurring her own thoughts of Doctor Polidori's end, of Aubrey Polidori's beginning—knowing they were one and the same.

"I don't see how there could've been any other outcome, any other destiny," she muttered, still entranced by the shock of what occurred less than two-hundred years previous. Her forearm lay along the length of his thigh, her hand nuzzled within the warmth just above his knees. Her love of this man had begun in college, escalated during the Shelley research, evolved during her time with him at 38 Great Pulteney Street, and was now agonizing in what it could and could not be. "Why didn't you tell me who you really were when I arrived in London?"

"Would you have believed me? Would you have stayed at my residence? Would we be where we are right now?"

"No." She glanced up into his face. "What happened after Brighton Beach?"

He reassured his tender grip and pulled her close as he explored their reflection in the window.

"Whether due to trauma, or grief, or lack of blood, I was beyond any real sensibility. Somehow, I made it up to the village and hired a cabriolet. The horse pulled me through the night, the deepest sense of my loss blurring my vision, numbing me. I must have appeared a grief-stricken madman. Wavering between life and death. Aware. Unaware. Indeed, I didn't know which was my reality.

"I felt an insatiable need to return to my family, to see them once again and feel their affection. To somehow receive condolences for a love and a loss I could not possibly reveal, even to the ones I held most dear.

"Thirty-eight Great Pulteney Street loomed large when I arrived. My father was in residence, entertaining a gentleman for supper. Any of my attempts to be part of those proceedings must surely have appeared sorry and I excused myself to my suite and curled up on the bed. Then I pulled the flask of tincture from the pocket of my frockcoat and guzzled its contents—not to end my life, but to subdue the pain that racked my every movement and thought. I suspect it was the diminished volume of blood coursing through my veins, a fact that should have seen me weak and still lying on the pebbles of Brighton Beach. It was my father who found me, and for that I am forever regretful. Such pain no father should ever bear. The coroner deemed it a visitation by God. *Not by God*, I would have told him. I lay in state amongst the memories of 38 Great Pulteney Street's front parlor for seven days. And then I was buried."

Rachel recalled standing with *Aubrey* in the tombstoned gardens of St. Pancras Old Church. She met his gaze in the train window's reflection. "How long were you in the ground?"

"Aware or unaware?"

She was thoughtful. "Unaware," she said.

"It might have been minutes. Indeed, it might have been days, weeks, or months. All I knew when I awoke was that I was underground, and that I dared not pull my bell string, lest its tintinnabulation cause dread to myself and those loved ones still above ground."

She leaned her cheek and ear to the heat of his breast. The beating of his heart was slow but strong. "And aware?" she asked.

"Three years," he said.

Rachel bit her lower lip.

Three years.

1824.

"The combination of your basement safe."

"It was a time I needed. To come to terms with who and what I was. And only when I was certain of myself did I tear through the disintegrating shroud and dig up through the sod to rejoin the living."

The train slowed to a stop at Gatwick Airport before continuing on.

"And Officer Hamilton?"

He stared at his boots for several long minutes that she dared not disturb.

"Have you heard of the Obscure Sorrows, Rachel?"

"Only one."

He nodded. "There are many. With Hamilton there was a Moment of Tangency. An escape from the sorrow. A glimpse of what might have been. Two soul mates, our lives parallel, but like parallel lines never meant to meet. I will always love him, but that night caused us both irreparable damage neither of us can confront or willingly endure by being in each other's company. Any semblance of my dearest friend's true nature was lost in the ocean almost two centuries ago. We grieved our loss for decades, but both agreed it best to go our separate ways."

Rachel closed her eyes, comforted by the beat of heart, and heat of the man who held her in his arms.

But her thoughts were of her husband and the words she needed to say.

CHAPTER EIGHTY-ONE

Rachel closed the last page of the ledger, astonished the events of Brighton Beach had been documented in Polidori's hand. The elegance of the copperplate had diminished into a scrawl that twisted and sloped down the page among ink splotches, smudged fingerprints, and incoherent ramblings in English, Latin, and Italian. But every facet was there, described in abhorrent and incredulous detail. Right down to the copious layers of Lady Walton's gold silk and gauze gown. A discrete anomaly of time she could not explain any more than she could the occurrences at Chillon during her research for the Shelley bio.

Rachel's cell phone lay upon the scarification of her name on Polidori's desk, recharging after her ten-hour call with Adam. Moonlight shone through the windows, casting the room into silvered shadows.

A soft knock at the door. "May I come in?" Doctor Polidori asked.

"Of course, John. Please," she said.

He was in his black silk, dragon-embroidered dressing gown. "You were on the phone quite a while. How are you?" He sat against the edge of his desk, his sleeves rolled high, muscled forearms tensing as he gripped the edge of the mahogany.

"I told him everything. Every aspect of my research. Every nuance and thought. Every contradiction, conclusion, and dream. My fears. My love. My uncertainty. And . . . my certainty."

He nodded. "I understand if you can't go through with this, Rachel. It's no light matter. It will impact every aspect of your life." He reached over and thumbed a nervous tear from her cheek. His face softened. "What were his last words to you?"

"That he trusts me, and he loves me without condition. He always has and always will." They fell into a silence, the creaks of 38 Great Pulteney Street gentle about them, the clock in the downstairs hall chiming the midnight hour.

"He's a beautiful man," Polidori said. "One I gladly would have met under different circumstance."

Rachel leaned into him, slipping her arms around his waist. "He arrives at Heathrow in the morning to take me away from here."

So, we have only tonight?

Yes. And I gladly give it to you.

He pressed his lips into her hair, kissing her gently. *Thank you.*

For a moment they held tight to each other, a moment Rachel wished would last forever but knew could not. She stepped back, and he reached for his document box and slid it to the front of his desk. He flipped the latch and urged the lid open, then lifted out the tray with its threadbare cobalt-blue silk. For several moments he stood immobile, his thoughts his own, before he turned back to her and touched the backs of his fingers to her cheek. His hand trembled, the intensity of his chestnut eyes deepening as he loosened his sash and nudged the dressing gown from his shoulders, folded it and placed it within the box.

The cool heat of his nakedness was agreeably unbearable, electric, drawing her close as she discarded her own gown, letting it drop to their feet. She felt raw before him, bewitched by every aspect of who and what he was, her every thought she'd ever had of his life, his death, and his relevance to who she was. And who she'd become. His gaze drifted across her face, his features gentle and kind. An immutable love. He glanced down as he removed the piercing from his nipple and tossed it into the silk-filled box. Then he twisted Jess's wedding band from his pinky and slipped it onto her finger.

Will you take this ring as a reminder?

Of the evil in the world?

No. Of the love, and the hope.

She placed her hand on the pleasant fullness of his pectoral to feel the beating of his heart. He was flushed, his body hot, slicked by sweat. His nipple was hard, pressing into the softness of her palm. With their gaze held firm to each other's he gently grasped her wrist and skimmed her hand down the undulations of his flesh.

Right there.

He was firm beneath her touch.

Polidori pressed his lips to her forehead as Rachel tightened her grip. The skin pulled back, exposing the tenderest part of him as she thrust the splintered oak stake from the document box into his abdomen and up behind his rib cage. His heart popped and ripped with an audible squelch. He fell back from her against the desk, two hundred years of weariness dropping from his features, an innocence and sincerity glowing from deep within, a sheer happiness and vitality invigorating his countenance and body.

Thank you, Rachel. My dear sister.

The light in his eyes dimmed to null but then returned with an astonishing brilliance. He combusted around her. The intense and loud glass-like shattering of brilliantly lit memories scattering and filling the room and her mind. Memories of Shelley, of Byron, of Jess, of Hamilton. Memories of eras and circumstances Rachel had only ever witnessed on the history channel, in movies and documentaries, in her mind's eye when doing her research. And still the all-consuming noise of breaking crystals of emotion enveloped her. He shared his innermost thoughts with her. His failures, his fears, his dreams, his happiness. Aspects of any man, of anyone, seldom shared with another. But willingly he did, allowing her to see reasonings and events that had never been written or photographed or painted or spoken. Concepts of a life that was lived to beyond the fullest across the vast time he had. The memories collapsed in on themselves, spiraling into a tight pinpoint of light through which Rachel could see his future. A future with Jess who had already passed through the twilight. The joy she knew they deserved. The joy promised all mankind.

Thank you.

The mote of concentrated light abruptly ceased, the noise of a shattering life passed, leaving her alone within the quiet of 38 Great Pulteney Street.

Aware and awake.

For love may break the downward spiral by driving in the stake.

CHAPTER EIGHTY-TWO

Rachel sat on the green leather bench in the National Portrait Gallery, room 18. Mary Shelley's enigmatic smile beckoned from canvas and oil. Polidori's reminisced of love beyond the frame. A glimpse of happier times with the ones he loved.

She looked up as Adam straddled the bench beside her, with Henny fast asleep against his chest.

Her first and only thought was *God, I love him.*

She pulled sleeping Henny into her embrace and held tight to Adam's tender gaze, hand in gentle hand. No need to talk. No need to kiss. Just knowing they loved each other without question.

Their lives, their future, their destiny held only the promise of joy.

THE END

Acknowledgments

Though writing might appear to be a lonely enterprise, any author is seldom alone. Every waking (and somnambulistic) moment is filled with the subtle whispers and possibilities of characters, events, intrigue, romance, adventure, and emotion that demands to be conveyed by words (or omission of words). There is barely a second where the one who holds the quill or sits in the dull glow of a computer screen is ever by themselves.

Perhaps the only true distractions are those friends who are not of the author's creation. Family. Work colleagues. Fellow authors and poets. Editors. Publishers. Virtual friends. But even they tend to seep into the mix, merging with the flux of imagination, of opportunity, of story-telling.

Some of my acquaintances *might* find themselves within these pages. If not by temperament then by given or family name as a nod to our friendship. Rest assured any inclusion is from a viewpoint of love and appreciation for how you have enriched my own life.

P.J.

About the Author

An avid reader and researcher, novelist P.J. Parker has traveled and lived extensively around the world—intrigued by cultures and eras of historic interest and buildings of architectural significance.

P.J. currently lives and writes in the beautiful Pacific Northwest.

Novels by P.J. Parker

Roxelana and Suleyman

"Fascinating" "Intriguing"

America Tuwaqachi: The Saga of an American Family

"Masterful" "Unforgettable"

Fire on the Water: A Companion to Mary Shelley's *Frankenstein*

"Tremendous" "Impressive"

Origin of the Vampyre: A Companion to Doctor Polidori's *The Vampyre*

Your feedback and reviews are always welcome.